REVENGE OF THE CHUPACABRA

REVENGE OF THE CHUPACABRA

KYLE ABERNATHIE

ISBN 1940816114
9781940816111
or for ebook
ISBN 1-940816-12-2
978-1-940816-12-8

Acknowledgements:
Many thanks to my newish, caffeine-addicted friends for their encouragement: Bryant, Peg, Lorri, Rachel, and Elizabeth.
My Baristas (2013-2015): Alex, Anita, Eduardo, Wileesha, Orlando, Aleesha, Elijah, Felicia, (breath) AhnnaBeth, Itzalina, Hannah, Holland, Halston, Hallie, Shelby, Shelbey, Chelsea, Chelsey, Frank, Chad, Chase, George, Dave, David, Maddie, Mattie, Mary, Barry, Brentha, Bri, Taylor, Taylor, Tina, Tracy, Keely, Kaleigh, Kaitlyn, Kyle, Caleb, Katie, Justin, Jacob, Lauren, Laura, Raymond, Robert, Sam, Sam, Ben, Ben, Ben, Emily, Emily, EmmaLeigh, Stephanie, Tiffanie, Tabitha, Jessica, Jessica, Joseph, Justin, Megan, Michael, Eumir, Omar, Danielle, Victoria, Amy Jo, Keanu, Cori, Tristan, Stormy, Celeste, Celene, and effing-LEE!
Love and thanks to: Brant, Bruce, Brad, and Heather for their valued friendship and support.
Special thanks to: Ben Donley (Yoda), of Jock & Lola Publishing (www.jockandlola. com) for his knowledge, patience, and friendship.
Cover art: Ben Schultz (www.artstation.com/artist/bentheevilclown)
Cover art concepts: Sarah Lowe & Ben Donley

Author's Note: While researching the setting for the first two-thirds of the story, I became interested in the *Nahua* (Aztec) culture, and particularly in its language, which is still spoken by more than a million people in Central Mexico today. I chose to use certain words and phrases from the *Nahuatl* language in the text, and where those words appear, I put them in a different font to separate them from the rest of the text. Hopefully, the *Nahuatl* words and phrases are surrounded by enough context so that you, the reader, will understand their general meaning and they won't slow you down. For those who are curious, there are several Spanish/Nahuatl translation glossaries online, and even one, abbreviated English/Spanish/Nahuatl translator. You might be interested to find that quite a few *Nahuatl* words have been appropriated as common terms by the English language.

For Sarah, Connor, and Andrew

YOU CAN BELIEVE EVERYTHING YOU SEE ON THE INTERNETS, PERIOD.

Laugh if you will, but imprinted on our simian synapse exists the rationalistic presumption that, if you can *SEE IT, TASTE IT, FEEL IT, HEAR IT, SMELL IT, or... READ* it.... it's *REAL,* therefore, it is *true,* period. You can guffaw, hem-haw, and deny it all you like, but that cock done crowed, Pete. Imprinting is one step removed from instinct on our bio- evolutionary survivalist checklist.

Ergo, let's assume that if a person or group of persons can be made to believe that anything they are told or shown is THE TRUTH, then the opportunity exists to manipulate those persons by controlling the information presented to them. The individual or entity with the means and the will to exert that mantle of control over a large number of people would possess great power indeed, and he, she, or it would be invaluable and indispensable to politicians, Wall Street, the advertising world, and the government itself.

William Randolph Hearst knew this very well. Hell, he invented a good portion of the game. He was the Pasha of print media for the first half of the twentieth century, and print media reigned as the pre-eminent system of information dissemination for five hundred and sixty years; from Guttenberg's press until the Apple King came along and built a much funking better mousetrap for a new information super highway; a super highway that Al Gore helped bring out of University basements and into the wider world. (Look it up).

The empire that Hearst created was vast and influential and, though he took pride in his collection of semi-respectable trophy newspapers, he would also leave a legacy of yellow journalism as flotsam in his wake. In 1926, Hearst bankrolled a man who had worked for his publishing empire for a number of years, William Griffin, for the purpose of starting a new publication that would one day be known as the *National Enquirer.*

At its inception, the publication was known as *The New York Evening Enquirer* and, whether Griffin knew it in advance or not, his sugar daddy had intended to use the newspaper as a testing ground for new stories. If Hearst liked a particular story being prepared for the *Evening Enquirer,* either for its gravitas or for sensationalistic value, he would cherry-pick it for use in one of his better broadsheets, insuring that his flagship publications got the lion's share of emergent cultural, and political material; thus allowing Hearst to maintain his upper hand in American spheres-of-influence. The *Evening Enquirer* was left with mostly second-rate material and their bottom line constantly suffered because of it, but it was okay, because *'Uncle Bill will make sure the heat and electricity stay on'.*

In the nearly ninety years since its birth, the *Enquirer* went through a great many changes, resulting in considerable growing pains; ownership changes, relocated headquarters (from New York City to Boca Raton, Florida, twice), and dramatic editorial paradigm shifts. One editorial, written by Griffin himself in 1942, earned him an indictment from a *United States Grand Jury* under the *Smith Act* for sedition. The editorial had taken up Charles Lindbergh's conviction of objecting to American involvement in the war, but the charges against Griffin, for undermining the morale of our brave troops overseas were eventually dropped, and the *Enquirer* returned to bread and circuses.

In the 1950's, the magazine made the name change to *The National Enquirer,* and its editors initiated the practice of publishing stories about sex scandals of the rich and famous. During that decade, the *Enquirer* also faced allegations of mob involvement between the paper's new owner and mob boss Frank Costello. The 1960's saw the magazine shifting to stories of shocking suicides, and gory, visceral photographs of automobile accidents, crime scenes, and close-ups of unopened-parachute aftermaths. In the 1970's, the tabloid ushered in the trend of stories about UFOs, Bigfoot, the Loch Ness monster and other tales both supernatural and preternatural.

The *National Enquirer* was both the pacesetter and the business model for a dozen other subsequently launched 'scandal sheets' that had proliferated since the late forties and, together, the *tabloids* titillated Americans with yarns of witches, monsters, serial killers, aliens, and dozens of other conceptual distractions designed to entice the supermarket line-waiter into forking over that $1.25, or $2.50, and eventually the $3.50 (current suggested retail price).

The Alien/Monster/Witch fare carried the tabloids through the 70's and 80's, but in the 1990's, America's pop-culture appetites returned to all things celebrity. 'Who's dating who', was a big draw, and, of course, 'who's cheating on whom?' Then, there was the most effective magazine rack eye-catcher of all time...'*Look Who's Fat*'...aaaaand....'*Who looks terrible at the beach!*'

Nope, you just couldn't beat that kind of crap.

PART I

Chapter 1

Bologna. It had to be the bologna. Or the mayo. The noisy mini-fridge in the tiny, sweltering motel room the previous night had been able to keep the sandwich and bottle of water cool, but nowhere near cold. John had bought the sandwich at a bag'n'wag in Irapuato at dinnertime the night before, eaten one half and saved the other for breakfast. It turned out to be a bad move.

He had been throwing up at ten-minute intervals since he left the motel two hours earlier. The first few times, he had pulled the rental car over and made complete stops, but he had three hundred fifty miles to cover before sundown tonight and, since his stomach had discharged all of its contents early on, the rolling-chunder it was; pulling the car over to the shoulder, slowing down, then holding on to the steering wheel with his right hand while he opened the door with his left so he could lean out and heave. The simmering heat made the yak-breaks even more unpleasant, but his nausea subsided after the first hour on the road. He still felt clammy though, and every time he caught a glimpse of his face in the rear-view mirror, he thought he looked very pale.

John Maddox's target destination was the remote, Central Mexican village of Santa Teresa where, six weeks earlier, the only semi-credible photo of the quasi-mythical beast, known colloquially as the Chupacabra, had been taken. Maddox had been doing freelance work for *The National Enquirer* for nigh on three years, and was now pursuing a follow-up story with the woman who had taken the photograph.

The National Enquirer, heh! John smiled to himself whenever he recalled being a young boy, standing with his father in line at the supermarket and laughing along with him at stories of:

ALIEN CORPSE FINALLY REVEALED IN AREA 51,
or
MAN MARRIES PIG HALF HIS AGE,
and at grainy black & white photographs of,
President Bush (no middle initial) **taking a walk with Alien Leader on the grounds of Camp David.**
and
Disembodied Chicken Head, Still Clucking After Seven Days,
("There's got to be something religiously significant in that one",
Dad had quipped).

The point had always been understood that they were silly headlines and pictures meant to entertain you in line or catch your eye enough so you'd pop for the $1.19 to find out *Just how long did that fucker cluck anyways.*

John Maddox's father was a newspaperman and, from a young age, John seemed to instinctually understand what that eponym really meant; it meant that Pops did an important job, and that a large number of people read what he had to say and took it as the truth. Not surprisingly, the curious, world-minded boy grew up wanting to be just like ol' Dad and he pursued his desire for a future in journalism starting in high school, taking preparatory classes and serving on the yearbook staff.

His father, Jeffrey Maddox, had been a reporter for the *Washington Post* in the late 1970's when the sweet bouquet of Woodward and Bernstein's journalistic coup still lingered in the air at that esteemed paper of record and, though his father had never scored the high profile, journalistic home run that all such correspondents secretly hope for, he retained a high standard of integrity and had never stopped pursuing THE TRUTH. He was still at it, in fact, though he now wrote for the increasingly tabloidish *Projo*.

The Providence Journal, in Rhode Island; *Projo*, as it was known locally, had its critics like any newspaper, but it did have a bona fides as the oldest continually published broad-sheet newspaper in the country, a fact of which the senior Maddox frequently reminded the owners and editors when it became clear that they were steering the esteemed news-vessel straight into the fog of *Infotainment*. John was proud of his Dad for maintaining a high standard of journalism in the face of the dumbification of news, via the Populist Media Movement. For Rhode Islanders, the political corruption surrounding the Barrington Bridge project was big news, and Jeffrey Maddox was the lead investigative reporter who had first uncovered the scandal.

John's own journalistic career began the year he graduated from NYU with a Masters degree in journalism and a desire for employment with a creditable news agency. Serious news; that was his goal, and John's post grad job search had begun in earnest during his sophomore year. He had refused his dad's nepotistic offers; determined to find his own path and reach the desired brass ring with his integrity fully intact. Unfortunately for him, as the advent of Internet "News Blogs" (*sneeze* i.e. *BULLSHIT*) had hit their stride during his college tenure and somehow gained a taint of credibility, the broadsheet papers of record were in a battle to retain subscribers and come up with new tricks in order to maintain readership. Grudgingly, the owners and editors of the larger, long-established newspapers had started to acknowledge the font on the wall. The future, as predicted, would be virtual.

As a consequence of these changes, the newspapers were hiring fewer apprentices every year, and even the mailrooms were down to one or two high school kids on work/study programs. Competition for a coveted staff-writing position was fierce and, yes, often nepotistic.

John was young, idealistic, and ready to start a career, but the scarcity of desirable jobs in the field made prospects bleak, and he had grown discouraged. Just when he began to feel desperation creeping in, the *National Enquirer* had broken a story that, at first, sounded like just another sensationalistic sex scandal, characteristic of that publication's fare. Even though the scandal centered around a major figure in the political arena, John hadn't paid much attention to it at first; not until it started getting play from credible news agencies.

With a page ripped from the NYU course he had taken on Situational Ethics, he had taken the opportunistic step of reconnecting with a girl he had briefly "dated" at NYU who had taken a job at the *Enquirer*. He would come to regret his initial, cynical motives, as their renewed relationship had eventually grown into a real love. They were currently cohabiting and working in the same field, though those two factors had caused some trouble of late.

Back when they had first reconnected, during his post-grad job search, John had feigned a mix of amusement and nonchalance when Victoria had bragged to him that the *Enquirer* had finally hooked a big fish. He snickered when she insisted that it was serious, legitimate news, but, when she described the details of the scandal, John's instincts were piqued. The thought of Presidential Candidate, John Edwards, who, at the time, was the front-runner in the Democratic Primary for President, having an extramarital affair exposed just after an announcement that his wife, Elizabeth, was in a battle with the Dread Pirate Cancer? It had whetted John's journalistic appetite.

Trying to get his foot in any door at that point, he had begun making regular submissions to the *Enquirer* as a freelance writer, in the hope that the Edwards story, (for which the *Enquirer* would receive a Pulitzer Prize), was a bellwether, and that he would get in on the ground floor of a new direction for the rag.

It was a ridiculous thing to expect; a fact of which he was now painfully aware as he drove through central Mexico on his way to the small village where the photograph of a Chupacabra, of all things, had been taken.

—⚹—

The road rolled along over terrain dotted with scrub-brush, juniper, and mesquite for as far as he could see. He was driving through the foot-hills of volcanically created mountains, and the occasional outcropping of sharp, white rock contrasted with the long dark lava flows that John figured must be many thousands of years old. The little village was in a valley somewhere just up ahead, and his food-poisoned body was antici-pating the end of the journey when, suddenly, a large shape darted out of the scrub brush and ran directly in front of his car.

"WOAH!" he exclaimed out loud as he swerved to avoid the animal. "Dammit!"

But it was only a coyote; as common in this part of Mexico as jack-rabbits on the Texas Plains had been during one of his last location assignments. The piece, printed in the *Enquirer,* had been about presi-dential candidate Texas Governor Rick Perry's addiction to painkillers and, though John hadn't broken the story himself, the controversy had contributed to the Governor's premature withdrawal from the race.

Recovering from the near collision with the coyote, John drove on over the roller-coaster road, now keeping a better eye on the shoulder of the highway. After a few more miles he crested a hill and was greeted by the sight of Santa Teresa nestled in a little river valley. The highway ran parallel to the river on his right, and John turned left onto the only dirt road leading from the highway into the village. It was a tiny burg, and he found his hotel quickly, it being the only such establishment in the village. He pulled off of the dirt road into the gravel parking lot of a long, ranch house-style structure, its adobe walls painted bright white and contrasting sharply with the dark, chocolate colored, heavy wooden framing & beams. The office was on the left end of the lot, and he parked the car underneath the big, block letters **HOTEL** painted on a stretch of wall to the right of the office door.

John had tried to call the inn from New York but, although he had taken a crash course online to learn the language, his Español was still *no buena*. It turned out that Rosetta Stone's method of full immersion offended his autodidactic sensibilities. Couldn't they just give him a damn translated VOCABULARY LIST? Fuck total immersion. Now, he wished he would have just taken the 'Beginning Conversational Spanish' class offered by the Learning Annex.

At the registration counter, the hotel owner, Señor Sanchez, smiled politely as John read from the 3X5 index card on which he had written Spanish words and phrases he thought would be helpful. Even with the card, he felt awkward during the registration process but, when they were done, John was amused when Señor Sanchez, from behind the front desk had said, in perfect Englais,

"If you need mor towlss, you gotta wait. Maleenda don't come till mañana. Dinner is in one hour. Don't lose the key, por favor."

The small hotel had a half dozen guest rooms of varying sizes, and John's was tiny. Carpet with the nap worn down to slick; a single bed/cot with a small sink beside it; a tiny bathroom barely big enough to turn around in containing a toilet and a cramped shower stall. But none of that bothered him, having become used to the minimal accommodations on the handful of assignments that had taken him out of Manhattan. The *Enquirer* would occasionally spring for expenses in advance, but John was paying for this trip.

This expedition to Central Mexico was not his dream assignment. He preferred to pursue stories of a political nature, even if it *was* for the *Enquirer* (i.e. the Jonathan Edwards gift from heaven), and John Maddox was here under protest. Since his graduation, the *Enquirer* had bought several of his political pieces, and the publishers were proud to get a leg up in the 'hard news' arena, but the bread and butter of America's top tabloid remained the simple half-page **Eye Catchers**. An impeccably dressed, expensively coiffed John Edwards was eye candy to be sure, especially when superimposed behind his Blondie and Love-Child, but, *come on!* a Chupa-freakin-*CABRA*!! Hombre please. That was front-page, eye-catching supermarket-queue GOLD in any politico-cultural atmosphere, and John had an apartment in Tribeca on which rent was due, so…here he was; Santa Teresa, Mexico; home of the now infamous, *real,* Chupe.

It mattered little that most people didn't know what a real chupacabra looked like. There were lots of hackneyed photos of Sasquatch, but not the Chupacabra. Until relatively recently, the existence of these creatures was apocryphal at most; an old folk tale told by parents to keep their kids from venturing too far from home. It wasn't much different than a thousand other such tales, from Sea-Monsters to Grimm's inventions, to the generic bogeyman. The difference between the Chupacabra and the other ersatz raptorial monsters was that, until the mid 1990's, tales of the Chupacabra had been exclusive to certain areas of Mexico and Guatemala. The appellation 'Chupacabra' had not been bandied about in the wide world until 1995, when a woman in Puerto Rico had told her neighbors that she had seen the 'dog' that her neighbors had suspected of killing the sheep, goats and chickens. Only it wasn't a dog at all.

As the woman had described it, the creature was larger than a dog, with sharp spikes running down it's back, and it was bent over and hopping on hind legs like a kangaroo. She had revealed that the thing hadn't disemboweled or eaten her stray sheep, but only sucked it dry of blood and left the carcass behind. After that story hit the airwaves, Chupacabra sightings started appearing semi-regularly in Mexico and South Texas but, even in an age of proliferating video cameras, smart phones and home security cameras, the sudden purported expansion of the creature's range was unrealistic; silly, really. There was a plethora of videos out there (yes that's what I said, a plethora) of tornados, hurricanes, train wrecks, bear attacks, and runaway, child-carrying, UFO-impersonating weather balloons, but where, oh where, was any footage of a dreaded Chupacabra? nowhere, mon frère.

As with all bogeymen and monsters, whether or not the Chupacabra actually existed was irrelevant. The world was getting smaller, and it needed a new preternatural threat for the new age; one that could move and hide better than the giant, sluggish monsters of antiquity. *Nessie* was ridiculously large for her little Scottish bathtub; Photos of *Big Foot* were mostly just laughable, and had begun to look like dudes you might see on 'Duck Dynasty' or, perhaps, pitching for a Major League baseball team. And the *Yeti*? You just knew that all the Sherpa(s) had a good laugh behind the backs of the... whatever Sherpa called their Everest-bound clients when asked about the Snow-monster.

Yes, the world needed a new, stealthier, less photographically documented creature for the new millennium; one onto which the populous could project their darker fears, and the Chupacabra was evidently reptilian (always a popular psychologically primal fear). Geographically speaking, a person would have to go to some effort if they wanted even a chance at sighting the Loch Ness Monster or the Yeti, so those monsters were not a realistic threat to most folk. Bigfoot, on the other hand might access your house through the front door (might even knock). But this new monster, the terrifying, bloodthirsty Chupacabra, you would never even hear coming. Your livestock would die first, then your dog, and when *your* time came, there would be no escaping. The windows, doors, attic, and chimney were all vulnerable portals, and nothing could really make you feel truly safe from this threat. And, when the end came, the devilish beastie would slip in with deadly stealth, and the only sound you would hear might be a quick hisss before it grabbed you from behind and pinned your arms to your sides with surprising strength, as it sank its long fangs into your jugular.

—∽∿∽—

The Sánchez Hotel offered its patrons the perk of home-cooked meals twice daily and, as the hotel's only guest tonight, John was invited to join the family who owned and operated the hotel for the evening meal. So, after a cooling shower to wash off the road-grime, he put on jeans and a white t-shirt, but went to dinner barefoot after noticing that it seemed to be an acceptable behavior amongst the family members he had seen walking around earlier.

The family was kind to their American guest, and they were all accommodating of his lack of Español. The lady of the house made a *pescado* especially for him, while the rest of the family, John noted, ate what looked like ground beef with bits of green peppers from small bowls, using rolled up corn tortillas as utensils. In the center of the large table, within reach of everyone, was a big platter with vine-grown tomatoes, onions, and more peppers. Everyone, including John, was also served a bowl of something mushy that looked like it was made from corn as well. It all tasted very fresh and full of flavor, even the fish, and the meal was an unexpected treat for the big-city dweller.

The children were a little girl of two, and three boys in their early teens, who obviously spoke English well, but mostly communicated by mugging faces at each other and laughing at themselves and at John. As he worked on the big, bony fish, John brought up the subject of the Chupacabra, but discovered that the family already knew why he was in their remote village. They were all very aware of the photograph taken by their neighbor, and the fact that it had been printed in an American magazine and, though the kids seemed amused by John's serious questions about the monster, their parents spoke of the creature somberly if not matter-of-factly, as if the creature was not a mere folk legend or a tongue-in-cheek children's tale. To John's ears, it sounded like they might as well have been talking about any of a handful of reclusive, or nocturnal creatures that they seldom saw, but whose existence was a part of their local rhythms. When Señor and Señora Sánchez related incidents of mischief that had been blamed on the Chupacabra, however, they spoke of them as occasional annoyances, but evidently not every day, or even weekly occurrences.

Toward the end of dinner, the grown-ups gave their guest a tasty tidbit concerning a Santa Teresan tradition that went back many generations, and was still practiced today. On the first night of every full moon, they explained, certain livestock were tied to an old tree (now a big stump) as a symbolic sacrifice; a healthy sheep, a small calf, or a fat chicken in a wooden cage. No goats, John was told very specifically; no goats!

"*No una cabra. Eso sería un insulto.*"

In accordance with tradition, they explained, if the sacrificed animal was still alive after two nights tied to the stump, it was set free and allowed to roam untethered in the village square, eating scraps thrown out by residents. Those animals who survived the first two nights were referred to as *bendito,* or 'blessed' and, if that particular animal was still alive by the time of the *next* full moon, it was *santificado,* or 'sanctified', and it was never killed or eaten, but allowed to live a long life and die of old age. Curiously, according to Señor Sanchez, only a small percentage of the animals who were tied to the stump survived to reach *santificado* status.

Evidently, the majority of Santa Teresans considered the ritual a harmless tradition, akin to keeping alive the belief in *Sánta Clos* for the children, and it was common knowledge to all residents that the animals who were sacrificed and 'didn't make it' had only been taken home in the night by one of their hungry neighbors (usually the original donor) and made a meal of. Part of the tradition, amongst the adults of the village, was that whoever took the animal didn't admit to the deed afterwards. But, Señora Sánchez added that, for every three sacrificed animals that disappeared from the plaza completely, there was always one carcass left intact, still tied to the stump, but completely drained of blood.

John flashed to the parallel of the North American tradition of leaving a glass of milk and a plate of cookies out for Santa Claus on Christmas Eve. He remembered that, for the delight of his brother, sister, and himself, their Dad would drink the milk left out for Santa and take a couple of bites of cookie while he was assembling the train set, or doll house on the night before Christmas.

He thought the story he was being told was nuts, but he was obviously in the right place. When the kids had left the table, the señor offered him an after-dinner shot of mescal and, after the third one, the assignment stopped seeming as much like a joke to him. In his mildly drunktified state, he began to think that he might actually get an interesting story out of this trip. As they sat around the table talking and drinking, he watched the eyes of the señor y señora carefully to see if they shot each other looks that said they were having him on. But there were no looks. The Sanchez's were sincere. However, when John asked if they would introduce him to Constançia Delgado, the lady who had sold the photograph to the *Enquirer*, they did indeed exchange looks with each other before the señora told him coldly that the woman wasn't from there, and they didn't know where she lived. Then they quickly changed the subject.

According to John's main contact at the *Enquirer's* business office, Pete Daia, Señora Delgado had asked that her compensation check for the rights to print the photograph be made out to her son, and the check had subsequently been cashed in Torreón, the nearest town with *una banco*. That was the lead he would follow in the morning. John wanted to start the story at ground zero, and he would need Mrs. Delgado to show him where she had taken the infamous photograph.

The mescal haze did not rob him of the fantastical scenarios described by his hosts, and John's dreams that night, as he knew they would be, were full of vivid, dramatic visions. He *was* going to enjoy this assignment more than he had thought he would, and if he could return to New York with a story that was both entertaining to the appropriate number of *Enquirer* readers, and impressed the magazine's editors, then, maybe, they would put him back on the story he had been kicked off of the month before; the one he really wanted. Needed.

Chapter 2

The American journalist opened his eyes and saw peeling paint and chipped plaster on the ceiling above, reminding him that he was not in his New York apartment. The small cot had been surprisingly comfortable and, when he hopped out, stretched long and hard, and dressed for breakfast, John felt none of the road weariness from the day before. This cheap, but cozily spare hotel was his jumping off point for the investigative piece that would illuminate the facts on the ground for the world about the illusive Chupacabra, and the village to which he belonged.

The home-style meals offered twice a day were served by the Señora de la Casa at whatever time the rest of the family ate. There was no convenience store, no grocery, not even a general store in this remote mexi-hamlet so, if you showed up late for a meal, you went hungry. The previous night, Señor Sanchez had explained that most of the villagers grew bountiful gardens full of vegetables and herbs, and many kept chicken coops and livestock as well, so if one neighbor had a surplus of something he had grown, another one might have a little extra of something the first one needed. The barter system was alive and operating well here, and John guessed that it made for a fresh and varied diet.

Everyone had what they needed and the community's collective cooperative was strong.

On this unseasonably hot Tuesday morning in early November, John found the morning *comida* (breakfast) absolutely wonderful and, as on the night before, it was served in the little dining room between the office and the kitchen. The white plaster walls of the vaulted room were accented with the same heavy, chocolate, wooden beams that he had seen on the outside of the hotel, and sitting on the clay tiled floor next to the kitchen door was a large, round table that could have easily sat ten people. The table's top was laid with tiles in beautiful designs of terra cotta, ochre, and several shades of blue and, when John arrived, the places were already set and the family were gathered 'round it. The comida was fresh eggs (straight out of the cloaca and onto his plate) scrambled with peppers, cilantro, onions and other spices; *atole*, the soup-like treat made from corn that he'd had the night before; and fresh squeezed guava juice to drink.

Mid-way through the comida, John again broached the subject of Mrs. Delgado and her son, but the result was the same as before. These people were definitely trying to avoid talking about the woman, he thought. Before he left New York, John had discussed the goals of the assignment with the editors of the *Enquirer*, and the point had been made that, although this was ostensibly a follow-up story about the woman who had taken the photograph, it would be a ridiculous waste of time and resources to make this long journey and not spend some amount of time actually looking for the creature. So, as he had promised them he would, John had to carve out a chunk of time to do just that; though he couldn't imagine spending very much time doing it. He figured the sliding scale of how silly and pointless it seemed to carry on with the hunt would help naturally determine the length of the search window.

One of the first journalistic concepts John absorbed while in college had been demonstrated for him in the first story he had worked on after graduation; published in Star magazine. The axiom stated that, when writing about any subject, the journalist should try to cultivate the human angle whenever and wherever possible, and his professor had said that the reader's attention could be better held if they identified with at least one person in the story. No matter how freaky, fantastic, or otherwise superlative the story might be, the lack of an opportunity to feel sympathy toward a character (animals also worked, btw) could reduce the ultimate impact of the story on said reader. John now thought about that lesson and the interesting way it applied to his current situation. The *Enquirer* wanted a piece about the Believe-it-or-Not-Freak-Lizard-Monster whose picture it had printed in an earlier issue of the magazine but, because John would most likely have no contact with, or even a sighting of the main subject of his story, he figured he had better start by meeting the fine people of Santa Teresa and the residents of the surrounding river valley. It would be their tales and recollections, he had decided, that would form the backbone of his story.

That would prove to be more difficult than expected. Soon after breakfast he set out on foot through the dirt streets near the hotel and began by trying to make eye contact with whoever would lift their gaze to his. After several failed attempts at contact, John finally got a young man in his mid-twenties to speak with him, but he instantly found that his weakness in the Spanish language was going to be a bigger problem than he expected. At dinner and at breakfast, he had been relieved by the ease with which he could communicate with the Sánchez family, but he now realized that his hosts were obviously more conversant in the English than were most of the citizens of Santa Teresa.

Another Manhattan-based freelance writer, René Hernandez, also a frequent contributor to the *Enquirer*, had wanted the Chupacabra story for himself but, at the last minute, the assignment editor tapped John for the job instead. Now, John knew it had been a mistake, and that Hernandez would have been the wiser choice. Not only was René fluent in Spanish, he had grown up in Central Mexico to boot.

After the fifth person with whom John attempted communication walked away in frustration spouting a string of ¿insults? John returned to the hotel and struck a deal with oldest teen of the Sanchez family to translate for him. He offered the boy ten dollars a day (U.S.) for his services, and the boy, whose name was Tomás, accepted enthusiastically. After John had cooled down with an ice-cold *Jarrito's* soda-pop (yellow), the two headed out the door and down the street but, before they even reached the first street corner, the teenager's Madre leaned out of the hotel office door and shouted what sounded like a strict warning in Español to her son. The words weren't meant for John, but he did pick out the name, 'Delgado'.

The reporter quickly learned what a great deal he had made. Tomás was fifteen-years old, very friendly, helpful, and was obviously popular among villagers of all ages. Soon the two were collecting stories about lost pets and livestock whose disappearances were inevitably blamed on the creature in question, though most of them sounded tongue-in-cheek to John's cynical ears. The Chupacabra, it seemed, made a handy scapegoat for any otherwise unexplainable nocturnal mischief.

Between interviews, he spoke with the boy and soon realized that the teen was of above average intelligence and knew quite a lot about the world outside of his little village. As Tomás explained, when he had reached school age, the Sanchez's had been one of the first families in the valley to take advantage of the services of a Satellite Dish company that had opened shop sixty miles away in Torreón. Besides providing dozens of TV channels for hotel guests, the "dish" had brought the entire family access to the Internet, and his parents had taken full advantage of the educational possibilities presented by it.

Primary education is mandatory in Mexico, John knew, but Tomás explained that, though there was a school in a nearby village that provided a free education for all children in the area, courtesy of the state, many parents in the valley chose to keep their kids at home to work. To that end, a child's opportunity for education here depended on his or her parent's willingness to let them participate. The satellite dish gave the Sanchez offspring the opportunity to do both. When the three boys were needed, said Tomás, they did their chores in the hotel, and, after the work was done, their parents insisted they take online lessons for several hours every day.

The Internet was the Sanchez family's window on the world and John was impressed at how, at least in Tomás' case, their utilization of technology had really paid off. When Tomás offered John his assessment of the cultural and ideological differences between the *New York Times* and the *National Enquirer*, John could find no significant flaw in his mature and astute observations, and, the more they spoke, the more he thought the kid also seemed to understand the direction John wanted to take with the piece he was working on now.

More than half the people he and Tomás spoke to this first day had some personal story about the creature; something their *Mia* or *Tio* or *hermano* had heard or seen; never a clear sighting or definite identification, only some, mysterious... something. Several villagers told of finding exsanguinated corpses among their own livestock, and many people spoke of dogs barking a lot more during the full moon, *la luna llena*. But, there were many superstitions connected to the full moon, and the mere baying of hounds could not be attributed exclusively to the Chupacabra.

John knew he had to get to woman who had taken the first Chupapic and, several times during the course of the day, he solicited Tomás' help in finding the Delgados. But Tomás had slyly ignored or postponed the subject. Finally, in the late afternoon, as they were walking up a long, sloping road, Tomás stopped in mid-stride after yet another inquiry about los Delgados and stood thinking about it for a moment. Then, he turned to John and said,

"Okay Señor Juan, mi Madre does not like Señora Delgado and thinks that she sent a fake photograph to the newspaper." Tomás looked down at his feet as he continued. "She thinks that the señora's photograph has made our village into a joke for the world to laugh at, and she hopes that you will write a serious story for your magazine; a story with no pictures that will give respect to the traditions of our village. Mi Madre knows the thing is real because she has seen it."

John was struck by the boy's sincere tone, and confused by the odd assertion that the Delgado photo could be considered a fake by a woman who claimed to have seen the creature herself. He tried to remember what he had been told about the photograph itself.

Señora Delgado had sold it to the nearest newspaper in Torreón, which had, in turn, attached a short accompanying story and sold it to the El Norte paper in Monterey. The El Norte had then put the story into the Associated Press system. The first editor, at the Torreón paper, had been savvy and kind enough to look out for Señora Delgado's interests, and had her sign what was, essentially, a management agreement wherein he would assure that she would be paid a little money each time the photo was re-sold. That editor wrote the copy for the first accompanying piece, and he got his cut when he sold that package to the Monterey El Norte. When the *Enquirer* finally purchased the rights to use the photo, Señora Delgado had received yet another check; the one her son had cashed.

The first time John saw the photograph himself, it was lying on top of a stack of papers on the desk of the *Enquirer's* assignment editor. He had picked up the pic thinking he knew what he was about to see, but, when his eyeballs focused on the image, both orbs went ***aOOOOga!*** The creature looked nothing like the recent video he had seen of an animal captured on the dash-cam of Sheriff's patrol truck in a rural, South Texas county. That shaky, poor quality image showed what had looked to John like an old coyote with the mange, galloping along with a canine-like gait down a dirt road in front of the vehicle. There was nothing unusual looking about the creature until the end of the clip, when the animal turns its head to the side and, for less than one second, the viewer can see a large, elongated skull that appeared out of proportion to the rest of the skinny dog's body. It was that short snippet of footage that had aroused the crypto zoologists, kooks, and conspiracy theorists, as well as the pop culture obsessed general public in the United States, whose over-stimulated brains thirsted for anything interesting or different.

He remembered that a first round of reports from supposed 'experts' had speculated that the animal in the video was most likely a hairless coyote with scabies. But, at the request of the Texas Highway Department, the Animal Sciences department of Texas A&M University took over and performed DNA tests on the carcasses of similar looking animals found in nearby San Antonio, and it was concluded that these biological outliers were the product of crossbreeding between a hairless coyote and a Mexican Red Wolf. Case closed? Not by a long shot.

When the subject of the 'Texas Chupacabra' had come up in conversation with the Sanchez's the night before, the señor had mirthfully revealed that, when Santa Teresans had seen the video on TV or the Internet, they had all laughed and challenged the Texans' assertions.

"Eso es sólo un coyote o un perro." The villagers had said. (Just a coyote or dog).

All citizens of the Santa Teresa Valley knew, either from ages-old local folklore, or from eyewitness descriptions, just what *their* chupacabra looked like, though, without exception, every person who claimed to have actually seen the beast admitted they had only caught glimpses in varying degrees of twilight. Nevertheless, in the village that claimed the Chupacabra as its own, the accepted description was as follows.

The actual, factual, *REAL* Chupacabra was the height of a short man and stood hunched over with a curved spine. It hopped on muscular hind legs and only used its smaller, front limbs when bending over to sniff the ground or, presumably, to clutch the struggling body of its prey as it drained the life from the poor beast. Some, who claimed to have gotten better looks at the creature, said that its eyes were large, red orbs that seemed to glow from an inner light, and that the pupils were black, narrow, vertical slits. There had evidently been heated arguments between neighbors over whether the Chupacabra's leathery, slightly hairy, reptile-like skin was dark brown, or greenish-grey, but everyone agreed that the creature had spikes running from the back of the head down its back, each one between two and four inches long, and most also described hind feet equipped with lethal talons. These were provocative features to be sure, but the two most terrifying attributes of the Chupacabra, agreed upon by all who claimed to have seen the monster, were the four, sharp, long curving fangs, protruding two up-two down from its opened mouth, and sharp, spiked claws at the end of its short, bony arms. Not as common among the villagers was the claim that the Chupacabra had a pair of vestigial wings, the functionality of which had evidently been discontinued by whomever, or whatever was in charge of evolution.

After Tomás' admission that his family did, in fact, know the Delgados, and that his own mother was among those who had caught a glimpse of the creature, the investigative journalist in John studied the boy's eyes, and looked for the telltale signs of bullshit in his demeanor.

"What do *you* think, Tomás?" John asked. "Do you think your mother saw it? And, do you think the Chupacabra is real?"

Tomás turned his head away and looked back down the road.

"Oh, I know it's real, Señor Juan. You see...I've met the... I've *met* him face to face."

At hearing the provocative pronouncement, John's investigative momentum was temporarily thrown off course. He needed this boy for his translation skills and didn't want to insult him, so he suppressed an urge to laugh.

"Met *HIM*?" John asked, trying not to sound perturbed. "What do you mean 'you met him'? You mean you've seen him."

"No, sir," answered Tomás confidently. "I *MET* him; he spoke to me."

Now, John was dumbstruck. Actually, he just felt dumb. This kid seemed too young to joke with such dry humor and way too smart to believe he could fool the American reporter, but John could see no trace of a smile on the teenager's lips. He fixed a doubtful gaze on the teen, trying to provoke a retraction or admission, but Tomás didn't break. Finally, John broke the silence and said, slowly,

"He? *Spoke* to you? *With* you? Come on, Tomás, I thought we had a good working relationship here. You've been very helpful, and I appreciate everything you've done, but come on!"

Tomás looked away again, this time toward the distant hills.

"Why are you making this joke with me? John asked. "And why aren't you laughing?"

"I am sorry, señor," said Tomás, still staring into the distance. "I thought I could tell you. I thought you were different...smarter, maybe."

"I don't understand," said John, flummoxed.

"Everybody laughed at me when I told them." Tomás' voice was quavering slightly, "Even mi Padre. The other kids called me '*HABLADOR DE CABRA*'. It means 'Goat talker'. But *they* are the ones who are stupid, not me."

Tomás sensed that the gadfly of his trust was about to be smashed by the swatter of betrayal, and he turned and started walking back down the road toward the hotel. John thought about stopping him, but he was frustrated by the teen's ridiculous claim, and stood silent, feeling like he'd been had. He prided himself on having a better than average bullshit detector, and writing stories for the *Enquirer* had taught him to ferret out phonies even more, but something about this proclamation did not compute. Tomás was very intelligent, and John just could not reconcile the cock-a-mamie tale with the mature kid with whom he had spent several hours in intermittent conversation. He let the boy go.

The sun was beginning to go down and, with the departure of his translator, John decided to throw in the towel for the day as well. He knew that his best play was to apologize to Tomás and then try to delve into his motivation behind telling the tall tale.

Just as he turned to go, his sight was drawn to a rickety mailbox on the side of the road, hanging precipitously from its rotting post by one, rusty screw, and three orange construction cones beside it that blocked the street entrance to a long, recently poured driveway. The driveway stretched to the front, left side of a small house set back from the road and, when John took another look at the mailbox, he saw the sloppily painted, uneven letters on the side.

CoNstaNçia DELgAdo

Chapter 3

This was interesting, thought John. Señora Delgado's casa was here on the edge of town, not two city blocks from the Sanchez Hotel. Even though Tomás had made it clear that his Madre didn't want them speaking to Señora Delgado, the teen had seemingly ignored his mother's wishes and led him toward this house anyway.

John needed to repair his relations with Tomás, and he knew that dinner would be served at the hotel soon, but he had just found the most important lead thus far, and he just had to knock on the Delgado's door. Dark patches still showed in the fresh cement, so he walked beside the driveway in the dirt and, when he stepped onto the narrow, cinder-block porch of the little white, stucco house, he could hear music playing inside. Before knocking, he stood listening for a moment, and smiled when he recognized that it was Elvis (the dead one) singing "Burning Love".

Suddenly, the curtain in a window to the left of the door flew open causing John to jump backwards off the stoop. Glaring at him through the windowpane were the bug-eyes of a woman sitting in a chair just inside the front door.

"*¿Que quieres?*" barked the irritated woman, her voice muffled by the glass.

"Quiero hablar con Señora Delgado por favor," attempted John.

"Erés Americano?" she asked with a politer tone.

"Si, soy Americano," he answered. Worried he would get in over his head Español-wise, he added, "I am from the *National Enquirer*, señora".

She looked him up and down as if to confirm his assertion and then, in a softer tone and with the beginning of a smile on her face, she said, "Espera."

The curtains fell closed and, as he waited, John turned his gaze to the west, where the sun was sinking toward the distant hills. Still plenty of light, he thought. When the door opened, the woman's smile was more welcoming, and she excitedly invited him in.

"Si, si, Enquirers! Me llamo Constançia Delgado. I took that picture for you. Come in, come in. Me hablar un poco Englais".

John stepped over the threshold onto the thick wine colored carpet of a dimly lit room and the smell of a lit cigar stung his nostrils. When his eyes adjusted, he saw layered waves of smoke floating in the air, and then spotted the still-smoking cigarillo in an ashtray on the arm of the chair by the front window to his left. Large tapestries depicting dramatic scenes in rich, deep colors of red, green, gold, and ecru covered the walls of the small den so completely that John could see no actual wall. Against the back wall opposite the door, was a burgundy sofa angled slightly toward a large flat-screen television that was positioned at an angle in the corner. The channel was tuned to what looked like a Mexican version of 'Wheel-of-Fortune', and on a TV tray beside the sofa sat the boombox, still blasting Elvis at a prohibitive volume.

As Señora Delgado crossed the room to turn off the music, John sized her up with the eye of a journalist. The woman was shortish and stocky, and she had reddish-brown hair cut in a messy shag style to just below her ears. Friendly now, she looked at him with a pleasant smile, and John saw a shiny gold tooth twinkling at him in the light that came from the kitchen door to the left of the sofa. John looked into the kitchen and saw a very large man in an olive green undershirt and baby-blue boxer shorts, who looked to be in his early thirties. The hulking Mexican had long, jet-black hair pulled back in a tight ponytail, and he was working a large cast-iron skillet with the steel end of a wooden handled spatula.

"¡*Es el enquirers, Chuy!*" Señora Delgado called to her son. "*Ven a saludar.*"

"Estoy cocinando, mama," replied the big man.

"I'm sorry, enquirers," the señora apologized. "He does not mean to be rude. He will come shortly. Please sit, sit."

She motioned John to a club chair in front of the kitchen door to the left of the sofa. Draped over its back was the same sort of heavy tapestry that covered the walls, only this one was threadbare and faded, and the scene it depicted was hard to make out. But John wanted to test the squeaky hunk of furniture before he sat and, when he bent over and mashed on the cushion, he looked at the picture more closely and thought he could just make out the figure of a brave bullfighter in mid-quité.

The señora said she was anxious to speak with him, but then she sat back down in the cigarillo chair by the window and took her time lighting up another Tiperillo. It gave John a moment to consider the fact that the photo this woman had taken, and the attention it had brought to Santa Teresa, had no doubt made her the talk of the town. But he knew if Tomás' mother had any influence on the town's gossip, the talk may have placed a crown of infamy upon Señora Delgado's head in the bargain.

"Stay and eat with us por favor, enquirers."

"Please," said John, thinking about getting back to Tomás. "I appreciate your invitation, but I need to get back to the hotel."

"But, my son Chuy...he is a good cook, si? He is frying up los pollo y papas. Don't it smell good?"

"Yes it certainly does, señora," John said truthfully. "But I really can't stay. I am sorry to call on you so late, but I wanted to introduce myself and ask if I could have your help with something tomorrow."

When he asked if she would take him to the clearing in the woods where she had seen the Chupacabra, she agreed to his request, but then ardently repeated her dinner invitation several more times while the sound of pots and pans rattled in the kitchen behind John's back. He really wanted to stay and pick the brain of this odd little woman right now, but she had consented to meet him the next morning, and he would ask her all of the questions he wanted then. The señora walked him to the door and John was about to say his goodbye, when an interesting object behind the cigar-chair by the window caught his eye and he asked her about it.

"Oh, sí, sí!" she said as she picked up the colorful, twenty-inch long metal bar and handed it to him. "This is Chuy's idea of protection. He don't let me keep a gun in the house."

The curiosity was made of solid iron and painted black with flames of red, orange, and yellow emblazoned down the sides and, as John held the weighty weapon by the end with the bright orange handlebar grip and turned it around in his hand, admiring what he had to admit was a pretty freaking cool looking *flame-stick*, the señora told him that her son had made it in middle school shop class the year her husband had died. A serious look came over her face as she described how the teenaged Chuy had sawn the length of iron, sanded it down, painted it, and brought it home, where, in the absence of the boy's father, the weapon had become a sort of protective totem for he and his mama.

As John opened the door to go, he couldn't resist playing the muckraker and turned to ask the señora if he could first interview her at the Sanchez Hotel before they went off into the woods. The stout woman's hackles rose and she sharply refused his request en Español. John put a hand over his mouth to hide a smirk.

"Come at ten o'clock tomorrow," said the señora, irked. In just short of a slam, she shoved the door closed, leaving John alone on the porch.

—⚏—

The western horizon glowed orange as he walked away from the house, and, this time, he tested the new cement drive and found that it had cured enough to support a person, but maybe not the brand new, dark green Nissan Sentra parked in the grass on the east side of the house. Instead of turning to the right when he got to the dirt road, which would have taken him back to the hotel, John made a left at the rusty mailbox and headed toward a ridge at the top of the rise, where the road appeared to end. There was still a little light left and, though he needed to apologize to Tomás tonight, John's plan for the morning was to ask Señora Delgado to show him where she had taken the photo; somewhere out in the scraggly, scrubby brush land that began just over this rise. According to Tomás, that was where the dominion of the Chupacabra began, after all, so he decided he would miss the evening comida and try to catch the teenager before bedtime.

Only one other house stood between the Casa Delgado and the crest of the hill and, after he passed it, the road narrowed rapidly from two-car width to a one-car lane, then to a footpath that started at the crest of the hill and plunged into an arroyo. At the bottom of the little canyon, the first path hit another trail that ran parallel to a dry creek bed, so John turned left and strolled along in the failing light, but in less than a minute, the absurdity of his twilight excursion hit him and a spontaneous laugh bursted out. What was he doing? Walking along in half darkness looking down at the ground for...*what*? WHAT IN THE HELL WAS HE DOING?? He was searching the ground for Chupacabra scat, that's what. Not that he would know the difference between that and dog shit.

Today of all days, he had wanted to be in Washington D.C. covering one of the biggest political events in U.S. history. While he was driving through Central Mexico the day before, the United States Electoral College had chosen America's first (half) black president. It was a huge story and one John had enthusiastically anticipated, but here he was, almost five thousand miles away in a foreign country, searching the ground for Chupa-dookie. Not only had he missed the election itself, but he knew that, today, the airwaves, the Internet, and the Halls of Government across the United States would be filled with shouts of

"*RECALL*" from the political right, and delighted but slightly dismayed "*HURRAHS*" from those on the left.

Unfortunately for John, he had pissed off the wrong person in the *Enquirer* assignment office. The intrinsic politiks rampant in the journalistic circles in which he operated were fierce and often quite petty and divisive, and John had recently stepped in the doo-doo. Now he found himself searching for fresh Chupa-CRAPra in the high desert of Central Mexico while most of his peers back home basked in the Obalmy sunshine of a nuevo American dawn.

The daylight faded faster than he expected, and he turned back for the village. As he clambered his way back up the hill in the moonlight, a single pair of red eyes watched him struggle clumsily back up the ridge and, when he got to the crest, John stopped and turned his head to the side. But he was a city boy and didn't even try to fool himself into thinking he could tell one sound from another. For a few seconds, he listened to the symphonette of the emerging nocturnal biosphere before heading back down the road, past Casa Delgado, and on to the hotel.

When he rounded the street corner, he saw Señor Sanchez standing in the open doorway of the hotel office, enjoying an after dinner smoke. As he approached the smiling man, John heard the sound of dishes being washed in the kitchen, announcing that he was too late.

"Ahh, you meess a good one tonight sir," said Señor Sanchez. "Terésa do her especial *Molé de Puerco*. You get lost?"

"That really sounds delicious," John responded. "My bad. I hope the señora will forgive me. And yes, I did get a bit lost."

The man chuckled and stepped aside, and John walked past the registry counter, crossed through the dining room with the big table, and poked his head into the kitchen, where the señora was standing at a large, steel sink rinsing pots and pans while her youngest son dried.

"Señora Sanchez," he said politely. "I'm sorry for missing the evening meal. I got a little lost."

John didn't mention where he had been. The mischievous muck-raker was hungry now, so he kept his mouth shut about his conversation with Constança Delgado.

"I save a plate for you, Mister Juan," said the Señora without smiling. Then, to her son, "Javier, calienta el plato en el microwave."

Javier removed a white dishtowel from a plate on the counter, put it in the microwave, pressed, **start**, and resumed his dish duty.

While John was sitting alone at the big round table eating the heavenly, slightly spicy concoction, Tomás suddenly appeared in the kitchen doorway.

"So," the teenager asked with a sideways grin, "you spoke to Señora Delgado, yes?"

John nodded and took one last bite of food before answering, but before he could, Tomás walked past him without another word, then continued through the office and past his father before turning left into the parking area. The chef and her helper were no longer in the kitchen, so John got up and took his dishes to the sink and washed and dried them before going after Tomás.

It was dark now, but still hot, and the white gravel of the parking lot glowed with a dull yellow cast from three dingy light bulbs that were suspended from an electrical cable stretched between two telephone poles. The yellow bulbs were aswarm with every flying insect know to man, and they swung gently but independently of each other in the welcome evening breeze, creating a disorienting effect as John walked in a wide arc around the light to avoid the bugs.

Tomás was sitting on top of an overturned metal trashcan near John's hotel room, swinging his legs and humming to himself.

"Listen, Tomás," John fawned. "I didn't mean to upset you with my reaction to your... to what you told me, but...well...it took me by surprise. I didn't know what to say. No offense meant at all, but I thought you were having fun with me. I didn't think you were being serious. But now, I understand that you were."

Tomás looked at his swinging shoes for a few seconds, then said,

"Look, Señor Juan, I know what you are here to do. You are here to write an entertaining story for your magazine. I have read about American tabloids on the Internet. I read a lot, sir, and I know that most Americans laugh at your stories and think they are mostly lies or made up...*mierda*. But, in Santa Teresa, what you have come here to write about is not thought of as a joke. I think this is like a funny game to you, but most people here believe in the Chupacabra. You heard all of the stories today, and you know about the rituals and customs we use to honor the thing that cannot be tamed."

John was taken aback by the maturity of the plea, and he stood impressed as Tomás jumped down off of the trashcan, took a step forward, and faced him confidently.

"The photograph?" said Tomás, "...the one Senora Delgado took? It's real. I have seen the creature also and, when I saw the photo that the señora took, it was the same. That is just what he looks like, and it doesn't matter if you or nobody else believes me. He is out there; he is real. And he can talk."

This was the second time that John had been confronted with this ridiculous claim and, just as he had the first time, he paused to let it sink in and tried to maintain a professional distance as he considered the source. This obviously intelligent and surprisingly world-wise teenager, whose company John had shared for several hours, was dead serious about his alleged contact with a chatty chupacabra. The reporter rolled it over in his mind, but couldn't suspend his own disbelief enough to take seriously what Tomás was telling him and, in mid roll, he just stopped himself from laughing out loud; not at Tomás, but at himself for taking a full ten seconds to wage the internal debate. NYU Journalism had taught him to avoid becoming personally involved in a story; it could affect the reporter's impartiality and taint the objectivity of the piece. So, John reset his parameters and, from an intellectual distance, launched into 'Interviewer' mode.

"So, Tomás, what did the, uh...what did the creature...say...to you?"

Before the teenager could answer, John held up a hand to stop him. This wasn't the right way to interview someone, he thought. He got it together and began again.

"Hold on, Tomás, let's start with the circumstances. Where were you, and what were you doing when you saw...*it?*"

Tomás took a step back and looked into the distance.

"Well," he squinted, "two or three times a week, I go to mi Abuela's casa early in the morning to collect huevos frescos...fresh eggs...por mi Madre to cook for the morning comida. And on that morning, I opened the gate to her side yard, trying to be quiet like always because mi Abuela is not awake that early. I went to the chicken coup and, before I opened the little door, there he was, standing behind the coup just ten feet from me. He was just staring at me with big red eyes. I didn't know what to do. It didn't run away like most animals do when they see someone, he just stood there, very still like me, and I could hear him breathing."

"Tell me exactly what you saw, Tomás," asked John.

"Okay, well. He was as tall as me, and stood up, you know, on its hind legs, I guess. His skin looked like, umm...scales. Kind of like the back of an armadillo. And it had some little hairs in some places on its body. You know, like the underside of an armadillo."

He looked at John and asked,

"Do you know what an armadillo is, señor Juan?"

"Well, yes," John answered. "I mean...I couldn't draw you a picture or anything, but...little prehistoric looking animal, right?"

"Si, that's right" Tomás agreed. "With long claws for digging."

"What else do you remember, Tomás?"

"Mostly the eyes; I couldn't look away from his eyes. They were large and dark red like big ripe plums and, even though the sun had not come over the horizon yet, his eyes kind of glowed, you know?"

John nodded.

"And, of course, the teeth, and claws, also. Sharp fangs and claws."

"So, what did you do?"

John was being pulled in, eager to hear the answer.

"Well, I turned to run, but he reached out with his hands, or his claws, like this".

Tomás held his hands with the palms facing up, and the reporter squinted at the teen and searched his eyes, his bullshit detector cranked up to eleven.

"Then, I heard the voice," said the teenager bluntly. "At first, I thought there had to be someone behind me, but I was afraid to turn my back on the thing. But then, his scary mouth opened, and he said, '*Wait*! I couldn't move. I wanted to turn around and run but the big red eyes were just...like...*holding* me."

Screw intellectual distance, thought John now. He was hooked, mesmerized, and hung on the boy's next words.

"Then, señor..." Tomás sounded conspiratorial, "...he said...'*Can you hear me?*'"

Now it was Tomás' turn to analyze John, and he studied the reporter's eyes trying to figure out what was going on behind them. Both parties were silent for what seemed like longer than it really was.

"Holy shit, Tomás," said John finally. "What happened next?"

"I looked at him like this," Tomás opened his eyes wide, "and then my brain goes '*WHA?*' And I run as fast as I can and don't look back...I didn't look back. I went into mi Abuela's casa and looked out her window into the back yard. I saw nothing of the animal, but the door of the chicken coup was open, and chickens were running all over the yard, *loco-loco!*"

John's heart was beating faster now, not merely from the words, but also the apparent conviction behind them, which added to the teen's dramatic delivery. This kid seemed to really believe all of this had happened to him. The reporter was befuddled and wondered what question he could possibly ask after the yarn just spun by his subject. After a beat, John finally flumbered,

"What did his voice sound like, Tomás?"

"It was like a person, but kind of like...high pitched and...umm... kind of, uhhh...*gurgly?*"

"You mean raspy-like?" John asked.

"No, gurgly. Kind of like he got bubbles in his throat."

"Okay then," John agreed amusedly. "*Gurgly*."

After a pause, John asked, "Have you seen him since that morning?"

"YES," Tomás was excited again. "Well...no, I didn't see him. But I think I heard him at my bedroom window that night, and every night for a week after that."

Tomás cocked his head slightly and a furrowed frown formed on his forehead, as he added, "But that part could have been my imagination. I had dreams about him for several nights after it happened. And, even during the daytime, I kept hallucinating that I saw him."

In John's experience soliciting a piece for tabloids, you had to acquiesce to a certain degree of fantastical whimsy in your writing if you wanted to attain the level of grocery-line, eye-grabbing gold that the *Enquirer*, in particular, was known for. The writers who were on staff at those rags, John had learned, used loads of literary license in most of their pieces and, these days, they cranked out nearly all of them without leaving the solitude of their cubicle-farms. But, John wouldn't need to festoon or embellish this one. This one was going to write itself.

"You refer to the creature as *he*," said John. "What made you think it's a male?"

"I don't know, exactly. I guess I could just tell. His voice was high-pitched kind of, but it still seemed like a... un hombre."

"Did you tell your Abuela?"

"Si, and she was nice and sweet to me about it because she is very nice and sweet to everyone, but she didn't believe me. She told me I had only seen a big dog or maybe a wolf." Tomás looked at the ground. "But... then, I told her about the talking, and she asked me if I was on drugs."

John couldn't resist and asked,

"Were you on drugs, Tomás? **Are** you on drugs?"

"No, señor. I have smoked the *móta* before, but not on that day".

There was a charming sincerity in the teenager's demeanor, and John thought the kid could probably pass a lie detector test if asked about the encounter with the creature. He weighed his response before speaking because he needed Tomás with him in the morning when he interviewed Señora Delgado and didn't want to offend him by saying something that might insult him now. The señora spoke barely pass-able conversational English, and John worried that he might ask her a question that was difficult for her to understand, or that she might give an answer that overshot his own grasp of Español. So, putting aside his personal feelings that the story he just heard was too weird to be true, John faked astonishment and apologized for doubting the teen's tall tale. The deception was manipulative to be sure, but it had worked for him surprisingly well in the past as a vehicle for expediency.

Before calling it a night, Tomás answered a few quick questions about his mother's encounter with the dreaded Chupacabra. It had evidently been just a brief sighting, and there had been no verbal interaction, but the glimpse had convinced Señora Sanchez, and Tomás explained with an impish grin that curled up on one side, that his Madre stood up for him now whenever his Padre derided him about the subject.

—⚭—

John crawled underneath the white cotton sheet, exhausted from the heat, and thought about how this assignment was shaping up. He might be missing the flurry of action back home, but, at least the booby-prize wasn't turning out to be boring. Granted, he would still only be writing a piece relating anecdotes and encounters with what, in all probability, was just a misidentified known animal, but the eyewitnesses that John had spoken to this first day were all true believers, and their recollec-tions had seemed to charge the atmosphere.

He knew there had to be more tales to be told by other locals, and, in the morning, he would interview the woman he intended to make the centerpiece of the story. As he drifted off to dreamyville, he count-ed fanged lizards as they bounded over Tomás' Abuela's back chicken fence; half hopping, half flying as they followed each other into the vanishing distance. The last hopper to hurdle the fence turned its head and called something out to him, but John was already too deep in sleep and never understood the words.

Chapter 4

On Thursday morning, John arose earlier than even Señora Sanchez, which was no easy feat. In his younger years, before he had stopped smoking, the early reveille would definitely have required a cigarette, and the old habit still pulled hard at him. But, he had learned that a bit of physical exercise would allay the nic-fits, so he put on tennis shoes and a pair of athletic shorts and took off, trotting down the road in the opposite direction of Señora Delgado's house. It was not yet seven o'clock, and he had some time to kill before calling on her.

As he jogged, he began to see more early risers, and he smiled and waved as he passed. Most waved back, but every one of them eyeballed him thoroughly. Santa Teresa was small, and the community grapevine had already alerted everyone to the American journalist staying at the valley's only hotel.

The day before, Tomás had explained that the printing of Señora Delgado's photograph in an American magazine had reignited local talk over the Chupacabra, and disagreements between some neighbors had resulted in them currently not speaking to each other. Evidently, the debate over the existence of the creature had been roiling for longer than the oldest resident could remember, with some villagers regarding the legend as a quaint, familiar superstition, and others proudly claiming the tales as a reality, unique to their beloved Santa Teresa.

When the photograph first appeared in the Torreón newspaper, the scuttlebutt pot had been stirred, and, with the arrival of a reporter from the American version of the *Enquirer* in town, the fire had been stoked and the pot was now boiling ferociously. Among residents who accepted the fact that there was something out there destroying livestock and taking *el sacrificio de luna llena,* there was also a side bet over the nature of the beast. Was it a wolf? A large dog? Coyote? Jaguar? Some suggested that there could even be a deformed, freakish, human outcast, living off of the land and the occasional chicken, goat, eggs, etc. For residents who kept livestock, the occasional lost or killed animal was an accepted risk, and there were known, rapacious, raptorial animals in this high desert who did take advantage of the 24-hour buffet that was the Santa Teresa stockyards. But to have a predator drain the blood of an animal without then consuming the flesh? That one continued to befuddle the citizens.

On John's first night there, the Sanchez's had told him about the sacrificial stump, and, when he had questioned Tomás about the curious ritual during their errands yesterday, the teen confirmed that the tradition was still practiced regularly. Now, he thought about the stump as he jogged toward a group of structures that looked less like dwellings and more like businesses. When he got closer to the first shop, he noticed, on the broad wall on the side of the building, a crudely executed painting of a hammer, a saw, and a nail. As he slowed to a walk and rounded the corner, the village square came into view.

The open, unpaved plaza was twenty meters across and surrounded on three sides by verandaed, stucco and wood structures housing a handful of small shoppes. In the courtyard, the hard-packed carpet of dirt was speckled with sparse sprigs of grass clinging for dear life on to the dry, desert soil and, from the side where John stood, the ground rose gradually to a wide, flat mound on the opposite, open side of the square. In the center of the flat mound, beside a small gazebo that was freshly painted light green with baby blue trim, sat a large tree stump that he instantly knew was the one spoken of.

John put his hands on his hips, shook first one leg then the other to keep his muscles loose, and breathed deeply to re-infuse his blood with oxygen as he ambled towards the mound. The stump itself was huge and stood just short of waist-high. With a wide, flat top more than a meter in diameter, and big, thick roots that plunged from the base of the trunk deep into the ground, he thought the tree must have been quite impressive when it was alive. But now, it was bare of bark and looked less like a noble giant watching over Santa Teresa, and more like a place you would sit to eat a laid-back sack lunch. At some point after the big tree was felled, someone had chosen to paint the entire stump white, but now most of the tint was washed out, and John hadn't even noticed it until he got nearer.

Stepping closer, he knelt to look at the strange symbol carved into the side of the trunk. It reminded him of the crude, simple pictographs he had seen while vacationing in Colorado years ago; drawn by long-deceased Native American artists. A horizontal, upward-bending arc with four small triangles spread out across the top of the curved line. He rapped his knuckles on the wood next to the carving and found that the smooth trunk was hard as stone.

John stood up again for a better look. He had just noticed a slack rope snaking along the ground that was looped and tied around the bottom of the stump on one end, when he suddenly felt a cold, wet nose and a quick puff of hot breath on the back of his bare thigh. His heart jumped a beat, and he spun around to see a sheep about the size of a Golden Retriever looking up at him through its sheepy orb-eyes with the creepy, horizontal-rectangle pupils. The animal lowered its head and brushed against John's leg with a *baaaaa*, and he smiled and reached down to sink his fingers deep into the thick wool on the back of it's neck.

"Hey there, fella!" he said. "So, you're one of the lucky ones, huh?"

The sheep baaa'd again as it circumnavigated the jogger's bare legs, leaning against him with enough force that John had to apply equal counter-force to keep from being knocked over. The spare clumps of grass scattered across the mound didn't look sufficient to support even one grazing animal for long, but then he noticed that some kind soul had supplemented the animal's diet, as a few wilted leaves of lettuce lay scattered here and there on the ground. He continued to duel with the gregarious sheep in its game of 'Gringo Knock-down', but he was startled once more by a voice from behind.

"Be careful you not standing too close when the Chupacabra **grab** him, heheheh."

Approaching from across the square and chuckling as he came, was a short, skinny man with a bush of wooly, gray hair sprouting from his chia head. His dark, sunbaked complexion made it hard to tell his age for sure, but John thought he was at least seventy years old. When he was ten feet away, the characterful man squatted, and the sheep left John and trotted over to the old timer, who put an arm around the animal and patted its neck.

"So, you met mi niña?" he said with a gap-toothed grin. "Es una hermosa niña. She don't make too much noise at night."

The skinny old man scritched up underneath the sheep's chin and it leaned against him, stretching its neck out for more. John smiled at the reciprocal display of affection.

"So, you live near the plaza then?" John asked.

At first, he didn't think the man had understood the question, but then his old eyes lit up.

"Oh yes señor. I stay right there."

The man crooked a thumb toward a wooden porch behind him. Sitting a few feet to the left of a shop door, in the shade of the eaves, John saw a weathered, wooden bench that looked about as wide as the old man was tall. Nailed to the facade above the shop door was a hand-painted sign with the letters **PANADERÍA** in blue on a white background, and John's sparse *vocabulario español* just happened to include the word.

"You are the baker?" John asked, giving the man the benefit of the doubt.

"Oh no señor, I stay right there in front. *Yo soy Centinela;* I watch the animals."

My god, John realized, this man must have seen some real shit go down here. Okay, time to hear some more crazy. Ready? Interview Powers…ACTIVATE!!

"Could I ask your name, señor?" he began.

"Si, me llamo Raphael. But everyone calls me *Corto.*"

"Okay Corto, do you sleep here every night?" John asked, hoping to god the answer was yes.

"Si, most nights I do, unless it's too cold. Sometimes in the winter, I go to mi hermano's casa, but mostly, I am right here, watching."

¡PAYDIRT!

"So, then you are the man to ask about the…" John faltered, "…the creature. Is it real? You must have seen it, right?"

A sly smile curled up slowly on Corto's lips.

"Ohhhhh, *tu eres el Americano que se queda con los Sanchez.* You are the guy from the magazine, si?

"Yes señor, I am writing a story about your Chupacabra."

Corto removed his arm from the sheep and stood up straight and proud.

"*No MI señor Chupacabra,* no no no. He is not *mine*; he belongs to all of Santa Teresa, to *all* of us. *Nos pertenece a todos nosotros.*"

John paused for a moment before rephrasing the question to think about the angle he was after. He wasn't here to write about the actual Chupacabra. His assignment was to write a piece about the Santa Teresans themselves, who not only seemed to have a collective belief in the phenomenon, but even claimed it as a sort of village mascot. Before him stood a colorful character who spent his nights beside the totemic sacrificial tree; potential for dramatic tension? *CHECK!*

"Corto," John started again, "what happens to the animals that are tied to the stump?"

The old man muttered something to himself in Spanish. Then, he looked around the plaza and down the road in both directions, giving John a conspiratoristic impression that the old timer was about to disclose some information that other villagers might not want the world to know.

"Wellll you seee," said Corto as he looked at John and scratched at his white, three-day whiskers.

"La mayoría de los animales, ummm…Most of them…they go back where they came from. Back to the owners; whoever bring him, take him back, *lo matan y se lo comen*."

"And what about the other ones, Corto?" pushed the reporter.

A blank look came over Corto's eyes, and John could see that a battle was going on behind them. He had an idea why and prompted the answer using the man's proper name to throw him off guard.

"Raphael, do you ever take an animal?"

He watched Corto's expression carefully, then added, "Or maybe some eggs… sometimes?"

Corto hesitated, and, after a few seconds, said "Okay senior…you see… I am *el Centinela*. It is my job for me to do. The people here…" he held his arms out wide. "…they take care of me, you know? It is expected for me to… sometimes…*take* an animal sometimes, eh? Eet ees okay for that."

"And the other times, Corto?" John increased the tension, "what about when the animal remains here, but only the blood is gone? What has happened then?"

The old man's posture changed, and he chuckled and said,

"Well, for that Señor," he stroked his whiskers again, "I sleep very soundly, you know, and sometimes I don't see everything that happens. Maybe I am a bad Centinela sometimes, heheheheh."

You've got to be kidding, thought John to himself. This was the answer he was getting? *Hail* no! He had travelled a long way to write this story, and he was not about to let him off the hook that easily. This grizzled old scarecrow was the only person who had the regular opportunity to see whatever it was, if anything at all, that was being spotted.

"Raphael, come on now, don't do this to me," John's voice was mock desperation. "Tell me yes or no, HAVE YOU SEEN A CHUPACABRA? Don't let me down now!"

From John's first question about the creature, Corto had shied away from eye contact, but now, he looked directly into the American's eyes, sucked in his bottom lip, put his hands in his back pockets and, after a long, considered pause, said,

"I do not know you señor." Corto's tone was sober. "You do not live in Santa Teresa and you don't know our ways. Sí, I have seen things. I have seen many things in my seventy-four years, but...some things are things that a young man cannot understand, and you are a young man, señor. I am more than just the *Centinela* of the square; I am the guardian of *los tesoros y secretos de Santa Teresa.* My people trust me to watch and not to tell.

John's shoulders dropped and he let out a sigh of frustration. The energy from the jog suddenly sloughed away and, as he stood looking at Corto unhappily, he was already pondering other alternatives to this disappointing dead-end. His mind shot to his ten o'clock appointment with Mrs. Delgado and, perhaps most promising from an exploitably sensationalistic point of view, his further conversations with Tomás, who had given him the juiciest account of the Monster yet. Before John could excuse himself, the old man said,

"I got to go now, señor. Okay?"

Corto was looking over his shoulder toward the veranda in front of the Panadería, where John saw the baker, dressed all in white, standing in the open doorway. The man gestured and called out *"Corto!"* and when he walked back into the shop, Corto turned back to John, bowed his head, and then shuffled off towards the porch.

The exchange with the old man had been fruitless, but it was nothing new for John. Often in his profession, he had found that promising leads could crumble in your hands or, at the very least, not pan out the way you wanted them to. An effective journalist was part writer, part sleuth, and, when he hit a roadblock, sought alternate routes to the objective. In two hours from now, Señora Delgado would take him to ground zero but, before that, he wanted to get a better feel for the little village, so he trotted out of the plaza through a space between the buildings at one corner of the square, and resumed his workout.

John was a city boy through and through. Born in Washington D.C., raised in Providence, and now living in Manhattan, he was an affirmed urbanite, but he enjoyed watching this sleepy little village come to life. Most *Enquirer* pieces being created in-house, preparing a story for them almost never required any travel at all, so this was a real treat and, although a snipe hunt in the middle of nowhere was nowhere close to his dream assignment, he had to admit that these village people intrigued him. He was determined to get the most out of the day's intercourse.

John knew that the business model of all tabloids was to provide readers with an escape from their, either humdrum, or stressed-out, anxiety-laden lives. But those readers had to first be hooked by enticing photos and provocative headlines, and he was hep to the delicate discipline of straddling the line between believability and fantasy, both with the images on the cover, and the stories within. Anything that seemed overtly commonplace or too 'real' was deemed too boring and, unfortunately, when a yellow-journalist's imagination failed him, the (accepted?) modus operandi could include the rehashing of old stories, raiding other publications for material ('Cookie-Jar Hand'; a legal/medical term), or, if the editor of the particular tabloid was foolhardy and brazen enough, they had been known to let slide stories created out of whole cloth, without regard to legal consequences.

The fact that the *National Enquirer* had been the top selling tabloid in the U.S. for decades came with the unfortunate upshot of being the scapegoat for, not just their own questionable practices, but those of all frivolous rags in general. They had squandered the opportunity presented them by the John Edwards scandal, and the *Enquirer* was currently experiencing a brand-identity crisis and, as John trotted along on the hard dirt road, he wondered if a story about a Chupacabra would help their bid to be seen as a source for hard news. He guessed probably not.

What about one with a *talking* Chupacabra? Definitely not. No, this piece would be red meat for the idjits, but if he turned in a winner, maybe it would give him the leverage needed to work his way back into the political blender where he wanted to be.

—⚹—

There were no vending machines in the Sanchez Hotel, and its owners were not down with the modern custom of providing guests with bottled drinking water, so, John had slipped a few U.S. dollars into his shoe before leaving the hotel room this morning, in case he found a place or person who would sell him a couple of bottles of *agua fría.* Having experienced *'Montezuma's Revenge'* once on a trip to Cuba, (that one might have been *'Batista's Revenge'*), he knew that the tough, leather-jacket wearing bad bacteria in the local water supply could beat the crap out of the fluoridated, bleached, and otherwise chemically treated water that his American body had arrived replete with.

It wasn't as hot today, but the jog had left him cotton-mouthed and parched, so he decided to circle back toward the hotel. Just as he turned around, someone called out to him, and he turned to see a pretty, young woman wearing a white apron over a knee-length, dark-green dress. Her black hair was tied up in a red scarf and, as she waddled toward him from an herb garden between two houses on his right, John saw that she was heavy with child.

"Ola, señor," said the woman with a welcoming smile. "You look lost. May I help you find something?"

Her accent was heavy, but John was glad to hear that she spoke at least some English.

"Gracias señora," he answered. "Can you tell me where I could buy some bottled water, por favor?"

"Haha, no señor." John found her laugh adorable. "No stores in Santa Teresa. But, mi Padre has water. *No le gusta el agua.* He buys it by the case in Durango."

"I'm sorry to bother you, señora," John appealed, "but do you think he would sell me a couple of bottles

"No, no, you don't got to pay him. Él le dará un par de botellas."

She motioned for him to follow and waddled towards her front door. When John stepped inside, a tall, imposing man with stern features rose from his chair to welcome his daughter and the stranger she had brought.

"Hola, niña," said the man, "¿Quien es este?"

"Papa, por favor dale dos botellas de agua."

John took his cue and stepped forward with an outstretched hand.

"Forgive me, señor," he said, "let me introduce myself. Me llamo John Maddox, and I'm here in your village to write a story for a magazine."

In an instant, the welcoming smile turned upside down as if a switch had been thrown. The tall man shot a severe scowl at him and stormed out of the room, waving his arms and unleashing a torrent of not-particularly beautiful romance language as he disappeared into the back of the house. The woman turned to John with an apologetic look.

"Uno momento, por favor, señor."

She wobbled off after her father, leaving John standing just inside the front door, not knowing whether he should stay or leave. But, his parched throat, as well as his curiosity, made him linger and, as he listened to the heated words coming from the other room, he was reminded for the second time today that his presence had caused disquiet in the tiny burg. Santa Teresans were a passionate and superstitious people, and any mention of the Chupacabra was sure to meet with a zealous response. In John's estimation, that was going to make for a great story when he put it all together. These people really believed this stuff, and now he stood in the living room of an angry man who possessed what might be the only supply of untainted drinking water for miles. *La passión y la superstición de Santa Teresa* were being acted out for him as if scripted.

At this point, it didn't matter whether the daughter was able to calm her father and score some *agua* or not; John knew his exit would be uncomfortable either way. So, he decided to stay and see what happened, and, while *los argumento el Español* continued in the back room, he casually surveyed the room he was standing in and did some light stretching to stay loose. Just above the frame of the front door was the same odd symbol he had seen carved into the stump in the town square; only, this version was slightly different. It was painted in vivid colors directly onto the wall and, although it had the same curved line with four triangles along the top, the dominating feature here was a large red eye below the line, with a vertical pupil like a cat's eye, or more likely, he thought, like the eye of a reptile.

"I am sorry for mi papa. He is not so rude most of the time."

John turned around and the young woman handed him three beautiful blue plastic bottles with an apologetic smile.

"Por favor tome el agua," she rattled off quickly. "The water is free for you, but you must go now."

She put a hand on his shoulder and pushed him out the door. As he was turning back around to show his gratitude, the woman shut the door behind him with a SshWACK between the words *thank*, and *you*, leaving him alone on the porch.

John had two hands, but three bottles, and he fumbled with them as he started off for the hotel; juggling as he jogged. He made it back in time for a shower before another wonderful comida with the Sanchez family, during which the kids were in a silly mood and happy to have the American stranger to entertain once again.

During the meal, both John and his young translator were careful not to mention their coming errand, and Tomás did his best to avoid his mother's gaze, but it was clear that Señora Sanchez had already guessed their plans. The darts shooting from her eyes bore directly into the top of her son's lowered head. When they finished, Tomás waited for his family to filter out of the dining room and kitchen before making two pimento-cheese sandwiches, which he then wrapped in a paper sack and carefully put inside a backpack on top of the two remaining bottles of water and a tube of sunscreen for the pasty American.

It was at last time to venture into Chupacabraland with Señora Delgado. They left the hotel and started off toward the woman's house, both uncomfortable from the conversation the night before, and silent as they walked around the corner and up the hill. The coming interview would be the story's most relevant recounting and, though neither spoke it aloud, both thought the same thing; this was definitely going to be interesting.

Chapter 5

"Hola, Señor John," Señora Delgado welcomed them. "I am ready to go!" Then, calling over her shoulder, "¡Vamos, Chuy, *Vamos!*"

The giant man that John had seen in the kitchen the night before entered the room and walked up behind his mother. Unlike the previous night, Chuy was fully dressed in jeans, heavy hiking boots, and a blue flannel shirt, unbuttoned, revealing a white undershirt underneath. His shoulder length, raven-black hair was pulled back in a ponytail and the colorful knapsack slung over his shoulder reminded John of the material and designs unique to traditional Guatemalan weaving.

The señora was a chubby, middle-aged woman with a slight limp, which made the uphill walk a struggle for her. She was panting when they reached the top of the road, so they paused at the crest for a moment to let her rest.

"Es~~~bueno vert~~~Tomás," the señora said between breaths. Then, still speaking to the teenager but switching to English in deference to the American reporter.

"You~~~have not come around~~~mi casa~~~in a while. Cómo está tu Madre?"

"She is well Señora, thank you," said Tomás in a polite voice. "I will say that you asked."

"Si~~~bueno. Tu madre es~~~una buena mujer."

"Gracias señora."

When the woman had caught her breath, she led the way down the other side of the hill into the arroyo and made a left turn onto the same footpath John had taken the night before. The reporter followed Chuy, who walked closely behind his mother, ready to catch her if she stumbled on the uneven trail, and Tomás brought up the rear. But the pace was too slow for the teenager. He was used to bounding along on paths like this at must faster speeds, and now he walked right on John's heels.

After a couple of hundred meters, the arroyo opened onto a wider creek that would have flowed toward the river valley to their left had it not been bone dry. At this point, the señora crossed the creek bed, turned right, and started up a long slope made of slight, undulating moguls scattered with trees and juniper. For the next five minutes, the party followed her up and down the shallow knolls that climbed steadily until they came to a narrow clearing surrounded by short pine trees. The woman halted, breathing heavily, and said,

"Okay~~Señor Juan~~~ this~~~is the place."

With one hand on her hip and the other gesturing toward the clearing, John smiled, thinking she looked like a broke-ass 'The Price is Right' model.

"Here... right *here* is where I take the picture."

"What brought you to this place, Señora?" John asked. "And how did you come to have a camera with you just then?"

"Well, I come here sometimes to pick up the piñon nuts, and I see him three times before that..."

The woman was speaking her best *Englais,* but she talked fast and with no pauses, and John had to consult Tomás several times for help.

"So," the woman continued, "I tell Chuy and he buy me a camera in Torreón when he go the next time and so he get me a little paper-box kind that take twelve pictures then you throw it away so you only use one time, si? But I only took one pictures of Chupacabra so I use the rest to take pictures of mi hijo y mis trofeos y mascaras de lucha then Chuy tomó la cámara a Torreón para que puedan revelar las fotos for, how you say...?"

"Develop, Mama," said Chuy, helping. "They developed the photos."

"Si, that." She pointed at her son.

"Can you remember any other details about what happened señora?" John delved further.

"Oh yes señor. It was on a Monday morning very early and it was nice outdoors, bonito-bonito. Not too hot. When I come to this place, I seen it and I was *READY* for him that time though, okay?" Then, holding up an imaginary camera. "The two times before, I just barely see him but this time I know what it was and I was ready for him, okay?"

"Ha! See?" Tomás interjected quietly, "She said 'him'."

Señora Delgado ignored the interruption.

"*IT*..." said the señora, ignoring the interruption. "...was crouch down with ees back to me." She mimicked the action. "And... he got something in his hands, in the claws...and right when I lift the camera up to my eye I turn the little wheel on the top and it make a sound, the little click click click. So then, Chupacabra spring up and turn around. I think he is jumping at me and I didn't even know I push the camera button because I turn and run fast as I can. But then I trip and fall down into the creek bed and I think it is *ON* me! So I yell! But, when I look back again, there is nothing."

The señora's rapid-fire account had been succinct and short on embellishment. Not a lot to work with, thought John. A moment of silence passed as he thought of what to ask next.

"Anything else that you can remember, señora?" he asked finally. "Any details?"

"Only...the hiss," she said, "It give me a '*hisss*' when it turn around."

"Tell me more about the appearance of the creature. What did it look like?"

"Well," she shrugged, "you saw the picture didn't you? That picture shows more than I see, okay? Because, right after I *click*, I run run run.

Later, when Chuy come back from Torreón with picture I say 'si, si, yes, yes that is what I see."

After trying different questions and angles from which to ask them, a discouraged John decided he had gotten all that he was going to from this woman. He thanked Señora Delgado and remained behind in the clearing with Tomás as they watched the Delgados hike back toward the village.

As far as the photograph and the woman who took it were concerned, John had now fulfilled his obligation to the *Enquirer*. He had hoped for more from her, but his real interest at this point was in spending more time with his teenage guide/translator who, so far, had told him the most compelling tale concerning the creature that he had heard since arriving in Santa Teresa. Tomás, however, was still tight-lipped and cold to him.

The day before, the boy had trusted John with the same tale that had brought him mockery and ridicule from friends and family alike. He had trusted that the worldly New York Cityman would take him seriously, and John had not handled it well. Who would have, he wondered? This reporter took pride in having an open mind that traveled liberally beyond even the required objectivity of his chosen field but, this week, that open mind was really being tested. For the last two days, his enlightened brain had run headlong into a wall of personally-delivered accounts of things he would normally have written off as superstitious bullshit and filed away in his brain's 'folklore-folder', but the percolating sincerity in these stories had caught him off guard. When he got back to his writing nook in Tribeca, it would be easier to deny credence to the ridiculous fairy tales, but here in Santa de Teresa, he was 'In the Shit'; as his Dad, a former Vietnam War correspondent would say. It was strange, but John felt that a hook had dropped into his gaping mouth, and he knew he couldn't let it set.

Alone again in nature with Tomás, he was able, after some effort and faux-sincere coaxing, to convince him to open up again and, sure enough, the boy gave him a hot tip that would lead to a promising new element. Tomás divulged that a little farther up the rise was the rim of an ancient volcanic crater, and the teen sounded like a tour guide as he explained that, eons ago, the crater floor inside had collapsed, creating a wide caldera basin that spread out nearly as far as one could see. He went on to explain that the side of the caldera that they were nearest to was covered with winding dirt roads that had been cut through the brush, trees, and juniper bushes by generations of young people in cars (and some not so young) as they raced and chased each other around a mazelike dirt racecourse.

It all sounded very familiar, and John remembered participating in similarly impetuous activities when he was younger. He and his high school buddies had called it rat-racing and, though the 'Wheeler-Wheelers' didn't have an extinct volcano back then with an awesome racetrack like the one Tomás was describing, their off-road enduros were almost always preceded by over-consumption of alcohol; a custom that he guessed was probably practiced here as well.

As Tomás spoke, it became clear that he had been a participant in the impromptu rallies more than once, at least in a passenger/navigator capacity. He went on to reveal that some of the older kids who careened around the course after dark had reported spotting Chupacabras out beyond the outer circle of the track in the wide band of thicket that grew in the shadow of the crater wall. Some, it seems, had described pairs of red eyes glowering at them from inside the brush, and a few even claimed to have seen the full-monty; a creature hopping just out of sight of the car's headlights as the driver tried to follow it.

To John, this sounded like a much better place to commence a farcical pursuit of the creature. The ludicrous exercise would be a snipe hunt anyway, but this sounded better than traipsing through acres of the rocky scrub brush that surrounded the village on three sides and rolled on for miles. So they continued on over the little hills; up and down, but always up, and moving farther away from the village.

When at last they reached the base of the crater's steep slope, they both climbed to the top of the escarpment and John looked down and out into the broad caldera. He thought it must have been an impressive volcano in its day, and he tried to imagine how it would have looked when it was active; a vast crater bubbling with all shades of red and orange as it fumed and belched its sulphurous gases. John smiled at Tomás' impressively detailed comments as he explained that, when the fire had gone out long ago, the volcanic rock had cooled and crumbled and been pulverized into ash by erosion. The ash had mixed with the surrounding Pleistocene fluvial, as well as ubiquitous, intercontinental dust, borne on the wind from the corners of the globe, resulting in the perfect conditions for a future bad-ass dirt race track; like it had been part of God's great plan all along.

The flat, caldera floor was thirty feet down from where they stood on the rim of the crater. Up against the base of the steep crater wall below, and all the way around the inner periphery of the caldera, was the wide band of trees and brush that Tomás had described and, beyond that brushy thicket was a broad apron of dirt encircling the racecourse. The track itself was a maze of single-car width ruts, which carved interconnected figure eights into the caldera floor and left a dozen or more oval shaped islands marooned within; each one varying from ten meters in diameter, to over two-hundred towards the outside edges of the track.

"No cars right now," John pointed out. "Do they only race on the weekends?"

"Yes, or a week night, sometimes. It's funner at night, but en Sabadós por la tare…sorry," Tomás apologized for the slip. "They also race most Saturday afternoons."

Away to the right, John saw a steep, ramp-like road that had been cut into he bluff and climbed from the caldera floor to the crater rim. From where they were, getting to the ramp would mean backtracking down the slope and back up again farther down, and John could feel the top of his own head broiling in the sun. He decided that he would rather have the rental car to drive down there anyway, so they tromped back down the slope and started back towards the village. It was midday now, and the pair kept their approaching lunchtime hunger at bay by wolfing down the pimento cheese sandwiches from Tomás' backpack as the walked. After climbing out of the arroyo and cresting the final hill, they marched past Casa Delgado and John noticed that the brand new, dark green Nissan was now parked on the new driveway.

When the intrepids reached the hotel, they found that the family had already eaten. But, Señora Sanchez had saved a lunch for them (*puerque rojo* served on homemade stone ground bread; deeelish!), so they kept mum about the sandwiches and sat together at the big table, soberly discussing the preposterous claim Tomás had made the previous day. Although they both spoke more candidly now, it was soon obvious that Tomás had, pretty much, spilled the tastiest beans already, and so John changed his line of questioning to find out what life was like for a fifteen-year old in this tiny town.

In turn, the boy asked John many questions about America, especially about life in New York City and, when the chat turned to the subject of John's own chosen profession, Tomás' eyes widened and he admitted that when he finished his online classes every day, he liked to practice writing short stories. The earnest, knowledgeable young man once again impressed, and John thought he might stay in touch with him after he got back to New York; possibly in a mentoring capacity, if the kid was interested. John thought that he might be.

Chapter 6

Reporter and translator finished eating lunch, and John excused himself to his little hotel room. After releasing the Kraken, he went to the sink and freshened up, then headed out to the parking lot, hopped into the rent-a-Buick, and set out for the caldera. Not that it helped him, living on the grid that was Manhattan, where everything was up-down-east-west, and his only concern was remembering to recharge his Metro-Card occasionally, but John was good with directions, and he found the road to the caldera with little trouble.

When he had picked up the rental car at *el Aero Puerto Internaçional Benito Juarez* in Mexico City four days earlier, he had discovered that his driving faculties were atrophied, and it took a while before the reflexive minutia of the task returned. During his high-school rat-racing days in suburban Rhode Island, he had developed what he considered above average skills while zooming around in a baboon-ass red, Mazda 626, purchased with money saved from a paper route he had worked since sixth grade. With a turbo kit, a low spoiler on the tail, and a motorized, oscillating air-conditioner vent in the dash that waved slowly back & forth from the driver's side to the passenger seat, the sporty little car had been a blast to drive.

Today, however, he would have to settle for getting his off-road kicks in a not so bitchin' Buick. Gathering road speed as he approached the base of the volcano's cinder-cone, John stomped on the accelerator a half-second before hitting the last, inclining slope, and powered the sluggish, urban vehicle up and over the rim. He took his foot off the gas and the car plunged down the ramp. When he hit the flat caldera floor, he made a couple of cautious circuits around the labyrinth of tracks to familiarize himself with the race course before pulling the dust-covered Buick onto the outer apron and killing the engine.

A westerly wind had now blown in, making the air feel somewhat Novemberier. He got out, tilted his head back, closed his eyes and listened to the breeze as it swished through the long grass; a few songbird calls; the distant sound of a truck on the highway; and several nearby animalian sounds that he couldn't identify. Field mice, maybe? Ground squirrels, rabbits, and shrews, skittering through the bushes; a coyote or two, maybe; possibly even a fox, but probably nothing bigger than that. Anything larger would have a hard time finding cover in the scraggly trees and low brush that covered the inner islands of the dirt track.

When he opened his eyes again, he took a better look around and noticed narrow trails going this way and that and slicing through the vegetation of the scrub-islands as they crisscrossed the racetrack. The pathways looked too narrow to have been made by humans but, stepping closer to a trail that led off across one of the smaller islands, John pulled aside the tall grass that bowed over the path and saw cigarette butts and cerveza bottles on the ground, along with plastic bags that had been snagged by thorny barbs in the brush on either side and flapped helplessly in the wind like gonfalons of shame.

A couple of especially narrow trails disappeared into the wide outer ring of growth behind him and, as he walked over to inspect, he wondered why the lion's share of vegetation grew around the base of the bluff, leaving the rest of the caldera floor a mix of grass, scrub brush, pitiful trees, and lots of bare ground. Thinking of Tomás and his tour guide patter from earlier, John deduced that because he hadn't seen any pools or ponds, dry or otherwise, in the middle part of the caldera, this band of trees and thick underbrush must have been fed by the rain runoff, and then fertilized by a high concentration of fertile, volcanic soil at the base of the crumbling crater wall. He attributed the abrupt halt of the thicket at the racetrack's outer ring to decades of spinning car tires, which had routinely beaten back the flora beneath generations of *Los Duques de Condado Hazard*, who had sliced, diced, and coated their hallowed auto-playground with layers of sacred dust.

As he looked out over the wild copse, John imagined a Chupacabra bounding through the brush. Despite the preposterocity of the notion, he was both amused and creeped out a skosh, but he had come a long way for this whacky story and figured he'd better poke around in this bramble for a few minutes. It was an odd position to be in, he thought; the idea that any time he spent tracking down the object of his story was actually time wasted.

The temperature had dropped quickly, and John pulled a breath of fresh, brisk air deep into his lungs in preparation for the preposterous promenade, and plunged into the bosk. The pungent fragrance of juniper, mesquite, and a scattering of flowering plants gave him an instant, Euell Gibbons vibe.

"If only I had a bowl of Grape Nuts right now," he said to no one.

Curiously, there was no trash on this path; no cigarette butts, no beer bottles or cans, and not one plastic bag, which was especially strange in light of the abundance of potential bag-snaggers all around. Using a low-aiming breaststroke as he walked to part the tall grass growing over the path, his mind drifted to his peers and colleagues in D.C., who, probably at this very moment, were waiting for press conferences to begin, or on phone calls with their White House sources, or hunched over a hot laptop in their sequestered cubicles banging out reports and/ or opinions of the first days of the Fresh Prez. Though it rankled that he was missing the action at home, he tried to relax and just...be here...

in the moment, as Victoria would tell him if she were here. Being out of the city was a treat for him and, though this place was not Xanadu by any means, it did have a unique, rugged kind of beauty.

As he neared the bluff, John's daydream of D.C. was dislodged by a strong breeze that kicked up in an instant and whished and whistled loudly through the trees. The path split off in a T when he reached the bluff, and he turned left and made his way along the wall. When he looked out over the tall juniper bushes towards his rental car, he couldn't see the Buick for the boscage, and a very real, and very American sense of 'automobile-separation' flared up in him. Adding to that nagging anxiety were two scratched-up legs, from several prickly bushes he had scraped against on the path, and a quickly germinating disenchantment with the snipe hunt in general. All of these factors compounded and he decided that the search window for tracking Chupacabri was now closed, and his all too brief love affair with nature had expired. *"The city is strong in this one,"* John laughed to himself.

After following the wall for fifty meters or so, he veered left onto another trail that cut back through the thick stuff. As he walked, he looked down at the path, trying to avoid brushing against outlying thorns, and also, to keep from stepping on the handful of small mammals, which he could identify by broad classification, and a couple of lizards, who moved a bit sluggishly in the cooling breeze. In the bushes and trees all around him, there were also birds; many, MANY birds.

Just as he noticed the odd, fowl proliferation, all of the winged creatures took flight in a single, loud, fluttering body, causing an eruption of sound that splintered the air like a shot had gone off. He ducked to avoid the wings of two large crows that flapped past his head, and then decided that the birds probably knew something that he didn't, so he speed-walked behind the flock, trying not to step on any of the small furry somethings skittering past his feet.

When he was halfway through the thicket, and the last bird had outpaced him, the breeze cut off as quickly as it had whipped up, and John stopped dead still in the sudden, eerie silence. The car was still twenty meters from where he stood, but he was afraid to move. He closed his gaping mouth, took in a deep breath through his nose, then held it as he turned his head from side to side, listening. But all he heard was his own heartbeat in his ears.

Frozen in a defensive posture, with limbs taut and eyes squinted, sharp and keen, as if his monkey brain was getting ready to flick the **ON** switch for the trusty ol' flight-response mechanism, John cracked a nervous smile and suppressed a chuckle at the ironic potential of becoming the first confirmed human victim of a Chupacabra whilst preparing a story about the beastie for the *National Enquirer*, priceless.

His uneasiness impelled him to employ a trick he had learned as a kid, and he bellowed out loudly in a deep, boomy voice.

"OKAY CHUPEY, I'm READY for you! LET'S DO THIS!!"

It was meant to diffuse his own nervousness as well as scare away the coyote, or bobcat, or whatever other predator had spooked the birds, and he felt emboldened, just as he had when he first discovered the trick at the age of eleven.

It was the first time young John's parents had left him home alone after dark. They had gone to see the Providence Symphony perform, and only left him alone for a couple of hours, but it made a lasting impression on the youngster. That night, he had taught himself to deal with his own fears in an interesting way. Before his parents walked out the door, he had told them,

"I'll be fine. Don't worry about me. I'm not a little kid anymore."

And his bravado had lasted all the way until the paneled, family station wagon had disappeared around the corner at the end of their street. They might as well have vanished from the face of the earth, and his youthful imagination had fired up, kindling his paranoia. Thirty minutes after his parents were gone, he was convinced that someone was trying to break into the house, and the eleven-year old decided to make the fail-safe call to his grandparents, who lived less than five minutes away. Before he dialed the last number on the rotary telephone, however, he thought about his mom and dad, and how much he didn't want them to think he was too young to be left alone, and he took his finger out of the 3 hole, and put the receiver back in its cradle.

T'was then he set about devising a surefire strategy; one that would enable a young boy to frighten away a bigger, stronger opponent, be it Monster, Alien, or bad guy from central casting. That evening, he had been sure that at least one of the three was laying in wait for him somewhere in the house and, as he tiptoed around corners, expecting someone or some *thing* to jump out and grab him at any moment, he had the epiphany; **a gun**! Of course! A huge .357 Magnum or a sawed-off shotgun. He could still remember the satisfaction of wrapping his young fingers around a huge, imaginary, shiny silver pistol, and feeling its cold warmth beneath his grip.

"OKAY MOTHERFUCKER!" The cursing made him feel especially invincible. "THE JIG IS UP!' Come out, you Sunnuva**BITCH!** I know exactly where you are, and I have my Dad's .357 Magnum! I want you OUT of here... ***RIGHT NOW!***"

With the barrel of the invisible weapon leading the way, he had moved methodically through the house, barking out warnings all the while as he leapt confidently around corners and fearlessly flung open closet doors. '*This is the real stuff*', young John had thought, and it felt like he had taken a giant step towards manhood as he brandished the weighty, shiny, hypothetical gun.

"I'll give you to the count of twenty to get the **hell** out of this house, or I start shooting. Then, I call the cops!"

He had counted loudly and menacingly and, when no one or no *thing* had come out, he had relaxed a bit. What criminal *or* monster could possibly fail to respond to his strong, pre-pubescent, high alto voice booming out the warnings, he had wondered. At that moment, and for the first time in his eleven years, he had felt what he thought it must be like to be a grown up, and the former scaredy-cat had lionized the conquering of his childish fears by watching the scariest movie he could find on television; his imaginary weapon reassuringly tucked beside him on the sofa.

The psychological trick he had used back then worked for him now, and he felt emboldened in the face of the unknown. Still, although the rational part of his brain knew that whichever local, Central Mexican Plateau predator had prompted the flight of the birds and smaller animals would probably not be a threat to a grown man, he had to admit that the collection of tales about the fanged, razor-clawed, blood-sucking giant lizard, which he had heard from the mouths of convinced natives, had left his pristine skepticism blemished. His reference points were shuffled into a jumbled mess. How could he be afraid of a creature that he didn't even believe existed, he wondered. An existential conundrum, indeed.

For what felt like a long time, the city boy stood listening for any sound. Eventually, the music of nature faded in again and, when the birds started to return and John was relatively sure he was not about to be forcibly relieved of his blood, he ran-walked back to the car and jumped in. The flight-response had served him well and, just as he slammed the door behind him, a shiver ran from the top of his head down his spine, and out into the beige upholstered, foam rubber seat cushion. The rush of adrenaline had done its job, but he tried to relax and switch it off again as he turned the key in the ignition.

He didn't consider himself a particularly macho guy, but the smidgen of that attitude that John did possess now came out, and he laughed triumphantly and bumped the shifter into DRIVE, then proceeded to spin around the dirt track, going faster and faster until he was Tokyo-Drifting around curves. A smile crept across his lips at the thought of justifying the adolescent behavior on a professional level. *Oh yeah*, this was research for the piece, right? It was a way to get into the heads of the citizens of *Chupacabraville* so he could better understand their way of life, si? Yeah, right.

The reckless joyride ironically seemed to calm his nerves, and he was thinking he would come back after dark to try and collar a rat-racer or two for a quick interview, when he suddenly caught sight of a car flying over the crater rim and plunging down the steep ramp. Immediately pulling off the track to what he thought was a safe vantage point on its outer edge, John looked again and noticed a second car, almost completely hidden by the clouds of dust billowing in the wake of the first. When they hit the flat caldera floor at the bottom of the ramp, the two cars jockeyed for position down the straightaway on a trajectory that would bring them alongside John's parked Buick before they reached the racetrack.

In the lead was a mid-90's model, burgundy-colored Chevrolet with a disintegrating, formerly white, ragtop. Emerging from the dust cloud on the Chevy's left rear bumper, a bondo-grey, Ford pickup truck challenged the lead as they sped towards John, who was thinking that the youngsters were not observing the venerated 'Safe-distance-between-Cars Rule', nor the recommended 'Guidelines for Safe Passing'. He could see that the side windows of both cars were darkly tinted, but the driver's windows were down, and, when they exploded past him, John clicked a mental snapshot of the two men, who weren't teens at all, but maybe in their mid-thirties. Both men had glanced at John briefly, and, as he stood in their dust cloud, he smiled at the flashing image of the Chevy driver with one hand on the steering wheel, while the other lifted a cervéza to his lips.

The rat-racers ignored the American stranger as they chased one another around the course nonstop for twenty minutes. More than once, they found themselves hurtling toward each other from opposite ends of a blind curve, only avoiding collision when one or both drivers chickened out and steered their chariots up and out of the one-lane road-rut, onto a brushy island. When the adult carousers eventually stopped two hundred meters from him to download their cervezas on the other side of the track, John saw his chance. He made a sharp U-turn and drove towards them, not too fast, not too slow, but they jumped into their vehicles before he could reach them, and both racers zoomed back up the ramp and out of the caldera, the late afternoon sunlight holding the dusty haze that hung in the air above the crater rim.

John didn't think it wise to follow them. He gave it a couple of minutes before heading back up the ramp himself and, when the Buick entered the still dissipating dust plume at the top, two pairs of eyes watched from below through the diffused red glow of the car's taillights as the big, loud machine disappeared over the escarpment. They had been watching the noisy sport from a safe distance and, though the spectacle was not new to them, it remained a curiosity.

—ɯ—

After yet another pleasant and delicious meal that night with the Sanchez family, John visited the caldera once again, hoping, on some level, that he really would see something intriguing; red eyes glowing at him from the trees; a figure hopping through the brush; or, more morbidly, the corpse or carcass of some poor dispatched victim laying in the dirt.

But it was not to be. On this particular night, no cars or trucks came to the caldera and, when his headlights swept over the thicket, he saw nothing of any crypto-zoological interest peering at him from the brush. It was a predictable anticlimax for the non-believer, so he made the best of it and took several more circuits around the racecourse; kicking up thick clouds of dirt, and then driving through them again and again.

Chapter 7

John Maddox awoke before dawn... *he put his boots on.* He took a shit and a shower and he... *walked on down the hall.*

All six of the Sanchez Hotel's tiny guestrooms sat side-by-side on a wing that stretched from the main building to John's cubbyhole at the end of the row. In addition to a front door opening onto the parking lot, each room also had a rear door that opened into a long hallway, which ran the length of the guest wing and provided a covered corridor through which one could access the dining area. John followed his nose down the hallway but, just before he reached the dining room, he saw another doorway on his right that opened onto another annex. This second wing, which he guessed was the domicile of La Familia de Sanchez, was at a ninety-degree angle to the first, and extended straight back towards the hill behind the hotel.

When he entered the dining room, the family were already in their seats and waiting for the morning meal to come bursting through the kitchen door, which was just behind Señor Sanchez's chair. Knowing that this would be John's last meal with them, the *Señora de la Casa* had outdone herself with a *comida espeçial* for their guest, or Señor Juan, as the entire family now called him.

Today, Señor Juan would begin his long return journey to Mexico City, followed by a direct flight (thank god) straight back to the big 'Mac-symbol' (double entendre alert). He had spent three interesting days in Santa Teresa, meeting fascinating characters and stockpiling their strange and sincere recollections, which he would use to decorate his story.

There was plenty to work with and, as he breakfasted with the family and pretended to listen to their spirited banter, John thought about how this piece was practically going to write itself, and the realization helped keep a smile on his face. No need for embellishment or fabrication with this one. It would be a simple matter of relating the anecdotes, punching-up the story with some titillating adjectives, and then committing the whole thing to binary code, which he would then surrender to the *National Enquirer.*

It was a shame, really, he thought as he took turns eating, smiling, and complimenting the cook. The reporter didn't know whether or not his objectivity had been compromised, but he had definitely been bewitched by the strange magic that percolated in the atmosphere here. He was beginning to think that, despite the preposterousness of the preternatural phenomenon, this piece might actually transcend the slop that was de rigueur for the *Enquirer.* Not that he hadn't written pieces for that magazine in the past that he felt should have appeared in more legitimate publications, but those stories had been in the realm of politics.

When he had taken this assignment, he figured he would meet a few kooks who believed the Chupacabra was real, or at least friends of Señora Delgado who agreed that her photograph was genuine, but he had quickly discovered that there were more than a few on both accounts. At least two-dozen Santa Teresans claimed to have personally laid eyes on the big lizard, and, amongst those who had not seen it themselves, John found no one who didn't think the *thing* was 'out there'. If he was thinking critically, the profusion of witnesses seemed to suggest that the most likely explanation was the 'misidentified desert-animal theory', but there was something else here; something unique to this particular culture.

In the final analysis, it mattered not. No matter how interesting his piece turned out, and despite the fact that he was not actually employed by the *Enquirer*, he had nevertheless taken this job specifically for that tabloid and, as with every assignment he had worked for them, the editors would insist that he sign a release, surrendering his rights to their Editorial Department. The story would then be fed through the overly censorious method used by their hack editors and come out the ass-end as magazine-stand fodder and, alarmingly soon after that, be used to line bird and hamster cages across the United States and abroad.

Whenever John became dispirited about the direction his career was taking, this fatalistic mindset would creep in, but he knew that he only had himself to blame. The arrogance he had shown in turning down offers of intern positions from more estimable newspapers had set him on his present course. Several of his former classmates had already done their time in the trenches at *The Post, The Chicago Tribune,* and *The Houston Chronicle,* and they were all well on their way up those corporation's ladders. His two closest friends from NYU, Sam Morgan and Taylor Grant, had started on the bottom rung at the 'Gray Lady' herself, and now, four years out of college, they were already on staff at *The Times*; the number-one dream job for most journalism grads who were serious about their chosen vocation.

Although he had graciously refused the help of his father, who had offered to finagle an internship for him through his contacts at *The Washington Post,* John did have avenues to exploit when it was time, and he knew that time was fast approaching. This assignment had turned out to be much more interesting than he had expected, and he was looking forward to writing it, but it was NOT REAL!! Even a story as interesting as this was not going to open any of the doors through which he wished to walk.

—ɯ—

After breakfast, John returned to his cramped room to call his girl-friend, Victoria. When he had touched down in Mexico City on Monday, he had called to let her know he made it, but they hadn't communicated at all since he got to Santa Teresa. When Victoria answered, she said she was doing research on the former pastor of the new President in her cubicle at the Enquirer, and she would call him back in a few minutes.

John, himself, had been following the controversy surrounding certain inflammatory statements made during sermons by the Rev. Jeremiah Wright; statements that had been characterized by right-wing pundits as irreverently anti-American and used to fan the flames of prejudice during the campaign. Following the election, the provocative nature of the right reverend's rhetoric lost some of its fire, until con-servative critics found a new angle. The story that Victoria was working on now focused on the heated, final days of the Democratic primary, during which Democratic Senator Hillary Clinton had also made use of Rev. Wright's remarks to cast aspersions on her opponent by asso-ciation. The momentum of her opponent's campaign was too great by that point, and the tactic was ineffective. But now, there was specula-tion that the President elect planned to nominate Senator Clinton to be his Secretary of State, and the caustic, conservative caterwauling, which Reverend Wright had sparked, was flaming up again.

The fact that the *Enquirer's* assignment editor had given Victoria the go-ahead on the Clinton story while John was reporting on a giant lizard monster in Central Mexico stuck in his craw, and the palpable tension between the cohabiting lovebirds had not abated by the time he had caught the cab for LaGuardia on Sunday. Adding to that minor strain on the relationship was John's belief that some major flirtation, plus sev-eral late night dinners, between Victoria and her boss, Managing Editor Benjamin Rantz, had apparently led to indecorous conduct in the form of story-assignment favoritism.

Despite John's status as a freelancer, the *Enquirer* had bought almost every story he had submitted to them, and they did pay well. The editors were aware of his preference for political assignments and, though they seldom covered anything in that realm, John was their go-to guy when they did. But, that had not been the case lately. He and Victoria had always been supportive of each other's careers, but when Ben Rantz, who oversaw but didn't normally delegate assignments, gave her the Hillary Clinton story, John was torn between being happy for his girlfriend, and pissed off at being passed over for a breaking story that was clearly in his bailiwick. In a moment of jealous indignation, he had walked into Ben Rantz's office and implied bad form. The Editór had responded by telling John that he could forget about the *Enquirer* accepting *any* of his political pieces for the time being. When John then suggested that the editor attempt to perform several anatomically improbable maneuvers on himself, Rantz hotly told him that the **ONLY** story he would accept from him at this point would be *"THIS ONE"*, and flung the Delgado photograph on his desk before storming out of his own office.

John Maddox and Victoria Magaña had met in a Media Law class during John's junior year at NYU and were immediately attracted to each other both mentally and physically. They had decided to not date 'officially', because both were dedicated to making the most of their college careers, and neither wanted to get distracted. That did not, however, stop them from having really great sex as often as possible, wherever they happened to be when the wild called. The fuck-buddy nature of their relationship had continued for over a year, during which they both went out with other people as well but, when her relationship with one of those *other people* developed into something more serious, John and Victoria had cooled it off.

Then, a year after graduation, John had visited the *National Enquirer* offices to submit a piece he had written about war profiteering in Iraq. The piece had been rejected for lack of frivolity, but he had reconnected with Victoria, and they began seeing each other regularly. Within seven months, they took an apartment together and, since then, things had gone smoothly, until the recent Victoria-Rantz-Clinton debacle.

Now, the long distance phone call between John and Victoria was uncomfortable and filled with long pauses, made all the more awkward by the absolute clarity of the two-thousand-mile International cell-phone connection. Victoria was not at all happy about his decision to confront Rantz, especially in her 'place of business' (she kept repeating the phrase) without having first talked to her about the situation. The terse call ended without concession from either party and, just as John pocketed his cellphone, there was a knock on his back door.

He swung it open to find Tomás, holding out a cervéza to him with a half grin on his mug. John took the offered bottle, then stepped aside and directed the boy to the single rusty metal folding chair beside the bed. With the long drive ahead of him, John didn't really want the beer, but it was a nice gesture. He used the edge of the side-table to pop the cap off, and sat on the little bed, facing Tomás.

"I want to thank you for all your help, Tomás," said John after a sip of mexi-brew. "I couldn't have gotten those interviews without your introductions and translation."

"It is *me* who wants to thank *you*, sir," Tomás responded earnestly. "That is why the beer. I am studying to become a journalist, just like you. And you showed me up close how it is done in the field. *Muchas gracias.*"

Tomás reached behind his back and produced two sheets of paper that were folded lengthwise and handed them to the reporter.

"I have written a story about the people we talked to," Tomás explained. "Por favor, would you read this...John?"

Hearing the teenager say his Anglicized name caught him off guard. While the rest of the Sanchez family had taken to calling him Juan, Tomás had always referred to him as sir or señor; a courtesy that he hadn't paid attention to until now.

"Sure Tomás," he said. "May I take this with me? I'm trying to get on the road as soon as..."

"Actually, sir," Tomás cut him off. "I thought that...if you would read it now, you could tell me what is good and what is not so good, and I can work on it more."

The hopeful look in his eyes told John that he couldn't refuse the appeal from this smart, kind-hearted kid, who was obviously enchanted with the idea of being a writer, and who clearly looked up to John. The impatient reporter wasn't immune to the overt flattery in the boy's desire for his opinion; he could take a few minutes to read the story.

Although he expected Tomás' story to be readable, and possibly even *good*, he thought to himself, as he took the papers from the boy's hand, '*Please God, don't let this be a piece of doo*-doo'. He immediately found that it was absolutely not a piece of doo-doo. The story was concise, grammatically cohesive, and, as John read on, he grew increasingly uncomfortable with the similarities to how he had planned to lay out his own piece; the focus on the characters, their belief in the creature's existence, and the fact that they viewed the Chupacabra as, essentially, the Village Mascot of Santa Teresa. It was all there.

When he finished, he handed the pages back to Tomás, then leaned back on his hands and looked at the boy's eager face.

"What can I say, Tomás?" John said with a sigh. "It's great, really. You wrote this all on your own?"

"Yes, of course by myself." Tomás was defensive. "Who else would help me? I speak better English than anyone in my village."

"Of course, Tomás, forgive me. It's very good, and you should be proud of it."

A big smile spread across the teenager's face as he carefully folded the papers and held them in his hand. Then, John saw a very serious look come into Tomás' eyes as he furrowed his brow and, after a pause said,

"Take me with you, señor John. Take me back to New York with you."

John opened his mouth but could only produce a slowly creaking croak.

"I want to learn to do what you do, sir. I think I might be able to get a passport in Torreón," Tomás put his hands together as if in prayer. "If you agree to sponsor me or be my mentor."

Not completely surprised by the request, but at a loss for a response, John sat with his mouth open and ran through a mental list of reasons to say no. Sensing the American's hesitancy, Tomás added,

"I know you will say that I can write on blogs and other places on the Internet, but isn't New York City the best place to go if I want to get a job writing for a newspaper like you do?"

Well, Tomás," John tried to field the question in the gentlest way possible, "every decent sized city in America has at least one newspaper. Yes, New York is at the pinnacle in the publishing business, but most people who get the kind of positions you're talking about have had between five and seven years of a college education at a laudable University to prepare them. Not to discourage you, because what you've written here is very good, but have you considered aiming a little lower than the very top? At least until you have some experience under your belt."

"Si," said Tomás, looking up at John, "I know...but I thought that...if you liked my story, you could help me get a start in the big city, the Big Apple."

Tomás' smile widened.

"If I make it there, I could make it anywhere, si?"

So, Sinatra's aphorism had penetrated even the remote regions of Central Mexico, John mused. That cat was omnipotent...**baby!**

"You're right about that, Tomás," John measured his response. "It is the toppermost of the poppermost, but I don't think you are quite ready for that scene. You're what, fifteen? To be honest with you, I had already considered asking you if you wanted to start a correspondence with me. The sort of arrangement where you email me your work, I read it, and we have a discussion about it...*by email.* I might could give you some advice...if you were interested."

The smile on Tomás' face ebbed, and his shoulders slumped.

"I figured you would say that, but I thought I would try anyway. I mean, that is very nice of you to offer that, but..." His voice trailed away.

"Look, Tomás," the erudite reporter consoled, "it is very, *very* expensive to live in New York City, especially in Manhattan. And... I like you Tomás, I really do, but I could not support you there. To be honest, I'm having a little trouble with my girlfriend right now, and things are a little dicey in the domicile."

John held out his hand and see-sawed it. With his arsenal of excuses nearly exhausted, he was relieved when Tomás finally acquiesced to the impractical nature of his request. In the lighter air, they spoke more realistically about staying in touch through emails and the occasional phone call.

"You're a young man, Tomás," John assured him. "Don't be in too much of a hurry. There will be plenty of time for you to pursue your dream. Believe me, you should enjoy your teenage years, because you only get one go at it. If you're really determined to be a writer I could help you find a University, and if you need student loans, I could help you with the application process as well. Then, you study hard and really learn the craft inside and out and, when you get your degree, there will still be a world out there to write about."

After they had exchanged email addresses and phone numbers, Tomas excused himself and went off down the hallway. John stuffed his things into his big backpack, then threw it and his laptop into the back seat of the Buick, and walked across the parking lot to the office. He had left a cash deposit when he checked in to the hotel on Tuesday, and now, he paid the balance plus a hefty tip for the housekeeper who had cleaned his room and turned down his pillow on Wednesday. As he stood in the office watching Señor Sanchez scribble out a handwritten receipt, John wondered how the placed stayed in business. Santa Teresa was located just off a small highway that served as a secondary route between Torreón and Durango, so it was not heavily travelled and, in the three days John had been here, there had only been one other guest, who had stayed only one night.

The Sanchez's had low overheads to be sure. With the exception of the part-time housekeeper, Malinda, who happened to also be a cousin, the family did all of the work themselves. On top of that, they kept a big garden behind the house, so all of the fruits and vegetables they served to their hotel guests and ate themselves as well, were economical and wonderfully fresh. In November, no less; a pleasant surprise to the American north-easterner.

When he slapped the extra large tip down on the registration counter, John suggested that the bulk of it should go to the chef. Señor Sanchez smiled and said,

"I be sure to tell Señora you say that, Señor Juan. She like serving you, She gonna be happy you say that."

"Gracias por su hospitalidad," said John, not wanting to waste the last phrase he had written on his index card.

With business concluded, the rest of the family, toddler included, came into the office to say adios to Señor Juan. He thanked them all, high-fived the kids, and then got into the rental car and pulled away from the hotel. To break up the long drive to Mexico City, he planned to get a room in Ciudad de Leon tonight, as he had done on Monday; the fateful night he had eaten that vile, demonic, bologna sandwich that had made a series of repeated appearances early Tuesday morning.

—⚭—

When John was working on a story, he liked to take a couple of days, if he had the luxury, for the collected source material to foment and ferment and take shape in his head. On his last night at the Sanchez Hotel, he had pulled out his laptop and punched out some rough notes and an outline, but the ingredients hadn't had time to germinate yet, and he knew from experience that the mixture wouldn't fully effervesce until he was back in his own writing-nook in Manhattan.

He had developed a fondness for the quirky little village of Santa Teresa and, though there were many miles to cover, there were two full days in which to do it. Before he left the baby-burg behind, he figured he could take a few minutes for a last look around, to fix the place in his mind. The thought of returning the rental car to the airport in Mexico City was slightly depressing and bittersweet. It had been a long time since John had driven a car at all, and the pleasant solitude of being alone in a vehicle, plus the freedom to choose when and where you wanted to go and how fast you wanted to get there, were not options for most New

Yorkers. Mass transit had its advantages, but it was largely a necessary compromise and, as John drove a final, slow, circuitous route through the village, he kept thinking about the caldera, and images began to rat-race through his mind of the fun he had had down on the dirt track. The thrill of slamming the pedal to the floor and gliding around those curves; the G-forces pushing and pulling you this way and that? It was fun as *SHIT!* You just could not do that in the city.

And so, before hitting the highway, John headed for the crater once again. He had been a bit cautious on the two previous joyrides, but this time, he was going to *GO FOR IT!* As the Buick tipped over the rim of the crater and hurtled down the ramp, he thought of the smiles on the faces of the rat-racers the day before, and when he hit the gentle curve at the base of the ramp, he **punched** it and flew over the straightaway at sixty miles an hour. Having negotiated the dirt racetrack many times by now, he knew that the first slow right-hand curve, and the second, much sharper left, were the most deeply carved and steeply banked turns on the course so, when he was a hundred yards from the dirt track, John took his foot off the gas, coasted into the first turn, and then punched it hard.

The machine hurtled through the long right curve and, when the zig began its zag, John let up on the accelerator for one second before whipping the steering wheel back the other way, punching it hard again, and leaning into the sharp left-hand curve. That's when it happened!

Someone, or some...*thing* was just around the bend, crouched in the middle of the rut and reaching for something on the ground!! Too big for a coyote or bobcat; was it a person? There wasn't time to tell. The front grill of the Buick bent the figure in half and the torso slammed onto the hood before hurtling into the windshield. John's body jerked forward from the force of the impact, and the airbag exploded in his face. It deflated just in time for him to see the...***Holy Shit!***

It couldn't be. Just...**couldn't**...*BE!* John tried to gather his wits, but a rush of thoughts instantly flooded his mind, one of which was, *'Did I* *sign that collision waiver at Hertz?'* In spite of the airbag, he had bumped his head on something, and he had a pain in his chest where the seat belt had cut diagonally across his torso. But he didn't think any of his injuries were serious and, with the threat of his own demise off the table, the altruistic lobe of his brain took over, and he tried to get out of the car *FAST!*

He quickly cut the engine and then grabbed the seat belt release with his right hand as he reached for the driver's side door handle with his left. With his shoulder pushing against the door, he pulled up on the handle and fell out onto the dirt, then scrambled to his feet and stumbled to the front of the car, sure that he was about to see the bloody-guts worst, and it took a few seconds for him to process the scene.

Nothing! In the spot where a body should be crumpled in a heap on the dirt and dying, there was nothing. John looked at the Buick's broken grill, then at the shattered windshield, and then back down at the ground. The cloud of shock was starting to dissipate, and he noticed the small, black, syrupy pool of blood seeping into the dirt, surrounded by numerous dark specklettes of splatter that had already been absorbed.

He didn't think he had hit a person...thank God, but he had definitely inflicted severe trauma on something. John estimated that he had been going around forty-miles an hour when he slammed, dead center, into the body-mass of, whatever his victim was, and he couldn't believe that anything could have jumped up and split so fast. Once, while driving through Louisiana, he had hit a deer when the graceful animal came out of nowhere and glanced off of his Audi's right headlight, then staggered and stumbled backwards for a few yards before careening back into the woods. He had gotten out to look and found blood and hair on the shattered headlight, but the deer was long gone.

This time was different. He had hit this animal dead-on. Now, he stood beside the dark, wet spot, making a 360-degree turn, but saw nothing on the track in front of the car, nothing on either side or behind the vehicle, and, when he dropped to his stomach to look underneath the battered Buick...*nothing.*

It had to be an animal, right? Please God, he thought to himself, let it be an animal. On closer inspection, he saw furrows in the dirt on the passenger side of the car, where the animal had dragged itself from the track onto the brushy island. The grass on this hillock was taller and thicker than on most of the smaller islets and it was flattened slightly where the drag marks left the track, but he could see where the disturbed foliage stopped dead a few feet in. There was no footpath here so, praying he wouldn't step on a snake, or a cactus, or some other treacherous vegetation, he waded into the tall grass and walked in the direction of two pitiful looking trees that grew side by side on the far edge of the little butte.

Scanning the ground ahead of him for any sign of the animal, John stopped halfway across to listen, but he only heard the sounds of insects and his own nervous breathing. He considered himself an animal-rights kind of guy and felt awful that he had more than likely killed the poor creature, but he had a schedule to stick to, so he surveyed the environs one last time before he decided to abandon the search.

Doing a quick about-face, he tromped back to the Buick, and then stood massaging his sore shoulder and chest as he inspected the damage, trying to determine if the vehicle was road worthy. The broken radiator grill was only a cosmetic matter, and the shattered windshield was a problem, but it didn't look like it was going to fall out. Aside from obstructing his view somewhat, the smashed glass shouldn't prevent him from getting on the highway. Besides, he thought, what could he do about it at this point anyway? There was no automotive service of any kind in this remote area, and he didn't think AAA could get to Santa Teresa any time soon. He climbed back into the driver's seat, tore the deflated air bag from the steering wheel, then took a deep breath to clear his head and turned the key in the ignition.

The effed-up rental car pulled slowly forward, bumping over the disturbed hump of earth where it had plowed to a halt. After cautiously completing the interrupted left curve, John left the race track behind and, as he accelerated up the steep ramp-road, still trying to remember if he had signed that insurance waiver, one pair of red, raging eyes followed the damaged death-machine up and over the crater rim.

PART II

Chapter 8

They were both foraging on the ground for the glass cruets when the loud machine crested the rim of the Arena and careened down the ramp toward the racecourse. From his vantage point fifty meters away, Esteban called out to her in warning, but she either didn't hear him, or was actively ignoring his cries.

In the recent days and weeks, he had been more protective of her even than usual. Their child would come soon, and it made him nervous for her to be out here at all, but his Beloved had convinced him that the golden elixir would be good for the baby. The tall bottles, tossed from open car windows now and again by the Workers as they raced and chased each other around the Arena, were like little treasures hiding in the tall grass, and she loved the small sip of warm, golden liquid that awaited her at the bottom of each one. If she found them too soon after the big vehicles had discarded them, finished their exposition, and departed the Arena, the contents of the glass containers might still be cold, but if she rolled one back and forth in her hands for a minute, the amber nectar warmed quickly to her taste.

From his vantage point, Esteban could see that her view of the huge vehicle was blocked by the blind curve and she was in imminent danger from the oncoming threat that was now swerving onto the track. He vaulted over bushes and hurtled through the tall grass, screeching out her name in warning, but it was clear that he was going to be too late. When she finally looked up, she saw him bounding towards her, but the sound of the roaring engine booming around the curve from behind caused her to whirl around, and the automobile slammed into her belly, bending her in half and sweeping her legs from under her. Her body flew towards the windshield and, just as she landed with a terrible, thudding *¡CRUNCH!* the big vehicle lurched to an abrupt halt, launching her crumpled form back over the hood, where it landed in the dirt four feet from the car's bumper.

Thick clouds of dust billowed over the whole scene as Esteban made the final leap and landed beside his Beloved. Grabbing her under the arms, he dragged her limp, broken body away from the still rumbling machine and into the brush, trying to get her as far away and as quickly as possible in case the worker attacked again. The lithe actions were automatic, but he could feel shock already coming on. He couldn't make sense of what was happening. How could this be? he wondered. Why would the Workers attack their Queen? The driver of the car must have gone mad.

Trying for now to shut out the why and focus on the what, Esteban picked her up and carried her to the far side of the knoll. She still had breath in her when he set her down beneath one of the two small trees near the edge and, as he bent close to her face, he whispered,

"*No...no my love. You must not leave me. Stay with me... **MY LOVE!**"*

Tears welled, but he knew he couldn't let them flow; must not let her see the desperation that washed over him. He *must* be strong…must think. *What now?*

He lifted his gaze from the beautiful face of his Beloved and saw that the demented worker had gotten out of the death wagon now and was standing in front of it. Suddenly, the lunatic turned and started straight towards them through the grass, his eyes scanning the ground as he walked. Esteban tried to marshal his thoughts through a fog of adrenaline. Was the worker coming after *him* now? Why would he want to kill his King?

He returned his gaze to the peaceful expression on his Queen's face. With her body cradled in his arms, he held his hands behind her head over the large hole at the base of her skull and felt her life fading rapidly with the warm blood that pulsed slower and slower through his fingers. His Beloved did not open her eyes again, nor did she respond to his pleading whispers.

"My love, you will live!" He comforted her. "You *MUST* live. You are my Queen. Please…open your eyes…look at me…*my dear*!"

A teardrop fell on her now untroubled face, and Esteban whispered, wept, and wailed desperately, but as quietly as possible so he wouldn't give away their location. When he looked up again, the murderer had returned to his car and was now alternately scanning the Arena and inspecting the front of the big machine. He didn't take his eyes off the worker again and, as he locked onto every movement the man made, Esteban sensed himself slipping into the unrestrained, savage haze that he always felt at the start of a hunt. But, just as he was about to lay his Beloved's body down and spring towards his prey, the worker got back in the machine and pulled slowly away, up and out of the arena.

He was alone with his Queen once again and, with the threat withdrawn for the moment, he held her and rocked back and forth, begging and praying, but he knew she was gone. Having watched his mother, father, and brother die, he knew all too well what it looked like, and his heart, as it had with each of them, ached in his chest. The anguish and outrage that he had stifled until now was reaching its rubicon and he began to shake with fury. Letting her broken body slip at last to the ground, he got to his feet, opened his clawed hands towards the heavens, and filled his lungs with air as he closed his eyes and, with tears streaming and saliva stringing from his opened mouth, released a long, desperate wail that burned his throat and caused him to struggle for the next breath as if his lungs were paralyzed by despair.

From inside the wretched awareness that his world had just disintegrated before his eyes, a thought pierced his brain like a white-hot spike, pinning him to reality.

"THE CHILD!!!"

The unborn prince was still in her womb and, when he looked down at her stomach, he saw the baby writhing inside and he felt his own stomach drop at the sight of the undulating waves. He could not lose them *both!*

Crouching over her, he spread his sharp, curved claws around the large belly and felt his child fighting for its life beneath his trembling fingers. The panicked thought came over him to rip into her stomach and pull the baby out, but he couldn't bear the idea of doing that to his Queen, and instead leaned in to the pear-shaped bulge and pushed down with all of his strength. If he could force the head out first, he thought, maybe he could pull the child's body from the womb, and so he pushed and sobbed, and sobbed and pressed hard, down and out.

The paroxysms suddenly ceased, startling him into a moment of stillness until a panicked reflex kicked in and he pushed again even harder. There was no movement now, however; no breath, no shake, no twitch, no signs of life anymore at all.

He removed his hands from her stomach, collapsed onto his back, and rolled into a fetal position beside her body, moaning and mourning the extinction of his race. But *la raza* was not going to go quietly. With no conscious thought on his part, Esteban's body jerked to life and he sprang up onto his knees like a puppet on strings and, in the measured swipe of a single digit, sliced a major arc across the belly of his Beloved. The flayed flesh did not bleed, though, and he could see that his sharp claw hadn't cut deep enough, so he pulled back the loose flap of skin with the claws of one hand and made a second incision to open the womb with the other.

The fetus fell from the opened womb and he caught the limp body just before it hit the ground. It was a male, just as he had predicted to his Beloved, and he gazed in bewilderment at the terrible sight in his hands. The last in the long and venerated line of *Rey Lagarto*, the Kings of their race, was dead before he could draw his first breath. And on the ground before him lay his *Beloved*; his sole companion since the death of his own family. Their child, *que Pilli*, had been slaughtered; murdered in cold blood by the Workers, who, until this moment, had protected the *Lagarto*, shielded them from the danger of the outside world, made sacrifices to them, and even worshipped them as Gods; living totems of Santa Teresa and of the natural world that surrounded them all; the plants, the animals and birds, and all other subjects of the King and Queen.

Time seemed to freeze. Esteban was immobilized by shock as birds circled in the air above him, and lizards, rabbits, foxes, and coyotes, as well as other smaller animals who were nearby moved closer to the tragic scene. He remained unaware of anything but the shattered shards of his life lying inert before him and, for uncountable minutes, he held the dead child's body and rocked back and forth, his gaze shifting from his son to the tranquil face of his Beloved.

When the sun was directly overhead, he bent down and laid the baby in the crook of its mother's arm. Just as he placed her hand over the tiny body and rose to his feet, the breeze picked up and he became aware of the sound of insects, the birds circling overhead, and other animals on the periphery. When he lay down beside his Beloved and child, he looked skyward once more and saw the birds flying languorously and deferentially off into the distance.

Above him, the sun labored lethargically across the sky, and Esteban watched it crawl as he laid beside her, closing his eyelids occasionally to rest the swollen, wet, red orbs. After the golden disc finally disappeared over the Arena's rim, rational thought began to seep back in and, as the stark reality of his predicament became clearer, he began to dig. The absent-minded scraping in the dirt was instinctive at first, but the more he scratched, the deeper his long claws dug into the hard, dry earth, until they reached the cooler, moist soil. T'was then he realized what he was doing and his actions became more deliberate. Although he knew the task was necessary, it was an unpleasant one, and he was content to let his instinctual impulses do the work at first. But quickly, his conscious mind caught up to the intrinsic, and the rage-driven motions became machine-like; instinct and reason working together to kick the soil higher and farther.

Esteban stood straddling the trench now, digging harder and faster with his shorter, front claws, as the larger hind talons kicked backwards, throwing the dirt up and out of the hole and, surprisingly soon, there was an impressive trench; not very wide, but three or four feet deep. As he laid his Beloved in the pit and placed the child in her arms, the bloated rage surged in him until his head felt like it was about to burst his skull to bits. His sentient mind struggled to keep it together so he could finish the sacred burial, and he fought to maintain control as he pushed the dirt over the bodies of his Beloved and *el Último Rey*, the Last King of the *Lagarto*.

Heartrending ancestral visions whirled in his mind like poisoned taffy as he mourned his progenitors with the images, memories, and tales related to him from birth by his parents, grandparents, and other elders of the tribe; epic legends and yarns woven by generations into a rich tapestry for his royal pleasure and purpose.

—⁓—

As *Rey Lagarto* stood on the earthen mound, stamping the cool dirt and consecrating the grave with his tears, he could feel the power of *la Raza del Lagarto* rise in him. His father and mother had articulated the faces and deeds of those who had gone before using such vivid words that the images played now like a comprehensive docudrama in his head. They had told him of days when *Lagarto* dwelt dauntlessly in caves in and around the volcano when the fire pits had still regularly belched rivers of lava and pushed them through lava tubes and down the hill to the river, many ages before the Workers had come to the valley.

By the time the human migrants arrived in the valley to exploit the fertile soil along the riverbanks, the volcano had aged and the eruptions become much less frequent. On occasion, during incidents of particularly inclement weather, some of the pale newcomers had sought shelter in the shadow of the inner crater walls on the opposite side of the caldera from the *Lagarto* tribal settlement and, though they had initially maintained a respectful distance, those few, brave pioneers would be the first to form a cautious, but ultimately symbiotic relationship with their overlords.

After the settlers had determined that '*worker*' was not a regular part of the *Lagarto* diet, they ceased to view their overseers as a threat, and some of the more intrepid ones, after poking around in the caves and hollows on that side of the crater and finding them free of any other threatening predators, had moved in semi-permanently. As the number of settlers in the valley grew, even the neophyte cave dwellers had eventually decamped to the collection of dwellings springing up between the crater and the river that would one day be called Santa Teresa. But, in those early days of diffident interaction between the two species, the *Lagarto* had saved many lives by acting as an Eruption Early-Warning System for their ignorant co-habitants whenever fissures in the semi-dormant crater threatened to flare.

When Esteban was young, his *cihtli* (*Abuela*) had explained to him that his *Lagarto* ancestors, having lived in and near the volcano for centuries, had developed a heightened sensitivity to the signs of a coming eruption. They could detect rising heat levels and smell the sulphur gas seeping from invisible fissures long before magma bubbled up through fumaroles and surface vents, dozens of which were scattered across the flat table of the caldera and, when the Lagarto had recognized the Worker's obliviousness to the coming eruptions, they had, from a distance, alerted them to the threat, (although, it had never been clear to the young prince just how). The pale-skinned Workers had quickly learned to heed the warnings and scram, only returning when they saw that the *Lagarto* had done so, thus signaling that the caldera was safe again.

Although they had learned that the immigrants collectively called themselves either **Mexicatl**, or Nahua, the *Lagarto* had watched from a distance as the settlers made tools, constructed shelters, then houses, and, over time, invented and built complicated machines. It was because of these industrious abilities and attributes that they came to refer to their pale, vulnerable subjects as '**Tekitini'** (Workers).

Eruption warnings weren't the only way the *Lagarto* protected the Workers. In those long ago days, there were large predators roaming the caldera that were legitimate threats to the slow, defenseless humans. Bears, Red Wolves (called *"perros del diablo"* by the Workers), Jaguars, Mountain lions, and the occasional rabies-crazed Coyote were all definitely *on* the *Lagarto* menu, and the Workers were grateful that the bounds of the village were regularly beat by their protectors, who fed on the blood of the lesser carnivores and left exsanguinated corpses for the scavengers. It was a service that Esteban had performed for his subjects during his reign, up until now.

The height of the synergic interaction between species was illustrated by the celebrated legend of **Amoxtli**, the *Lagarto* who had saved a young village boy from attack by a large jaguar and ushered in a new era; one in which the *Lagarto* were viewed as sovereign protectors. As his grandmother told it, the young worker had wandered away from the village, and the big cat picked up his scent and stalked him all the way to the volcano's edge. As the child was toddling along the Arena's rim, fifty feet above the caldera floor, the predator had been about to pounce, when **Amoxtli** appeared from out of nowhere and jumped onto the puma's back, sunk his talons into its muscled body, and plunged his long fangs into its neck. A fierce battle ensued in which many deep wounds were suffered by *Lagarto* and savage feline alike but, in the end, the big cat lay dead, and the young boy, though also frightened by the giant, bloody reptile, had smiled in thanks at the creature who had saved his life, and then toddled back towards the village.

The story not only recounted how the *Lagarto* had become ennobled as protectors, but also commemorated the first time a worker had heard the voice of *la Lagarto*.

"*Paina chantli, telpochtli!*" Amoxtli had instructed the child. "*Tzicuini isiukak!*"

Following the jaguar incident, the Workers had begun the tradition of honoring their guardians with sacrifices, made at Cuahmeh Tlamanalli (Tree of offering), a giant old sycamore at the edge of the village. The sacrifice consisted of a sheep, or a calf, or a piglet with one end of a rope tied around its neck and the other end looped around the trunk of the tree, and the offering was made so that the *Lagarto* king could enjoy the sweeter blood of a domesticated animal once every full moon (thence leaving the others alone, they hoped).

In spite of the fact that *Lagarto* primarily sustained themselves on the blood of a desert or woodland mammal that happened to wander too close at dinnertime, it was tradition for *Rey Lagarto* to acknowledge the gracious tribute by ceremoniously siphoning the blood of one sacrificed animal every fourth full moon. On the subsequent *trés lunas llena*, the beasts were left untouched and unharmed by the king, as a return bequeathal to his subjects.

The tradition of the sacrifice had continued into the modern age, but the interspecies interaction had decreased steadily over the recent several hundred years, until the accord between the *Lagarto* and their vassals had dwindled to only minimal contact.

During his own lifetime, Esteban had watched helplessly as a terrible sickness had tragically taken the tribe one by one. As the number of Mexicatl settlers to the valley grew, more and more small groups of *Lagarto* had fled the caldera out of fear that the newcomers were somehow responsible for the deadly malady, until the tribe had been winnowed to just the Royal Family and a handful of faithful others. Now, a thousand moons hence, the Workers had, for some perplexing reason, decided to wipe out the *Lagarto* race forever.

—⟨⟨⟨—

As he knelt on the fresh grave trying to make sense of the betrayal, his sweeping, reverential remembrances were interrupted by the sound of cars booming down into the Arena once more. The murders of his Queen and child hadn't been enough; now they wanted to kill their King as well.

There was no time for a goodbye. Esteban left the grave and hurtled through the tall grass, then bounded across the outer ring of the dirt track and shot through the thicker growth and into the lava tube that was his home. Mentally wrecked and physically exhausted, he collapsed twenty feet inside, out of breath, his arms and legs trembling and aching from the exertion of digging hours before. He lay on his side with his head resting on his arm and watched through eyes still swollen with tears as huge shadows, generated by car headlights, moved back and forth over the Arena floor.

Until this tragic day, the big machines zooming around outside of his front door would not have been a threat. On the contrary, he had always known the nocturnal contests of speed and daring as entertainments, presented by the Workers semi-regularly to delight their *Lagarto* overseers. His father had told him that the first exhibitions had happened before he was born, not long after the clever creatures had first built the noisy vehicles, and the King often took the young prince to the edge of the trees, where they would watch the huge machines whirl around the track, kick up clouds of dust, and occasionally bang into each other before the drivers, through some method that his father had never quite been able to explain, declared a winner somehow and chased each other back up the ramp and out of the Arena.

He could still recall his father's laughter, as they stood side-by-side and thrilled at every dusty spin and wipeout. Now, however, the sight and sound of these harbingers of death frightened and angered him in equal measures. Why had this happened? What had changed in the symbiotic accord that would suddenly make his subjects want to destroy the *Lagarto* race?

Compounding the despair and confusion was his ambitious aspiration, prior to this tragedy, of re-establishing the direct interrelation with the Workers that had been severed long ago. He had always felt an unexplainable affinity for the Workers, and dreamed of a reciprocal relationship akin to the one his *Lagarto* ancestors had enjoyed in antiquity with their Workers.

As he watched the light and shadow show dance around the walls of his front door, *Rey Lagarto* brooded and desponded on this, the unrivalled worst day of his life, and a furor swelled that threatened to sweep away any empathy that remained in his heart for the Workers.

"*They will pay for thisss*," he seethed through clenched fangs. "I will find the driver who killed my *Beloved*...and he *WILL* pay...with his **LIFE**!"

The wretched worker's face had only flashed in his view for a split second, and he didn't know if the killer behind the wheel had seen the King, but the King had seen the killer, and now the face was seared into Esteban's reptilian brain. With fists clenched in anger, he dug his claws into his palms, and a trickle of blood ran down his knuckles, dripping onto the dusty floor.

Chapter 9

*R*ey *Esteban Edúardo Salazar Tepiltzin Huemac Lagarto, Necuametl Cuetzpalli*; son of *Chicahua Ortega Morales Tlazohtlaloni Rey Lagarto*; Protector of the village of Santa Teresa, the caldera itself and the world that surrounded the river valley; and, the last in a long and venerated succession of Kings; *Último Rey*.

The name Esteban had been in his lineal family for generations, and Esteban had ruled under the shortened sobriquet *Esteban Rey Lagarto*, as had his great-grandfather and many other ancestral antecedents. Every male offspring in their line had taken the title of *Rey*, for they were the Royal Family, and Esteban was now, lamentably, the infecund king.

His full, unexpurgated name attested to a closer, symbiotic contact between two separate, but neighboring species at some point in the past, as the appellation itself contained tributes to the human settlers. For, just as the Workers had, over time, learned to speak *nauatlajtoli*, the language of the *Lagarto*, and even referred to themselves by the borrowed pseudonyms *Nahua* or *Mexikatl*, so had the *Lagarto* eventually adopted certain words, names, and titles from *la lengua del la españioles*, the language the Workers had been forced to learn from the ominous, pernicious, and portentous shiny metal men (*tepehuani*), who came from beyond the stars many moons ago.

According to the elder's legends, the giant 'Shiny Men' had arrived in the Santa Teresa valley from over the distant hills riding on the backs of even gianter subjugated and shackled quadrupeds, which they had brought with them. The tales described the men as being cloaked in gleaming silver and carrying long, vertical poles with yellow banners tied to the tall tips that swished in the wind as they rode, single-file, into the river valley.

The imposing beings declared that they had come to bring the Sun God to the primitive workers of the valley, and when the primitive workers countered that they already worshipped 'that one', the information did not sit well with the Shiny Men. Until then, and for many generations before, the *Nahua* had cultivated the river valley, but they had blasphemously worshipped multiple deities and prayed to them for the blessing of their crops, a fact that angered the Shiny Men, who had to kill many Workers and their leaders with swords and diseases before they convinced the ones still alive to worship the Sun God, and *only* the Sun God (who lived with the Shiny Men in outer space, and in whom all other gods were consolidated and united).

The elders had taught Esteban that God had created the *Lagarto* in his own image. They also explained that their appearance was frightening to the Workers, and when he was old enough to ask why this was so, his father told him that God had used an *enchantment* to make the *Lagarto* appear vile and hideous in the eyes of the Workers. When Esteban asked what God's intent was in creating the illusion, the King had delivered his twofold answer thusly.

First, his father had grandly stated, the hallucination generated in the hearts of the Workers a prudent fear of the *Lagarto*, *"...as all creatures should fear their Gods and Kings, and tremble in their presence."* The second, logical consequence of the illusion was that it made it irrefutably clear which species was superior to the other and, therefore, which was naturally meant to rule the land as Kings, or, more specifically, God's chosen, cherry-picked leaders. Every *Lagarto* knew of the contorting trickery that the enchantment played on human eyes, and the tribal elders passed an official decree that, unless it absolutely could not be avoided, the *Lagarto* should stay hidden from their subjects at all times.

Esteban's curiosity made the temptation too great, and he had defied this tribal dictum on multiple occasions. As a young Lagarto, he had oft ventured into the cluster of casas to spy on the simple, yet crafty beings, and observe their way of life. But, it takes a tribe to raise a young one, and Esteban's father was *Rey Lagarto*. The King had many eyes, and when he learned of the young prince's subterfuge, he had chastised his offspring severely.

The shenanigans were attributed to youthful restlessness, but Esteban didn't understand why the King should be hidden from his subjects and, as he matured, he refused to accede to the Royal Edict. In his adolescence, he had once brazenly challenged his father.

"Let the Workers see us," he had said boldly. "Let them tremble at the sight of us, *if* that is what will happen, but we should allow them to *SEE US!* Let them hear the voice of their King. They deserve that privilege."

The King had responded to his son's obstreperousness by appealing to his common sense. Keeping out of sight was also a matter of self-preservation. He calmly explained that, although most Workers were good, well-meaning creatures, some of them were not, and you couldn't tell which was which from a distance. Some of them were not, and couldn't be trusted. Esteban was young and impulsive then, and, though he had nodded in understanding at the time, juvenile arrogance dulled his full appreciation of his father's admonition. Even then, the future *Rey Lagarto* had absolute confidence in the preeminence of *su Raza* and, unlike the elders, believed that the *Lagarto* should interact with the xochipepe. The words of his father nevertheless remained firmly embedded in his consciousness, and the warnings still echoed in his head.

"Never, EVER, speak to the worker. Our voices will destroy their minds and blood will run from their ears."

As a child, he could never understand why the 'blood-from-the-ears' thing had not been mentioned in the tale of 'Amoxtli *and the jaguar*', but when he was more mature, he saw the purpose behind the ruse. The grimm warning was just a cheap trick to frighten young *Lagarto* from approaching the village. But it hadn't worked with him.

He didn't know why he felt so drawn to the Workers, but he always thought that the elder's decree was misguided. When everyone else was dead or gone and he and his Beloved were the only ones left, he had wanted to reveal his agenda to her, but his Queen didn't share his dream of slumming it with the unwashed. She had, unfortunately, bought the line of theological excrement from the elders and didn't trust that the Workers wouldn't try to hurt them, out of fright or frenzy.

If there was any chance of that happening at all, Esteban had reasoned, then he should test it first on one lone worker, in case he was wrong and they were right. It wouldn't do to reveal himself to all the villagers at once only to set off a clusterfuck of crazed, bloody-eared, red-necked humans, holding their heads as they ran around the village square shrieking in panic and pain. And so, not long after the deaths of his mother and father, and unbeknownst to his Queen, he had tested the bloody-ears theory and appeared before the old worker who watched the sacrificial stump (all that now remained of the once imposing *Cuahmeh ica Tlamanalli*).

The encounter had been frightening for him, but also thrilling and vindicating. He was right, and they were wrong, and the interaction with the old one, while mutually awkward and stilted, had been even easier than he had hoped. Encouraged, but curious about what the rest of the workers were like, he started prowling the village at night, hiding behind rocks, bushes, and trees as he moved from house to house, listening to the conversations of the fascinating creatures through open windows.

He was intrigued by the way they spoke to each other, and when he had eavesdropped on an exchange between one young worker and his father, in which the young one out-maneuvered the older using cleverness and logic, he thought that he might have found his next guinea pig. He returned several times to that particular window, and even started following the boy in the daylight to hear the words he made with the others. Something about this one set him apart from the others. In addition to his unsullied, youthful purity, which the more grizzled ones lacked, he was curious and intelligent; attributes that Esteban thought would make him more open to an encounter than the others.

It was also evident that the young worker, whose name was Tomás, was very independent for one so young, and a bit of a loner as well. But, the most interesting ability this young one possessed was the gift of a third tongue. Esteban had heard the strange sounding language before, but only once or twice, and Tomás seemed to be more adept at speaking it than the other villagers who attempted it. On the few occasions when he had heard the boy use it with others, he almost seemed to be teaching them through encouragement, correction, and helpful suggestion.

Of all his fascinations with the traits and habits of the Workers, speech was the one peculiarity that captivated him the most. *How did the Workers learn the language of the Lagarto?* The closest interaction between the races must have been much cozier than any of the tales or legends described. His grandfather always talked about how the *Lagarto* had gifted their minions with speech, *but how?* Though the question had always been in the back of his mind, he had never been cheeky enough to ask Abuelo exactly how it all had happened.

On the morning that he decided he would reveal himself to Tomás, he arrived at the boy's house just before the orange sliver of the sun broke the line of the horizon and followed him to another dwelling a short distance away. When Tomás went through a gate on one side of the house into a fenced *piomeh tepankali* (chicken yard) to collect eggs in the empty basket he was carrying, Esteban had slipped around behind the yardbird shack and quietly hopped the fence into a narrow gap between it and the coop, then listened through the wood as the boy gathered the eggs from under the cooing hens. When the young worker finished, Esteban had summoned his nerve and popped out in front of him, trying to look as unthreatening as possible. Knowing that any loud noise would bring other Workers to the yard, but having no idea what the boy's reaction would be, he had been ready for a hasty retreat, just in case.

"Can you hear me?"

The young worker hadn't yelled or screamed at hearing the *Lagarto* voice, but neither had he answered, and they had stared into each other's eyes for several seconds before Tomás ran for the big house, leaving a trail of eggs behind him that fell from the overfull basket. In those few seconds, and despite the fact Esteban had already had a (sort of) conversation with the old man at the tree, he felt that the new era he had dreamed of had finally begun, but that didn't mean he hadn't been scared shitless of what would happen next, and he had turned and cleared the back fence in one long leap, then hopped back to his sanctuary as fast as he could.

For hours, as the sun rose in the morning sky, he had waited for the Workers to come streaming down the ramp into the Arena en masse, either to bow down in fealty to *el Rey Lagarto,* with whom they had craved conciliation for so long and who had finally given them the go-ahead, or to barbarously hunt for Esteban with dogs baying in between sniffs in voracious anticipation of finding his hidey-hole.

—⁓—

The incident in the chicken yard had happened several *lunas llenas* ago, and he hadn't known whether to be relieved or disappointed that they hadn't followed him. Now, in the aftermath of a direct attack on the Royal Family, Esteban was even less sure of what would happen next. As he lay a safe distance inside his front door, watching the three loud machines circle the track again and again, their headlights sweeping the bushes for their prey, he wondered, with the paranoia that makes all sentient monarchs eventually come to distrust their vassals, if these workers were here to finish him off for good. *KILL THEM ALL!* He couldn't fathom what perceived harm or injustice on his part could have turned the segregated yet harmonious accord into a revolutionary coup. The Workers had left a sacrificial calf at the stump for him only a few days ago.

While the three-car death squad continued its circuitous sweep outside his Palace, he hazarded a guess. Maybe they had decided to wipe out the last vestiges of an outmoded system that they no longer venerated, and had, perhaps, even come to resent. Regardless of whether his hypothesis was right or not, his own frame of reference had undergone a dramatic change, and in a very short amount of time. Things were very different now, and the Lizard King's mind was reeling as he struggled to catch up, for the sake of his own survival. The murder of his Beloved and child had severed the sovereign line of *Lagarto* forever, and the world he had known, as well as his yearning for a more hopeful future, lay in ruin. As he watched the loud machines, he saw the face of the worker who had killed his Queen, and fury frothed inside his skull.

Although the palace door was well shielded by trees and overgrown brush, his sanctuary felt suddenly vulnerable when one of the cars circled away from the other two and began prowling along the perimeter of the thicket. As it pulled even with the narrow trail that led through the brushwood to the cave opening, the rumbling machine slowed to a crawl, then veered away in a wide arc before cutting sharply back toward the brush. Twin shafts of light swept over the copse and Esteban shrank back against the wall as the bright beams passed over his front door. But, the car rolled a few more inches before it halted, and the headlights stopped a few blessed degrees beyond the opening.

When the driver emerged from the machine, his silhouette loomed in the indirect glare. He was very tall and, when he stepped out in front of one of the headlights, Esteban could see a bright, red cloth tied around his forehead over long, black hair. The big worker casually lifted a cerveza to his lips as he sat down on the front of the vehicle, and neither his manner nor his comportment suggested an aggressive posture. His bearing didn't indicate that he was on a hunt of any kind and, when he relieved himself into the bushes, got back into the big machine, and followed the other machines noisily up the ramp and out of the Arena, Esteban felt a tentative relief.

But, in the subsequent silence, questions started to nag. Why had the search ended so abruptly? Why had there only been three cars? Would they come back again, but this time with an army? Maybe the Workers would return on foot with the dogs and nets and weapons! The royal residence now seemed not so much a sanctuary as a capricious refuge.

With the immediate danger gone for the time being, he returned to the grave beneath the tree and curled up on the mound of broken earth. Sinking his long claws into the dirt, he pressed his cheek to the still cool soil, and he wept until exhaustion brought desperately needed repose. The sleep was shallow at first and he awoke several times with a start, expecting the next wave of attack. But, the only sounds were the caldera's nocturne, and fatigue eventually overcame his anxious restlessness, submerging him in a deeper sleep; deeper even than the horrific sorrows of the day just passed. These dreams echoed the idyllic life he had known until now; the world that was all but gone. He dreamt of his life as a prince, and then as the King of a proud dynasty; a race that lived in harmony with the world around them, and whose traditions, folklore, and spiritual convictions, handed down through generations, attested to their kindred's supreme role as the protectors and guardians of their domain.

—m—

When he awoke, the sky was a canvas of blue velvet framed with a blood-orange ribbon along the eastern horizon that coaxed him from the comforting cocoon of slumbering calm as it grew. His body had rested, but he still felt drained and weak. The reality of his circumstances stung even worse than it had the night before, and his isolation loomed before him like a stark monolith. While the sun rose on the disparately beautiful day, he lay on the mound of dirt, trying to feel something... *ANYTHING*, of his love below, but there was nothing but cold earth underneath his belly. Now, he was *completely* **alone.**

...Or was he?

Through a despondent haze, his father's words echoed again.

"...but some of the Workers are bad..."

SOME of the Workers were bad... Did that mean that most of them were good? The young worker, Tomás, hadn't tried to hurt him. Nor had he squawked an alert or called for help during the encounter. Most of the Workers he had spied on recently seemed more intelligent than the elders had intimated, but Tomás stood out from them all. He was smarter than the rest and wise for one so young. That first contact in the chicken yard had been brief and trivial, but it hadn't been a disaster. Maybe, Esteban reckoned, just maybe, the young worker could tell him what in the HELL was going on. Why had his subjects turned on him? And, why did they kill his Beloved and child and why did they now hunt him like a devil dog???

The thought was nearly inconceivable to him but, if the Worker's had resolved to reject their King and end the *Lagarto* line, then his only option was to abandon the caldera forever; leave his ancestral home ground and wander the unknown lands beyond the valley, searching for a new home in a wide world of which he could not perceive. Where would he go? Should he just choose a direction and shove off? Towards the distant mountains, maybe; they had always been a curiosity, and now he speculated that they might be his best chance of finding caves. There was no point in staying here to try and defend his kingdom. His true home had perished with the death of his Beloved; eviscerated at the hands of one of their own vassals.

He would seek answers from the boy, but not until the night came again. Esteban wanted to have all of his senses about him for the all-important undertaking. He returned to his palace of pumice, curled up in his den, and slept through the day.

Chapter 10

His home and Palace was the largest of a handful of lava tubes perforating the porous rock in the northernmost wall of the dormant crater. Each of the long, horizontal tunnels sloped gently downward from the crater-cone to the river valley a mile away, and they all had once acted as pressure-release valves for volcanic gases as well as escape routes for the bright, orange and red magma exuding from the roiling, bubbling crater. The tubes had formed in the latter part of the volcano's active stage, when the surface of the broad lava-pool inside the crater had cooled and hardened, and the extreme pressure caused by the decreased, but still considerable volume of molten rock vomiting from below forced itself through the weaker points in the cooler, porous rock of the outer cone.

When the old volcano finally petered out, its last effusions emptied out along the riverbanks, leaving near pristine tunnels in the void. A thousand years after the last fiery flows hardened, the entire caldera floor had collapsed, exposing the open mouths of the tunnels in the inner crater wall, and, in the ensuing years, the cylindrical caverns, the wide caldera, and the river valley itself had been pelted, pummeled, beaten and battered by water and wind, eroding and re-shaping the landscape and transforming the porous rock into nitrogen-infused soil. The combination of rich earth and a flowing river created a fertile, green valley, which drew animals, birds, beasts, and eventually human settlers to what those settlers would one day name the Santa Teresa Valley.

Along with their servants and sycophants, Esteban's direct ancestors had occupied the longest and largest tube since God gave birth to the earth. The Royal Residence had two attributes that made it more suitable to the status and function of a monarch than the other tunnels. It was the only tube that hadn't, over time, fallen victim to collapse from erosion. The others had all experienced occasional cave-ins on their subterranean courses from the caldera to the river, which had to be dug through or burrowed around. But, the nearly pristine hallway was not the only facet unique to the Imperial digs.

From the two-meter wide palace entrance in the crater wall, the passage traveled horizontally for fifty meters and then sloped gently down for another fifty, the diameter of the conduit narrowing slightly as it went. The basalt rock floor was carpeted with a layer of fine, brown dust that had blown in from the dry caldera, but, at the point where the tube began its slow decent, the brown dirt gave way to even finer black silt, the result of centuries of foot traffic pulverizing the pumice into dark dust. Beginning at the downward slope and continuing through the rest of the palace, ancient generations of *Lagarto* had hacked, hewn, and carved living spaces back into the tunnel walls using their own sharp talons and claws and, in later years, crude tools that they 'borrowed' from the Workers. In time, the lava tube had been transformed into an elaborate complex of coves, cubbies, hollows, and pillared dens and bedrooms; a Royal Palace for the reptilian potentates and their progeny.

Most remarkable and impressive, however, was the feature that made this particular subterranean sanctuary most suitable for the King. Midway between the front door and the (mostly) blocked back door at the river end, the floor leveled out again before opening into a cavernous cathedral. The expansive Throne Room had formed in the volcano's active stage, when the tremendous push of magma had become backed up halfway through the tube, causing the weakest spot in the shaft to bulge. When the pressure finally burst through the blockage, the swollen vesicle disgorged its load of lava through the back half of the conduit and out along the riverbanks, leaving in the breach a glorious throne room for future generations of *Lagarto* Kings.

The room's vaulted ceiling was much closer to the surface than were the roofs of the tunnels leading in and out, and there were half a dozen small fissures in the cupola where, in the short rainy season, water dripped and dribbled into small, shallow pools scattered across the Throne Room floor. When the seasonal showers concluded, rainwater seeped through the porous bottoms of the little basins, seeking the water table further down, but the majority of surface seepage through the fissures streamed down the dome's uneven contours and spilled into deeper pools that curved around the perimeter of the hall. The bottoms of these narrow pools were lacquered with mineral deposits from the surface, making them less porous than the smaller ponds, and they held more water and for much longer.

All but one of the larger pools had been used for either bathing and washing (the Royal Family only), or for frolic and play (the young princes and princesses and their playmates). The exception was a large, rectangular, solid-bottomed pool, which had been carved out of the harder rock at the base of an immense, conical flowstone formation near the center of the room. *In Atl Tepatilistli* (the Sacred Pool) was shallow, but much wider than the other pools, and its sole function was for *Lagarto* to cleanse and purify themselves prior to tribal ceremonies as a gesture of respect to the King. Looming above the pool from atop the rock pyramid was a tall dais that had been hewn from the hard flowstone, and at its pinnacle was a large knob of even harder calcite, out of which the throne itself had been cut, shaped, and sculpted into a broad, horizontal, stone slab with an arching, raised contour on the front end like a sort of backwards-facing chaise.

The throne was the highest point in the room, overlooking a semicircle of a dozen terraced platforms that had been carved and worn from the rock surrounding the Sacred Pool by ancient generations. Ten meters directly above the dais, one fissure in the domed ceiling had eroded into a small hole, allowing a shaft of light to pierce the cool, dark, damp air of the cathedral for an hour or so each day (depending on the solar season), and bathe the Royal *Lagarto* throne in a pool of golden luminescence. The royal recliner had been meticulously sculpted and polished to a smooth sheen, and it was the seat of authority from which every *Lagarto* King had issued decrees, passed judgments, and granted benevolent mercies during their reign. And, when servants & family left the monarch alone for an hour of solitude, it was the rock on which every King had basked in the warm sunshine during his midday meditation.

Esteban had lived in the royal residence as heir apparent until his father and mother had died. Soon after he ascended the throne, the parents of his Beloved also fell to the sickness and she had joined him there. After the last of their Royal attendants died in his arms, Esteban and his Queen had occupied the huge Palace alone as the last Royal Couple, and it would be their sad destiny to reign over the final days of the tribe until the eventual exodus or expiration of everyone save themselves and their estranged, subject Workers.

—◊—

He awoke in his den, alert and fomenting about the task that lay before him. Tonight, he would make contact with the young worker, Tomás. But first, he needed sustenance; a provender to quell his hunger.

It had been three nights since he and his Beloved had drained a stray sheep they found wandering beside the river, and the horrendous events of the two, intervening days had robbed Esteban of all vitality gained from the blood of the beast. Though it was not his habit to kill livestock animals unless one was offered to him at the tree of tribute, the red nectar from domesticated animals tasted so much sweeter than the blood of the wild, desert creatures. He didn't know why, but sheep's blood was the tastiest of all, and sometimes he just couldn't help himself.

The *Lagarto* appreciated their place in the natural world and understood that they were firmly entrenched in the ranks of carnivores. Esteban knew he was a killer. In the course of spying on the Workers, he had seen them eat vegetation as well as the charred, dismembered carcasses of animals. Although he was aware that many other creatures also fed on plants, he had chewed on a vegetable once as a child and instantly found that it was not his color. The *Lagarto* obtained all the nourishment they required from their exclusively liquid diet. And, when their hunger was satiated, the carcasses of their prey were left as carrion for the buzzards; for scavengers were also God's creatures, and they figured equally in the great design that bound all living things together.

Tonight, he could not afford to be picky. There was no time to search for strays. He needed to catch a quick snack and get on with the task at hand, so he went to his front door and looked out onto the caldera floor, trying to detect any motion or heat. The moon was just going down behind the Arena's rim and the land would soon be all dusky shadows; perfect cover for the hole-and-corner he would be about tonight.

Esteban was a deft and clever hunter with superb hearing and big eyes with long, vertical pupils that dilated to capture any available light, giving him sight in almost complete darkness. From the cave opening, his ears quickly fixed on the sound of a small, nocturnal forager skittering through the low brush along at the bottom of the escarpment wall to his left. Before he set eyes on the critter, his other senses told him that it was warm-blooded and that it was moving straight toward him. Suddenly, however, the instincts of his targeted prey triggered a warning for it to flee in the opposite direction, *FAST!*

But, the little brown rabbit was not fast enough. Esteban shot along the wall in a second and, in one movement, snatched up the ball of fur in his claws and sank his three-inch fangs deep into its neck, feeling the little, double **pop** as the twin daggers pierced the creature's soft flesh. Within seconds, the struggle was gone from his victim, and only a single drop of blood fell on dusty ground as he flung the little bunny aside like an empty can of V-8 and turned for his front door.

The last sliver of moon tucked behind the crater rim as he reached the opening, and he started down the dark tunnel at a full-speed, galloping hop. But, when the life-essence hit his system several seconds later, the gallop rapidly faded to a slow lope. He knew that in a few minutes, the infusion of iron-rich syrup would replenish his own depleted system and strength would return but, for now, the King was on the half-nod. At an ambling, but steady pace, he passed the coves and dens on his left and right, and the drip-dropping sound of water grew louder and louder as he neared the Throne Room.

As a child, he had played with other young Lagarto in the deeper pools along the walls of the great room for hours at a time; splishing and splashing, but always watching and listening as his father received members of the tribe, giving them counsel and advice. Now, Esteban washed himself in the waters of the Sacred Pool, purifying his body, mind, and spirit in preparation for a task that could well be the most pivotal and determinative action he would ever take as the King; the last King--*Último Rey*, the last of his race; *Último Lagarto*. Scooping water onto his head, he ran through a short list of possible outcomes, but even his resourceful mind could not fathom the events this night would set in motion.

When his body & soul had been depurgated, he left the cool pool and gave a vigorous shudder to shake the water from his leathery hide. Then, he scampered up the corkscrew steps of the pyramid, serpentining from the front to the back and then climbing out onto his *Tepatlachtli* (throne). A narrow shaft of ambient light from outside entered through the fissure in the dome, and, although the moon was gone from the night sky, the pale, purplish beam contrasted with the near pitch black of the Throne Room, piercing the darkness and bathing him in a pool of violet luminescence. He stood up and pulled himself to his full height and, with the spotlight lighting his face, raised his hands to the light, spread his clawed fingers wide, and pleaded,

"**Tatzintli, Nantli, ehuacan** *axan chicahtoc ica tequitl!!*"

Other than his own sobs of agony and cries for revenge immediately following the catastrophic deaths of his Beloved and child, he had not spoken out loud, and the tone of his voice ringing out in the big room surprised him so that the last few words of his plea trailed off. Through the skylight above, he could see one bright star twinkling frantically, and he imagined that it was a sign, guiding him and anointing him with the courage he needed this night. With a final shimmy to shake the moisture from the hairs on his sinewy form, he leapt from the top of the dais and hit the floor beside the Sacred Pool, then bolted toward the far side of the room and through the large doorway into the back half of the lava tube.

Unlike the Palace's long entryway, the shorter, rear passage had experienced minor cave-ins and was almost completely blocked at the river end. But, despite not being as long as the front hallway, the pumice here had been more extensively carved and hulled, and this section of the tube contained twice as many cloistered dens and nests. In the remote, inner sanctums that riddled the walls here, Esteban had been conceived, hatched, and nursed, and had spent a good part of his young years playing in, and exploring every deepest recess, corner, and crevice.

In the last stretch of corridor before the blocked back door was a long row of a half dozen, roundish holes in the conduit's arched ceiling. The openings were spaced several meters apart from one another, and each one was larger than the last as the tube neared the blockage. These apertures were the bottommost openings of vertical vent-ducts, drilled into the terra firma from above by water erosion through a parallel surface rift that mirrored the length of the lava tube. When seasonal rains brought flash floods, the rainwater rushed through these vertical conduits and collected in stone basins that had been carved out underneath each one. The shallow basins had provided Palace dwellers with fresh water, and a row of carefully placed stones diverted the overflow into a Royal Sewer System that ran downhill to the river outlet.

Three of the ducts were big enough to crawl through and the widest, which was the next to last one in the row, was known by all *Lagarto* as *'Cuahmeh Itlatlacoyocton'* (tree hole). For a thousand years, the *tree hole* had been the means of egress used by every *Rey Lagarto* to pop out and take the offering left for him every fourth full moon. It was also the only one of the shafts with ladder-like rungs carved into the rock, and its surface opening was only forty yards from the Offering Tree. Just a hop, skip, and another hop to accept the tasty treat from the Workers to their King, who would fill his belly before returning to the Palace, where he would then share the blood of the sacrifice with members of his own family and, in a gesture of benevolence, with other 'chosen' tribe members through a ceremonial method of regurgitation, the details of which are not necessary to recount here.

Because of the edict commanding all *Lagarto* to remain hidden from the Workers, the surface-access vents were off limits to all, save the King. But, since the humans had begun to arrive in the river valley, long before the houses and buildings had sprung up around the big tree, every *Lagarto* King had defied the command, for the good of the tribe, and granted themselves permission to study the pale, scale-less, upright-walking creatures. In his adolescence, Esteban had viewed this practice as hypocrisy and insisted on bringing up the subject with his father on occasion.

Now, as he lumbered past the last of the dens and made for the Tree-hole, the pow-pow-power in the bunny's blood started to hit him. His pace quickened with his heartbeat and, when the smaller vents began to appear overhead, he picked up speed. Then, just as he had done many times before, he made a triple-hop and launched himself from the edge of the basin underneath the hole, his powerful legs propelling him upwards into the meter-wide opening. His long claws crunched into the sharp, abrasive rock on the second ladder-rung from the bottom and he swung his legs up, grasped the lowest rung with his hind talons, and pulled himself inside. The porous rock beneath his claws turned to softer earth as he scrambled the ten meters to the surface. There had been no rains for some time, so the normally moist, cool soil was now mostly gritty dirt, but it was still easier on the pads paws & claws than was the pumice in the lower part of the duct.

The vent's opening was camouflaged inside a thick clump of scrub and juniper that encircled the trunks of two old oak trees growing alongside the eroded rift, and Esteban shivered involuntarily as he emerged from the hole into the cooler surface air. With limbs bowed out to the sides and his belly low to the ground, he scurried along the narrow passage that cut through the brush, stopping short at the tunnel's end, as he always did, to survey the panorama before venturing out into the open.

Through a space between the buildings surrounding the old tree trunk, he spotted the familiar figure of the old man asleep on the bench, wrapped up mummy-like in multiple blankets, his head completely enshrouded by a red neckerchief. Despite the lack of moonlight and the forty-plus meters between himself and the bench, his sharp eyes could see the whole pile slowly rising and falling, and his acute hearing picked up the familiar snore. The old one, who was called 'Corto' by the other workers, had lived beside Cuahmeh Tlamanalli, sleeping on the same bench beside the bakery door, since long before Esteban had first seen him, on a *luna llena* long ago, when his father had allowed the young prince to come along and watch from the bushes as he took the offering.

On that night, the old man slept while his father, *Rey Lagarto,* had hopped confidently out to the stump and feasted on a small calf which, the King had warned him in advance, took more time than did most of the sacrifices. His father usually took the blood of a young sheep or a piglet or a fat **piomeh** (pollo/ chicken), and he always complained about the latter, because it required him to remove the flapping, struggling bird from a tricky cage, delaying the silencing of the animal for an embarrassing extra few seconds. Once, when Esteban had asked him why the *Workers,* without fail, specifically sacrificed a *calf* every twelfth full moon, just as the weather was turning colder, the King had answered,

"The calf comes on the twelfth oyuaualiumetsli when the Workers are celebrating their harvest. We are grateful for it, and I will receive the gift and share as much as my belly can hold."

That first night, just as his father had predicted, old Corto never budged; never even shifted his sleeping position while *Rey Lagarto* drained the life from the calf a few meters away.

"The old one is a sound sleeper," he had commented afterward.

When Esteban ascended the throne himself, the same scene had played out over and over, as, on all but three occasions, Corto had slept through the sacrifice without a stir.

But the old timer couldn't be blamed for dozing through the proceedings. Although Corto may have been a harder sleeper than most, Esteban had been trained in the art of killing from the time he was a hatchling, and his process was nearly silent. In the first lesson she had given him, his mother taught him the two most important goals when dispatching one's quarry; *'Silence during the kill'*, and the all-important tenet that *'Your prey should never suffer longer than necessary'*. Both objectives were achieved in a solitary strike; a single, powerful, well-aimed bite that crushed the larynx, pierced the carotid artery, and started the swift transfer of blood all with one swift maneuver.

In his own estimation, Esteban thought that his fascination of, and longing for contact with the odd Workers must be stronger than any *Rey Lagarto* before him, and one bright full moon he had decided to be a little clumsy with the sacrifice. He knew that his mother would have been appalled if she had seen the way he allowed the chicken to screech and flap in his claws before he delivered the death chomp. And, as if that wasn't ill mannered and sloppy enough, he had followed that with a *'Sschluurrp!'* **¡Dios mío!**

He could still recall the mix of uncertainty, embarrassment, and mischievous delight he had felt as he watched Corto stir on his bench, sit up, and then spring to his feet. Esteban had stood crouched, clenching the chicken in his jaws as the distance between himself and the porch seemed to shrink in an instant like the zoom shot of a Hitchcock film. The two had locked eyes in an awkward standoff for what felt to both of them like forever until Esteban finally got the courage to move. Being careful not to give away the location of the Tree Hole, he had dropped the fowl carcass and hauled ass around the corner of the nearest building.

He had roused Corto again on the following full moon with slurpings and yummy-sounds, resulting in a slightly longer standoff before the spell had broken. But, on the third *luna llena*, when Esteban peeked out from his hole in the brush, the old worker was already awake and ready for him. He had crossed the ten-meter span of dirt and grass, snatched the little piglet, and stood beside the stump with his back to the porch, looking over his shoulder at Corto, who bowed his head in deference and respect while the King took the sacrifice.

At the conclusion of that ceremonial suckfest, he had turned around with the dead animal still in his grasp and *Lagarto* and Worker had studied each other in silence for several minutes. When the Mexican Standoff ended, he had dropped the piglet and casually loped away in the opposite direction, hoping Corto wouldn't go searching in the brush for the Tree-hole, and, knowing his Queen wouldn't approve, he hadn't told her about the encounters. In deference to her stand on the issue, he had stayed away from the village for a while.

Now, things were very different. His Beloved was gone and everything was at stake on tonight's errand. Corto was not on the agenda this night; he would let the old man sleep. Tonight, it would be the young one.

Chapter 11

Not much happened in Santa Teresa after midnight. On weeknights, the citizens were indoors by ten p.m. at the latest, and even on weekends, most socializing wound down by ten or eleven, with the exception of a handful of hardcore carousers who sometimes caroused until midnight or later. These young inebriates, after pelting down mas cervezas, would race their loud machines either up and down the Durango highway, which ran parallel to the river just north of the village, or around and around the Arena's dirt track, kicking up dust and forcing the *Lagarto* to go farther afield for their nocturnal hunts.

It was nearly three a.m. when Esteban left the sleeping Corto in the village square, and all was quiet as he made his way through the town. With senses on full alert, he hurried across dirt streets, peered around corners, and moved from bush to shed to tree, navigating the shadows between dwellings all the way to the long, white building, where he knew he would find the boy nestled in his bed. After crossing the treeless band of dirt road in front, he started across the parking lot, but got slightly dizzy from the disorienting canvas of yellow whorls coming from the three light bulbs swinging overhead.

He made his way to the annex on his right, and when he reached the corner, he tip-taloned around to the back side, being careful not to wake the dog that he knew would be sleeping on the small porch at the far end of the rear wing, near the hill. Staying low to the ground and close against the plaster wall, he slunk past several rooms, and then turned right at the inside corner and crept past two more windows before crouching beneath Tomás', where he sat thinking about his next move.

On his previous sorties to this place, the young worker's window had been left open a few inches, but this time it was closed, and Esteban didn't know whether to just stand up to his full height and hope the boy was awake and saw him, or try to wake him with a pointy-clawed tap if he was not. It wouldn't do to wake the other workers by making too loud of a sound, but if Tomás awoke and saw a shadow looming in his window, he might yell and wake everyone in the house, resulting in the same cluster-fuck situation.

As he was mulling over the conundrum, the choice was snatched away from him by the sound of paws thump-thumping on the dirt to his right. They were coming on fast, and before he could bolt toward the hill behind the hotel, the dog careened around the bend on two wheels and instantly locked its eyes and nose on him. With teeth bared and hackles at full sail, the big yellow mongrel pulled to a halt a few feet from him, baying and barking ferociously. Esteban knew he could rip the beast a new orifice with one swipe, so the canine was not an immediate physical threat, but a worker with a gun, that was a different story.

When a light blazed on in the next bedroom, he turned to face the mutt and, with his weapons fully displayed, aimed an inhumanly vicious, snarling hiss at the dog, who backed up, whimpering and peeing itself. Esteban turned his head to the side for one last look into the boy's bedroom before wheeling back around and bounding off full speed across the stretch of ground between the building and the hill.

It had all happened so fast, but, as he navigated the steep slope and made his way between the huge, craggy boulders, it flashed in his brain that, in that last glance, he had seen Tomás staring directly at him through the closed window of the darkened room. He ducked behind a big rock near the top and listened for raised voices or opening doors, but all he heard was the dog, who had taken up his resolute barking again, only now it was from the safety of his stronghold under the shingled canopy over the back porch. When he was sure the beast was not coming after him, he clambered on top of the huge boulder at the top and looked down on the scene.

The dog was standing by the back door, pointing in his direction and howling and yelping in a bid to reclaim its dignity. Framed in the bedroom window, Esteban saw the silhouette of Tomás, his hands pressed up against the windowpane, and from the tilt of the boy's head, it was clear that the he had seen the retreat up the hill and was watching him still. When Esteban realized that they were making direct, if distant eye contact, and the young worker wasn't yelling for help, he thought this might not have been a fool's errand after all.

Suddenly, the bedroom light blazed on, and Tomás yielded his post to an adult male, presumably his father, who hurried to the window and looked out into the darkness, turning his head this way and that and trying to set eyes on whatever the family pet was yowlping fiercely at. The ordinary, nightly barking of a bored canine might not have roused the father, but these particular barks, growls, and snarls evidently signaled a greater level of danger, and the mutt was now looking back and forth, from the top of the hill to the bedroom window, as it progressed through a canon of warning-whines and whimpers.

The boy took a step back so the adult couldn't see that his gaze was still focused on the giant lizard atop the hill. So far, the young one hadn't given away his position, which Esteban took as a good sign, but then Tomás further encouraged him by raising a hand behind his father's back and waving slowly. The hand snapped back down in an instant when his father spun around and rushed out of the room, but before Esteban could resume his non-verbal communication with the boy, the sharp warning siren of baying hounds hit his ears, and the cacophony sounded like it was moving in his direction, (on the hoof, or, on the paw, as it were).

He had won foot races with packs of dogs before, but the contests had been too close for his comfort and, on one occasion, he had been forced to turn around and defend himself. The results had not been pretty, and he had felt a mix of fear, anger, and guilt at leaving a visceral mess of blood, fur and bone on the ground that a few seconds before were probably treasured companions of one or more workers, for whom they felt great affection. He had also guessed (correctly, as it turned out) that it would surely be *he* who would be blamed for the canine carnage on the outskirts of town.

Resigned to a retreat for now, he looked in the boy's direction one last time and raised a hand in the air, uncurling his long claws only slightly so as not to appear threatening. Then he spun around, leapt from the top of the rock and bounded off over the other side of the hill, feeling confident that he had enough head start that the hounds would give up before they could close the gap.

—⁂—

The baying stopped by the time he was halfway to the crater rim. He was cut off from the vents at his back door and didn't dare go back yet, so he gamboled down the dirt ramp and across the Arena floor, then up the slight grade through the trees to the front door. Once again, he had fled before he could make contact with his subjects. The damn curs were always in the way. He should have tried to stand his ground and frighten them away, he thought, but a combination of flight response from raw fear, and the imprint of the Royal Decree on his brain, affixed there by elders and family, overcame him, and he had bolted once more.

So what now? Should he risk going back tonight, he wondered? The boy's family had been roused and might still be awake, and the dogs would surely be on the alert for his return. He thought he could be silent enough to get past them, but the wind was blowing into the village from the direction of the caldera, and they now knew his scent. If only he had been born with the gift his ancestors had possessed, he thought. The power of **flight!** (That's levitation, 'homes).

His own, useless wings were just soft, thin, slightly stretchy skin pulled taut over hollow, light weight bones. The appendages projected from a secondary pair of humeral ball joints just below his shoulder blades, then extended vertically to big knobby, calcified joints right behind his spiked skull, on which he occasionally bumped them. From the big knob-joints, the long radii were redirected down the length of his curved spine to the metacarpals and the wing tips which, when the wings were folded flat against his back in their relaxed position, ended just behind his kneepits. Had he been able to spread them fully open, the wings would have spanned five or six feet, but alas, he could only lift them off his back slightly and wiggle them up and down, which tired him quickly and hurt badly if he tried to raise them past a certain point.

When he was a child, young Esteban had gathered around and watched, along with the other members of the tribe as, during special ceremonies, his father would spread his wings wide and display them before the entire assemblage. The others were always duly impressed and *oohed* & *ahhed* in admiration, even though several of the older adults also possessed the ability. He admired his father greatly and, in his youth, assumed that the King's ability to fully spread his wings meant that he could fly, but as he grew older, he learned that the great *Rey Lagarto* was ground-bound just like everyone else. When he had once summoned the chutzpah to ask his father why he could spread his wings so impressively, but could not fly, the King answered, but Esteban had heard a hint of humiliation and shame in his voice.

"My Grandfather's brother was the last of our kind known to have flown," he had said. *"And it was said that, in his youth, he could attain a great height."*

His father had followed the melancholy tidings with more upbeat, prideful tales, handed down from long ago, that told of a time when many *Lagarto* took wing together in deft displays of proficiency, circling and swooping in the sky above the caldera and amusing their *Nahuatl* co-inhabitants with mid-air simulations of battle as they challenged each other's aerial skills and abilities. He was never sure if his father was just trying to entertain him with the fables, or if the stories really were true, but as he grew into adolescence he learned to take with a grain of salt most of the tales that the elders would ramble on about. All he had ever known for sure was that he could not get his wings to unfold even halfway, and thinking about his shortcoming had always brought the somberness of an unfulfilled promise.

Now, as he sat staring out into the Arena from the safety of his home, he watched and listened in case anyone had followed him. But, there was nothing and no one and, when his eyes fell on the island in the middle of the track, and then on the grave where his Beloved and child lay cold and dead, the elation of making contact with Tomás, and seeing the boy wave to him, faded. It was replaced by the image, playing over and over in his head of his Queen being cut down by the huge metal machine; the car slamming into her belly; the face of the worker behind the wheel; the body of the infant laying limp and lifeless in his hands. All of these fresh memories and the deep anguish they brought, rekindled the flame of rage and made his brain burn white-hot once again.

The errand had distracted him from the reality of his hopelessness, but now the lust for revenge came rushing back. Only, this time, the scope of his recriminations widened to include not just the driver, but *all* of the Workers. He couldn't contain his rage.

"Why would you kill your QUEEN?" Esteban cried, imploring. "You must ATONE FOR THIS TRANSGRESSION!"

He took a few steps out of the opening and looked to the sky in the direction of the village.

"All of you who caused my Beloved to die, there is no need for you to kill ME, because I am already ***DEAD!"*** He thrust out a finger; "You killed me when you murdered my Queen! You have killed me, and you have destroyed ALL *Lagarto*....YOU HAVE DESTROYED TEN-THOUSAND YEARS!!!"

The seething tirade continued as he galloped through the brush, over the dirt track, and on to the island. With three, long leaps through the tall grass, he landed with a thud on the burial mound, muscles taut and blood coursing through his veins. With a banshee-like wail, he cried,

"I will avenge you my love, even if it is the final act of my life. **I will kill the killers!**"

He fell to his knees on the grave, his chest heaving with the pounding of his heart as he knelt in the dirt, oblivious to anything other than his own misery. But, after a few minutes, he became aware that he was making a commotion in the middle of the Arena at the very spot where the genocide of his race had commenced and was more than likely going to recommence at any time. He gathered himself, kissed the still fresh dirt, then rose to his feet and started back to his sanctuary, thinking of a new plan of action as he sluggishly trod along.

Tomorrow night, he would return to the village. And it would be Tomás once again. He knew now that his intuition had been on target. The young worker had kept his secret and, although his anger still burned for the other Workers, Esteban knew that this intelligent, sensitive boy, whose words and actions he had studied on three separate excursions, could not be involved in this barbarous genocide.

But how could he get Tomás alone? Another attempt like the one tonight would most likely end the same way or worse, he thought, and he felt certain that Tomás' father would not be thrilled to find a worker-sized, long-clawed, sharp-fanged *ketsalkuetspalin* hanging around outside of his son's window. Maybe there was a way to lure the boy to the cave.

Rey Lagarto was engrossed by the puzzle as he slipped through the growth, but, just as he approached the cave door, a low growl coming from his right broke his concentration. On the ground at the bottom of the escarpment, a coyote was feasting on the remains of the little rabbit Esteban had dispatched earlier, and the brownish-grey furred canine snarled at him through a clenched jaw, his teeth clamping the limp rabbit tightly.

He stomped his foot playfully at the animal, feigning a challenge, and the coyote scrambled away along the wall with the hare in tow. But then, just as Esteban stepped over the threshold into the cave opening, he heard the voice behind him.

"Wait"

Chapter 12

A combination of shock from the awful calamity that had befallen him the previous day, and the draining of his well of anxious energy during tonight's sortie into the village, had left him sapped of strength, if not his very will. But the survival instinct is strongest of all, and when Esteban heard the voice behind him, the last drop of adrenaline dripped into his blood and he whipped around, teeth bared and hissing, ready to pounce. But it hit him in mid-turn that he knew *THAT VOICE*, and when he saw Tomás' alarmed face, he was just able to repress the impulse to strike before he decimated his only potential ally and possible only chance to survive.

Human facial expressions were difficult for him to interpret, but the look on the boy's face didn't look like one of panic and fear as much as astonished wonderment. But, Tomás had instincts too, and it took all of the young worker's will to repress a shudder of fear and stand his ground as he looked directly into the Chupacabra's deep red, plum-sized eyes, and said,

"Yes…" then a pause before, "Yes I *did* hear you…that morning with mi Abuela's chickens."

Esteban gaped at the boy in awe and his jaw was ajar as they stood several feet apart and studied each other from head to toe. Each knew that this would be a life changing moment, but their individual perspectives were worlds apart, and neither could comprehend where this encounter would lead. As far as Tomás knew, he was the first human ever to interact verbally with a Chupacabra (now for the second time), whereas Esteban knew that there had to have been close contact between worker and Lagarto in the past; how else would the boy be able to speak to him here and now in *lengua de lagarto*. In either case, both knew this was a historic incident for *Lagarto* and Worker alike, and the significance of the moment weighed heavily on them both. Two species that had had no literal contact with each other for hundreds of years were now figuratively, and literally, standing on the threshold of a new connection; one that *Rey Lagarto* had spent his whole life envisioning. He wanted to savor the moment.

When the Chupacabra finally spoke, his high-pitched voice was squeaky, pinched, and..... *gurgly*; just as Tomás had remembered.

"You are called by Tomásss, are you not? Asked Esteban.

Tomás nodded.

"Do not fear me, Tomáss," he continued. "I will not hurt you."

The boy was stunned at hearing his name spoken (hissed) by a creature that was not human, but who he could no longer think of as merely animal. He stared at the long, curved fangs protruding over wet lips and, though the pronunciation was distorted and strange to his ears, he realized that the big lizard was speaking the old language; the *Nahua* tongue. It was the original language of the *Mexicatl* people, to whom both of Tomás' parents' claimed direct lineage.

"*Quemah*." The boy answered. "Sí...that is how I am called. *Me llamo* Tomás."

Tomás could see Esteban trying to think of something to say, but the silence felt uncomfortable, so he added,

"Do you have a name?"

"I am called Esteban."

"Esteban...Esteban?" Asked Tomás with a skosh of a crooked grin.

"It is the name given to me by my mother and father," Esteban responded proudly, feeling affronted somehow.

"Yes, of course, lo siento. So... there are more...Chupacabra?"

Esteban winced at the word. He knew it was how the ignorant Workers referred to the *Lagarto*, and this young one had not meant it as an insult. Still...Goat Sucker? It was so crude.

"Please," he asked calmly with squinched eyelids, "do not say that word. It is a coarse insult. Very foul."

"I'm sorry, I did not mean to offend you. What do I call you?"

Esteban hesitated. The word *LAGARTO* was a sacred sobriquet, both to him and to those who were now gone, and it had not been spoken in everyday conversation. Use of the moniker had been reserved for either addressing the King himself, or when referring to the tribe in ceremonial parlance during formal gatherings, and the thought of a Worker uttering the name seemed improper. Nevertheless, since he was the only one left, he answered,

"*LAGARTO*...that is the name for...my tribe. It is a word no doubt familiar to you for it was adopted by my ancestors through you Workers, from the Spanish Men of God; the pale, brown-robed ones who came with the Shiny Gold Men from the heavens. There is an older word, used before they came, but it is difficult for Workers to say. And, as for your other question...there were many of us...*once*." He looked past Tomás, his thoughts far away. "There were many *Lagarto*.........but they are all gone now."

"Where did they go?" asked Tomás innocently. "Will they come back?"

The cauldron of anger started to burble deep in Esteban's belly again, but he tried to keep it in check as he spoke slowly, through a clenched jaw. "They are all dead. They will not return."

The young worker wanted to ask what had happened, where they had gone, but guessed that it was not a good idea. Instead, Tomás steered the subject to the mystery that puzzled him the most.

"How do you...how can you...how is it that you talk? *Tlatoaya?* Who taught you to speak?"

Esteban was confused by the question.

"Taught? Well...once again, of course my father and mother *taught* me to speak."

"But who taught them?" Tomás tried again, imagining some mysterious mountain hermit who must have befriended one of these creatures.

"I do not understand your question, Tomás. We...*the Lagarto*, we gave the gift of speech to the Workers. Long ago."

"Who are the workers?"

"YOU are the Workers." Esteban tilted his head to the side, befuddled. "That is what we call you because it is who you are."

Both fell silent as they tried to adjust to the major reality shifts that had just shaken the embryonic accord. After drawing a deep breath, Esteban spoke first, and in a sedate tone.

"There are many things that we do not know, or...understand, about each other, quemah?"

Tomás nodded in agreement.

"We have lived side by side for many suns," continued Esteban, "yet, our ways seem to be curiously unknown to you."

"No, I mean yes...uhmm..." Tomás fumbled for words, "this is...*esto es una locura*. This is crazy. I mean...you know a lot about us, but we...I mean *me*...I know almost nothing about you. This is...kind of...unreal." Then, as an afterthought, he added,

"...most people don't even believe that you exist."

The words were a blow to Esteban's gut, physically doubling him over. Confused and reeling, he wondered how this could possibly be. If the words of the young worker were true, then what *was* truth? What had he been told all of his life, he wondered? Had they all played some cruel trick on him? The elders, his mother and father? And for what purpose? A dagger of doubt pierced through him, and he turned without responding. Like a wounded beast trying to avoid further injury, he started to drag himself back into the cave.

"Wait," Tomás pleaded, "I have seen you. I will tell them about you. They will have to believe me, now."

Esteban stopped, but didn't turn around. He didn't know if the young worker was trying to deceive him by catching him in some kind of trap that he could not fathom, but he decided to challenge the boy nevertheless. Trying to recover his composure and think through the mistrust that now muddied his mind, *Rey Lagarto* turned slowly to face Tomás, and said,

"Then...what of *'Cuahmeh ica Tlamanalli'*, the tree of offering? What, then, of the tributes to *Rey Lagarto*?"

Tomás was barely able to stifle a laugh at the name Lizard King. The idea was comically absurd, but a rubric had been crossed now. He was actually speaking to a Chupacabra. This was all through the looking glass and, from now on, all previous bets were off in this new, strange, backwards, and a few degrees off parallel world.

"Why do the Workers leave offerings for me on **omahcic metzli...**" asked Esteban with his arms spread in an exasperated posture, "...if they do not think I am their King?"

Tomás put his hands on top of his head and scrunched his fingers in his thick mop of black hair as he looked off into the distance and analyzed the conundrum aloud.

"Well...that is a good question...let me see." He looked back at Esteban. "Wait...who is Rey Lagarto?"

At hearing the question, Esteban's fast-sinking narcissism plummeted as his heart dropped onto his stomach with a thud.

"I...am REY LAGARTO!" he shouted, making Tomás jump backwards.

"Yes, I'm sorry," Tomás suddenly felt in danger and averted his eyes downward. "Lo siento...*Rey Lagarto.*"

"So..." Esteban asked again, "...what of the offeringss to ME?"

"Okay..." Tomás' fingers went to his hair again. "I know that *Árbol de Homenaje* is an old tradition going back a long time...before the tree was a stump. Most... sacrifices... they stay tied to the stump for a while, and then they are allowed to roam around for a few days. If the person who donated the animal doesn't take it back and butcher it before a certain number of days have passed, it is said to be *bendito...i teoyohtica*; it has been blessed, and someone will take it home and keep it as a pet."

Esteban listened silently with a fixed, despondent expression.

"Every once in...a... while..." Tomás said haltingly, beginning to make the connection, "...Sometimes...the animal is found dead and... drained of blood... but... not eaten."

"*THAT ISss ME!!*" Esteban squawked feverishly.

The boy grinned his crooked grin once again, and said, "I thought that it might be."

"Then they MUST know me. They must know that I am *Rey Lagarto*. I AM THEIR KING!"

Tomás' urge to laugh was again thwarted by the creature's obstinate zeal and, even with human eyes and ears, he sensed the conviction and consternation as *Rey Lagarto* continued to justify his character, if not his very existence.

"The old man at the tree," Esteban implored, "he has seen me. He has watched me take the *tlamanalli* (offering). Surely he tells the rest of you what he sees."

"Ah, si, Corto! Señor Raphael; he calls himself *el Centenía*. He says that he watches for the Chupaca...that he watches for YOU. But, most people don't take him too serious. They think he is *loco* because he sleeps out of doors on the bench beside la Panadería, even though su familia are just across the river."

Between awkward silences, during which each tried to recalibrate his brain to accommodate these bizarre new realities, the initial shock of the encounter began to wane and, without either being aware of it, they began to feel more at ease in each other's presence. Sitting on the ground together just inside the cave opening, the odd pair set about (merely) reassessing their entire perceptions of the world they had known til now. But, just as the pow-wow was getting past the necessary, fundamental translation and vocabulary phase and on to an exchange of cultural curiosities, which both found fascinating, the coral, morning light kindled outside, which made Esteban feel uncomfortably vulnerable. He beckoned Tomás to come further inside the cave and, sensing the boy's uneasiness, said,

"Do not fear me, Tomáss, I will not harm you. Just step further inside in case the...cars come back."

Tomás looked out into the caldera toward the earthen entrance/exit ramp and said,

"There won't be any cars here this time of the morning. But, I must return home soon. My father and mother will worry if I am not within shouting distance when they wake up."

"Wait, Tomáss!" Esteban was ardent. "I sought you out because I have suffered a great tragedy, and I do not understand why it has happened. You are the only one who can help me. I chose *you*."

Rey Lagarto closed his eyes and lowered his head, and his shoulders sank in a half-defeated posture.

"I have learned much from you tonight," he continued, "that iss difficult for me to understand. You...Tomássss...are the only one who can explain *why*. Why do the Workers seek to destroy us ALL!"

The boy, who was just a boy, suddenly felt more important than he had felt in his short life, and it scared more than a little of the shit out of him. Someone... some... *thing*...needed him. Out of everyone in Santa Teresa, this creature had specifically chosen him for help in an important matter, one that could have an impact on everyone he knew. Esteban stared at him, waiting for a response, but Tomás was distracted by the thought of himself escorting the dreaded and fierce Chupacabra into the village square, his family and neighbors waving and shouting their admirations for his achievement. He tried to picture the looks on their faces when he introduced a theretofore-unrecorded species to the world. It suddenly hit him like a giant banana-cream pie in the face that this would be monumental news. Not just the fact that the Chupacabra actually existed, and right here in his hometown, no less, but the revelation that the dreaded Lizard-Monster also **SPOKE!!** Holy Guacamóle! That was news of the world.

As he pretended to ponder the Lizard King's question, he ran through a quick mental list of animals that could either mimic human speech or communicate non-verbally, but the list was short. Parrots, of course, and macaws and mynah-birds, all of which could respond to learned stimuli but had no idea what their mimicked rejoinders meant. Then, there were the apes and dolphins he had learned about in his on-line zoology class, who had been trained to put together simple sentences using rudimentary signals and symbols. Those larger-brained animals clearly had the power of reason and/or rationalization, but they didn't possess the physical apparatus needed to produce vocal sounds, at least ones that could mimic human speech. Esteban Rey Lagarto, the self-described King of the Santa Teresa valley, however, could vocalize with sounds that were nearly identical to human speech.

The King was becoming irritated by the young worker's lack of response, and increasingly nervous due to the brightening sky outside, so Tomás agreed to go further back in the tunnel. It would give him a little more time to think of how to answer the question. His Padre y Madre would be worried when they realized he was AWOL, but he knew they would have to forgive him when he came waltzing up to the hotel's kitchen door with a Chupacabra in tow.

Esteban motioned impatiently for the boy to follow him inside, but soon, the light from the ever-shrinking cave opening behind them was not enough for Tomás' unaccustomed eyes. He felt uneasy when he could no longer see the shape of *Rey Lagarto* in front of him, and when he started to stumble over invisible, uneven places on the floor, he became frightened and stopped short.

"Do you ever use a fire to cook your food before you eat it?" he asked nervously. "Or, maybe... torches... for light?"

"I see very well in the dark, Tomáss," answered Esteban, enjoying the novelty of using the boy's proper name, "And I do not burn my 'food', as you call it, with fire. The *Lagarto* do not eat the flesh of our prey. We...I mean I... I am nourished and sustained with only the life-giving blood;

something you must surely know from the crude name the Workers have for us."

"Yes, of course," said Tomás, embarrassed. "I knew that...of course. I'm sorry. Besides, it would probably fill the whole cave with smoke if you lit a fire in here."

"There is no need to apologize, Tomásss. Once again, there are clearly many things that we do not know about each other."

"Do you mind if we go back a little way towards the door?" Asked Tomás timidly, looking into the black void and waving his fingers in front of his face. "A little closer to the opening... if that's okay."

Without a word, Esteban reached out to grab the boy's wrist, but, at the first gentle touch of his clawed hand, Tomás gave a yelp and jerked away, tripping and stumbling backwards over the uneven floor before his back thumped against the cave wall, breaking his fall. Esteban had seen the clumsy ballet and blurted out,

"No, Tomásss! I meant no harm. I was only trying to guide you to the door. Please, do not be afraid. I am sorry for startling you."

"I'm okay," said Tomás, trying to catch his breath. "Forgive me, but your claws freaked me out a little. I wasn't expecting them, and it caught me by surprise. Those things must come in handy for catching dinner, huh?"

"They serve me well," Esteban responded tersely as he took the boy's hand once again.

The disparate pair found a spot in the corridor that suited them both and sat on the cold floor, facing each other. Over the ensuing minutes, Tomás came to understand the malevolence *Rey Lagarto* now felt toward the villagers as he recounted the tragic murder of his Queen and their only child with sibilant fury as vitriol spewed from his speech-impeded lips.

When Tomás heard that it was a blue car that had hit and killed the female lagarto, he put two and two together, and they equaled JOHN MADDOX. The last time he had seen him, the reporter was behind the wheel of the blue Buick, zooming past the hotel on his way out of town.

At the time, Tomás had noticed the car's badly smashed windshield and broken radiator grill, which, curiously, had not been damaged when Maddox left the hotel parking lot a half-hour earlier, but he kept these damning facts to himself for the present.

In the low light, he could just see the outline of Rey Lagarto, his sharp, curved, weapon-like fingertips gesturing wildly to punctuate his spittle-spraying diatribe. The savage display of acrimony unnerved Tomás, but he relaxed a bit when he was able to shift the subject away from the genocidal crime Maddox had committed and focus instead on the history and reality of the *Lagarto*.

As the blue disk of sky turned lighter, *Rey Lagarto* recited a long list of events, both from his own experiences and from the oral traditions of his ancestors. He revealed that, despite the elder's insistence to the contrary, he had always known that there was more out there, beyond the horizon. But the *Lagarto* were a completely isolated phenomenon, and it was clear to Tomás that they had been largely occupied in the business of survival. The world of the *Lagarto* was small, flat, and finite.

The fact that Tomás was as well educated and world-wise as one can be with the Internet as your main resource didn't help him when he tried to explain cities and airplanes and television and computers in terms that the lagarto could understand. He had expected it would be like explaining things to a child, but was quickly dispossessed of the notion. *Rey Lagarto* was an adult, and seemed to be accordingly judicious and mature in thought. Describing the world outside the valley to the Lizard King was more akin, Tomás thought, to blowing the mind of a native tribesman, who lived deep in the Amazon but, though he might be wise in the ways of the jungle, whose life is far removed from any semblance of a grid, making him ignorant of all but the remedial technology he observed from a distance. What *Rey Lagarto* knew of the 'real' world, he had gleaned from the Santa Teresa villagers; not exactly cosmopolitan fare, and, several times during the discourse, as Esteban spoke of his lifelong desire to have contact with humans, it began to dawn on Tomás that sudden exposure to the world at large might not be in this introspective being's best interest. Indeed, it could very well destroy him.

But the wily young worker saw his chance. He did feel a smidgen of guilt when he thought about the naive creature's shock post-coming out, and he didn't allow himself to even consider what might happen physically to *Rey Lagarto* when governments and scientists got hold of him, but the revelation of this self-possessed Last of an Ancient Breed would indeed be the story of the decade, if not the century, and it presented the ambitious teen with an opportunity for advancement that he couldn't refuse. He now had *Acceso Exclusívo* to a story that would blow John Maddox's fluffy follow-up piece on *"Superstitious Citizens in Quaint Mexican Puebla"* completely out of the water, and he had to take full advantage of being in the right place at the right time. That's what a 'real' reporter would surely do.

It was completely doubtful, however, that anyone would believe anything he said or wrote about *Rey Lagarto*, without The Lizard King of Santa Teresa at his side (live action; on-site; real time). If a fifteen-year old Mexican home-schooled kid had a hope of piercing the bubble of skepticism and doubt in the outside world, he would have to march the giant, terrifying, and deadly fanged and clawed reptile down Disney's Main Street. Then, the image would be burned into the public consciousness for all times, no take backs, no crosses counted, and Tomás knew that, anymore, images had much more impact than the written word on the world at large.

Still, the twang of his conscience twung whenever *Rey Lagarto* raised the prospect of entering the public eye and, for now, Tomás steered the conversation ironically away from the subject.

Noon was approaching, and the mismatched confederates huddled in the cave's hazy gray light and decided that there was far too much at stake to make any hasty decisions apropos of a 'Coming-Out Party'. They would part and sleep on it for a night, so that both had time to ponder the misadventures that could befall them if they followed through with the plan that, though they had only begun their association a few hours ago, was beginning to take shape. It was a scheme, which, ultimately, would rip a thread from the fabric of public perception for good.

From the shaded safety of his front door, Esteban watched Tomás climb the ramp up and out of the Arena. Now that he had been enlightened to a new reality by the young one, he was forced to accept that the Workers, as a whole, were oblivious to his preeminence. The accession would allow him to focus the surplus paranoia and anger on one, specific individual. He *would* find the driver of the car who had run down his Beloved and, when he did...*yeh cocotona huacatl potoni, ihuan inon nacaocuilin chihuilia miqui!!!*

—m—

Walking back toward the village in the noonday sunlight, Tomás came up with a cover story to explain his absence to his parents, who were no doubt getting worried by now. He would make a detour to his Abuela's back yard and gather a few eggs in his shirttail-basket before heading home, and just hope that his Madre, who would probably be cleaning up after the noon comida, bought the ruse.

As he marched, he reflected on all he'd just heard from the creature's mouth. In the deep hours of darkness, *Rey Lagarto* had told of an ancient, regal tribe of beings who, according to its lone survivor, had once thrived in numbers in the Santa Teresa caldera, and who had viewed themselves as overseers in a strange sort of feudal system; one in which the human Workers played the role of serfs to their ophidian overlords.

Tomás had, at first, found the claims of royalty outrageous if not comically ridiculous, but, as the morning sun had risen over the world outside, the Lizard King had woven a rich tapestry for him from *la Saga de los Lagartos,* and he had learned of a brave, proud clan who exhibited more similarities with their human counterparts than he could have imagined. These anomalous beings had wanted the same things for their kindred-familial as humans wanted for their own loved ones; safety and shelter; food and water; and *a little **privacy** in the **BATHROOM**...if you don't mind...PLEASE!*

Tomás was bright, but he was young, and his worldviews had not yet fully cured. In only one night, he had developed an empathetic bent for the plight of, not just *Rey Lagarto*, but of the entire vanished race. If the dramatic tales he had heard were *lo juro por dios*, honest-to-god ***TRUE***, then reality was upended and it was the humans who were living in an absurd, veiled reality in which they had no record or cognizant memory of any shared history with the creatures. He didn't think the seemingly sincere King had the capacity to deceive by invention, and, even if he did, he wouldn't lie to someone who was trying to help him, would he? All signs pointed to the likelihood that Tomás' own ancestors had replaced the truth with quaint, superstitious fables.

Although he knew that his dream to become a successful writer and journalist would someday take him away from his home, Tomás had a great ancestral pride for Santa Teresa that had been instilled in him from an early age by his parents and grandparents. He respected the people of the valley and their traditions, and now that he knew there was much, much more to the story than he had previously been told, his native reverence would expand to include *la Raza Lagarto*. This fusion was the stew that would make him the perfect co-conspirator for *Rey Lagarto*.

When he considered the slings and arrows that might accompany worldwide attention, Tomás felt ill-prepared and underequipped to protect the Chupacabra. Adding to that anxiety was the cold truth that he, himself, would be the one to unleash the onslaught, and the guilt that he hoped to profit from it in the bargain weighed on his conscience. His only comfort was the fact that *Rey Lagarto* wanted to reveal himself to the world. Was it his fault that the creature was ignorant of the Pandora's box he would be opening in the process?

It was clear that the King's boiling blood-lust for Maddox was the real motivation behind his reinvigorated resolve to appear before the villagers, and that his ultimate intention was to avenge one murder with another. But Tomás liked Señor Juan, and was conflicted about participating in something that could lead to his harm, or worse. He'd been able to deflect *Rey Lagarto's* questions about the driver of the big blue machine, whose face he had described almost as well as Tomás could himself, but doubt was growing in the teenager's mind about how and why the tragedy had happened in the first place. It was more than likely just an accident, but, whether it had been intentional or not, the American reporter had nonetheless committed the more nefarious crime of genocide, and who was Tomás to stand in the way of Old Testament justice.

So, to accommodate them both, the impending 'Big Reveal' was expedient and necessary. Tomás just thought there should be a cautious delicacy in how the whole thing went down.

Chapter 13

"**W**e missed you at breakfast this morning, Tomás. *Y ahora la comida*. Why do you have more huevos with you when you got a whole basketful yesterday?"

"Lo siento, Mama. I couldn't go back to sleep after Pancho's barking woke me up, so I went for a long walk. And, as for the huevos, I kind of wanted them for dinner tonight and didn't want you to run out in the morning. Would you make them for me...por favor...Mama?"

"Huevos for dinner? You don't usually like them for dinner, but if you want huevos tonight, I will surely make them for you. Sit down now and let me feed you something.

Señora Sanchez whipped up a quick lunch and, after wolfing it down, Tomás helped his mother clean up and then rounded up his brothers for their daily chores. All day long, he felt about to burst, wanting to tell someone, anyone, about his experience in the cave. But he couldn't say anything, not yet. His youthful impulsiveness made it hard to keep the secret, but he was wise enough to know that, when the world's radar picked up on this monumental revelation, his little village would be cast in the global spotlight, and it would change the lives of everyone he knew. So, he would hold his tongue until the plan developed further.

When all of his own chores were finished, and he had checked to make sure his little brothers had done theirs, he went to his bedroom, closed the door behind him, and lay down on his single bed for siesta. In his dreams, he was weightless and floating over progressing dioramas of his own impending fame; T.V. appearances, talk show interviews, movie premiers, literary award acceptance speeches etc. But, always behind the curtain or lurking in the background, there was the Lizard King, vowing retribution on anyone who had anything to do with the death of his family, seething and frothing through wet lips and fangs just as he had when he delivered his castigatory covenant to Tomás in the cave.

The echoing memory of *Rey Lagarto's* flashing temperament, which the previous night had made him a touch frightened for his own life, eventually overpowered Tomás' dreamy visions of self aggrandizement, and he awoke in a sweat. He sat up, rubbed his eyes, and thought about the deadly oath he'd heard from the lips of his new acquaintance, realizing that this relationship wasn't going to be anything like the one between the odd-headed creature E.T. and Elliott, his young rescuer in that old movie. No Reese's Pieces in this story line. This wasn't kid stuff. This was very REAL!

One festering thought bedeviled him throughout the day and nagged even stronger after he awoke from the dream. If he were going to truly be the confederate of *Rey Lagarto*, he needed to nourish the bond, and he knew that meant bringing something more to the alliance. Gaining the King's trust could give the fifteen-year old more influence over the intimidating creature and help him minimize the destruction by controlling the path of the building tornado once it was released on the public at large. It might not be a trail of candy-coated chocolate treats, but Tomás had something even more enticing to use as bait. He knew the murderer.

There was a risk his new partner would be angry that he hadn't revealed he knew who the killer was before, and Tomás figured he wouldn't even mention the fact that Maddox had been welcomed, harbored, and fed by the Sanchez Hotel, but to show loyalty, he would give a name to the face that was the target of *Rey Lagarto's* rage. It was sure to lead to more questions about the reporter and why he would come here from so far away to kill the *Lagarto Pietà*, but since there was no way the creature could get his claws into the American long-distance, and Tomás had disavowed him of the notion that the Santa Teresans (along with all the rest of humanity) were out to destroy his entire species, *Rey Lagarto* could focus his ire on the reporter and not Tomás' family or neighbors.

The King would want to know everything he could tell him about Maddox, of course, and Tomás would be compelled to answer. The most damning and salacious scoop he could reveal was also the bit of info that he himself found suspicious and beyond ironic. Maddox had run over and killed one of the very creatures he had come to Santa Teresa to write about, and then sped out of town without so much as a sideways glance at Tomás, who had been emptying the waste bin in the hotel parking when the smashed-up vehicle zoomed past *El Hotel Sanchez*. The shattered windshield had made it hard to tell if the driver had seen him or not, but it bothered him that Señor Juan hadn't stopped to tell the family about the mishap before getting on the highway. It had all the earmarks of a hit and run, actually.

But, *Rey Lagarto* was not human. When Tomás considered the crime in actual legal terms, he knew that no court in the world would press charges on an off-road kill incident such as this, whether it had been an accident or not. It was an animal, and there had probably not been any malice behind the killing anyway, unless Maddox was part of some larger plot that Tomás couldn't fathom. If he were to reveal the reporter's identity to the intelligent, but potentially dangerous *Rey Lagarto* and Maddox somehow wound up dead because of it, however, Tomás wasn't sure that he couldn't be considered an accessory to murder. Irony.

When he had recovered from his post-siesta fog, Tomás stood and stretched his limbs with a spasmodic shiver. Then he hurried down the hall to the tiny room beside the kitchen, where the family computer awaited him like a familiar friend. In an attempt to quell his doubts, he trolled for answers with a friendly but cleverly worded email to *jmaddox@gmail.com.* Careful not to jeopardize his exclusive access to the Chupacabra and squander his opportunity for a rocket-propelled entrée into a dream career, the missive was not deceptive as much as dishonest by omission.

> *John:*
>
> *When you were in Santa Teresa, you told me I could write you anytime about my wish to be a journalist and writer. You also mentioned that you might be able to help me get into a University so I can learn the proper way to write. Is that offer still good? If so, could you suggest a few College websites that I could search for information about applying?*
>
> *Also, are you going to use any of the story I wrote in your piece for The National Enquirer? If you do, won't I need to sign a release, or a contract or something? Thank you for your help and any advice you could give me.*
>
> *Tomás Sanchez, P.S. I saw you when you were driving out of the village, and it looked like you had hit something in your rental car. I was just wondering what happened.*

After reading and re-reading the email to be sure that the tone was right, he pressed **Send**.

—⚒—

The dinner hour came and went, followed by an evening that dragged by so slowly that Tomás wanted to pull his hair out.

"Why you can't sit still in your chair, mi hijo?" his father asked. *"You jump around like you got los cucarachas en tus pantalones. Whatchoo think, the* **Chupacabra** *ees after you?"*

Tomás laughed at the remark along with the rest of the family, but the laugh was nervous and hollow, and he dug his fingernails into his palms to stop himself from blurting out his real thoughts.

When the family at last turned in for the night, he went into his room, closed the door, and made a Clothes-Tomás in the bed, using a fútbol for his head. Then, putting an ear to the wall, he waited for his father's nightly snorefest to begin. He knew that his mother could never fall asleep until after his father but, when the paternal, glotal buzz saw fired up, the softer, sweeter, maternal snore was never far behind.

As soon as the dual signal began, he crept out through the office door and into the parking lot, then hurried around the corner and up the rise, past Señora Delgado's casa to the top of the hill. Sideways-skipping down the steeper side, he turned left at the dry creek bed and followed it to the winding dirt road, where, with the moon lighting his way, he jogged to the crater, and then gamboled down the ramp to the caldera floor. When he was halfway down the path through the thicket, he could make out the shape of *Rey Lagarto* pacing back and forth in the cave opening.

Their second confab began at midnight and, as they spoke, Tomás found that the creature's words were more understandable than they had been on the previous night. The hoarse, pinched voice was still strange to his ears, but the way *Rey Lagarto* put words and sentences together was eerily familiar and, though Tomás didn't want to reopen a debate about who-taught-whom, he couldn't help being intensely curious about who, indeed, had taught these otherwise primitive beings to transform their guttural grunts and sibilant hissing into words. Probably not an easy task, he thought.

Before Tomás broached the subject of the American reporter, he first tried to give some context by explaining the concepts of celebrity, fame, and the media. But, as he did so, the King struggled with the ridiculously human conceits and seemed so confused that Tomás wasn't sure whether he could ever fully grasp the momentousness of what they were planning or the immanent perils of the precipice on which he teetered. After approaching the subject matter from several different angles, he came upon an idea he thought might work. In their previous encounter,

Rey Lagarto had regaled him with stories about his tribe for hours without pause, and so, with that in mind, Tomás tried again.

"So...*Rey Lagarto*," Tomás croaked. "There is a man who came here from a big city far away. This 'Worker', as you would call him, has the job of Storyteller. Only, instead of telling his stories out loud, he writes them down on paper."

"Paper!" yelped Esteban excitedly. "*Quemah*, I know about that."

"Sí, *quemah*. There are many...Workers...who read the stories that he writes. If his stories say that something is true, then most people who read it believe it as the truth."

Esteban looked confused. He turned his head to the side and said,

"But, the telling of a story is meant to teach a lesson, or to give an account, or to entertain. Storytelling is not truth, for the story is at the mercy of the one telling it. Only *TRUTH* is truth."

The crude logic struck Tomás, and he let it rattle around in his brain for a few seconds before he replied.

"Sí, *Rey Lagarto*, but this kind of storyteller is called a *reporter*, and... I guess that he...kind of...tries to make a point, or...sort of...teach a lesson by describing something that happened to the reader, who wasn't there to see it for themselves, but describing it in a way that might influence the reader the way the reporter wants it to, whatever his motives might be."

Tomás had nearly tied himself in a knot with the clumsy job description, but Esteban just sat stoically, staring out into the caldera through squinted lids. After an uncomfortable silence, he looked into the teenager's nervous eyes and asked,

"Thiss worker who writes the truth on paper...was it he who murdered my Beloved and destroyed our child? MY CHILD...the heir of our RACE!?"

Esteban had caught the scent of his prey, and his tetchy temper began to flare once again. Tomás knew that this was the moment of truth, and his next words would paint an indelible target on Maddox. But, the seeds of suspicion had been planted in his mind when the reporter had zoomed past him on the way out of town, and they were now taking root, choking out his resignation about exposing the killer-journalist.

"Sí, Rey Lagarto," he said. "His name is... John Maddox. And he was the driver of the car."

Esteban was silent for a moment, then he seethed,

"The big, blue machine that killed my Queen?"

"Sí, but I think it must have been an accident," Tomás backpedaled, suddenly afraid he had made a mistake. "I talked to him myself, and he did not seem like a bad man."

"You have spoken to the murderer? Tell me how to find him, Tomásss...you MUST TELL ME!"

A torrent of questions followed in rapid succession, which Tomás did his best to answer, but it took much decoding and paraphrasing of ideas and, when he again attempted to explain the mass media to his associate, and how information is distributed to, and consumed by millions and millions of Workers every day, hour, and minute, the discourse bogged down. The *Lagarto* communicated with each other almost exclusively verbally, and even the pictographs and crude characters that were painted or etched into the rock in some of the older dens and cubbies were so ancient, rudimentary, and vestigial that they basically served as the Chupacabran version of interior wall decoration.

Sensing the King's growing agitation, Tomás steered clear of mentioning the possible media frenzy and its resulting tumult when the press, the police, and the public (gawkers, crypto zoologists, and kooks) descended on Santa Teresa in their numbers.

"*Ihuan*, Tomáss," said Esteban, "this...news-paper you speak of...it is meant to entertain Workers?"

"Well, there are many newspapers," explained Tomás, "and their purpose is to give information to people. But, because there are so many papers competing against each other, they use tricks...kind of...to persuade readers to buy their papers. They put big photographs on the front to catch your eye; pictures of something interesting, or funny, or terrible."

"Catch... your eye? Esteban asked, tilting his head again.

"The picture is a gimmick to make you either happy, sad, mad, or curious, so that you'll want to read the words of the story to find out more. And it's not just photographs. They also print words in big letters on the top of the paper, which say outrageous things to tease you into paying money for the newspaper."

"Tomin, quemah. This is all very strange to me," said Esteban, confounded. "I knew there had to be many more of your kind beyond the valley, but there must be more Workers than I perceived.

The troubled look on his face told Tomás that Esteban's reptilian brain had reached its maximum capacity of mind-blowing, revelatory information, and he fell silent while *Rey Lagarto* put the pieces together.

"I wonder," said Esteban dubiously, "how did this...Maddockss... know how to find me? How did he come to be in the *Arena, icihuahuatzin mictin*? Why would he travel such a distance to do this terrible thing, if what you are telling me is true?"

The teenager felt challenged and without considering the consequences, he blurted out,

"Señora Delgado"

Tomás said the name before he could stop himself and, just as the last syllable took flight, he wished he could snatch it back. He saw the King's long, diamond-shaped pupils dilate instantly and widen across his big, red orbs as he hunkered into an aggressive posture.

"Thisss...is the name of a Worker?" His voice was rapacious.

Tomás tried to steer the subject back to Maddox, but Esteban had latched on to the name ***Delgado*** like a pit-bull on a blood-rope, and he wasn't going to let it go. So, Tomás relented and reluctantly explained the connection between the American reporter and the photograph taken by the señora.

"The female worker that I frightened one evening," said Esteban confidently. "She flashed a bright light in my eyes, so that I couldn't see her running away."

"That's right," confirmed Tomás. "That's when she took the photo."

"So it is just as I thought," Esteban hissed. "There is more that just the one worker in league to destroy the *Lagarto*! How many Workers are hunting me, Tomásss?"

"No, NO!" Answered a flustered Tomás. "I ...I don't...I mean...I didn't mean to say anything like that."

"But, if it were not for this old female, Delgado, as you called her, the Storyteller would never have come to Santa Teresa."

What had he done? a panicked Tomás asked himself as the full impact of his blunder came clear. The controls had suddenly been ripped from his hands and he was left a helpless passenger on a runaway locomotive that was out of control, throttling up, and heading straight toward Señora Delgado. The more he tried to backpedal by downplaying the señora's culpability, the more *Rey Lagarto's* paranoia was unleashed until he became more savage than civilized. Tomás knew that Señora Delgado's life was def in danger.

If he had underrated the potential of the Chupacabra's raging fury before, the next few minutes rectified Tomás' miscalculation. The transformation was dramatic as *Rey Lagarto's* percolating temper mushroomed into a spitting, frothing frenzy and he commenced half-hopping, half-galloping in wide arcs up and down the walls, making figure eights around Tomás, hissing and cursing in Chupacabran. When the wheeling gyrations began to move farther back into the dark tunnel, Tomás saw his chance and inched backwards towards the front door and the deep, purple glow beyond. The Lizard King gave no indication that he was aware of the retreat, and a relieved Tomás backed out of the opening and into the trees, then turned and ran down the narrow path through the copse, across the dirt apron, up the ramp, and out of the caldera.

The mockingbirds made their morning reveille for the beginning of what was to be a beautiful day but, as Tomás trudged home under the brightening blue sky, a little storm cloud hung over his head. The excitement he had felt the night before now faded with the dread realization that he had given the fearsome creature the name of a very accessible alternate target on whom to focus his anger. And, it was his neighbor, the odd-bird old lady who lived up the lane.

While John Maddox might be out of his reach, this was one very pissed-off Chupacabra, and anyone who was caught off guard by the rampaging Goat Sucker (and who wouldn't be?) would be in serious danger. Tomás tried to imagine what the savage, enraged, erratic, saber-toothed Lizard King would do with the new information. He wouldn't have to wait long to find out.

Chapter 14

Constancia Delgado was fifty-two years old; a short, stocky woman with a slight limp and a gold capped tooth, both reminders of her twelve-year stint in Mexico City as a *luchadora* in the *Lucha Libra* wrestling league. She had been known as *"LaDiabolica"* and, in her prime, she had held the middleweight belt on two separate occasions and was a regular crowd favorite.

When her career began at the age of sixteen, Constancia had married her manager, and soon after, she bore him a son, Jesus, who they called Chuy. Chuy would travel with her throughout her wrestling career, not missing one match in fifteen years, but by the time she was thirty-five, LaDiabolica's fame had faded, followed by the disappearance of her career and, soon after that, the couple's money. So, *la poco familia* relocated to her husband, Caesár's home town of Santa Teresa. Only a year after they moved to the little village, Caesar was stabbed in a bar fight in Torreón and died a few days later, leaving Señora Delgado a young, widowed mother in a village where she was not a native.

Constancia had spent her childhood in Torreón and moved to Mexico City in her teens but, to Santa Teresans, even the smaller of those two municipalities was considered the 'big city', making her suspect from the day she set foot in the village. Her outsider status was not the only reason that she had a hard time fitting in. As in most small rural communities the world over, everyone in the village of Santa Teresa knew everyone else's business, so no secret was kept for long, no matter how small, and Constançia's scandalous secret was well known. She had been a **LUCHADORA** in Ciudad Mexico; shame & scandal.

The *Lucha Libra traditión* was a popular entertainment in the larger cities, but twice a year, the league put together 'Road Shows' that drew people like flies from rural villages throughout Mexico and Guatemala into towns the size of Torreón or Durango. Rural folk were provincial and often prudish in their attitudes toward entertainers and big-city folk in general, but, as in any community where the local codes that dictate morality seek to repress the human urge to cut loose and have fun on *una loca Noche del Sábado*, there were hypocrites in Santa Teresa. When she arrived in the tiny village, Constançia had recognized the faces of several of her neighbors (mostly men) as having been fans of LaDiabolica when she was in her heyday. These Santa Teresans had travelled to Torreón many times to see her grapple in the ring, but those same men and women wouldn't make eye contact with her when they passed her on the road. They had cheered for LaDiabolica in Torreón but, in this little village, *Luchadora* was considered a disreputable job for a woman, which made her persona non grata.

Even the women who had never seen her wrestle only spoke to her politely, and rarely invited her to their homes or on their group shopping trips to Durango. Because of her status as an outcast, Constançia came to depend on her son more and more as he grew into manhood. He was her companion, roommate, and Señor Fix-a-lot whenever things around the house needed repair, or required the strength and/or height of the sturdy, six-foot, four-inch Chuy Delgado.

It broke his mother's heart when, in his early twenties, Chuy had moved back to her childhood home town of Torreón to live with relatives while he sought employment. He met a girl there who gave birth to a daughter the day after their wedding, but the marriage only lasted a couple of years, and when Chuy lost his job soon after the split, he left his baby daughter with his ex-wife and moved back home to live with Constançia. Since then, he had looked out for his Madre, cooked for her, and protected and defended her against all offenses and insults, whether real or perceived. He even built her a sort of shrine beside the television set in their den, on which he had displayed her *Lucha libre* mask, the ribbons and medals she had won, and newspaper clippings honoring the career of *LaDiabolica*.

Three days a week, she and Chuy worked the Santa Teresa community garden, where they watered, tended, and harvested fruits and vegetables for several other families in the village in exchange for discounted bread, from the *panadero*, and meats, from the *carnicero*. On the other days of the week, Chuy was employed at a grain elevator thirty miles down the highway and, as of late, the drive had been made much more pleasant thanks to the brand new, green Nissan Sentra with dark-tinted windows, a powerful air-conditioner and a Bose sound-system that Chuy loved to show off by blasting loud music with the windows down as he cruised the dirt streets in town.

Mother and son had made a large down payment on the new automobile with the stipend earned from selling the Chupacabra photograph to both the U.S. version of the *National Enquirer* and *El Norte* newspaper in Torreón, who had actually gotten the jump on the *Enquirer* by printing the photo and a short, accompanying story two days earlier than the American magazine. The Delgados had poured a concrete driveway to park the car on, and then spent the remainder of the substantial windfall on a variety of purchases in Durango and Torreón.

The publication of the photo had caused quite a stir in Santa Teresa and, while most residents were excited to have their village mentioned in a popular American magazine, some were of the mind that it made them look foolish to outsiders, and a few even suspected that it was a tacky publicity stunt designed to revive the career of LaDiabolica. Señora Sanchez, of the Sanchez Hotel, was in the latter category, but her criticisms included the prediction (accurate, as it would turn out) that the magazine article and photo would bring unwanted attention to their quiet burg.

Whatever the opinions of her neighbors, the Chupacabra incident only added to Constançia Delgado's level of infamy in the community. But, she was stubborn and tough, and had decided to give an implicit badfinger to all of the *punta pendejos* who had derided her by thoroughly enjoying her boobie-prizes. She even convinced Chuy to move LaDiabolica's shrine over three feet from its honored position in the front corner of the den, to the middle of the wall underneath the evaporative air-conditioner that sat in the window, making room for the brand new, forty-eight inch Samsung 1080 flat screen television, placed diagonally in the corner so it dominated the room from its wedge of power.

—✠—

In spite of her bad hip and knees, Señora Delgado liked to take walks in the late afternoon or early evening, from her casa at the top of the hill down into the arroyo and then up the long slope of hillocks that lay in the shadow of the crater. On her good days, she trekked all the way to a certain, small clearing on top of a low ridge, where she would pause to catch her breath and reflect on her day. Before starting back towards home, Constançia would always say a prayer to Saints' Joseph and Nicholas asking them to watch over *su hijo* if anything should ever happen to her. It was in this quiet little clearing that she had seen the Chupacabra, not just on the evening that she took the photo, but twice before as well, which was the reason she had the camera with her the third time.

On a Monday evening, four days after she and Chuy had guided the nice American reporter to the clearing, Constançia was returning from one of her evening walks just as the sun was relinquishing its post for the day. She saw that the new car was missing from the driveway and guessed that her son had gone to visit his friend Miguel, who lived alone in a little hovel a few miles south of the caldera, out in the middle of no-where. Chuy was never gone for too long on those Monday nights when he went to visit his hermetic, junkie, high school amigo out in the desert to take him some fresh produce, and make sure he wasn't laying dead and decaying into his sofa.

The crime rate in Santa Teresa was virtually non-existent, and most of the citizenry never bothered to lock their front doors. The Delgado's casa had no locks at all, but on the day they brought home the giant new television from Torreón, Constançia convinced Chuy to install a locking doorknob and a deadbolt set. They had gotten a bit lax about locking it lately, however, especially when she went for her walks, and on this night she wasn't surprised to find that her conscientious son had left it unlocked for her. She'd peed just before her walk but already needed to go again and so hurried inside, slammed the front door behind her, and held her thighs tightly together as she ran from the knees down into the hallway to the left of the kitchen and into the tiny bathroom between the two small bedrooms.

Ever since her 'Chupa-photo session' in the woods, Constançia had occasionally seen visions of the fearsome creature standing right in front of her, poised for attack with its claws and fangs a-twinkle in the camera's flash, so, when she returned to the den after taking care of her bathroom business and set eyes on Esteban, who was standing just inside the front door, she thought it was just her imagination running away with her again. After a beat, she realized that this was no phantom, and her eyes opened wide as her jaw dropped into a silent scream. She tried to force a yell but, before she could produce a sound, words came from the mouth of the creature! Words! Not growling or snarling, but real *words*.

"It wasss *YOU*, señora!" he seethed. "*YOU* are the one responsible for bringing the killer to Usss, and *YOU* are to blame for the murder of my Beloved. What you have done hass brought an end to uss...your protec-tors! *Te mictia calpolli.* You must tell me why, Delgado...why did you bring the murderer here?

Constançia gaped in disbelief and stared at the fanged mouth of the Chupacabra, who continued in his shrill rasp,

"Why would you do such a thing? You musst explain to me. *Tu in aquin tlami cihuapillahtocatzintli ihuan tu cocotona calpolli.*"

When the wail finally emanated from the woman's open maw, it wasn't a high, piercing screech, nor a feminine *eeek*, but a guttural roar, and, with it, the luchadora struck a defensive posture with her legs bent, torso taught, back arched, and arms ready to grapple. ¡LaDiabolica was back and ready for action!

But this was not the wrestling ring, and when Constançia took another look at the monster's long claws and sharp fangs, she decided to find a weapon to even the odds in the battle that was about to be on like 'Comicon'. Chuy kept a lead pipe behind the chair next to the front door for protection, but the giant lizard was standing between her and the door. Her mind flashed to the wooden baseball bat she kept under her bed for her own protection, and she spun around and speed-limped to her bedroom at the end of the hall without looking back. She dropped to the floor and squeezed her plump body underneath the bed, but the weapon was just out of her reach on the other side where she slept. Twisting and wriggling frantically and pushing backwards with her feet wasn't getting her anywhere, and so, with adrenaline-fueled strength, Constançia arched her spine and lifted the entire bed off of the floor with her back, then stood up and let it fall behind her, where it landed on its side athwart the bedroom window.

Holding the Louisville Slugger (José Conseco model) firmly in her grip, she turned to face the Chupacabra, who was standing in the bedroom doorway with his hands out and palms up in a pleading gesture.

"Wait, woman!" he screeched. "You must talk to me! *Cihuatl, tlahtoa nohuan. Chihua ne acicamati TEICA?*"

"I DON'T KNOW WHAT YOU ARE SAYING TO ME!" Yelled Constançia. "I don't talk that Aztec mierda."

"Why did you bring the Maddockss here?" Esteban implored. "*TEICA?* WHY?! You have KILLED US ALL!!!"

"I DON'T KNOW WHAT YOU ARE SAYING TO ME! I don't know what you're talking about! How can you speak!? GO AWAY!! *Salir de mi casa!*"

Rey Lagarto was starting to get pissed off. No longer apprehensive about speaking to a worker, he was frustrated that the old woman wasn't communicating with him in the way he wanted her to. It would do no good to let his rage get out of control, he knew. She obviously didn't understand the *Lagarto* tongue. But he needed a rejoinder, needed to understand why she had set the boulder rolling that landed up crushing his Beloved and child. This woman, he calculated, must have the answers.

Constançia stood ready to swing, shifting her weight from foot to foot as she held the bat up behind her shoulder, wiggling the tip like Roberto Clemente. Esteban feared that his pleas and petitions had sounded too aggressive, and he continued to make pacifying gestures, bowing low and trying to be as unthreatening as possible.

When he had left his Palace minutes before, he had been in a violent, vengeful frenzy, but his reason had resurfaced just before he entered the señora's casa. He couldn't kill her, at least not yet. There could be no answers from the dead. Besides, she wasn't his ultimate target. It hadn't been her behind the wheel, that was the Maddocks, and this female worker might be his best chance to get to that *tepolli ica ocuilin.* Tomás had explained her connection to the murderer, and if they could somehow force her to bring him back, Esteban could avenge the entire *Lagarto* race with a swift and violent disembowelment. In both his night and day dreams, he had imagined the evisceration happening on the stump of *Cuahmeh maca tlamanalli* while all of the villagers looked on.

If he was going to get his claws into the man's skull, he first had to calm this frightened woman. Using the two short phrases in the woman's language that he had tricked Tomás into teaching him, Esteban tried to mollify her and explain that he only wanted answers.

"*Te digo nada. Sólo quiero respuestasss.*"

"Answers to *WHAT?* The woman squawked. "What do you want with me? *¿Qué quiere de mi monstruo?*

Esteban couldn't understand her response. His scanty *Español* was exhausted, his poorly thought out plan was crumbling fast, and, as he was trying to think of a new one, Constançia yelled and charged.

"No chingues con La Diabolica!"

The baseball bat came whooshing down with surprising force from the middle-aged woman, and when he put his right arm up to block the blow, it hit with a *CRACK*! He yelped and recoiled as he stumbled backwards into the hallway. From the level of pain, he guessed that she had broken his arm bone, but there was no time to further assess the injury as the rampaging woman came at him, ready to strike again.

Cradling the wounded limb in his good arm, he turned and scrambled back into the front room, but when he turned around to look, LaDiabolica was on him again, swinging the weapon wildly as he ducked and sidestepped and staggered backwards. The Returning Champ had stopped her caterwauling, and the only sounds Esteban heard as she chased him around the room were her laboring grunts and the whoosh of the bat as she swung it. But the Lizard King was lithe and agile. He quickly regained his footing and began to bob and weave as he retreated backwards over the furniture until she finally pinned him against the tapestries in the corner, beside the shrine to *LaDiabolica*.

Trapped between the woven images of the Virgin de Guadalupe on one side and a prancing rooster on the other, he was cut off from escape and knew that the next swing would connect. In a split second calculation, he decided to take the coming blows against his back instead of to his head or arms, and so dropped to the thick, wine-colored carpet and folded up like an armadillo. When the blows began, they came one after the other, buffeting into the hump of muscle to the left of his spine, and, with every wallop, an involuntary *HhmmfPh* was expelled from his lungs along with a blast of air.

Through a haze of pain, Esteban realized this errand was a lost cause, and that he was now in a fight for his very life. After more than a dozen, crushing *THWACKS* from LaDiabolica's cudgel, he sprang up and wheeled around, slashing backwards with the claws of his left hand as he pirouetted. The outside edge of his hand first crashed into Constançia's jaw and, when he followed through, he felt the buttery soft flesh of her neck give way beneath his razor-talons. In one motion, his swipe severed the woman's carotid artery and perforated her trachea. LaDiabolica looked at him in wide-eyed disbelief and fell backwards onto the coffee table, smashing the glass top into a thousand little blue-green cubes.

As the last tinkling of glass died away and he stood over Señora Delgado's body, observing the cascade of blood disappearing into the deep red carpet, he was struck by a pang of remorse at all the liquid-life going to waste. The woman's eyes were opened wide and locked onto his, and he watched as her essence ebbed away until the penultimate moment when the eyes became glassy and soulless, and then... Constançia Delgado was gone.

Esteban kept his eyes on the motionless ex-LaDiabolica for a few seconds to be sure she wasn't going to get up again. But this Chupacabra didn't get his sustenance from any grocery store. The face of death was familiar to him, and he detected the very moment that life had been vanquished. He turned away from the señora and scanned the room, nonplussed that the mission had gone so wrong so quickly, and wondering what he was going to do now.

It had all happened so fast. The deadly swipe was an instinctual, reflexive action, delivered when his lucid mind had surrendered and his lizard brain sprang into action, keeping him alive for another day on the planet. The adrenaline fog began to lift, and, in a moment shared by all cogent beings in the seconds, or minutes, or years after they have taken the life of another soul, the full impact of what he had done smacked him hard in the face. *Rey Lagarto* had killed a WORKER!

The warm, wet crimson dripped from his fingertips as he stepped over Señora Delgado's corpse and stood stunned in the middle of the room. His mind rushed through the tales related to him by the elders and his parents and grandparents, but, try as he might, he couldn't think of one yarn, or narrative, or even a myth or fable that told of a Worker being killed by a Lagarto. It sickened him, the thought that this, the first execution of a subject Worker in the tribe's history (*calpolli cemiac*), had been levied by the hands of Esteban Edúardo Salazar, *Rey Lagarto*.

When Tomás had told him of the woman's complicity in the destruction of the *Lagarto* race, Esteban had been provoked to a terrible furor, but, even in his rage, he had only meant to confront Señora Delgado in a bid to understand why the tragedy had occurred. Now he had not only committed this offense against nature, but also annihilated his best bait for luring the murderer, Maddox, back to him; all in one backhanded swipe.

Both halves of his brain united in a flight response and he looked for an escape route. The front door was not the best option. He knew he couldn't exit the crime scene on the side of the *casa* that faced the road, so he turned and started for the back kitchen door, but, just when he rounded the club chair in front of the kitchen doorway, the sound of the front door opening behind him made him spin around, and he saw the giant frame of Chuy Delgado filling the portal.

The big man's long, un-ponytailed, raven-black hair flew wildly around his head in the strong breeze rushing past him from outside, and his eyes shot back and forth from the bloody, lifeless body of his mother, *in situ* with her rear end through the glassless table top, to the fearsome, but frightened *Rey Lagarto*, standing frozen in the kitchen doorway with fresh blood on his long claws.

"*¡LA HOSTIA PUTA!* Chuy bellowed. "*¿*Qué pasó con mi madre? *¿QUE DIABLO?*"

Esteban was overcome by a wave of regret and panic, and he shot another quick glance at the woman's dead body. It was all the time Chuy needed to produce the solid iron flame-stick from behind the chair next to the door. He held the grip of the lethal baton tightly in one hand and slapped it threateningly into the palm of the other.

"*¡Maldito hijo de puta!*" Chuy yelled. "*Mataste a mi madre! Voy a matarte!* I'm gonna mess you up.... you...GOAT SUCKER!"

Esteban had tried his best not to harm the woman, but she was older and weaker than himself, and he had been reasonably sure he could overwhelm her if need be, but this was a very different sitch. The señora's son looked very strong and, as he brandished what looked like a deadly weapon in his giant paw, Esteban knew there wouldn't be any talking things out this time either. Round Two would also be a fight to the death.

Bracing for battle, the Lizard King assumed a fighting stance; back arched, feet spread, and claws splayed wide, ready for the clash, and, as they maneuvered around the room like wrestlers in the ring, the adversaries sized each other up like wild animals looking for an opening in their enemy's defenses; (that's right, double-simile). When Chuy moved right, Esteban pivoted left towards the back wall, leaping onto the couch to avoid the mess of blood, glass, and *ex*-señora. The move frustrated the angry man, and when Esteban hopped back to the floor next to the big television set in the corner, Chuy demonstrated the flamestick's deadly power by slamming it down onto the back of a small, wooden chair with a heavy *THWACK,* cleaving the flimsy piece of furniture in two.

This is really going to hurt, Esteban thought to himself as the huge man closed the gap and swung the weapon at his head. He ducked and swiped at the big hand that held the pipe, slicing to the bone and making the attacker drop the hunk of iron. Through clenched teach, Chuy grunted a guttural *Rrrgghhh* and slapped his uninjured hand over the splayed, pink flesh of his severely wounded paw. But, after a beat, the hulking Mexican pushed through the shock of the wound, crouched, and rushed his reptilian foe with a wail no doubt reminiscent of his *Mexicatl* ancestor's battle cry.

Esteban raised his hands to absorb the charge and Chuy's bloody mitts seized his wrists in their vice-grip. The momentum carried them both backwards and to the floor, with the big worker on top, pinning his arms to the thick, wet, glass-strewn carpet. The smaller Lizard King couldn't budge the arm injured by the blows from the señora's baseball bat, and his other limb seemed just as useless against this powerful beast, so he bent his hands inward, trying to reach Chuy's arms with his claws, but the man's grip was too far from his wrists. The only option was to use his other set of talons.

The sentient half of Esteban's brain took a breather and kicked back with a bag of popcorn for the show as the half that controlled the ophidian killing machine took over. *Rey Lagarto's* glistening fangs were inches from the giant's jaw when his powerful legs flew into the fray. Esteban's hind talons thrashed and slashed, and climbed their way up Chuy's shins, then thighs, and then the flailing weapons shredded the flesh and muscle of the man's gut, eviscerating his stomach and bowels. The sudden trauma robbed Chuy of his arm strength and, when Esteban felt the grip loosen, he pushed with his strong, sinewy thighs and launched the behemoth up and backwards, where he fell to the floor in a helpless spread-eagle, his innards all exposed and bleeding.

Adrenaline was coursing through Esteban's system like rushing river water through the penstocks of the Hoover Dam, and he sprang up from the floor, landing flat-footed on the blood-soaked carpet between the worker's spread legs. Chuy was mortally wounded, but he wasn't done yet, and he wasn't giving up. He put his hands on the floor behind him and was just able to push himself to a sitting position. Esteban took a giant step backwards and watched in repulsed amazement as the wobbly giant scooped up his own intestines in his big hands and, with considerable effort, rose to his feet. The gutted goliath had a glare in his eyes that was equal parts anger, disbelief, and wooz as he stood facing Esteban unsteadily.

The Lizard King had extinguished many beating hearts in his lifetime and knew how to end this beast's suffering quickly. From his first childhood lesson on, he had dispatched every victual-elect in exactly the same way, and, although he had never dreamed of implementing the move on a worker, he didn't think this repast would be much different than his standard fare.

The old woman's death had been unintentional and her essence had gone to waste, but now, the trigger of the Chupacabra's bloodlust had been squeezed, and this, his second taboo victim of the night, would not be drained in vain. Springing onto Chuy's huge, teetering torso, Esteban pulled the wounded warrior to his knees and pinned his only good arm to his side. With the claws on his other, battered and throbbing appendage, he grabbed the man's long, black hair and yanked his head back, exposing a thick, veiny neck.

Scimitar teeth sliced deep into flesh and muscle, and simultaneously pierced the carotid artery and crushed the larynx and, when the red nectar began to flow, the King drank deeply from the fount, his large eyes rolling back in their sockets and exposing the white hemispheres below their red crescents. His body was accustomed to consuming the blood of small, desert animals, or the occasional spindly lamb or fat hen left for him in the village square and so, after gorging on the life-force of this very large worker for over a minute, he collapsed and rolled onto his back, sated and sluggish beside the now lifeless body of Jesus "Chuy" Delgado, R.I.P.

With the immediate danger passed, and his last reserves of adrenaline depleted, he began to feel the full impact of the baseball bat in all the places where Señora Delgado had struck him. In the midst of the melee, he had been able to ignore the sharp pain of her first *whack* on his arm, but now it ached terribly. But, that was nothing compared to the damage that the multiple hard blows had done to his back.

Slowly rolling over onto all fours, he arched his spine and tightened his back muscles to test the damage and guessed, as he pressed gingerly on his trunk with his hands, that there were at least two broken ribs. But he wanted to be sure, and so, fighting through the pain, he flexed his backbone with a great, heaving *Hmmphh* and, just at the apex of the stretch, he heard, and felt, a loud '*POP*'. The strange sensation startled him, and he quickly inverted the curvature of his spine and pushed his shoulder blades together, which made an even bigger '*CRACK*'! followed by a feeling he had never experienced before.

The odd new tingle in his joints and muscles wasn't unpleasant, and the cracking action seemed to have actually relieved some of the pain in his back. It didn't feel like a fracture so much as a kind of mechanical release, and the useless bulk of bone and flaps of loose skin, which he had borne his whole life like a heavy knapsack that he could never take off, were moving up and down and wiggling more than he had ever been able to wiggle or move them before. He seemed to have full control of them for the first time, but, when he got to his feet and thrust his shoulders forward again, he felt a *WHOOSH* of air pass his ears and spun around to see who, or what, was coming at him from behind.

But, there was nothing and no one, and a rapturous wave of realization washed over him. Frozen in disbelief, a sly smile appeared at the corner of his mouth as he considered the possibility. Collecting his wits and pulling himself to his full height, *Rey Lagarto* took a deep breath and thrust his shoulders forward again with a quick snap, feeling the *WHOOSH* once again as he unfurled his wings and spread them fully open for the first time in his life.

Chapter 15

In the days following *los horrores en la casa de Delgado*, the sleepy village of Santa Teresa experienced a flurry of turmoil and commotion. Señor Vega, who owned the one small hardware store in the village, ran out of locking door knobs and deadbolt sets by noon on the day after, but, when he closed the shop and headed to Durango for more, a few panicked customers couldn't wait. They drove in the opposite direction to a hardware superstore in Torreón, where they stocked up on locks, window bars, bear traps, and firearms, for there was consensus among villagers that, based on the nature of the injuries inflicted upon the Delgados, these attacks were indeed the work of a vicious Chupacabra, though a few holdouts harped on the absurdity of the idea. The interruption of their daily monotony was titillating and entertaining, but, for most of the citizenry, the quaint, colloquial belief in the creature was now, sadly, cast in a new, more sinister hue.

The bodies of Constançia and Chuy Delgado had been found in their home just before noon on Tuesday after they both failed to show up for their morning shift at the community garden. State Police came from both Durango and nearby Coahuila, and the Federáles were brought in to assist the local Constable in a double homicide investigation that lasted for three days, but turned up no conclusive evidence. Neighbors, relatives, and co-Workers of the deceased were questioned, but no significant leads emerged. Forensic detectives saw no sign of forced entry, and they could find no fingerprints on windows or doors other than those of the Delgados. They did, however, find scores and scratches on the brass, front-door knob that looked recently made, as well as what appeared to be fresh claw marks of an as yet unidentified animal dug into the blue-painted door all around it. It puzzled the investigators in light of the fact that the killer, or killers, had left the back door standing wide open when they left.

Upon the discovery of the bodies, it was clear to the *Policía* that some scavenging desert carnivore had smelled the blood, entered the dwelling, and helped itself to the dead bodies, which made it difficult to determine, from a cursory inspection, which wounds, if any, were inflicted prior to the animal(s) evisceration of the corpses. They knew an official autopsy would have to be performed in Durango before an official cause of death could be announced. Aside from the lack of a murder weapon or any evidence pointing to a human killer, the investigators were also perplexed by the trail of the animal footprints themselves. The blood-soaked, wine-colored carpet made it impossible to see any prints around the bodies themselves, but there was a trail of bloody footprints in the kitchen that led across the yellow and white linoleum floor and out through the open back door.

The tracks were made by long, narrow, four-toed, clawed feet like those of a lizard, but these were too large to be those of any local reptile, and they were set side by side in parallel pairs instead of staggered, like those of a quadruped would be, suggesting that the animal had stood upright on hind feet and, apparently, hopped away from the crime scene. When a member of the first responding group of deputies followed the tracks out the door and over the hill behind the house, she noticed that the pairs of tracks became progressively farther apart and slightly offset from each other, like those of a kangaroo at full gallop. But, just as this mystery hopper had hit its full stride, the tracks disappeared suddenly and completely, as if the beastie had been scooped up and carried off into the sky by eagles. The officer and her cohorts were left scratching their heads and reaching for their radio transmitters to request a K-9 unit from Torreón.

By mid-afternoon, the police had set two hounds onto the trail of the bloody animal footprints and two more sniffing for any scent of a human killer. The first unit followed the scavenger's trail to the spot where the tracks disappeared, but this time, the dogs picked up the scent again a few meters farther on and followed it for a few more before it disappeared once again. The intermittent pattern repeated several more times in a game that seemed to delight the hounds, but at the delta of the dry creek bed and the larger flood wash leading to the river, the trail vanished completely. The two other mutts were at a loss from the start and ended up begging for leftover pieces of pimento cheese sandwich from their human handler on the Delgado's front porch.

In addition to the disappearing trail, los *Policía* y los *Investigatores* were stumped by the fact that neither Central Mexico nor the Chihuahuan desert had any native mammalian, or marsupial, or any other kind of 'hoppers' large enough to pose a threat to even the most helpless human being. And so, after the crime scene investigation and subsequent search for a double homicide suspect were concluded, the official reports would state that, though the opportunistic interloper could not be identified, the mystery scavenger was not responsible for the demise of the decedents, but had only taken advantage of a door left open by the killer(s).

Authorities instructed all law-enforcement personnel involved in the investigation to keep the details of the case confidential. But this was Santa Teresa, the village seen now more than ever before as the "Hometown of the Chupacabra", and the residents were beginning to take a more serious interest and pride in their local mascot. When the 'Chu-believers' learned about the lack of a human suspect, the door-knob scratches, and the bloody footprints of a large unidentified hopping beast, the local speculative-rumor pyre flared up like *Zozobra*.

La casa della morte became a curiosity for, not just Santa Teresans, but for people with inquiring minds from the surrounds who wanted to know. Some came from as far away as Mexico City, where interest had been stirred by an *¡artículo de periódico sensacionalista!* in the Capital-city based *El Enquirer Naçionale*, which hit the newsstands thirty-six hours after the murders. In a case of bad timing, unfortunate irony, and an employee in the *Enquirer's* U.S. office being asleep at the wheel of the AP machine, the American version of the *Enquirer* printed the story written by John Maddox on the day after the attacks in Santa Teresa. And, Maddox's piece was not a knockout headline about the murders, but a page-4 follow-up piece about the previously printed Delgado photograph and the people of the charming Mexican village who believed the Chupacabra was real. The copy was accompanied by a reprint of the infamous photo, taken by the woman who had now been killed by the very monster in question, and the article seemed antiquated in light of the new developments. If the *Enquirer* had waited one more day before printing the piece, they could have featured the **"KILLER CHUPACABRA"** headline like their sister publication in Mexico. As it was, Maddox's story would now only be seen by, *a)*. the coterie of dedicated and thorough *Enquirer* readers, *b)*. a few dozen casual *Enquirer* readers who were, unfortunately, suffering from constipation, and *c)*. several hundred parrots and parakeets who were not.

For Tomás, the killings were a horrible tragedy, and he felt directly responsible. He had revealed the geneses of the entire tragic drama to the murderous reptile, and now the corpses of the Delgados lay in the Torreón morgue being examined by curious pathologists and medical examiners from all over Mexico. There had now been *four* deaths that were anywise the direct result of Tomás practically handing road maps to, first, John Maddox, and then, *Rey Lagarto*. And, he was astounded by the irony that the exigent quarry of the pissed-off Lizard King was still alive and journalizing away up in *el Nórte*.

Tomás thought he had understood from his homicidal associate that Homo erectus was not on the Chupacabran diet, and he was stunned that the squirrel-sucking, sheep-siphoning, bunny-bleeding lizard had actually killed the Delgados. In spite of the fact that his mother had always looked down her nose at Señora Delgado, the former *Luchadora*, none of Tomás' family would dare wish any harm on their neighbors up the street. Tomás himself had found the lady fascinating, and he had always looked up to her leviathan of a son. Once when Tomás was young, a group of bullies had tried to steal his bicycle out of his very hands, and Chuy had stood up for him and made the *pendejos* apologize. Also, unbeknownst to Señor Sanchez, the quiet giant had been the first person to let Tomás get behind the wheel of a car (1960 Chevy Pickup; on the caldera race track, of course).

During his two, lengthy confabulations with *Rey Lagarto*, the longer-fanged one had asked most of the questions, but now Tomás had some of his own. He had been flung into this drama by forces beyond his understanding or control, and he desperately wanted some kind of absolution for his own involvement, which, so far, had resulted in eternal dirt-naps for four. He knew he wouldn't get any vindication from the King, and he was too scared to attempt a return to the caldera any time soon, so he decided he would bide his time until things calmed down again; if they calmed down, that is. At the very least, he wanted an explanation about why the Delgados had to die, but he found that he now had a creeping fear of the deadly creature.

Despite the fact that the *National Enquirer* in the United States had missed the breaking story about the murders, Tomás had been anxious to read Maddox's piece. He knew it wouldn't be the exact story that he had shown to the American reporter, but they had both been present when the interviews were conducted, and Tomás couldn't imagine that they could be much different.

—※—

Three days after the attack on the Delgados, Tomás went with his father to Torreón for supplies, and, when they went into the *tienda* so his papa could buy cigarillos, he spotted the new issue of the *Enquirer* on the rack with the *teaser* at the bottom of the front page directing the reader to turn to page four for more about: **"CHUPACABRAVILLE"**. He paid for the magazine, helped his father load up the pickup truck, then hopped up in the passenger seat and read the story over and over on the ride home; excitedly at first, but growing more and more incensed as he realized that this wasn't just similar to his own version, it *WAS* his version. It was the story he had handed to, and then watched Señor Juan read right in front of him. The words were switched around a little, and there were a couple of extra parts and some things missing, but this *was* his story, and he kept looking up at the byline as he read.

"Story by John Maddox"

Tomás was confounded. The man who had asked him to be his temporary apprentice and then had been so friendly and cool during their time together, wasn't cool at all. He was a thief. And the more he rolled it over in his mind, the hit-and-run of the Lagarto Queen, followed by the hasty exit of the American from the scene of the crime, reinforced a growing notion that John Maddox was a cold blooded murderer as well, an opinion that Tomás, now more than ever, was beginning to share with his new confederate.

Over the next week, he sent multiple emails to Maddox expressing his dismay over the perceived purloining, and left several voice messages on the reporter's phone in which he tried to hide his true anger so he wouldn't discourage the reporter from replying. Whenever he wasn't doing chores, he tried to stay within earshot of the telephone in the dining room, but the call never came, the phone never rang.

His parents were at first curious and then concerned, so Tomás showed them the *Enquirer* article and explained how his own story had been ripped off by Señor Juan, but, despite their love for their son and an acute awareness of his journalistic ambitions, the Sanchez's didn't seem surprised that a big city reporter would screw him over. They encouraged him to just let it go, and what he perceived as their unwillingness to try to understand frustrated him and made him wish there was

someone with whom he could sympathize. There was only one such being who fit that bill, and so, after two weeks of second and third guessing himself, during which he also worried that *Rey Lagarto* would be
captured and/or killed, Tomás decided he would take the chance and
wandered up the winding road to the caldera.

—ᗯ—

Throughout the two weeks that Tomás was fuming over Maddox's article, his slaughterous cohort was a prisoner in his own home. *Rey Lagarto*
nursed his wounds and, as he fulminated about the unfortunate debacle
at Casa Delgado, he realized that a line had been crossed, and the re-
percussions would be transformative and irreversible. In a few, short,
regrettable minutes, his decision to ignore the advice of generations of
Lagarto, who evidently knew what the fuck they were talking about, had
turned Esteban into the very monster of whom the residents of Santa
Teresa were now excitedly terrified. Regrettably, his ambition to rees-
tablish contact with the Workers suffered a severe setback when he had
shredded the Delgados like paper dolls.

Though his right forearm didn't seem to be broken, it was tender
and sore for days, but, as his aches and pains lessened, pangs of hunger
from an empty stomach increased. When an unfortunate coyote picked
a bad time to come sniffing around one of the surface vents, the King
snagged it and wolfed down the only nourishment he had consumed
since taking the blood of a Worker.

The lamentable episode with the Delgados did have one, undeniable
silver lining, however; his WINGS WORKED!!! He considered this to be
a gift from God (by way of his xenogeneic *Lagarto* progenitors), but it
took some time before he was convinced that the miracle was real and
the liberation of his wings had not been a fantasy. The anxiety of it woke
him from sleep the first few nights and made him stand to unfurl the
glorious novelties.

Every day, as his injuries healed and their pain faded, the wings were getting stronger and more flexible, and he wished he could give them a proper test run across the caldera floor. But, he couldn't risk being seen by the posses of Workers, who, whether it be in sunshine or in moonlight, had been casting a wide, collective search net across the entire Santa Teresa Valley since the murders, trawling for either a homicidal maniac with a big, sharp, butcher knife, or a chupacabra with blood underneath its claws. In the narrower parts of the lava tube, there wasn't room enough to fully extend his newly actuated webbed wonders, and even the vaulted Throne Room was too small for the novice aerialist to get any kind of decent running start. And even if it were, he never knew when he would have his sanctuary to himself anyway.

The groups of Workers, who tripped and meandered throughout his Palace with their bright torches, loud voices, and their musty smells, were certainly not the first humans to poke around in the caves, but they were the first in many, many moons to venture as far as the Throne Room, and in such numbers. This was Esteban's home, however, and he knew every nook and cranny. He moved stealthily and silently and used his scotopic advantage to play cat and mouse with the khaki-uniformed, flashlight-dependent Workers as, sometimes for hours, they stumbled around the cave, talking, laughing, and cursing.

On the last day of their manhunt, the uniformed Workers had brought three bloodhounds out in the afternoon, one of whom refused to enter the cave at all, the other two proceeding only reluctantly. They were spooked by the scent of an apex predator they had never smelled before, and Esteban used the dens, cubbies, hidey-holes, and system of surface-vents to pop in and out, sometimes in front of the posse, sometimes behind them, until the whimpering mutts were befuzzled and the authorities finally abandoned their search of the Palace in frustration at dusk.

Esteban had watched them from his front door as they disappeared over the rim of the Arena. He had fully expected the search parties to return the next day in even greater numbers and with braver and smarter dogs, but no Workers came to the Arena at all for two weeks; a fact which made Esteban both relieved and paranoid as if he were in the eye of a hurricane waiting for the back side to hit him in the backside.

—m—

A shroud of clouds moved overhead as Tomás crossed the flat expanse of the caldera floor and entered the path through the trees. He pushed through the overgrown trail in the sunless gloom and, as he cautiously approached the cave's door, he could just make out the shape of *Rey Lagarto* standing in the shadows a few feet back from the opening. With lagarto eyes, Esteban could see *him* perfectly, of course. He knew that human eyes needed time to adjust to darkness and, as Tomás approached, he studied the boy's expression, attempting to gauge his disposition. The Delgados had been neighbors of Tomás and his family, and Esteban couldn't guess what the young worker's reaction to the tragic misfortune would be.

When Tomás spoke, however, his voice did not sound angry or defiant, and the King was pleased that he used his proper title.

"Is that you, *Rey Lagarto?*" Called Tomás in a loud whisper.

"Yess, Tomáss. I am here. Come to me."

"Do you think that..." Tomás tone was diffident, "...that you could come out this way...a little bit?"

Although he didn't consider Tomás a physical threat, Esteban was equally apprehensive. As the King stepped cautiously forward, Tomás glared at the silhouette as the line separating shadow and light climbed slowly up the Chupacabra's body, stopping just below his chin, leaving his face still in shadow. *Rey Lagarto's* big, red eyes glowed at Tomás through the dark as he spoke.

"I have been waiting for you, Tomásss."

"What happened, Rey Lagarto?" Tomás got right to the soup nuts. "Why did you have to kill them?"

The red, luminescent glow switched off as Esteban closed his eyelids and considered his answer.

"I know that you must be disturbed by my actions, Tomáss," he began earnestly. "I doubt, however, that you could be more troubled by the outcome than am I. You must believe that my call on the señora did not go as I had planned."

He opened his eyes again and Tomás studied the glowing orbs, trying to measure their sincerity.

"What did you mean to happen?" Asked Tomás.

"It would be dishonest to say that I didn't want to harm her," Esteban continued, "I *wanted* to. But I wass going to let her live...if she had agreed to bring the assassin, Maddox, back to me. I believe that my appearance was dread to her, and she panicked. She did not cower in fear as I expected, however, but instead, attacked me with a tree limb. And, she clearly meant to beat me to death with it."

"Couldn't you have just run away?" asked Tomás. "Surely you can outrun an old lady."

"She backed me into a corner with her club and pounded me many times. I did not want to strike back, and I took the blows as long as I could, Tomás. Until I thought my life was in danger...then I struck her."

"And what about the big man," asked Tomás. "Her son, Chuy?"

"Oh, he was definitely going to kill me. He burst in and saw the woman on the floor and then attacked me with a flame stick."

"He had fire?" Asked Tomás, surprised.

"No, only a colored stick. But it stung like the flames with which it was painted."

"And you had to kill him also?"

"*Quemah.* I had to do it, Tomáss. If I had not defended myself, we wouldn't be speaking now. I would be dead like the rest."

As Tomás listened to the justifications, he detected a sly subtlety in *Rey Lagarto's* tone, which he took to mean that the creature thought the Delgados had gotten exactly what they deserved.

"You know they're looking for you, right?" Tomás said gravely.

Esteban took the last step out of the shadows and stood close to Tomás, but looked past him into the caldera beyond with his wrinkled eyelids drawn together over the large, red globes as he squinted into the light.

"They have been all through my home," said Esteban, pointing back into the cave. "And, all over the caldera and beyond hunting for me. But, as you can see, I am still here."

When their wariness of each other had eased somewhat and Tomás was fairly sure he wasn't in danger, the pair retreated into the tube and talked about how to proceed following the misfortune in the village. Tomás admitted that, although the boner had been a public relations disaster and didn't bode well for an encore appearance, the setback did have one bright side. At least now, the Workers knew *Rey Lagarto* was real, with the exception, Tomás had to clarify, of skeptics far away, who didn't believe anything that appeared in the *National Enquirer* and other such tabloids that pedaled to the more gullible or less educated workers.

Tomás took a run at explaining to a creature who lacked even the most basic reference points, the difference between public perception and reality in a modern, technological world, but he soon grew frustrated and so decided to steer the pow-wow to the subject that was bothering him the most.

"He stole my story," Tomás suddenly blurted out. "John Maddox stole my words and told the world that *he* wrote them. Then, he sold it to the magazine I told you about. And, probably for a lot of money."

Esteban detected discontent in the voice and, although he didn't think the theft of this boy's "story" was a comparable grievance to his own, he knew that any hope of luring his prey to Santa Teresa now lay with Tomás, and so he prodded.

"This Maddockss sounds like a worker of lowly character. The *chingada* murders, he steals, he takes trouble wherever he goes."

"That has turned out to be true," Tomás agreed.

"There is a question I must ask you." Esteban's voice was tentative. "Something that has me in doubt about you."

Tomás felt a lump in his stomach and a corresponding knot in his throat. He swallowed hard as he said, "What is it, Rey Lagarto?"

"It is very confusing to me..." Esteban's face contorted in chagrin, "... the stories that Workers tell... and write.... for each other. But, if I have understood you correctly, it would have been you, not the Maddocksss, who told all of... the world... that I exist, and... that I am here."

"Well, umm," Tomás stammered, limping to his own defense, "I am not like him, *Rey Lagarto*. I have much respect for you and only want to help you. John Maddox doesn't even believe that you really exist. At least he didn't before... before the...before the bad things happened. He does not really care anything about you, but I..."

"You would have made your story...and sold me to the world."

Groping nervously for a response, Tomás thought of the connection between money and power.

"You see, *Rey Lagarto*," he began, "money is kind of like a place-keeper. People trade it for things they need or want that make them feel either safer, or more powerful."

Esteban cocked his head, struggling with the concept.

"Let me say it this way," Tomás tried again. "Somebody, somewhere is going to tell the world about you, *Rey Lagarto*, and, if they can prove that you really exist, and they are smart and shrewd about it, they will make sure they get paid a lot of money for doing it. John Maddox has already done it, but it was in a magazine for entertainment, not serious news. In other words, most people don't take his story seriously. They think it was made up, and they would have thought mine was made up too, since it's the same damn story."

"But I am not... made up!" Esteban was defensive.

"Exactly!" said Tomás. "And, whoever proves that could make a lot of money; more than even Señora Delgado was paid."

"So, *you* will get the...money," Esteban puzzled. "That does not help me. I have lost everything, and money cannot change that, can it Tomás?"

"No, it can't," said Tomás, bowing his head briefly, then looking up and into Esteban's eyes, "but... money is...money is power. If you have

169

enough of it, you can sometimes use it to make others think what you want them to think... or even... to do what you want them to do."

"Can money make the Maddocks return to Santa Teresa?" Esteban was hopeful.

"It's possible, but I'm not sure. The *Enquirer* sent a different reporter here after you... I mean... after what happened to the Delgados. This guy was short and stocky and actually spoke Spanish. He looked like a broke-ass Emeril Lagasse."

The reference was lost on the Lizard King, and he stood silently and stewed while Tomás thought out loud.

"But, mayybeeee... if we can't make Maddox come back here..."

"Yessss?"

"Maybe I can... I mean, maybe we can cause some kind of misfortune to happen to him from here... long distance. I don't know how, just yet, but..."

A discouraged look came across the face of *Rey Lagarto*.

"There is a way," Tomás quickly added.

"Yess, tell me, Tomásss."

"I could go to New York myself... in your place...and... confront him. But, it would take a lot of money to get there, and a lot more once I do."

"You are wise for one so young, Tomáss. Do you have money?" Esteban cocked his head again as he asked the question.

"No... no I don't. *Mí familia* is not rich, and I don't get paid for my chores at the hotel."

Esteban felt defeated once again and bowed his head.

"We may not have money now," said Tomás, "but we have you, Rey Lagarto! I think I know how to get enough money so I can go to the United States and deliver your message in person. But, you'll have to trust me."

Esteban raised his head, looked deeply into Tomás' eyes, and said,

"I will trust you, Tomáss. So, what do we do now?"

PART III

Chapter 16

When John Maddox returned the damaged, blue, Buick rental-car to the airport garage in Mexico City on a Friday at noon, his yarn about hitting a coyote was met with skepticism by the Hertz rental agent.

"Thas a lotta damage, señor. You say that jus one coyote deed both of thees smashes?"

"Well, now that you mention it, there *was* more than one," John bullshat. "Three or four, maybe. Probably a pack, you know?"

"The coyote is a lone creature, my friend. They do not travel in packs."

The editors of the *National Enquirer* were kind enough to provide an umbrella insurance policy for any reporter, whether staff writer or freelancer, who they sent on an out-of-town assignment, and so John signed the paper work for the company's automobile collision claim, and then swung by the Duty-free for a couple of bottles of tequila before boarding an *Aero Mexico* 737, which whisked him away from Mexico and this whacky assignment. The flight unfortunately took him only as far as Houston, Texas, where he had to switch to an American Airlines jumbo, but, by seven p.m., John was back in NYC at his Tribeca apartment on Franklin and Varick, washing off the accumulated travel-grime in his very own shower.

With his hands flat against the familiar, blue and white checkered-tile of the shower wall, and his face directly under the showerhead, he closed his eyes and let the cool, clean water wash over him as he pondered how he was going to put this crazy story into words. Over and over, and against his will, the image of a body flying across the hood of his car flashed across the inside of his eyelids. Just what... *exactly*... had... he... seen? The more he tried to replace the phantasm with mental stock-photos of other animals who might be native to Central Mexico and were large enough to shatter the grill of a 2008 LaSabre and hull a crater into its windshield, the stronger the images reappeared, like the missing frames from 'THE EXCORCIST'; images of a...A... *DAMMIT!*

"This is ridiculous," he gurgled through the water streaming over his lips. "I'm just gonna say it was a deer."

Grabbing hold of the showerhead like it was a microphone, he sang out loud,

"IT WAAAS A fuuucking DEEEER...God Dammiiiiit!!"

After the shower and following an awkward phone conversation with his girlfriend Victoria, during which they agreed to have 'the talk' when she returned later tonight from a weekend at her folk's house in Connecticut, John tried to put relationship troubles out of his mind and sat down in his writing nook to hammer out the Santa Teresa piece.

He wrote the story he had he been constructing in his head while on the assignment; one that would entertain *Enquirer* readers with Chupacabra eyewitness accounts from Señora Delgado, Corto, the colorful old man in the plaza, and the best of the blips and blurps from other residents who had "seen things", or knew people who had "seen things. What he did not include was any mention of Tomás, or his ridiculous claim that he had spoken with the bloodthirsty Chupacabra.

Although he thought it absurd that any story could be too ridiculous for the *National Enquirer* to print, John had learned that the tabloid's publishers actually did have a (soft) ceiling on the level of disbelief-suspension they required of their readers. A story about a town full of people who believed that a Chupacabra lived in their midst was a great story in and of itself, and there was no need to add the ridiculous angle that the Monster could also *speak*. It was gilding the lily, and it just asked too much of even the dummies.

When John had finished the first draft, he read it through, and the omission of his own guide and translator's eyewitness account started to unsettle him. He was uncomfortably aware that his own copy read very much like the two-page story that Tomás had handed him in the little hotel room. A professor of John's at NYU, one of the most respected schools of journalism in the United States, had taught him that an investigative reporter must flesh out every bit of information at their disposal to get at the meat of the story, but John now felt caught in the most absurd catch-22 imaginable. He was actually burying the lead in a piece that would appear in a rag famous for foisting upon the public the most outrageous stories in the tabloidosphere.

After graduation, when he had spurned offers of internships in a rush to get his own byline in print as quickly as possible, he knew it was a gamble and had anted up by willingly lowering his expectations, but he had never intended to lower his journalistic standards in the process. His decision to submit pieces to the *National Enquirer* had been made in the wake of that publication's breaking the Jonathan Edwards story and the accompanying announcement of an intended editorial sea change for the magazine, but John quickly discovered that he had been hoodwinked when the wind whipped the sails right back around and *Enquirer* readers demanded that the low hanging fruit be put back in their diet. For the editors, the Edwards affair had only been about the sex, and the scandal, and the jilted, cancer-afflicted wife; they gave nary a crap about how the ramifications of the affair affected the ongoing political race.

John was treading water. He knew the *Enquirer* would never achieve legitimacy while still printing junk like this Chupacabra story, and the mag wasn't about to abandon its bread and butter fare of full color photos of Kardashian-Cottage-Cheese-thighs-type material. Professional pride compelled him to write the best piece he could with the information collected, but, as he pecked out the final draft, he knew that no one who operated in the leveled-up journalistic world to which he aspired was going to take this Chupacabra shit seriously; not unless Edward R. Murrow and Walter Cronkite themselves walked into somebody's living room with the chimeric beast hogtied and hanging upside down from a pike they carried across their shoulders.

He had swallowed his pride thus far and lived with his post-grad decision, but he didn't want to spend another year of his life in this rut. From the time he could read, John had been taught to view this kind of "journalism" as slop for the pigs and, on the flight home from Mexico, he had decided that this would be the last indignity he would allow himself to suffer. It was time to go vert and reach for the brass ring; *the New York Times.* He was more than ready.

Since the first issue of *The Times* rolled off the press in 1851, it had been the undisputed broadside of record for not just for the city it served, but the western world as a whole. Whether they admitted to it or not, news agencies around the globe looked to *The Times* for the current prevailing or ascendant stories, content, tone, and general shifts of public opinion concerning America's national identity. The only newspaper in the U.S. with a sphere of influence that rivaled that of *The Times* was *The Wall Street* Journal. The difference between the two was that the *WSJ*, being owned by Rupert Murdoch's *NEWS CORP.*, was generally viewed as a conservative, pro-business news agency, whereas the editorial creed of *The New York Times*, as printed in the newspaper's Inaugural Edition, was stated thus:

> *"We shall be Conservative, in all cases where we think*
> *Conservatism essential to the public good; —and we*
> *shall be Radical in everything which may seem to us to*
> *require radical treatment and radical reform. We do not*
> *believe that everything in Society is either exactly right or*
> *exactly wrong; —what is good we desire to preserve and*
> *improve; —what is evil, to exterminate, or reform."*

John was ten-years old when his father had read those words to him, and then explained exactly what they meant in terms that a boy could understand. It was the first time he had begun to grasp the higher concepts and ideals that he would later identify as profundity and integrity, and his comprehension would seed and grow throughout his adolescence, during his dad's time at *The Washington Post,* and finally bloom at *NYU Journalism.* The Maddox family had moved to D.C. a few months after President Nixon's resignation in 1974. In the aftermath of the debacle, in which two reporters from the *Washington Post* had exposed the conspiracy that would eventually lead to the resignation of Richard Nixon on August 9, 1974, an upheaval in *the Post's* internal power structure, and ensuing game of managerial musical chairs, resulted in an open position for John's father, Jeffrey.

Notwithstanding the respect he had for his father, or the old man's success at two of the country's top newspapers, John's ultimate goal was indeed landing a job at *The New York Times,* but on his own, earned, merits. He had taken the freelance work so he could make enough money to survive in New York City while he cultivated his skills as a writer, learned the trade from the inside, and had an actual, semi-regular byline in print, all of which were ultimately meant to serve as an autodidactic internship of sorts, and, eventually, garner him a staff position at *The Times.* Had he been stubborn or had he played it smart? John had gambled everything on the latter.

Subsisting on Ramen noodles, peanut butter, and New York tap water, in a rat-infested apartment on the Lower East Side, he had written and submitted stories to a plethora of publications, none of which saw the light of day. But, after a run of disappointments, he had sold a story to *The Star* magazine, a tabloid in the same mold as *The Enquirer,* and then parlayed that small success into writing pieces for *the Enquirer* and *The New York Post.* Soon after, he began to receive encouragement and accolades from a handful of writers at *The Times* who had known his father, and who were pulling for 'Jeffrey's boy'. They had, evidently, been following the trajectory of John's burgeoning career and were keeping up with his growth as a journalist and writer. He noticed, however, that these encouragements only came when his byline was affixed to a political piece, and *not* when he filed stories about Rosie O'Donnell's divorce, or even about 'pink slime' being served in school cafeterias. He was always grateful for the kudos, but the stubborn part of him felt the onus of knowing that, without his father's career, he would have received no such huzzahs.

His father's college buddy, *Times* reporter Frank Slater, was the first one to send a note of encouragement after the *NY Post* had printed John's piece about the troubles Texas Governor Rick Perry was having on the Presidential campaign trail. The note had been written on a single 3x5 sheet of *'From the Desk of...'* note paper; folded once, stuck in a small envelope, and delivered to John's dump of an apartment by his own father, who happened to be in Manhattan for a conference at the time, and had lunched with his old buddy Frank.

Yes, the 'Gray Lady' was the standard by which John measured all of his journalistic endeavors, starting with his sophomore year in high school, when his journalism teacher, Mr. Scarborough, who had acted in a sponsor/advisor roll for the student-operated weekly publication, had given the quixotic advice...

"When deciding the angle and gauging the tone your piece will take, ask yourself if you would write the story any differently if you were writing it for the New York Times? If so, how would it differ, and more importantly, WHY?"

The words were never more clearly illustrated than when delineating the difference between the *Times* and the *Enquirer.* The former was one of the world's most respected gazettes, and the latter, probably the least, owing largely to its success and its position at the top of the dung heap. The *Enquirer's* aim was for a decidedly lower journalistic standard; one more focused on the entertainment of its readers than with socially, culturally, or politically emergent material. Since John had entered the field, however, he had witnessed the line separating 'hard news' from 'entertainment' becoming blurred at an exponential rate. A new term had even been coined to describe the mongrel entity; INFO-TAINMENT.

Every news agency was fully aware of the reduced attention spans and lowered political awareness of the general public, and they used every tool at their disposal to gain and then retain readership in the midst of a technological revolution. Digital graphics, computerized enhancements, and other thoroughly researched techniques had been used in print for years to catch the eye of those afflicted by Attention Deficit Disorder as they walked past newsstands, and the techniques had found their full potentiality with the advent of the Internet. The six-hundred-year reign of the paper NEWSPAPER was in rapid decline, and the major players saw the bold typeface clearly on the wall. Any media entity savvy enough to survive the change would offer its wares under the banner of a website, thereafter supplanting the loss of subscribers and the closing of a thousand newsstands with millions of web-surfers and news-junkies whom they could buoy and addict. There was no stopping it; the genie had leapt out of the bottle and then smashed that bottle into shards on the sidewalk of history.

John had flirted, very briefly, with the idea of moonlighting as a political blogger when an old high school buddy, who knew of his career frustrations as well as his skills as a writer, asked him to contribute to his news blog. John was acutely aware of his father's attitude toward yellow journalism of any hue and didn't think his old man could handle the shame and betrayal of his son becoming a prodigal blogger. So, being careful not to insult his friend, he politely declined.

When the personal home computer appeared in the 1980's, a multitude of do-it-yourselfers were spawned in a number of fields, including music, art, commerce, business and, to the chagrin of all respected, and/or self-respecting journalists, the sacred institution of **THE NEWS**. The odious, embryonic entity would be known as the 'news blogosphere', and it was an entirely new can of worms whose contributing bloggers gorged themselves from the trough of source material on the World Wide Web, and then shat out a buffet from which literally anyone could pick and choose, recycling and exponentially expanding the trove of speciously researched conjecture and speculation. The inventions were typically agenda-driven, and their inventors attempted to give them a ring of truthiness by pilfering and appropriating the work of journalists who had diligently researched their subjects, resulting in an output that itself became a smorgasbord for both the web-surfing news junkie and the casual visitor who were hooked by the lead line of a Google or Yahoo search (or, for Chuck Berry).

It was irritating and insulting to anyone who had chosen the traditional pursuit of a formal education in preparation for their vocation. News-bloggers were rank amateurs who lacked bona fides and possessed none of the skills required to properly track sources and run down leads. Those facilities came from training, experience, and, most importantly, boots-on-the-ground field work, but the overwhelming majority of bloggers found it unnecessary to leave their cozy homes to investigate a story, or even attempt to correspond via Internet or telephone to corroborate any statement or substantiate any claim that might contradict their specific agenda. To the mind of the professional journalist, the news blogs were clearly pieced together with shmeers of randomly collected info from myriad, Internet-only sources, and they had no credibility as a news source, but were merely editorial in nature.

The whole clusterfuck shit-ball was antithetical to the ideals that John had inherited and, though he had backed the wrong horse so far, he didn't want to remain one of its jockeys and have his reputation hauled off to the glue factory without experiencing the satisfaction of, at the very least, a show. He would claim his birthright, offer himself up to the *New York Times*, and take his place in the dwindling ranks of those still defending the Old Guard. It was time to call in his chits, pull the trigger of nepotism and mobilize all other applicable idioms and antonyms.

But, he wouldn't ask daddy for help; at least not literally. John was a big boy, and he would go straight to Frank Slater and ask him to make the proper introductions. The worst that could happen would be the offer of an internship, but, at this point, he was willing to pay the dues he had tried so hard to avoid just to get a finger in the crag. Any shame he might feel for eating crow would be tempered by the approbation he knew he would receive from his parents. In his more honest moments, John admitted to himself that their approval mattered very much.

He printed out the finished copy and, as he always did before submitting a piece, sat back in his comfy chair in the den for one last go-over. Yes, he thought as he read, Tomás was going to feel ripped off. But, could he help it if the teenager had used the same angle he had already decided on? There was, of course, the trivial factor that John had read the kid's story before he had put his own onto the old, Dell hard-drive. But, John was the reporter the magazine sent on assignment to that god-forsaken place. He was the *professional*!! Not Tomás.

Fuck it, let the Legal Department handle it, John decided. He would deal with the fallout later. He hit SEND and fired off the final draft directly to Ben Rantz who he knew worked late, even on weekends. It would be his first communication with the editor since their confrontation in the man's office.

After almost three years of submitting pieces to the rag, John knew the rhythm of the *Enquirer's* publishing cycle and he estimated that, if Rantz gave it the go-ahead before the weekly printing on Monday, it would be on the newsstands by Wednesday.

—⁓—

Victoria returned at nine o'clock after a long drive from Northwest Park, Connecticut. She was very close to her mother and father, who had raised her in the quaint suburban neighborhood outside of Hartford, where they still lived and kept her bedroom exactly as it was the day she left for college. After a shower, she met John on the sofa for the tête-a-tête both had been rehearsing all day. They each began by expressing their love for each other, but John got quickly down to brass tacks.

"So what exactly *is* going on with you and Rantz, then?" He began.

"It was a flirtation that got out of hand. I don't have feelings for him, John. He's actually kind of an asshole."

"He definitely doesn't feel that way about you," John shot back.

"Not my fault. It's basically one way. Believe me."

"So how, exactly..." John asked with mock indignation, "...did it happen that I'm in B.F. Mexico interviewing people about a giant, goat-sucking lizard, while you're getting chummy with the new President's inner circle? How does that happen? Do I need to flirt with Rantz to get a good assignment?"

Victoria gave him a blistering look.

"KIDDING!" Said John, raising his hands in surrender, "I'm kidding... kind of. Come on!"

"Okay, that's slightly humorous, but let's let it go now, goofball. Just try to get along with each other please. He's my boss."

The couple moved past the rumpus over Rantz and went on to a discussion about their relationship in general. Where was it going? Were they in this for the long haul? Could they live together for an extended period of time without eventually wanting to strangle each other? These were the quintessential questions that every couple considering marriage asked themselves. There might be one or two others, but those were the big ones, and John had been having the internal debate for a while now. The recent rankle over Rantz had been a monkey wrench but, for the most part, his talk with Victoria tonight helped ease his doubts.

John had bought a ring two months ago, but only now felt confident enough to put the rock into play. It wouldn't be tonight, though; the reconciliation needed a few days to cure while he thought of a way to spring the customary question. A ring in her champagne glass? In the Chocolate Mousse? An ensemble playing their favorite song? He wasn't sure that a string quartet could pull off a Radio Head song, but maybe with the right arrangement.

—◊◊—

The reconciled couple made love that night and were in each other's arms when morning came. A fresh feeling followed them both through the day as Victoria went to work in the *Enquirer* office and John made an appointment for lunch with Frank Slater. He was to stop by Slater's office at eleven thirty and they would walk to Schnippers at the end of the block, but John arrived at the *Times* building early so he could catch up with a couple of friends and NYU classmates.

First, he popped in on Sam Morgan, master of all things graphically artistic and Internetual, and the *WSN's* former Art Director. The *Washington Square News*, named for the park that lay in the shadows of the NYU buildings, was the hip newspaper read by the students and faculty as well as the residents of neighboring Greenwich Village and 60,000 online readers and NYU alumni. During his tenure at the paper, Morgan had been responsible for re-designing and updating both the printed version of the *WSN* and their online website. He and John had run in the same circles and had worked closely together, Sam providing photos and artwork for most of the pieces John wrote while at NYU. Now, Morgan was moving quickly up the salmon ladder, as was the other school chum that John popped in on.

Taylor Grant was a laid-back over-achiever, who had been at the top of their class at NYU Journalism and was the first to be offered an internship at the *Times*. Everyone in their circle knew that if anyone were going to milk the opportunity to its dry bones, it would be Grant. In just four years, he had attained the position of Managing Editor for the Times Financial website page and, along with Sam Morgan, was the contemporary embodiment of John's ambitions.

"Still impersonating a journalist, I see," he joked as he walked into Grant's office. "I guess they don't do background checks at this dump, huh?"

A man with a boyish face and a black mop-top (like a skunk had curled up for a nap on top of his head) rose from his chair and walked toward John with an outstretched hand and a goofy, sincere smile.

"How did you get past security?" Said Grant in his characteristically casual tone. "Was the guard asleep again? I really need to remember to lock my door."

"Nice, very nice," John said sarcastically. "Cub reporter Taylor Grant. I still don't believe that's your real name. It's too 'movie star' sounding."

"So, what brings you into the Lady today? I haven't seen you for weeks. Didja finally decide to grace us with your talents?"

"Actually, I am indeed ready to level-up," John admitted. "I'm having lunch today with Frank Slater."

"Not a bad place to start, buddy. Slater's stock is high this month, and he has Marshall's ear of late."

Grant was referring to Andrew Marshall, *Times* managing co-editór. Known respectfully by the staff as 'Vice Admiral'; the man who steered the prominent gazette over the vast seas of culture, politics, arts and finance. Marshall didn't do the hiring of course, but, if he wanted someone hired, *his will be done*, and John hoped that if his lunch with Frank Slater went well, an introduction to the Vice Admiral would be forthcoming.

"How is Victoria? Asked Grant. "You two still in business?"

"Yeah, we're still at it. Been a bit bumpy lately, but it's good now. She's still working for Rantz."

Grant rolled his eyes sympathetically as John continued.

"But, she's great. It's all good now...I think. Uhh...I actually think I'm ready to level-up in that arena as well."

"Whoa, you're kidding? said Grant, surprised. "Already? Well, I guess you guys did have all that time on the down-low, unbeknownst to Celene and Rex."

His pal was referring to the friends-with-benefits-style tryst that John and Victoria had sustained at college under the noses of their official 'inamorati', who had eventually discovered the betrayal, comforted each other through their respective breakups, and were now married to each other. Taylor was still one of John's best friends, and as such was privy to insider info concerning the couple's personal lives.

"If you see Vic, don't say anything," John beseeched. "You're the only one I've told."

"Your secret is safe, buddy."

—⋙—

Lunch with Frank Slater went swimmingly and, just as John had hoped, his father's friend was encouraging about his entering the *Times* employ in a salaried position. He had added that if John would hold his water, put in some hard work, and not make any waves while doing it, he could probably garner a byline of his own in the not too distant future. When Victoria came home, late that evening, she was thrilled for him, but she made the mistake of mentioning Rantz, (still a tender subject), and what "Ben" would think of losing John, one of his top freelance contributors.

"Well," John replied, "I really don't think there will be much of a conflict of interest as far as content goes. It's kind of apples and oranges, really, at least professionally."

"Give it five years," Victoria joked facetiously, "and you'll have the Chupacabra on the front page of your precious *Times*. Then Ben Rantz shall have his REVENGE!!"

"Ben, Ben, Ben," John whined sarcastically, "Screw Ben Rantz and the Chupacabra he rode in on!"

It was said in a mocking tone, but he watched Victoria's reaction carefully until the ringing phone interrupted her half-hearted laughter.

Surprise! It was Rantz himself, calling to say that the Santa Teresa piece would indeed run on Wednesday. Though the similarities to Tomás' story were still nagging at him, it was good news for John's bank account. He had a card in his pocket left to play, if the need arose, but, at the moment, the high rent of his Tribeca apartment was due.

—⁂—

News of the Delgado killings took a few days to hit the AP wire. The first spark was its appearance in a police blotter report in Wednesday's Torreón newspaper, then it was fanned by the *Monterey El Norte*, who picked it up for its Thursday edition. By Friday, the story was set ablaze by the revelation that one of the deceased was the woman who had actually taken the first Chupacabra photo. The weekend editions of every newspaper in Mexico featured their own versions of:

"TWO KILLED BY CHUPACABRA"

John was walking down Hudson Street on his way home when Victoria called his cell.

"Have you heard the latest about your Mexican monster?" she asked. "It just came over the *AP*."

"You know I count on you for the hot tips. What's up?"

"*Chupacabra kills two in Central Mexico.* Actually, it said allegedly in there somewhere, but one of the deceased is that Constance Delgado from your story."

John nearly dropped the cell phone. This was some coincidence. A week after his interview with Señora Delgado, she was dead.

"Does it say if her son was the other victim?" he asked.

"Doesn't say. It's just a short item on the *AP*. Slow news day, I guess."

"Hey, don't belittle my work," John joked.

Victoria laughed, "Heheh, I just thought you should know that you are leaving destruction in your wake."

He had developed a soft spot for the little village and its citizens, and this news was disturbing. Maybe he had gotten too close to the story, John wondered. There was something about the murders that nagged at him, something aside from his natural sympathy for the human victims. The flashing images of the animal-collision continued to disturb him. If it wasn't a coyote or a deer on the hood of the rental car, he wondered, then what the hell was it? The whole experience had been a blow to his natural doubt and cynicism.

As he stood on the street corner trying to make sense of this new information, his cell phone rang.

"Well Maddox," said the voice of Ben Rantz, "looks like you came back a few days too early. It's getting more interesting down there all the time. Did you hear?"

"I heard."

"I've already sent René down there. He'll have an easier time with the language, I think."

"You're definitely right about that," John agreed. "It's best that I put some distance between myself and that story. It's beginning to mess with my mind."

Back in his apartment, he went through the emails he had been ignoring. There was a butt-load of spam, a couple of messages from his parents, one from his sister, Misty, and several splenetic diatribes from Tomás. As predicted, the teenager had read the story and was very upset. He demanded that his calls and emails be returned and insisted on an explanation as to why John's name had appeared with *his* story. The recording on John's answering machine affirmed Tomás' acrimony and, when he heard the pissed-off tone in the boy's voice saying that he had already contacted the *Enquirer's* legal department, he knew that he'd be hearing from them soon as well. The kid did not lack gumption, he thought to himself. John made no reply, just clapped the laptop shut in guilty frustration, and left the apartment again.

It had become a habit for him, whenever one of his stories went to print, to pick up a fresh copy at a certain newsstand on Greenwich Street, then walk to his favorite Starbucks and sit at his favorite table by the window, scanning the piece for typos. When he did so, he always treated himself to a French press (Sumatra: brought to his table by the cute girl at the register, with a small, white timer clipped onto it, because she knew he liked to press the plunger himself). The coffee was consistently good of course, but the staff was also great and, if he was lucky, the singing, dancing, and thoroughly entertaining barista, known affectionately by his co-Workers as '*Streisand*', would deliver an inspired, impromptu a cappella performance standing atop the counter or, better still, while strolling amongst the tables of friendly regulars in the lobby as he belted out 'America', from *"West Side Story"* or 'Light My Candle' from *"Rent"*.

John read through his story twice, and the piece had zero typos and misprints. It wasn't, however, going to make him a Pulitzer candidate. It wasn't even close to his best work and, as he read, he couldn't shake the nagging guilt he felt about Tomás. Why did it bother him so much, he wondered? He hadn't stolen anything from the boy, so why did his conscience feel so muddied? Maybe, he guessed, because he had been so impressed with Tomás. The boy had obviously looked up to him, and instead of helping him, John had betrayed him. At least that's how Tomás saw it now.

—⚬—

When the next issue of the *Enquirer* came out, René Hernandez's piece was featured on the front page with full color photos of the Delgado's bodies, draped with white sheets and being wheeled out of their little casa; the brand new, green Nissan parked on the concrete drive in the background. As he read René's take on the story, John had to admit to a skosh of Chupacabra-envy. He knew these people now, and not just the Delgados. He had learned a little bit about the mind-set of Santa Teresans in general, and he guessed the little burg was in turmoil at the thought that their village mascot was guilty of eviscerating two of their fellow citizens.

Hernandez had not mentioned Tomás in the article, and John wanted like hell to call the teenager to hear what he knew. The kid did, after all, claim to be on speaking terms with a Chupacabra, for God's sake, and he wondered if the creature might have spilled its guts to the boy in a trans-species murder confession. The idea made him smile, and he was amused at the thought of news crews arriving in Santa Teresa to cover the story with their tongues firmly in-their-cheeks. What if, John mused, the words being sarcastically delivered by the always-irritating talking heads when they reported on the mythical lizard-monster having shredded the Delgado's carcasses, turned out to be unwittingly accurate accounts of the tragic crime? What epic irony.

Although he had officially found the boy's claims to be ridiculous, something in the sincere assertions made John's 'Spidey-senses' tingle. Tomás was as sharp as a tack, and John guessed he had probably already written his own take on the killings. Summoning his testicular fortitude, he dialed the number Tomás had given him, but it rang for so long with no answer that the international operator came on the line and suggested that he try again later. When he checked his email again, there was a new angry missive in which Tomás dropped the names of specific employees in the *Enquirer's* legal department. After that, John did not reply to the contentious email, nor did he try the call again. Testicles... AWOL.

In the following weeks, tales of the *'Killer-Chupacabra of Santa Teresa'* flourished as fodder for American popular culture. Morning chat shows, late night talk shows, and even local, suburban news programs all expounded jokingly on the Phenom, but John remained troubled, and he stewed over the entire affair and the effect it must be having on the little village. Hopefully, the Sanchez Hotel's rooms were filled with morbid curiosity seekers and supernatural nature photographers, all bringing money to the local economy. It was the only positive thought he could summon whenever his guilty mind touched on the tragedy.

—◆—

On the Friday after Thanksgiving, John took Victoria for a wonderful, very expensive dinner in a restaurant overlooking Central Park. He played it cool during the meal and waited until afterwards to take her across the street and into the park, where he took a knee on the cold sidewalk next to The Pond and asked her to be his wife. They had only been living together for a few months, and Victoria was taken by surprise, especially in the wake of the Ben Rantz ripple, but she accepted, and then commenced planning the wedding and the honeymoon that very night.

The couple shared the news with their parents just before Christmas, and then spent three days with John's family in Providence, followed with three days in Connecticut with Victoria's, who, collectively, it turned out, were as nutty as a fruitcake factory. John had always been curious why she had never taken him home to meet the "rents' as he had done, and he quickly learned why. *Who would have known that such a seemingly well adjusted girl could be produced by such a family?* he would later entreat a co-worker.

Her older brother, Chris, was home on a courtesy, holiday-release from his stint at a State-imposed rehab facility; the demon white powder having interrupted his promising career as an MBA. He had been a salutatorian at Vanderbilt, but his last few months had been spent painting, taking long walks, and participating in group therapy with other wayward college grads.

Victoria's father had pursued a handful of vastly divergent vocations over the years including fishing boat captain, record store manager, donut shop owner, and short story writer. John found the man to be a dyed-in-the-wool eccentric and, during the course of his visit, the two had had the same conversation about the same subject on three separate occasions, with Mr. Magaña passionately defending a different position each time. On the third go-around, as the kook second and third-guessed himself on the subject of Nuclear Energy for over an hour, John just smiled at him and nodded.

Then, there was Victoria's mother, a peculiar woman who spent nearly all of her waking hours cleaning, tidying, and mumbling to herself. John politely pretended not to pay attention to the woman's mutterings, but secretly noted that they sounded like an argument between two or more of her inner selves, and occasionally, when her rambling dialogue became heated, it would end in silence from all parties. Whenever John struck up a conversation with her, however, she seemed perfectly normal and was very kind and accommodating.

Victoria's seventeen-year-old baby brother, Mark, didn't speak. He just...........didn't speak. They were all happy for the couple, however, and the family heartily welcomed John into their fold, a fact that, now that he had met them all, had a slightly unsettling effect on him. What had he gotten himself into, he wondered? These nutters were going to be the grandparents of his children someday? Holy crap.

When the holidays ended, they returned to a snow-covered Manhattan and John began the New Year just where he wanted to be. It was just a crappy, little grey cubicle surrounded by thirty others exactly like it, but he felt he was in the catbird seat. Nepotism might have played a part in his hiring, but now it was time to deliver, and he set to work diligently researching and working on follow-up pieces in the political sphere.

By March, he had wrangled his way into co-authoring a huge story that centered around a CIA operative who had destroyed ninety-two videotapes revealing harsh interrogation techniques that had been used on suspected al Qaeda combatants. John was tapped to do a follow-up interview with Jose A. Rodriguez Jr., the CIA's former head of clandestine services, who had ordered the tapes destroyed. It would be John's first byline for *The New York Times* and would be well received and widely quoted. He was in the mix, and he couldn't have been happier.

Victoria was happy for him, of course, though it made her even more self conscious about trying to make a silk purse for the piggish eyes and ears of *National Enquirer* readers. Alongside stories about celebrity excess, she churned out pieces that alluded to the President's Kenyan ancestry, a subject which never failed to rankle and rouse a new group of conservative-minded Americans calling themselves "The Tea Party". Unsurprisingly, the bullfunk surrounding the search for the Commander-in-Chief's Kenyan birth certificate was as far as the *Enquirer's* editors had been willing to delve into the political realm lately and, with the exception of an occasional update about the Chupacabra, or some other preternatural or supernatural crap, the tabloid's front page was predictably covered with giant, color photos of celebrities and their celeb-babies; the ensuing pages fleshing out the Hollywood scandals, pill-addictions, and games of musical spouses. America was celebrity-obsessed and with each passing day of the new Presidential administration, the country was becoming more and more politically apathetic.

Whether at work or not, Victoria was busily planning a grandiose wedding and an even grandioser honeymoon. Her parents were not wealthy people, and John knew that the celebration she was planning would strain even a royal budget, but he loved the girl, and thought she deserved the best of everything. He decided he would go along to get along and try to stay out of the way, which, in theory, should have been easy, but Victoria still called him whenever she had a new idea, and then her mother would call John to confirm that he had really meant yes when he had said *yes* to Victoria a few minutes before. It was maddening, just maddening, but he figured this was probably de rigueur and rode it out.

The small irritations in his personal life would be history soon enough, but there was a festering boil on the otherwise peachy complexion of his professional future. No lawsuit was pending thus far, presumably because Tomás didn't have the money to hire an attorney and, even if he had, John guessed that the teenager would have difficulty finding a barrister willing to take on the *Enquirer* in a plagiarism suit that centered on a page-four story about Santa Teresa's pet Chupacabra. Such a dispute would boil down to the word of a sixteen-year old, Mexican national versus that of a (currently) *New York Times* staff writer. Not even ambulance-chasing, shyster-bait was that!

Still, with his own illustrious career at the *Times* in its infancy, John knew that an accusation of plagiarism would cause a ripple that could tip his boat, if not set it aflame and scuttle it at sea. In an effort to get ahead of the threat, he visited the *Enquirer's* legal department, where he was advised to not answer any emails or phone calls from Tomás Delgado. He foolishly ignored the advice, however, and, assuring himself that he could use simple logic and reason to convince Tomás to back the fuck off, John engaged in a series of email debates with the teenager in which he argued that the similarities were due to them both having been present for the interviews. For his part, Tomás claimed that their stories weren't just similar, they were damn near IDENTICAL! In retort, John insisted that it was he, John Maddox, an actual, accredited journalist, who had conducted the interviews, and that Tomás had merely been along for the ride.

It was a tacky, infantile thing to say, and he immediately regretted pushing SEND on his final missive. The e-debates served no purpose other than to make Tomás angrier, and John came to realize that, in the ultimate assessment, all he had done was make the job of the *Enquirer's* legal department that much more difficult.

Chapter 17

In the days following his reconnection with *Rey Lagarto*, Tomás was caught in a taffy-pull of emotions. His loyalty to Santa Teresa, its citizens, and even his own family, was at odds with his desire to protect the creature he had only recently met face to fangs.

It was a fact, however, that the Lizard King had been in his life since he could remember; first as a children's tale, and now as a walking, talking personality. Tomás thought that the *Lagarto* deserved the respect of everyone who lived in the shadow of the crater. After all, in the mind of the King, just as the Workers of Santa Teresa belonged to him, he belonged to them, and, as the *Lagarto* had always watched over the humans and protected them from harm, so Tomás thought they should be *Rey Lagarto's* defenders and champions now. He was considering taking on that role quite literally, but there were several points about which he was still reluctant.

The sympathy he felt for the creature was very real, but *Rey Lagarto's* tragedies were not his own. Tomás' budding dislike of the American stemmed from his own squabbles with the man. Their ongoing e-banter only added to the enmity; the quarrelsome exchanges growing steadily nastier until the reporter stopped responding altogether. The King's demand of a death sentence went way beyond a fitting punishment for the petty crime of plagiarism, but Tomás still stewed over the very real fact that Maddox was also guilty of killing the Lagarto Queen and child, which, even if it had been accidental, meant that he was, technically, responsible for the genocide of an intelligent and ancient race of beings. A *Taffy-pull I say!*

He was caught in an intensifying vortex and, though a public execution seemed far too extreme, Tomás wanted to hit Maddox with something more personal than a lawsuit; something that would strike at the man's very soul, and he thought he knew how. It would take money, however. Not hit-man money, nor the bargain-basement option of a desperate crack head who would crack heads for a few bucks, but, if he could generate enough funds to hire a private investigator in New York City, maybe he could dig up something that would embarrass Maddox professionally. Everyone had skeletons in their closet, and Tomás thought that if Maddox had stolen *his* story, he had probably at least plagiarized others. If he could expose him as a serial plagiarist, the revelation would certainly heap shame and disgrace upon the man, and, if Tomás were then able to convince his reptilian cohort of the severity of the disgrace, he might possibly be able to steer the torpedo of revenge, which *Rey Lagarto* was busily arming, away from its present, bloody trajectory. That is, of course, if the very human concept of professional disgrace was pernicious enough to satisfy the creature's bloodlust.

Without money, the plan was dead in the water and, under normal circumstances, the enterprise would be next to impossible for an unemployed teenager whose family lived on a very meager income. But, his current circumstances were anything but normal. Tomás had *Rey Lagarto,* the key to a probable gold mine if he played his hand right.

Time was definitely of the essence, as Tomás had been keeping up with how the pop culture phenomenon was playing out in the U.S. and had noticed a downtick of late. The most recent round of Chupacabra references on American television had kicked off with Señora Delgado's photograph, peaked soon after her murder, and now, even the highest rated U.S. soap opera had written a story line about the monster into the show (as a comedic device, of course). The synergy in the American popmosphere was still ripe for capitalizing on the fad, but he needed to step it up before public interest waned again. *Gather ye pesos while ye may.*

The animosity *Rey Lagarto* felt for Maddox had not diminished. If anything, the solitude and loneliness of the creature's new reality had left a void into which he poured all of his rancor, malice, and acrimony. He admitted to Tomás that if he could get his claws on the murderer, the result would be visceral, but since that did not seem possible, he tried to grasp the alternate-requital scheme Tomás was presenting to him.

As far as American pop culture was concerned, the *National Enquirer* in the United States was the well from which '*el fenómeno del Chupacabras de Santa Teresa*' had sprung, and that tabloid was where Tomás planned to peddle a new set of photographs. This batch had to cut through the jaded, infamously short attention span of the American public, and he had thought of a gimmick that would make them look just shocking enough to kick it up a notch. That was, if *Rey Lagarto* consented to the undignified artifice. Any amateur could fake a photograph or manipulate an image using any one of a thousand Photo Shoppe-type programs, but Tomás had an idea that, coming on the heels of the previous Chupacabra stories, the *Enquirer* would just *have* to print, even if they thought they were fakes.

The King was baffled by the explanation at first, but he had come to trust the young worker and didn't think he would betray him.

"What will happen, Tomáss," he asked, bothered, "when you show the...fotograffss... to the other Workerss?

"People will come looking for you again...hundreds of people, maybe. They will come from near and far to capture you on video cameras and..." Tomás chose his words carefully, "...and some will probably try to snare you and put you in traps and cages."

Esteban's eyes widened in alarm as Tomás added,

"The ones who searched for you after you *ki*... I mean... after the Delgado's died? they will come again, and they will not give up so easy this time." He squinted and gave the King a grave look. "Most likely, *Rey Lagarto*...they *will* find you."

"Thisss is dread news, Tomásss."

"I don't think they will kill you, though," Tomás tried to sound upbeat. "There are Workers called Scientists who will want to study you.

They will want to protect you, surely...probably. I will be with you, Rey Lagarto, and I will not let anyone hurt you."

Esteban hung his head in confused despair trying to process the realities as Tomás described them.

"I promise you that," Tomás swore, then, soberly, added, "But... I don't think that your life will ever be the same."

"What life do I have now, Tomáss?" Esteban shot back without hesitating. "What is left for me here? I am not the king that I have always believed myself to be. I find myself without substance and of unclear purpose in whatever life I have remaining. Why shouldn't the... world... know about me and see me? Am I so frightening to your kind that they would want to hurt me?"

"Well, um," Tomás fumbled, not wanting to be dishonest, "actually, your looks would be frightening to people...I think. But, they can get used to it... like I did. The thing that will really freak them out is the fact that you can *speak*!"

—⁓—

Just as Chuy Delgado had done, Tomás bought a disposable camera at *los Rápida* in Torreón. Unlike the Delgados, he knew he couldn't give the new film to someone else to develop. The first Chupacabra photo may have slipped past the technicians at *la Pharmacía*, but with Chupamania now permeating the local air, he couldn't take the chance of handing over to a stranger, a full, twenty-four frame roll of color negatives of a chained and bound Lizard King. Thankfully, Tomás knew someone who could remedy his predicament.

Señor Vega at the hardware store was an amateur photographer and, for months now, he had been offering to share his hobby with Tomás by teaching him how to develop real celluloid film in a darkroom he had made from a converted storage closet in the back. And so, the man was all smiles when the teenager showed up one morning for his first lesson and, after an hour of going over the basics, Tomás was left alone to practice on a roll of Señor Vega's family photo negatives while his mentor counted screws and nails behind the counter in the front.

On the day of the photo session, Esteban was agitated when Tomás walked through the Palace entrance carrying a collection of ropes and chains, but eventually relented after being convinced that the restraints were only for the camera. As Tomás explained it, when the final gambit was played and Esteban appeared before the Workers (in... person?), it would be clear that he was an unrestrained, in-control, free-wheelin' lizard. Then, said Tomás, the world would see the 'magnificence of the one, true, *REY LAGARTO de SANTA TERESA*'.

The potentate was placated by the ass-kissing for the moment, but he was wary as he led Tomás through the corridor into the Great Room, and, when the boy came toward him with the props and lifted them up to drape them over his shoulders, Esteban chafed again and spat. It took considerable coaxing from Tomás and, only after the King took the implements in his hands, inspected them closely, and then draped them loosely over his own body, did the photo session begin.

Annie Leibovitz would have appreciated the surreal atmosphere of the vaulted Throne Room as a dramatic, diffused, blue light filled the space from the natural skylight above. With water drip-dripping from the domed, cathedral ceiling into the small pools all around him, Esteban stood frozen and tried his best to look 'captured'. But it was obvious, from the looseness of the restraints, that he could have freed himself with little effort. Only after heaped flattery and pleas from a frustrated Tomás about the waning light, did Esteban let the photographer place him in a (slightly) more distressed position and, even then, as Tomás was carefully tightening the ropes, the Chupacabra hissed and groaned and chirred out a high, guttural growl that sounded like nothing less than an extremely pissed-off *gato*.

—⁓—

The next day, Señor Vega was thrilled when his new apprentice returned to the store to practice developing with his own roll of negatives, and he gave the boy privacy to do so. Soon, Tomás had printed a stack of clear, precise, color images, and afterwards, though the señor said it wasn't necessary, his student insisted on doing two hours of morning grunt work in exchange for the lessons.

When he returned to the cave and placed the finished collection of photos in the King's clawed hands, *Rey Lagarto* was equal parts thrilled and baffled. He had only ever caught distorted glimpses of himself in pools of water and seeing his own face clearly on the small, rectangular pieces of photo-paper fascinated him. It reminded Esteban of pictures he had seen on the stacks upon stacks of brightly colored pages, found while rummaging through the garbage heaps on the far side of the caldera; images of very strange-looking, and oddly dressed Workers of undistinguishable gender, who's skin was as pale as an exsanguinated piglet. But, he had never seen his own likeness, nor that of any other *Lagarto,* in this way.

As *Rey Lagarto* held the paper gingerly and studied the photos, Tomás thought he looked like a baby discovering his own hands for the first time, and he elucidated for the King the power that the images could convey in the human world. Only after he began to perceive the photographs as an odd sort of tool with which he could communicate with, not just the workers of Santa Teresa, but, ultimately, the wider world that he had always known was out there... somewhere, did Esteban's lizard-brain begin to absorb the completely alien concept of *PUBLICITY.*

The mismatched duo stood silently, both speculating daydreamily about the course of their futures, but each from a very different perspective. While *Rey Lagarto* was reconnecting with and being canonized by his subjects as they returned him to his proper place as their Sovereign figurehead, Tomás was mentally enjoying his fortune and basking in the warmth of the fame that would surely come to a *hero* who had captured and tamed *THE DREADED CHUPACABRA.* Both superstars kept their fantasy endings to themselves.

—m—

Workers seldom visited the far southern perimeter of the caldera, even in the daytime, unless it was to dump garbage, and the remote area had always been a safe hunting ground when Esteban's body needed nourishment. Now, it served as a testing ground for his nocturnal flying practice.

Unaware of how ridiculous he looked, his first efforts of hopping around awkwardly and flapping the wings fast and hard produced only a slight buoyancy in his body weight, but he could never get his feet to leave the ground. After the inaugural attempts, he was unsure he would ever be able to actually take to the air and fly, but, day-by-day, his back muscles became stronger, and the soreness in his wing joints began to fade away. He soon learned that the secret was not about physical exertion so much as ground-speed, and, after a half-dozen tries gallomping along as fast as he could with his wings fully extended, the final piece fell into place. Just as he hit top speed on the next run, he tilted his wings on their horizontal axis and the batwing-like flaps of skin caught the oncoming breeze, stretched taught, and lifted him into the air.

He looked down to see the ground falling away beneath his dangling feet but, when he lowered his head, the motion caused him to drop, so he beat his wings furiously until a warm current of air caught the fleshy billows and buoyed him skyward once again. But, as the flying lizard climbed higher, an unpleasant ground-separation anxiety washed over him, and he had a sudden yearning to get his feet back on solid ground as soon as possible. Leaning his body-mass to the left, he banked into a gentle, downward spiral. As he circled, he found that he could steer himself back into the warmer pockets of air and climb again. When he used the rising currents, it took much less brute strength to remain aloft, and he hardly needed to flap his wings at all unless he was dropping too fast or wanted to change directions quickly. Soon, the acrophobic sensation disappeared completely and, as he soared, *Rey Lagarto* looked out over the vast horizon beyond the river valley, shrouded in pale moonlight, and reveled in the glory of his ancestral birthright as he climbed higher and higher.

On his third night of enjoying the new abilities, Esteban climbed up the steep rock wall of the escarpment and stood on the high crater rim, talons curled over the lip and wings folded behind him. Raising his clawed hands over his head, he 'Louganissed' off the edge, but instantly regretted his decision as he fell like a brick towards the hard, bramble-covered ground, but, with the thicket rushing toward him, the thin membranes of skin ballooned open with a *PFLOPP* just in the knick, and he sailed out over the caldera floor at a high rate of speed, the tops of the tallest scrub trees brushing past his undercarriage.

The King of the Santa Teresa Valley soared and dipped and dived, and, when he felt one warm pocket of air drop out from under him, he just tilted his wings, which only spanned five feet but bore the diminutive reptile easily, put his muscled back into it, and flapped his way into another one, riding it skyward again.

A fast moving object on the caldera floor to his left suddenly flashed in his peripheral vision, shaking him from his euphoric aerial ballet and instantly focusing all of his senses on the coyote loping along through the scrub brush below. It wasn't his meal of choice; the sweeter blood of the smaller desert animals was better suited to his palate; rats, squirrels, the occasional opossum. But, a coyote contained a greater volume of vital sustenance, and the King had not fed for several days.

Without taking his eyes off of the canine, he circled back so he could climb to altitude out of earshot of his prey. Then, Esteban chose his trajectory, queued on the target, synched its movements with his own, and dropped in on his victim silently. But, with only a few meters to go, he lost his nerve, abandoned the attack, circled back once again, and reset his approach. This time, his prey was engaged with a propitious snack of its own, and its radar didn't detect the threat from above. The coyote had no idea it was about to get got as, with a mighty, forward-scooping thrust of his wings, Esteban's momentum stalled and he dropped onto the canine's back, his front claws sinking into its coarse shoulder-blade fur, and his larger hind talons shoving the creature's backside to the ground. As they skidded to a quick stop, the animal rolled onto its side in submissive panic, giving the Chupacabra a perfect angle for his bite. In a millisecond, fangs penetrated coarse, neck fur, punched through soft flesh, and double-pierced the thick artery, starting the flow of life.

Esteban's eyes rolled back in their sockets as he drank heavily from the life source and felt the animal's strength fading away. When he could draw no more, he plopped the coyote's limp body onto the dirt beside him and, pushing through his own sated lethargy, pulled himself to his full height, thrust his chest out, popped his wings wide open, and blasted a victory screech that emboldened him as it echoed across the wide caldera. *Rey Lagarto* had discovered a whole new way of hunting, and he was greatly pleased.

Chapter 18

When Tomás googled **private investigator new york**, he was greeted with more than a hundred pages of results. Most of the websites presented little more than a list of official accreditations (if any), and the areas in which they specialized. The only memorable exception was a site featuring a lengthy bio of the agency's owner on its home page; an ex-NFL footballer who held a little, black Chihuahua up to his smiling face in the accompanying photo. The mustachioed man reminded Tomás of a low-rent Magnum P.I. from American television.

Because there seemed to be no significant differences between the first dozen sites he perused, he chose randomly:

AMES INVESTIGATION AGENCY

He wrote the telephone number down on a sticky-note, then sent a short email to **b.amesPI@yahoo.com**, asking how much he/she charged for his/her services, and if they accepted money orders. Next, he made an international phone call to the *National Enquirer* in the United States.

"I have photographs of a Chupacabra that I want to sell to your magazine," Tomás launched right in with the woman who answered.

"I'm sorry sir," she responded, *"but the Enquirer doesn't accept direct outside submissions."*

"This," said Tomás insistently, "is the same Chupacabra that your magazine has printed stories about lately. I am calling from Santa Teresa, Mexico."

The smile that he heard in the woman's voice sounded either amused or intrigued.

"Let me connect you to our Submissions Department," she said. *"Please hold."*

The hold was long, and, as he calculated how bad the international charges would be, he wondered how he could be holding for the Submissions Department if they didn't take submissions. After two minutes, a male voice came over the line.

"This is Caleb, who am I speaking with?"

"I have captured the Chupacabra of Santa Teresa," said Tomás proudly.

In the background, he heard the jangling of a metal watchband as Caleb motioned for a colleague to get on the line.

"And... you have photographs of this 'captured Chupacabra'?" said the man, with an audible smile.

"Please," Tomás implored, "I know this sounds crazy, sir, but it's true. I caught him and tied him up and I've been feeding him. And, I have color photos that I want to sell to someone, maybe you."

"Well, that's a new one!" The voice was acerbic. *"Do you have any video of this 'tied-up Chupacabra'?"*

"No sir," answered Tomás after a pause.

"That's really too bad."

Muffled chuckles in the background.

"Why don't you take a video of it?" said Caleb. *"If this thing looks anything like the animal in the Santa Teresa photo that we printed...and, the thing is still alive... well, you've got a helluva story there...what did you say your name was?"*

"Can I just send you the photographs first?" Asked Tomás, ignoring the question. "I don't have a video camera."

He correctly guessed that the man received a dozen such calls in a week, but Caleb nevertheless took mercy on him and, in a bored, matter-of-fact tone, gave Tomás the *Enquirer's* mailing address; adding that he should write **attention: Caleb** on the envelope. After a brief tutorial, in which he told Tomás how to protect his rights to the photos before dropping them in the mail, the man hung up without saying goodbye.

Though the call had ended abruptly, Tomás was excited to be out of the starting gate so quickly, and after his first try at that. On their next supply-run to Torreón, he snuck away from his father and crossed the street to *la Correos*, where he asked the postal-clerk to mark two, large, manila envelopes as REGISTERED MAIL (the poor-man's copyright) and, as he handed the clerk the thirty pesos for the postage, he was electrified by the thought of the unstoppable series of events this act would set in motion. After signing the proper forms, he stuffed the thicker envelope, which contained all twenty-four photos of the Chupacabra up under his shirt, then returned to the pickup truck just as his father was starting the engine.

"Whatchoo got in the envelope, mi hijo?" Asked Señor Sanchez. "I seen you go in *la Correos* with it."

"It is my future, papa."

The father smiled at the satisfaction in his son's voice and silently wondered what kind of shenanigans Tomás was up to.

Once they were home, he helped his father unload the truck, then hurried to the computer nook to find that he had already received a reply from B. Ames; Private Investigator.

Mr. Sanchez:

In response to your inquiry, I provide Investigation services & Information collection within the five Burroughs of New York City. Any work outside of NYC requires the client to cover any and all travel expenses and related costs. The initial retainer for my services is $3000 from which is deducted my hourly rate of $150. I would be happy to correspond by email or to meet you in person. Thank you for your inquiry.
Brent Ames,

Jesús Cristo! Three thousand U.S. Dollars! It was a huge amount of money, but Tomás had learned, through the village gossip-machine, that the American version of the *Enquirer* had paid Señora Delgado 53,000 MXN, around $4000 USD, and that the *Monterey El Norte* had also printed her photo and paid her an additional 19,000 pesos. That was a big score for one blurry photograph taken on the fly by a frightened old lady. Surely, he thought, his three shots of the monster in chains would bring at least that much. He had to hurry, though.

The *Enquirer,* and others of its ilk, dealt mostly in celebrity scandal these days and gave only limited coverage to the super- and/or preternatural. They had met they're Chupacabra-quota of late, and soon, the space they allotted to non-celeb news would be filled once again with Squatch, Nessie, Angels, and Anal-probing Extra-Terrestrials.

To Tomás, the American' obsession with fame and celebrity seemed petty and trite, but he knew very well what he was up against. Sitting in the tiny, computer nook, pondering the enormity of the challenge in front of him, he considered the jaded appetites of *el Norte* and amused himself by recalling a line from one of his favorite comedians.

"...it's like eating pancakes. All exciting at first, but by the end... you're sick of 'em."

—⚹—

With the cogs of his scheme starting to creak into motion, Tomás knew he had to tell his Mama and Papa what he had been up to, with certain omissions for their own protection. He loved his parents and couldn't let them be blindsided by discovering what he had been doing under their very noses, and so, after helping his mother clean up from the evening meal, he corralled them both in the family T.V. room and shooed his little brothers away with the toddler in tow.

"I have done something... " he began falteringly.

"What is so important, *mi hijo*?" asked his mother.

"I have done something...*big.* This thing...that I have done...it will bring much attention to our village and to our family."

The Sanchez's looked at each other worriedly.

"*Que es,* Tomatino?" his father asked. "What have you done?"

"Well...remember when I used to tell you that...that I had seen the Chupacabra?" Tomás said, watching their eyes. "You said that I had a big imagination and thought I was just trying to get attention?"

His parents nodded hesitantly and looked at each other again.

"And, when I told my friends," Tomás continued, "they all laughed at me and called me names? Remember that?"

The Sanchez's worried faces eased into amused smiles.

"Sí, we remember. *Sigue.*"

"Well...it *wasn't* my imagination. It was not a joke. The Chupacabra is real. Mama, you know. You saw him too, *sí?*"

"Well, I seen *something,*" replied his mother. "But just barely, and I never was sure what it was."

"Why you start this talk again, *mi hijo?*" his father asked. "You are sixteen years now. That's too old for these things."

"Papa, I don't mean to make trouble or embarrass our family but..." Tomás looked back and forth from one pair of eyes to the other. "You must know the truth... it's time." Pulling three photographs from under his shirt, he handed them to his parents, who held them tentatively in their hands, passed them back and forth, and exchanged bewildered glances. A smile gradually returned to the face of his father, and he said, approvingly,

"Aaahh, these are very good, *mi hijo.* How did you do this? Is that a costume? It looks so real. How... "

"Look closer Papa. It's not a trick... they are really real."

With a furrowed brow, Señor Sanchez whispered conspiratorially. "*Dios mío. ¿Qué has hecho?* How...what...what did you do, *mi hijo?* This... thing... is tied up with ropes and chains. How did you..."

Without revealing the more salacious aspects of the relationship, Tomás launched into his rehearsed explanation, but, when he mentioned that the creature could think and speak like a person, his parents looked at him like he had gone insane. Having interacted with *Rey Lagarto* for months now, yet being still occasionally dubious about whether it had all been a dream or not, Tomás tried to be patient and unambiguous in his explanations.

"So, where is this...*Chupacabra*, Tomás?" his mother asked.

"Actually Mama, he doesn't like that word. He prefers to be called 'Rey Lagarto'."

"*REY LAGARTO?*" shouted his father. "The "LIZARD KING? ¿Estás loco? Esto es una locura."

Tomás' parents had many questions, and he did his best to answer them without mentioning either the death of the Lagarto Queen or John Maddox's murderous guilt. Though they knew their son was angry at the man for his perceived plagiarism, the Sanchez's had enjoyed having the American as a hotel guest, and Tomás thought that a full disclosure of the reporter's worst crimes would be ill conceived. It could result in his loving parent's interference, as well as making them possible accessories to any impending illegal activities, so he left them ignorant of his involvement.

"Where is this... Chupacabra now, *mijo?*" Asked his father sternly.

"I can't tell you, Papa. I have promised *Rey Lagarto* that I wouldn't."

His father harrumphed at the name again.

"It looks like he's in the caves in these pictures." His mother chimed in. "Did you go down into those caves mijo? They aren't safe. You could..."

"Could what, Mama?" Tomás laughed. "I could meet a Chupacabra? I already did that... and he needs my help."

Tomás immediately knew he had made a mistake and braced himself.

"NEEDS YOUR HELP?!" Señor Sanchez bellowed. "What can you possibly help a monster with?"

"He is not a monster, Papa. He is a living creature just like us, and he has thoughts and feelings just like you and me."

"So there is only one of them here, then?" asked his mother. "What about the ones they seen in Texas?"

"I don't think those stories are true, Mama. Those people are just making things up for some other reason; probably to make money somehow. I have not asked *Rey Lagarto* about those other places, but he has never been anywhere else but here. He says that all of the others of his kind are gone or dead. *Es el Último Rey lagarto.* He is the last."

"*Bueno*," said his father. "*Gracias a Dios por eso, al menos.*"

Now, Tomás' brothers returned dragging the crying toddler by her feet and mercifully ending the discussion, but not before Tomás had secured a promise from his parents to keep quiet. It didn't take much convincing, as his mother and father were uneasy at the thought of being at the epicenter of the roiling scuttlebutt in their little village. Later, before bedtime, his father pulled him aside and said he wanted to see the creature for himself but, when Tomás told him that the ropes and chains were just for the photographs, and that *Rey Lagarto* actually remained unbound, his father said,

"I will just enjoy your wonderful pictures, *mi hijo.*"

—⚒—

A week after he mailed the photographs, Tomás received a reply from Caleb, who had been terse with him on the phone, but was more forthcoming in his written response. The man disclosed that the *Enquirer's* media analysts, while normally skeptical and jaded from having seen every manner of bogus photo and video imaginable, had admitted that Tomás' photos, while probably faked or manipulated, looked good enough to pass the *Enquirer's* Standard Level of Editorial Plausible Deniability. (SLEPD). He further revealed that he had spoken to the two reporters who had filed previous pieces on the Chupacabra and had shown them the photos as well. They had both evidently expressed their enthusiasm for the ongoing story. So, thought Tomás, now Maddox knew.

In his last paragraph, Caleb said that, although they had run several updates on the first piece already, the editors were willing to keep the ball rolling as long as readers were interested, and they wanted to offer Tomás three-thousand dollars for the exclusive rights to the three photographs. He closed by saying:

> *Since you evidently have direct access to the subject in the photos, we would be interested in seeing any additional photos or video that you think would be right for our website. If you choose to accept this offer, please sign and notarize the attached release form and return it to the address below, certified mail. We will remit to you a cashiers check upon receipt.*
> *Sincerely,*
> *Caleb Essbuck*

¡Three thousand US dollars! Exactly enough to cover the private investigator's retainer. It was fate! It must be, thought Tomás, though he was a bit disappointed that it wasn't as much as Señora Delgado had received for her crappy, blurry photo. But, he had never had more than fifty pesos in his pocket at a time, and he felt phase one had been a success. Besides that, he would use the money for a higher purpose than Señora Delgado's television, automobile, and trinkets; he would put the *Enquirer* check to work honoring *Rey Lagarto* and the legacy of Santa Teresa.

Three-grand was a lot of dough, but, it would all go for Brent Ames' retainer, and Tomás was now more determined than ever to get to New York himself when the time was right, which meant finding even more money, somehow. There was no way he was going to ask his parents for help. At this point, he wasn't even planning on telling them he was going to try to get into the U.S., because they would flip their lids. He still had an envelope full of alternate photos, however, which he had not offered to the *Enquirer* and to which, therefore, he would not be signing away his rights with this release. Although he was bothered by the slightly unethical maneuver, he thought he could sell a few more pics to the newspaper in Torreón before the *Enquirer* released his first three. If any circumstances were ever extenuating, he thought, these were they.

There was, of course, the video that Caleb had suggested recording, but Tomás had other plans for such a bombshell. If three photos of a static *Rey Lagarto* had fetched three-thousand U.S. dollars, video of a walking, talking Chupacabra could be worth... well, he had no idea how much. But, there was no way he was going to send video files across the Internet or through the mails. When the time was right, he would deliver them in person, and then use them as bait to lure Maddox back to ground zero.

—⚎—

Tomás' best friend, Diego, had recently received a smart-phone as a birthday gift from his parents. Diego's father was a co-owner of the local grain-mill, which made his family wealthy by Santa Teresa standards, and they lived down the street from the Sanchez Hotel in the nicest house in town. The two boys had been playmates since toddlerhood and, when other friends had derided and teased Tomás about talking to the Chupacabra, Diego had been the only one to stand up for him and tell the others to back off.

When he visited Diego on the morning after the email from the *Enquirer*, however, his friend was hesitant about parting with his fancy new present. It took some convincing, and the bribe of a *Pulparindo*, before he handed it over and showed Tomás how to use the video function.

The video shoot began in earnest in the late afternoon and, after taking a quick test video, Tomás showed the moving images to an astounded *Rey Lagarto*.

"Thisss, Tomáss, is why we refer to your kind as 'Workers'. Whereas the *Lagarto* are...that is to say... we... were...content to live a simple, contemplative existence, you workers build, build, build. You have hands that can perform tasks that I cannot; not with these."

He held his hands out, palms up, and wiggled his fingers.

"We have always been fascinated to see what your kind were able to create, and now, you show me thiss. It seems to me to be a kind of magic."

"I guess so," said Tomás. "It's sort of...just another kind of tool, I guess. It is cool, though."

There were no ropes or chains used this time, not only because the cinematographer thought it looked too contrived on video, but because Tomás was painfully aware that he had humiliated the proud reptilian monarch by asking him to pose in such a compromised way for the melodramatic affectation. He was determined not to repeat the insult, but was unsure about what he would direct, (or delicately request), the King to do on-camera? He had noticed the wings on the creature's back, but the pair had never talked about them. Tomás couldn't imagine what kind of Chupa-tricks his partner might be able to perform, if asked. Would the Lagarto feed in front of him? he wondered. Tomás doubted it, but... HOLY SHIT, would that ever make for a dramatic shot!

The smart phone's camera had a flash, but there was no continuous light source for shooting video and Tomás had forgotten to bring a flashlight. A dull, hazy, orange glow was all they had to work with, and they were rapidly losing even that, so the director quickly got set to film *Rey Lagarto* in all his glory.

"Action!"

But, Esteban didn't know what to do or where to look. He just stood stock-still with his arms to his sides, feeling an unfamiliar and bothersome self-consciousness. What followed was a comedy of terrors as Tomás held the camera and moved in a semi-circle around his subject, telling him to *"Hold up your claws"*, then *"Show more teeth"* and *"Hop around a little...or...something"*.

Tomás took three, short clips, but then realized, just as the ambient light was waning, that he had no video of *Rey Lagarto* speaking.

"What do I say, Tomásss?"

"How about just telling them who you are. Say your name, then...say whatever you want the world to know."

In the other three clips, he had framed his model's entire body in the shot, and he started with the same wide-focus this time, but, as his subject spoke, Tomás zoomed in slowly, until, in the last seconds, *Rey Lagarto's* face filled the entire frame.

A wide grin spread across the teenager's face as he looked at the image in the display. The world was not going to believe this.

Chapter 19

Esteban was alone. In spite of his growing bond with Tomás, he still *felt* alone. He slept alone, woke alone, hunted alone, and grieved... alone.

The regular visits that Tomás made never lasted long, and they were difficult for the King, owing to the pair's xenogeneic differences. In these pow-wows, they mostly discussed the murderer, Maddox, which only left him feeling more despondent when the boy returned to his own home and family.

Ever since the other *Lagarto* had all died or departed, his Queen had been his constant companion, and although he often thought about the ones who had left and ruminated about their fate, he knew that any *Lagarto* who left the tribe and journeyed beyond the bounds of the river valley could not have survived. The elders of the tribe had made that point clear, and even Esteban's father had issued a proclamation that warned of certain death for those who were considering deserting the tribe and joining the exodus.

In his present state of contemplative isolation, Esteban now suspected that the elders, and their elders before them, had used the predictions of death and damnation as a way to hold the tribe together by intimidation and fear. There was, after all, safety in numbers. Many had left during his lifetime, never to return. Some had been driven away by the increasing presence and influence of the Workers, who came more and more frequently to the caldera and whose loud machines and shouting voices frightened and annoyed *Lagarto*, but most left in fear of the horrible disease that first appeared when Esteban was young. The deadly malady was predictably blamed on the Workers, whom the *Lagarto* regarded as generally dirty and unhealthy creatures, and it killed its victims by first robbing them of strength, and then slowly suffocating them over the period of three or four days as their lungs filled with blood and other fluids, until the sufferer gurgled for his or her last gasp of air.

The invisible killer had taken his own mother and father six years ago, leaving Esteban to serve the last reign in the long line of *Lagarto* sovereignty. When the parents of his Beloved died a few months later, and the few remaining took their chances and disappeared over the distant hills, Esteban was left as a king without a kingdom. He and his *Queen* had wondered why they alone were spared, but they knew that God's ways were not to be questioned by his lowly creations, and so they decided to stay put and try to begin anew by having offspring of their own in the volcanic, Garden of Eden.

He had mourned all of his friends and relations, but lately, he found himself thinking of one particular female, who had left long ago but had been his constant playmate in their childhood. As the son of the King, he had grown up knowing that one day he would ascend the throne and, when he did, he would be expected to take a queen. He had always felt that his female, whose name was **Xochitl** (flower), would be his choice. She was kind, but with an acerbic humor and, as children, they had hours of fun chasing each other through the caves and tunnels during the day and, after dark, when it was time to feed, chasing the ground squirrels and rabbits through the trees and bushes together.

Xochitl's parents had taken her away long ago, along with her two older brothers, and Esteban had been crushed at the time as he had stood atop a tall hill and watched her family disappear over the horizon. Now, he smiled and recalled that, while everyone in the tribe, including his parents, had always called him by the informal and familiar Spanish name, *Esteban*, she alone had insisted on using the Lagarto name, *Xipil*, whenever addressing him.

Despite his fond remembrances, the suffocating nothingness was closing in around him, and Esteban *was* going nuts. He would soon re-unite with the Workers, his life's ambition, but he found himself feeling ironically more isolated with each passing day, and the constant chatter from Tomás about how they would somehow harm the Maddocks, but not kill him? He did not understand. The boy's descriptions seemed feebly inadequate, and Esteban sometimes imagined reaching out and strangling the young worker when he was rattling on about newspapers, and investigators, and public shaming, and... EVERYTHING EXCEPT DESTROYING THE *XIUHCOATL* (Weapon of destruction).

Esteban's white-hot inferno of rage for the murderer had burned in him for weeks afterward, but now, the wrath was a roiling cauldron in his belly; not as sharp as when he held the dead body of his Beloved, but just as painful in its dull ache. There was something that Tomás had called a 'wise saying' used sometimes by the Workers; something about revenge being a dish best served cold. But, all of Esteban's meals were quite warm, even in the wintertime, and he had no idea at all what Tomás meant.

In the months following the untimely deaths of the Delgados, Esteban didn't stay away from the village completely. Despite Tomás' claims to the contrary, the King still harbored suspicions that his sub-jects were out to get him, and he occasionally spied on them in an effort to determine whether or not they were trying to destroy his line for ever. It wasn't an unfounded fear, of course, and not just because the work-ers had repeatedly tried to flush him out of his own home with their flashlights and dogs, but because, when he visited *Cuahmeh tlamanalli* on the subsequent full moon, in the hopes that the Workers had left an offering tied to the stump for him, he had spied dozens of pairs of beady little peepers in the shadows, all locked onto the sheep-on-a-rope who, like himself, was not at all fooled by the worker's lousy attempts at concealing themselves.

The fat, healthy-looking sheep, which Esteban had noticed was one of the finer specimens he had ever been offered, had trotted from one side of the dirt square to the other, almost choking itself as it strained at the rope and pointed its muzzle toward the exact places where the workers were hidden. On top of that, the old worker, Corto, had not been on his bench; a big red flag. It was a comically pathetic attempt at an ambush, he had thought at the time; using the sheep as bait? Did they think he was stupid??

The Workers didn't get a show on that night, nor would they on the next two full moons, which were basically repeat performances, but, on the fourth *luna llena*, Esteban peered out from the brushy tunnel and detected no sign of the tiny, white, prying eyeballs. The old man was back on his bench asleep, and a small, spindly calf was standing beside the old sycamore stump with a rope looped loosely around its neck. Not a big healthy sheep, but Esteban had been happy to see any sacrifice at all.

On that night, he had rattled a branch while wriggling out of the bushes, which made the calf turn to look. But, the animal hadn't seemed alarmed, and they had stared at each other as Esteban crossed the field into the plaza, the calf becoming less curious and more frightened the closer he came, and the anticipation distracting Esteban from the fact that the old worker had left his bench and was standing, paralyzed, halfway between the stump and the store front.

When the figure appeared in his peripheral vision, Esteban had jerked around to catch the man staring at him with wide eyes and mouth agape. Though Corto had froze in fear, Esteban's frequent interactions with Tomás made him less apprehensive about humans and he had stepped to within a few feet of the old worker, the calf making a wide arc away from him as he passed. Corto hadn't moved a muscle, but his body language shouted that he wanted to turn and run.

"You are called by Corto, yes?"

"*Dios mío!* the old man had exclaimed. "*¿Qué es esto? ¿Hablas?*"

"Please speak to me in the *Lagarto* tongue," Esteban demanded. "I mean you no harm, old one. You have seen me at *Cuahmeh Tlamanalli* before, and you have even watched me as I fed."

"*Estoy sonando.*" Corto had answered in a shaky voice. "I am dreaming, sí? You are in my dream... speaking my name."

"You are awake, old one, though that is not usually the case." Esteban had pointed to the bench. "I have seen you there... and now, I have come to speak to you, Corto."

The old man had shut his eyes tightly and wiggled a finger in his ear while the King tried to put him at ease.

"What do you want with old Corto, Ch... Chu...Chupacabra?" Corto had stammered. To which Esteban had boldly replied,

"My name is *Esteban Salazar Tepiltzin Huemac Rey Lagarto, Necuametl Cuetzpalli*. You, are the watchman of *Cuahmeh Tlamanalli*, yes?"

"*Sí, yo soy...*I am *el Centenía.*"

Just as he said it, Corto had turned to look behind him at the bakery door, but it was late at night, and the villagers who had kept vigil during the previous three *lunas llenas* were all snuggled up in their beds and dreaming. There had only been himself, Corto, and the clueless calf looking on, oblivious to the significance of the exchange it was witnessing. When Esteban asked if the old man ever told the Workers about him, Corto had replied,

"I tell them all the time, but they just say '*Oh that is just Corto viejo loco having his dreams again.*' They would not believe their eyes...or ears, if they were here now."

"Well, old one," Esteban had told him, "they will not say you are crazy anymore. Things are about to change... back."

"What do you mean, change... Chupaca...whatever I should call you... *no puedo recordar ese nombre estúpido!*"

Esteban instructed him to use the formal *Rey Lagarto*, to which Corto had replied,

"Actually, if we are being formal... me llamo Raphael."

Esteban had bowed his head in deference, and then proceeded to tell the old man about Tomás, and how the boy had revealed to him the reality of the Worker's faithlessness and unbelief, to which Corto admitted, as he had scratched at the back of his Einsteinesque coif,

"That is true... *Rey Lagarto.* But, not me! I have known of you and seen you since I was a child."

"That was my father," Esteban had told him. "I have never see you when you weren't old."

"Si, si. I thought you look different than that one...I mean, *Rey Lagarto...*"

Their shared language put Corto slightly more at ease, and Esteban had taken the chance to divulge an abridged version of his plan.

"Oh, this is wonderful!" Corto had exclaimed. *"Doy gracias a Dio!* Finally, they will know that I'm not just Crazy Old Corto who sleeps on the bench and who sees monsters."

Corto had caught himself, and said.

"Forgive me, *Rey Lagarto.* I don't mean no offense to you, but that is how some people think of you... that you are a monster."

Esteban had tried to explain about the video recordings Tomás made, but Corto knew nothing of modern technology and had no experience with cellphones whatsoever. The old man had as much difficulty understanding the concept as Esteban did explaining it, but he had definitely understood the bottom line; the Chupacabra was planning a 'coming-out party' that would bring hundreds, perhaps thousands of people to Santa Teresa. It meant that Corto and his bailiwick would be at the center of the rowdydow. But, when Esteban asked the man to remain silent about it all until Tomás said the time was right, the man had balked.

"Soon, I will reveal myself to all of the Workers," he had told Corto. "Tomáss told me it will bring faimusss to me, and that it will be both good and bad. And, it will bring faimuss to you, as well, Raphael. But, you must keep my secret and tell no one of this meeting."

"Aww, no. *CHINGADO!!*" cried Corto. "*¿Por qué?* Why you make me not tell something like this?"

"Listen to me, *ueue*," Esteban had implored. "You have spent your life watching and telling others about me, which suggests that you know of the *Lagarto's* importance and imminence. You have never tried to harm me, and neither have you allowed others to harm or capture me."

"Si, *Rey Lagarto*," Corto had replied. "And it was the same between my father and your father, too. Although it will be *mui difficulto*, I will keep my mouth shut, *Rey Lagarto...Sí*."

The calf had bleated just then, and Esteban turned to look at the animal, giving Corto, who had been afraid to break eye-contact, the chance to eyeball the giant lizard more closely.

"So... "Corto had said when Esteban turned back around, "... are you gonna suck on that calf?"

"You know, old one, that I do not take every animal offered to me, *quemah*?

Corto had given a knowing smile.

"I will leave this tender one for you tonight, then?"

Corto nodded again, and Esteban had added,

"It is your custom, is it not? to burn an animal's flesh before you... consume it."

"Oh si, *Rey Lagarto*," Corto had said with a grin. "I will cook this wonderful veal on my greel over there."

The man had pointed towards the side wall of the Panadería, where sat a rusty, sawed-off oil barrel, and, after trading respectful and polite goodbyes, Esteban had hopped away and left a stupefied, yet exhilarated Corto alone in the plaza with the young bovine.

—⟋⟍—

It distressed Tomás when Esteban told him of the encounter, and he expressed his concern for the King's safety. What he did not express was the twinge of jealousy he felt at another Santa Teresan now being in on their secret.

Although he fully intended to capitalize on his relationship with the King, Tomás felt more and more that his objective in protecting his Golden Ticket had shifted from self-serving motives to a deepening loyalty. His growing malice for Maddox had strengthened his own patriotic devotion to Santa Teresa, its legacy and its history, and he found himself more determined than ever to help *Rey Lagarto* receive his vengeance, one way or another. It had not escaped him, the irony that he felt protective of a creature who, if physically threatened, could slice open most any opponent with one swipe of his claws, and then drain them of blood in a hot minute.

But, Tomás knew, that was only in a fair fight, and he warned his captain about the danger of firearms. Esteban, who had heard and seen guns in action when Workers came to shoot at, and sometimes hit and kill the caldera creatures on which he regularly fed, declared to Tomás that he was angered by the wasteful practice of killing the animals and then leaving their bodies to bake in the desert sun. Only occasionally, the King bemoaned, did the ignorant workers take their kill with them, and, more times than not, the carcasses were left to scavengers.

Rey Lagarto was not a scavenger and never fed on an animal that he did not kill. Neither did he kill any animal whose blood he did not take. All life was sacred to the *Lagarto*, and Esteban had been taught since childhood to respect all the gifts with which God had blessed them. To the *Lagarto* mind, the use of guns was proof that the *Workers* possessed *Yolotli ica piotli* (the hearts of chickens), and the respect they had for the human's ingenuity and resourcefulness did not extend to the use of a tool that was so quintessentially destructive. To kill from a distance, with no physical contact with your prey, could not be seen as anything but the laziness of a coward.

PART IV

Chapter 20

Señor Sanchez handed his eldest son a notice from the rural mail carrier saying that a certified letter from the *National Enquirer* in New York City awaited Tomás' signature at *el Correos* in Torreón.

The teenager had turned sixteen in the spring and was now languishing in the wilting, summer heat of the Southern Chihuahuan Desert, waiting until he could finally take advantage of the opportunity-of-a-lifetime that had literally presented itself at his bedroom window the previous winter. This letter, he knew, would contain the sizeable check from the *Enquirer,* but the entire thing was going to the private investigator for his retainer. Tomás needed cash to smooth his way across the border, with a little left over so he wouldn't have to sleep on a Manhattan sidewalk, if he was able to get that far.

He had an idea how to kill two birds with a single trip into Torreón and begged a ride from his father, who grumbled under his breath and motioned for him to get in the truck. When they arrived in the bustling city, they found *el Correos* closed for renovations, as Tomás knew it would be, but a sign on the front door directed them across the street to the large cinderblock building that housed the local newspaper. They followed the arrows to the postal service window and were greeted by a round, bespectacled clerk, who took the notice from Tomás and retrieved the certified letter, but insisted on the signature of an adult before he would release it to them. Without looking down at the paper and pen, Señor Sanchez scribbled his signature using muscle memory while glaring at Tomás, who took the envelope, smiled sheepishly, and thanked his father.

When they started back towards the front door exit, Tomás excused himself to the restroom and told his father he would meet him in the truck. Then he waited until the coast was clear and quickly tracked down the office of the managing editor. Finding no receptionist outside of the office door, he pulled the large, slightly damp envelope from under his shirt and swept into the room. Before the thin, grey haired man behind the big desk had time to look up from his paperwork, Tomás reached into the envelope and produced three photographs of a chained and bound Chupacabra and shoved them under his nose.

El Editór glanced down at the photos, then up again at Tomás, whose lips were closed tight in a sly, crooked grin. When the man looked down again, Tomás gave him the once-over and was amused by how his gaunt body was swallowed up in the bright orange, three-sizes-too-large dress shirt, and how his skinny neck disappeared into the two-inch moat between itself and a buttoned-up collar, festooned with a maroon tie.

"¿Eres de Santa Teresa?" Asked the editor in a much lower pitched voice than Tomás had expected.

"Si, señor," Tomás answered. "Señora Delgado was my neighbor."

"Ahh, sí...sí," el Editór's voice went deeper still. "I was very sorry to learn of her death, *y tambien su hijo.*"

Tomás bowed his head and nodded somberly.

"Señora Delgado came to me," the man confessed. "She brought me the photograph she had taken of the...whatever it is. I tacked on some copy and sold it to several other newspapers and magazines. It was even in the *National Enquirer* in the United States. Did you know that?"

"Si, señor."

The man picked up the photos again and looked at them more closely. Tomás had thought they would be shocking to whoever saw them but, as the seasoned executive studied the pics, his expression was unchanging.

"I have wondered many times," said the grizzled newspaper-man, "if the terrible tragedy was somehow connected to the señora's photograph."

If he only knew, thought Tomás, fidgeting restlessly and thinking about his melting Pop-sicle in the hot truck outside. The silence was uncomfortable, and his eyes wandered around the room looking at the framed diplomas, accolades, and family photos that hung on the walls, while the editor held a big, black-handled magnifying glass up close to his face and scrutinized the images. He seemed completely engrossed, but his peripheral vision sensed Tomás' gaze coming to rest on an au-tographed, color photo of *LaDiabolica*, striking a fearsome pose in her black and red leather lucha libre mask and pleather costume.

"You know that she was famous, si?" He said without looking up.

"Yes, she showed me her mask and trophies once when I was little. But she never talked about it much."

"Oh yes, big... BIG crowds came from all around to see LaDiabolica do her famous Flying Head-Scissors."

The man smiled as he set the photos on the desk, and he placed his hands on top of them, fingers splayed, and squinted at Tomás with a serious look.

"These are very interesting, of course, *jovencito*, but I must tell you, ahhh...I'm sorry, I did not ask your name."

"Tomás, señor. Tomás Sanchez."

"Okay, Tomás Sanchez. I don't completely understand this Chupacabra business that is going on in your village... maybe someone is very good at faking these photos and are having a good laugh on every-one, or..." his eyes narrowed to slits as he looked at Tomás, "...or maybe you do have a live Chupacabra chained up in... what is this, a cave?"

He stabbed a finger at the top photo on the pile.

"What I do know, however," he continued, "is that people want to see more Chupacabra. That first item did really well for us. And after the double murder, the whole thing really took off. There is still money to be made on this *mierda loco.*"

"Actually, señor," Tomás jumped in. "I have written a short piece to go with these pictures and I would like to sell you my story and photos together."

"I see," said el Editor, his curiosity piqued. "You have thought this through, eh? I'm impressed. Do you have this... piece... with you?"

Tomás reached inside the envelope again and pulled out a letter-sized plastic sleeve he had used as a sweat-guard for the single sheet of paper within. He handed his story to the editor, who held the page in one hand and used the other to fan himself as he read.

"Eye-catching title, *jovencito.*"

The editor's manner was matter-of-fact, as it was when he had looked at the photos, but he evidently was impressed, and made an offer then and there for both the pictures and the copy. When Tomás expressed concern for his Papa in the truck outside, el Editór pulled a leather-bound ledger from his desk drawer and drafted a check for him on the spot. As the man reached across the desk to hand it to Tomás, he offered sincere advice in his low, rumbling voice.

"I don't know what you have gotten involved in, *jovencito,* but, for your sake, I hope this *is* just an elaborate prank. If these pictures are not messed with, and you have actually captured something there... please tell me you will be very careful. This...thing...it looks dangerous... and angry."

After a quick goodbye, Tomás hurried down the long corridor with an ear-to-ear smile on his face, flapping the two cashier's checks in his hands as he flew towards the front exit. 75,000 MXN; almost five-thousand U.S. Dollars. And, not only did he now have enough money to implement his plan, but it came from selling his very own story; the first in what he hoped would be an illustrious journalistic career. This inaugural piece would, of course, play to the same seedy and sensationalistic side of the profession that the *Enquirer* catered to, but Tomás could live with that for now, because, apart from the ruse with the ropes and chains in the photos, his story had the virtues of being significant, consequential, and one-hundred percent true, even if no one knew it... yet.

He felt a cringing pang of guilt when he thought about the indignities he had asked Rey Lagarto to endure, but he reminded himself that they were playing the long game. The connivance with the restraints was meant to be shocking and sensational, but, while regrettable, it had been a means to a, hopefully, more transcendent end. Nevertheless, the conceit came with the burden that accompanies the sin of vanity.

As expected, Señor Sanchez was pissed off and sweat-drenched when his son finally climbed into the truck cab. Tomás kept his mouth shut about the supplemental windfall on the ride home, though it wasn't easy. He had hoped to put off telling his parents about his international travel plans until it was too late for them to stop him, but, in order to send money to Brent Ames in the United States, he needed the wire-transfer services of a bank and, as had been the case with the certified letter, he would need the signature and/or permission of an adult.

He gave it a couple of days, and then went hat in hand to beg for his parent's help. As expected, Señor y Señora Sanchez were quite upset, and their objections and comments made it clear that neither of them really believed the legitimacy of what they both called 'this Chupacabra business', nor did they understand his need to be involved in it. As far as they knew, their son had long since given up any hope of satisfaction from the *Enquirer's* legal department, and they hammered Tomás with questions and pleas for over an hour until they realized they couldn't stop their smart, determined son from pursuing what he obviously felt was his destiny.

Once they had resigned themselves to the inevitable, the Sanchez's did an absolute about-face and switched into support-mode so instantly that, though Tomás felt relieved, he was bewildered. His father was infamous amongst family and friends for his distrust of banks, and he was fond of stashing cash in hidey-holes, under mattresses, inside of books, or burying it in the garden. He only grudgingly set foot in *el Banco de Torreón* once a month to swap the hotel's credit card receipts for cash, and his complaints about it were de rigueur, so, when the father agreed to drive the son back into the city the next day to conduct the transaction, Tomás concluded that his Papa must have some degree of trust and confidence in him. It almost felt like acceptance.

"Papa," he asked as they drove, "why are you doing this for me?"

"Well, you figured out how to get this money. And, it don't seem like you done anything against the law. So... I figure you should be the one who decides what to do with it."

Tomás' mouth curled up in a grin, and he turned his head to the passenger window and watched the world speed slowly by.

After a minute, his father added, "If you gonna do this, I want you to have the best chance." Then after another beat, "Besides... you're a smart boy, Tomatino. I think there is more to all of this than you are saying, but something tells me you know what you are doing."

Before the pickup had come to a complete stop in the hotel parking lot, Tomás kicked open the heavy, creaking, passenger door, jumped out, and ran inside to the computer nook, where he logged in to his email account and, afore ye could say Jack Robinson, composed a message to Brent Ames that simply said... **LET'S DO THIS!**

—ɯ—

In January, Tomás had begun a cyber-sleuthing campaign in which he read and researched every piece John Maddox wrote for *The New York Times*, his new employers. He was hoping to find more evidence of plagiarism on the reporter's part, but it was now late June, and he had yet to turn up anything blatant enough to pursue.

The socially and politically relevant pieces filed under Maddox's byline were the same kind of investigative reportage that Tomás aspired to. He found himself frustrated by how good they were, and he bemoaned the fact that he now considered his former employer a bitter enemy. The truth was, though Tomás had learned what news blogs to read and which issues to follow, he was in over his head as far as processing the information and overly dependent on the Internet. He simply didn't have the academic chops to know how to put it all together, and he knew it. Maddox would have been the perfect mentor for his career, but the man had shown himself to be a liar, a thief, and a murderer, and because of that, Tomás didn't think he deserved his position at the *Times*. And, he was determined to prove it.

As he sat sweating in the little computer nook off the kitchen one, steamy, summer, Sunday evening, an item on the *Times* website caught his attention.

[Victoria Andrea Magaña & John Benedict Maddox announce their engagement. The nuptials will take place at St. Patrick's Cathedral on Saturday, July 18th of this year. In lieu of gifts, the couple request that donations be made to the Eleanor E. Malouf Scholarship Fund.]

So, he thought, the *pendejo* was getting married. Tomás would have another set of strings to pull when the impending showdown came, but the wedding was only three weeks away, which meant he had to get to New York... like **now!** The underage, unemployed Mexican National had long since researched all of his options for getting into the U.S. legally, but he had never followed through with any of them. Obtaining a Travel Visa in less than three weeks was out of the question, and with no job waiting for him nor employer to sponsor him, a Work Visa was right out as well. If the relationship with Maddox hadn't turned sour, a Student Visa might have been in the offing by now. Try as he might, Tomás could find no short term, U.S. Immigration initiatives that welcomed Mexican teenagers to America's bosom for the purpose of harassing and possibly harming its journalists. It looked like his only option was an illegal crossing into Texas, a difficult, and dangerous undertaking.

—⁓—

June melted into July, and the Private Eye began sending regular reports updating his new, foreign client on the progress in what he officiously referred to as a 'surveillance and information-retrieval operation'. Tomás had asked him to try and dig up anything that could be used to discredit or embarrass Maddox professionally; violation of corporate codes of conduct, misappropriation of corporate funds, misuse of assignment per-diems, inappropriate workplace behavior, breach of contract, porn-surfing on company time... anything!

When Tomás felt he had achieved a degree of rapport with the man, he broached the subject of joining him in Manhattan for a surveillance ride-along, but, when he hinted at the prospect of Ames possibly forging documents that could help grease his passage through some crack in the U.S. immigration system, he received a polite but firm reply that the agency's menu of services did *not* include human trafficking. Tomás sussed that Ames was an adept professional who appreciated the fact that his hefty rate demanded results, and so, when a month had passed and the investigator confessed he was unlikely to uncover anything that would disgrace the reporter, it was clear that a change in direction was needed. In spite of his status as a plagiarist and a murderer, Maddox was obviously a company man, who probably wouldn't risk ruffling the feathers of a golden goose by abusing his employer's trust, so Tomás made the decision to allocate the rest of his retainer with Ames on looking into the reporter's personal life.

He had considered it briefly before he first contacted Ames, and Tomás' teenaged imagination was still titillated by the thought of adult love-life scandals, which he envisioned as being like the *Telenovelas* he watched with his Abuela when he was younger, but hadn't wanted to lower the scope of the attack to the personal level. For a reason he couldn't quite figure out, it didn't seem commensurate to the crimes the man had committed, and it felt trite and petty to go after someone in that way.

When Tomás had first perused websites looking for private dicks, it had been clear that, along with insurance fraud and missing persons' cases, they also, unsurprisingly, routinely dealt with divorce and custody cases, which meant that Ames was probably proficient in all of the sleazy techniques used to document the cesspit of behaviors associated with that type of misdeed. The change in direction was just fine with the investigator, who emailed a reply that he was about to suggest it anyway, and so, with Maddox's wedding imminent, Tomás gave him the go ahead to proceed with Operation Tawdry.

—⁂—

Unbeknownst to Tomás, his fourteen-year-old brother, Téo, had been listening from around the corner of the family room when the discussions about *Rey* Lagarto had transpired, and he had followed Tomás to the caldera on several occasions afterward and watched him disappear into the cave with the Chupacabra. Téo also knew about the private investigator as well as Tomás' plan to go to New York City, and he wanted desperately to help his *hermano* in any way he could.

When he let the cat out of the bag, Tomás was taken aback by Téo's self-professed proficiency in sneaktitude, but admitted to his kid brother that he needed a way to communicate with the Lizard King while he was on the mission to America. Téo could be a pain in the ass sometimes, but he was basically a good kid, and he and Tomás had always been close. If there was anyone they could trust to bring into the circle, it was *su hermano*.

They had each taken the same cyber-classes, and not only was Téo smart, he was clever and very tech-savvy as well, and immediately proved his worthiness by demonstrating to Tomás a way they could communicate long distance without the hassle and expense of International telephone calls. The software program was called SKYPE, and it enabled anyone with access to the Internets to video-chat with anyone else, provided that person had the program installed on their own computer. Tomás knew it would be a definite benefit, and he was glad his kid brother was now on board.

—⁂—

When the rest of the family had gone to bed, Tomás grabbed a flashlight and headed to the caldera for a final pre-game with *Rey Lagarto*. In the last weeks, all of their meetings had been prearranged, and the King always knew, approximately, when to expect his young cohort. The visit on this night would be a surprise.

The Chupacabra hated flashlights and didn't like them brought into the cave for fear that the fulgurating beams would draw unwanted attention, but Tomás had never gone deep into the cave alone before. In deference to the King's aversion to 'battery-torches' he kept the light switched off as he entered the dark tunnel, stumbling over the uneven floor and feeling his way along the rough, pumice walls until he was far enough inside to risk switching it on again.

"*Estoy aquí!*" He called. "Are you here?"

The only sound was the slow, drip-dripping of water in the Great Room ahead of him, and the chirruping of crickets in the caldera behind.

"*Olaaaa*! Where are you, Rey Lagarto?"

There was no answer, and a germinating, uncomfortable realization that he was an intruder in someone else's home flushed through him. He tried to allay the fear by reminding himself that there was only *one* dangerous creature in these caves, and there was no reason for Tomás to fear him. Was there? *Rey Lagarto* wouldn't mistake him for an intruder, and then attack him from behind, would he?... WOODY??

Because his previous incursions into the cave had been in the company of the King, who always held him by the hand as he led him through the darkness, Tomás had never actually seen the coves and dens that were carved into the walls of the lava tube, and, when he shined the light on the carvings and drawings and paintings, he saw dozens of representations of animals and hunts, tribal events and activities, and clear depictions of Lagarto and Worker interacting with one another. He knew that a handful of archaeologists, associated with several different universities, had studied the pictographs in the past, but now that Tomás saw the drawings for himself, he was astounded that a bigger deal had not been made over them.

When he approached the opening to the Great Room, he saw, carved into the rock high up on either side of the doorway, the same odd symbol that appeared in multiple places in and around Santa Teresa, including one carved into the side of *el Árbol de Homenáje* in the village square. Even the non-believing villagers knew that the Redeye topped with four triangles was a representation of the Chupacabra, but, for reasons Tomás had never been able to comprehend, it was considered bad manners to draw attention to the symbol, or even mention it in polite company. It was just one of the strange customs, unique to his weird little hometown, that he had been taught not to question, and he hadn't devoted that much thought to it until recently; specifically, starting the morning that the most interesting chapter of his life had begun beside his Abuela's hen house.

He moved closer to examine one of the carvings and, as he moved the light back and forth over the surface of the motif, he saw that the artist had first sanded and polished a section of the rough, porous wall before etching the icon into the smooth(ish) canvass. Just as Tomás reached up to touch the Red Eye, he heard a sound and whirled around to see Rey Lagarto standing two feet behind him.

"This is not the night for us, Tomásss," Esteban rasped in his high voice. "Is something wrong?"

"No, Rey Lagarto," answered Tomás as he clicked the flashlight off. "Everything's okay. I'm leaving tomorrow, and I won't see you for a time."

Esteban looked troubled, and he tilted his head to one side.

"Because we'll be out of communication for a while," Tomás continued, "we need someone here who can help us. And, I think I know who could..."

"Raphael!" blurted Esteban. "It should be Raphael."

"You mean old Corto at *el Árbol de Homenaje*?"

"Yesss!" Hissed Esteban, baring his fangs in an awkward attempt at a smile. "The old one promised he would keep our secret until the time is the time that is the right time."

"I am sorry, *Rey Lagarto*, but I don't think that Corto...uhhh...that Raphael is the right person for this thing."

Esteban's head-tilt shifted from one shoulder to the other, as Tomás explained.

"I know that Corto wishes you no harm, and I believe that he may turn out to be an important ally before this is all over. But, he is old, and doesn't know anything about computers. My brother, Téo, would be better for what we need done."

The Lizard King was irked that his young confederate had exposed him to yet another worker without first consulting him. But since he had done as much himself when he unilaterally chose to interact with Raphael in the village square, he relented and agreed to let Tomás bring Téo to the Palace unmolested for an introduction before Tomás went away.

They said their farewells and Tomás left the cave and climbed up the caldera ramp under a ribbon of burnt orange, which widened along the line of the horizon as he trekked back home. He had trod the path so many times now that his feet knew the way, and he fixed his gaze absentmindedly at the ground in front of him while his mind clicked through a checklist of the elements of the intrigue. The most difficult, dangerous, and fateful chapter of his life would begin when he woke up tomorrow morning, and while he pursued his own destiny away up in *el Norte*, he would be leaving kid brother in charge of governing a large reptile with four-inch fangs, a quick temper, and an agenda. His stomach had been tied in knots for days, worrying every detail and fretting about his coming confrontation with Maddox. And now he could add Téo to his list of worries.

The creature had shown a renewed restlessness of late that Tomás took to mean he was growing ever more anxious for his moment of retribution, and if he decided to reveal himself to the Workers before Tomás had finished his business in Manhattan, it would be up to fourteen-year old Téo to forestall the formidable being. In all of his entreaties and appeals to Rey Lagarto, he worried that the lizard-brain had focused more on the words *SOON* and *IT WON'T BE LONG*, and not so much on *NOT YET* and *WAIT A LITTLE LONGER*, and if Tomás wasn't here to act as

Master of Ceremonies, and/or Advocate/Protector, the outcome could be disastrous for *Rey Lagarto,* the Sanchez's, and for all the citizens of Santa Teresa.

By the time he reached the outskirts of the village, the whole river valley was cast in hues of rich, radiating gold. Still in his reverie, Tomás' thoughts reached back hundreds of years to his own *Mexicatl* ancestors and, as he looked out over the panorama, he tried to envision the nature of what must have been their remarkable relationship with the fascinating and proud *Lagarto,* and, even more curiously, why had the contact between Aztec and *Lagarto* ended.

Whatever the reason, the ignorance and segregation of the intervening years would soon expire and perish, and Tomás was thrilled to be the person who would drive the stake through their collective hearts.

Chapter 21

In the escalating, late morning heat, all six members of the Sanchez family gathered around Tomás waiting to see him off. They were huddled next to the familial pickup truck, which was parked beside a small, concrete cabana on the side of the Torreón highway. In old paint on the side wall of the neglected, cement shack, the faded, barely-blue letters **BUS** were the only evidence that the little building had, indeed, acted as the Santa Teresa Bus Terminal in earlier times. Now, the solitary door in the rear of the bus-station was permanently padlocked, and, in the front, someone had taped a square of cardboard onto the inside of the tiny, broken, half-moon ticket window. The structure's only enduring purpose was as a beacon to bus drivers whizzing past on the Jiménez/Torreón highway, reminding them to look out for, and then pull over to retrieve the rare passenger.

The more Señor Sanchez thought about his son attempting an illegal border crossing, the less he liked it. They had decided not to try and stop their boy from leaving, but Tomás' imminent departure on this balmy morning overwhelmed his father's previous permissive posturing and, as they waited for the bus that would carry him away, the señor collared Tomás for one last warning.

"You know what will happen if they catch you, *mi hijo*?" He asked. "First, they will put you in a jail cell on the Texas side, and then another cell on the Mexican side. And, who knows when they will let you out."

"Papa, I know you and Mama are worried, but I *have* to do this," Tomás exhorted. "You know I wanna be a writer more than anything, sí? The *Enquirer* already printed one of my stories, and... "he looked down at the ground, "...even though they gave the credit *and* the money to John Maddox, they have already paid me for a second piece. Now, I just have to prove that John Maddox stole the first one from me, and this man in New York City is going to help me do that, Papa."

"Los Polleros will steal your money and leave you to die in the desert."

"I have it all figured out, Papa," Tomás retorted.

"Ah, of course you have, Tomatino!" The man's tone was loud and sarcastic. "How could it be any other way?"

Tomás' mother sidled up, carrying the toddler on her hip, and gave her husband a Leave-him-alone look, though, in truth, she was as worried as he was, maybe more so. She looked her son over, trying to remember every physical detail, in case she never saw him again.

When the bus finally came into sight in the west, Tomás pulled Téo aside.

"Okay, you know what to do, right?"

"Si," answered Téo, apprehensively. "I am a little scared to go alone, but I can do it. And don't worry, I won't tell Mama and Papa."

"Good. You'll be fine, Téo, but still, be careful. *Rey Lagarto* is not like you and me. He has a bad temper, so watch how you speak to him, and be sure to show *mucho respecto a lo*. If he starts to get angry, you get out of there fast, okay? Él podría rasgarse otro pendejo en ti."

The younger brother grinned nervously and nodded as the bus came to a dusty stop. Then, as rest of the family started to gather around for last goodbyes, Tomás whispered one last thing in Téo's ear.

"When I get to Manhattan, I'll send you an email giving you a time that we can SKYPE."

Both Señor y Señora Sanchez had tears in their eyes as they watched the coach pull away, taking their child from them. All of a sudden, baby Sister shook loose from her mother and scampered after the bus, disappearing into the billowing dust cloud in its wake as Téo chased after her, trying to catch the toddler before she made it to the highway.

Tomás was equal parts elated and exhausted from his late night meeting with *Rey Lagarto*, and he began his Great Adventure by falling asleep against the bus window, using his satchel as a pillow. Deep at the bottom of the duffel bag and rolled up in a white gym sock, were two, small thumb drives, each with an identical copy of the only surviving video of *Rey Lagarto*. Having downloaded all of his recordings onto the Sanchez's family computer, Tomás had been sure to then delete them all from the smart-phone before returning it to Diego, and yesterday, after saving the final edit onto the two thumb-drives, he had cleared all photo and video files from the family computer as well. His future was dependent on the little devices, and he would remain hyper-conscious of their location at all times while on the journey.

His first dream was a whimsical version of the encounter with the Chupacabra at his Abuela's house, but, as the bus rolled through Torreón and on to the north, the chimeric fantasies morphed into wildly presumptive scenarios, which were set in an, evidently, Pre-Columbian, pre-Santa Teresan caldera. A large tribe of *Lagarto* populated the scene under a pale, yellow haze that enshrouded the entire dreamscape, and when Tomás awoke with a sulphurous, rotten-egg odor in the nostrils of his imagination, he was amused by the thought that he had dreamt a smell (or smelled a dream).

He slept almost the entire way to Ciudad Chihuahua, and when he and his duffel bag exited the ADO coach in the big city, he yawned and stretched himself to life again before starting off on foot. For the past few days, he had studied Google maps, carefully planning his route from Santa Teresa to Manhattan on four printed pages (color, no less) that were now folded and tucked in the side pocket of his duffle for quick reference. But, he didn't need them here. Tomás had been to this northern city many times before for family reunions, and he knew its layout by memory. For as long as he could remember, *Los Convoyo de Sanchez*, which would include the Sanchez family along with mas cousins y Tios y Tias, several dogs, and an occasional, ribbon-seeking, livestock animal or two, had made its annual, multi-vehicle pilgrimage to *los Feria de Verano de Chihuahua* (the Summer Fair).

The city was not as large as Torreón and its neighboring municipality, Gómez Palacio, and, from where Tomás de-bussed at the eastern edge of town, it only took him half an hour to reach the northeast-bound highway on which he would hitchhike to *los Rio Bravo*, the natural waterway that served as the official border between Mexico and Texas. The hike was several miles in the mid-summer heat, nonetheless, and he was carrying a full satchel, so, by the time he found the truck stop that his father had told him about, he was exhausted and had to sit down with two bottles of cold water in the air-conditioned café for a few minutes before beginning the next leg of the journey.

Too hot and dehydrated to think about eating, Tomás gave a waitress a big tip for his table-rent. After he had recovered somewhat, he went to the restroom for a quick freshen-up before shouldering his pack and schlepping to the front edge of the parking lot, where he established a base-camp at the far, right-hand corner, so that any vehicle leaving the truck stop had to turn in front of him before pulling onto the highway.

He dropped the duffel in the dirt and crooked his thumb northward in the hopes of flagging down a traveler or a trucker willing to take him all the way to the border town of Manuel Ojinaga, where he planned to find a Pollero to smuggle him across the border. Human traffickers in Ojinaga were always ready and willing to profit from the desperation of others, and Tomás didn't think he would have to search very hard. His main concern was how much they would charge for their services. Manhattan would be very expensive, and the cash in his front jeans-pocket had to last until he could sell the Chupacabra video.

The reputation of the *Polleros* depended on who you asked. To the ranchers in southern Texas, who ran cattle along the river on the north side of the border, the 'coyotes' were considered a nuisance, and were usually presumed to be smuggling drugs into the U.S. on the backs of poor, migrant mules, who relieved the coyotes of the lions share of risk. South of the border, however (down Mexico way), opinions were varied. On one hand, the human traffickers were opportunistic and cutthroat, but, on the other, they provided a service to those who wanted to work and to join their families in America, where many jobs waited for migrant laborers. The danger was that the exploitative *Polleros*, who charged exorbitant sums of money, didn't seem to be bound by any form of ethical behavior toward their customer-clientele when the chits went down.

Los Polleros risked long prison terms if caught with their truckload of *pollos* on either side of the border, by either the *Federáles* south of the river, or Texas border guards on the north (U.S. Immigration and Naturalization Service [I.N.S]; or the Texas National Guard), and the coyotes minimized their exposure by jam-packing the airless cargoholds of their big, box trucks with frightened, desperate, people, whom, if the driver of the truck sensed impending trouble, could be abandoned anywhere along the route, depending on how wide the Polleros' window of escape from the Border Patrol was. And, the traffickers occasionally forgot to unlock the cargo doors, leaving a truckload of vulnerable *pollos* to fend for themselves in the dangerously hot desert climate, if, that is, they could first escape the locked cargo-hold. The coyotes, of course, always collected the money in full and up front.

As he stood thumbing and sweating in the afternoon heat, Tomás was discouraged by the big city drivers, who made wide turns around him and shot dirty looks at the human obstacle that was preventing them from short-cutting the curbless corner. He tried to tell himself that the impatient city folk probably weren't bad people, and they most likely saw him as just another border-bound country rube, but some of the cars seemed to be cutting it a little very close on purpose.

Not wanting to hitch and walk for fear of ending up far from the city in the middle of the night on a desolate, desert highway, he stuck with it at the same spot through the hottest part of the day. When the sun had vanished and the orange glow was fading from the western sky, he accepted that he just wasn't going to reach the border tonight and started looking for a safe-ish place to sleep, but, just as he threw the pack over his shoulder, a produce truck pulled over and the driver shouted that he could take him as far as Juan Aldama, a few miles down the road. It wouldn't get him far, Tomás knew, but he also knew that Juan Aldama was the only town of any size between Chihuahua and Ojinaga, and, when the driver offered him shelter underneath his fruit stand in that burg for the night, Tomás climbed up onto the flat bed and found a comfortable spot between the fruits and vegetables for the half-hour drive.

When they reached the produce stand, the driver of the truck made a bed for Tomás out of boxes filled with potatoes and cabbages, and after the man had spread a fairly clean, woven blanket across the palette, he tossed the tired, thankful teenager a couple of giant carrots and one, big, red apple, and said,

"My brother is driving his family to Ojinaga in the morning, and I'm sure he will give you a ride, if you want one."

Tomás said "Gracias" through a juicy bite of apple as the produce man walked off and into his trailer, which sat a few feet behind the stand. Having skipped lunch and then resisting the mounds of field-fresh produce on which he had lain in back of the truck, Tomás sat on the edge of his makeshift bed and enjoyed his free feast before laying down for the night. Before he drifted off to sleep, he saw the produce peddler twice peer at him through the trailer's sheer window curtains, either to see if he was okay, Tomás thought, or to make sure he wasn't helping himself to the boxes of fruits or vegetables.

—⅏—

He was jolted awake very early and quite suddenly when his good Samaritan yanked the blanket off and shook him hard.

"*¡Deberías ponerte tus zapatos rápidamente!*" The produce man was pointing excitedly at a truck coming down the road. "Mi hermano is here!"

As the vehicle was slowing to pull over, Tomás hastily pulled on his still sweat-damp Chuck Taylors. The flat bed truck was a produce vehicle nearly identical to the one he had ridden in the night before, with wooden side-rails and a closing tailgate. The side-rails were six inch boards separated by three inch gaps, through which Tomás could see several pairs of eyes peering at him as he followed the produce man to the big, blue cab. After a quick exchange between the vege-brothers, it was all set and, with a friendly smile, the driver motioned for Tomás to get in the back.

His fellow passengers were the driver's seven children, ranging in age from three-year old snot-covered urchin, to a pretty seventeen-year old girl with long, dark brown hair wearing a dark blue, summer dress dotted with peach-flowers. As soon as the truck pulled away and headed north on the highway, the curious kids began to pelt him with questions: What name was he called by? Where was he from? Where is THAT? What's in the bag? Where was he going? He would regret answering the latter question because, when he admitted he was going to los *Estados Unidos*, the pretty girl fixed him with her big, dramatic eyes and challenged him.

"You mean you're going to *TRY* to get into the U.S.," she said, dripping with sarcasm. "Do you even have a visa?"

"No, señorita," Tomás was indignant. "But I'm going to America all the same, and not to work on a farm, either. I am going to New York City to write for a newspaper."

Pretty girl laughed at the careless boast and teased Tomás relentlessly for the next two and a half hours, but he just remained silent and grinned like a Cheshire cat whilst fingering the pair of thumb-drives in his pocket and watching the mountainous landscape roll by. She could just find out about TOMÁS SANCHEZ AND HIS TALKING CHUPACABRA along with everybody else, he thought. *Joder esa chica.*

When the truck reached Ojinaga, it didn't stop to let him out, but kept going on through the town to its western edge before pulling into a huge, crowded parking lot across the street from a Market district, where two, long rows of warehouses sat on the edge of lush, green, farm fields stretching on to the west for miles along the Mexican side of the *Rio Bravo*. It was late Saturday morning, and the parking lot was packed with every kind of vehicle imaginable, so it took a few minutes before the driver found a space wide enough for the big truck. The instant it came to a halt, the children jumped out and, led by their sassy big sister, skipped off toward the buzzing hive of humanity that swarmed in the open-air, paved corridor between the two rows of buildings.

Tomás thanked the driver graciously, then followed the others through the parking lot. Once across the street, he passed underneath the colorful banners at the entrance, and immediately saw that it was the same kind of open market he had visited with his family in Torreón, Durango, and Chihuahua. A bazaar, flea market, and county fair all rolled into one, where farmers sold their fresh-from-the-field produce under big, open warehouse doors, and mercantile peddlers displayed their goods beside the colorful stalls and kiosks of garment merchants, while the aromas from dozens of food stands filled the air along with the sounds of children, chickens, goats, dogs, burros, and a mariachi band or two.

As he waded into the throng, he immediately spotted the requisite group of rowdy teenagers angling for mischief. He knew that pickpockets and thieves thrived in places like this and had been savvy enough to jam the thumb drives into the toe of his shoe and stash his cash elsewhere on his person. His caution was soon validated as, while pushing through a particularly congested area near the portable toilets, he felt a hand from behind him shoot like lightning into his front pocket, only to pull back pocket lint.

Soon, Tomás' breakfastless stomach began to grumble, and he ducked into one of the portable toilets to extract money in private. Breathing through his mouth the entire time, he first relieved himself, then hurriedly retrieved a few bills before escaping the malodorous fiberglass sarcophagus just as his breath ran out. He purged his nose-holes of the foul smell with a series of hard puffs of fresh air, and then used his revived sense of smell to track down a particularly aromatic food cart, where he bought *dos grandes tamales* and a grape soda for lunch, and two large bottles of *agua fría*, which he somehow squeezed into his already full duffel bag, for his journey.

Finding a spot out of the heavy flow of foot traffic, he wolfed down the tamales and soda and, with his hunger abated, set out angling for los Polleros. He knew they were here, somewhere, but guessed they probably wouldn't be conducting their illegal business out in the open, and so, as he shuffled through the crowd, he studied the eyes and read the body language of anyone he thought looked 'sketchy'. Anyone who fit that description and who returned his gaze as they passed, he whispered 'Polleros?' to, and, although everyone that acknowledged his furtive question gave him stern, disapproving looks, most pointed back over their shoulders in the direction of the far end of the complex.

The farther he went in that direction, the crowd was sparser and most of the big warehouse doors were shut and padlocked. He saw no one who looked like they were making any clandestine deals, but did notice two people glancing around suspiciously before they disappeared into a narrow gap between two buildings, so he followed them down the candy-wrapper strewn passageway. The gap opened onto a dirt road running left and right that separated a cabbage field from the back wall of the warehouses, and, when he stepped out of the breach, several dozen eyes shot him a quick look before resuming their business.

Three, separate huddles of nine or ten customers were gathered around one person in the middle of each and listening intently to their rapid-fire, take-it-or-leave-it offers. Trying not to draw any more attention to himself, Tomás shuffled up to the rear of the nearest bunch so he could hear what was being said. Suddenly, a huge, boulder-hand from behind clamped like a vice onto his shoulder, and he felt like a ragdoll under the strength of the clutch as the man gave an effortless twist of his big, knotty wrist and spun the teenager around to face him.

"You don't want to be here." The hulking, bald-headed behemoth was friendly but adamant. "You want that group down there."

He twisted the wrist again, spinning Tomás back around and, while holding him firmly in place with *that* boulder-hand, used the other big paw to point to a larger huddle of people thirty meters farther down towards the end of the warehouses.

"That's who you want," he said, twisting the wrist once more and leaning in, face-to-face with Tomás, who was starting to feel dizzy. "This man here is looking for mules." He gestured behind them. "You don't want to be carrying this man's goods across, do you mi hijo?"

The question hung in the air, and Tomás couldn't tell if it was a friendly warning or the start of a job interview. In either case, he wanted no part in transporting drugs, even for a discounted rate. He thanked the hulk and walked away toward the distant group.

When he was in earshot of the new circle, however, he heard the dispiriting words:

"TWO-THOUSAND DOLLARS...TWO-THOUSAND USD!"

The Pollero repeated the number over and over, tossing in the occasional... *"TÓMALO O DÉJALO!"* (Take it, or leave it.), in case there were any doubts.

A hunchbacked old woman standing just in front of the man asked if there was any way to get across cheaper, and *el Pollero* responded by pointing over her head toward the other three assemblages down the way. The answer was wordless, but understood clearly; Drug Mules get a free ride, everyone else pays.

Tomás had planned on finding the cheapest possible lodging while in New York, but he didn't know how long it would take to do what needed doing and needed at least enough cash to get back home if things were to somehow go horribly wrong. Even more pressing, he needed bus fare from Texas to Manhattan, and so there was no way he could pay this man's transportation toll. He had done his research, of course, and knew that traffickers could charge anywhere from $1000 USD to as much as $5000, so this hiccup was not a complete surprise to him. He had been preparing himself for the potentiality of a *wet* crossing.

Only three people in the circle accepted the deal and, as the trafficker of souls walked away with his *trés pollos* following him back through the gap that led to the market place, the remnant split up into smaller bunches to discuss their options. Tomás inserted himself into a group that included two boys who looked a few years older than himself, one forty-ish looking man named Miguel who was traveling with his twenty-something daughter, Anita, and a woman of around thirty who was traveling alone.

Miguel had crossed the border on foot twice before, once successfully. This time, he was there to help Anita, who, it turned out, was pregnant, though it wasn't obvious. When quizzed about the crossing, his only advice was predictably simple.

"Find a shallow place on the river, hide in the reeds until the Border Guard Jeep passes on the other side, and then run, climb, and swim as fast as you can for as far as you can."

In border cities where the rate of illegal crossings was the highest, Tomás knew the I.N.S. patrol Jeeps worked in teams of two or three. In Texas, that meant Laredo and McAllen, far to the east near the Gulf of Mexico; Del Rio, which was closer to Ojinaga but still on the east side of the cathedral-like mountain range in Big Bend National Park; and, at the far west tip of Texas, Juarez/El Paso. But, the border between Mexico and the U.S. was nearly two thousand miles long, running from *Las Palomas Wildlife Refuge* in the Texas' Lower Rio Grande Valley, to *Friendship Park* in Tijuana on the California coast and, in the more remote sections of that extensive boundary, the I.N.S. budget only allowed for single-vehicle patrols to work THE LINE. Not only that, but Tomás had seen two websites that revealed that there was no air support for the Border Patrol in lower-risk zones like Ojinaga and Presidio, its counterpart on the Texas side, and both of those attributes were why he had chosen this place to cross.

Even so, if one of those lone vehicles was after an individual runner, the Jeep definitely had the edge and was much more likely to catch its quarry. If a cadre of aspiring immigrants could get even semi-organized enough to time a run just right, however, their odds for individual success were much greater once they crossed and split up on the other side. Tomás considered mentioning the stratagem aloud but guessed that everyone in the group understood the same, obvious concept; there was safety in numbers.

Once the alliance of six had gelled and the decision was made to cross together, the coterie's members began to steal furtive glances around the circle, each calculating his or her own odds were a patrol jeep in hot pursuit. The two older boys would probably be the fastest, Tomás guessed, with Miguel and his pregnant daughter bringing up the rear. From the looks on the other faces, it was clear that the unspoken consensus about the father and daughter's odds was unanimous, and Miguel broke the silence to made it clear that he and Anita knew the risks, and were willing to take the chance.

The two older boys, Marcos and Emilio, disclosed the invaluable information that they had already scouted possible crossing spots for a mile or more in both directions, and thought they had found the least risky place. So, with a unanimous nod of heads, the sextet shouldered their bags and backpacks and fell in line behind the scouts, Tomás bringing up the rear. As the column in front of him marched north down the dirt road toward the river, he assessed his situation and relaxed a bit, for no matter how temporary or contrived the camaraderie, being part of a team seemed to ease the pressure some how.

At one point during the late afternoon trudge, it occurred to Tomás that, apparently, when scouting places to cross, apparently Emilio and Marcos had apparently chickened out, and had apparentlee gone back to the market to apparently fetch a group of decoys in order to, apparently, help them *increath their chanthethhzz....* then we jutht watch the *POWERBALL.* (Completely unnecessary, but funny reference: author)

When the river came into view, Emilio motioned for them to keep their heads down as he and Marco herded everyone behind a large clump of trees. With everyone squatting in a circle around him, Emilio put one forefinger to his lips and pointed with the other to the fence along the river, then to the cameras, and then at the two guard towers spread far to the left and right on the other side. The two boys then steered the band silently along the riverbank to their left, heading northwest. Everyone walked bent over at the waist, trying to stay behind hillocks, dunes, and structures whenever possible as they passed fields of carrots and celery on their left, and the inconsistent cover of undulating berms of sand and dirt held together with sparse grass and weeds between themselves and the river on their right. While the rest of the group hurried past the gaps in the dunes, Tomás lingered behind a bit each time to steal looks at the river.

Rio Bravo (or Rio Grande, on the U.S. side); the natural waterway that had been the subject of political and cultural controversy on both of its shores since the Texicans had pried the territory north of the river from the grasp of the Army of Santa Ana... long time ago. All his life, Tomás had heard stories, sagas, and superstitions that all romanticized the crossing of the *Rio Bravo* and of the journey into *El Norte*, beyond; the land of milk and honey in the forms of money and opportunity. Now, Tomás saw with his own eyes the logistical, quite un-romantic reality of the fence, guard towers, surveillance cameras, and patrol roads beyond the river, upon which border guard jeeps routinely zoomed back and forth, kicking up clouds of dirt as they hunted down people just like himself.

Soon, the entourage came to a concrete, irrigation pump-house tall enough for them to stand upright and stretch their backs and wide enough to conceal them all from the towers and cameras. They took turns peeking around the corners at the opposite shore, and, when his turn came, Tomás saw just what he knew he would. The river was more than fifty feet wide and flowing northwest to the southeast with a strong current that made the water too murky to guess its depth. The bow of the river here curved onto the Texas side, so the cyclone border fence was on the near bank, and, beyond the patrol road on the other side were large, fenced fields wherein small herds of cattle searched for sustenance in pastures stippled with clumps of cactus and scrub. To the north and west of the fields, the terrain climbed into the craggy foothills of the Chinati Mountains, which, from here, looked devoid of all but scant vegetation, and far to the east, he could just make out the taller and more dramatic cliffs of the distant Big Bend range.

Scanning the panorama, Tomás' hours of online Geology and Geography lessons suddenly found a practical application as it became clear that the foothills that climbed gently away from him towards the mountain range to the north, were actually an ancient lava field where, in antiquity, streams and rivulets of molten rock had flowed from the volcanic cones and peaks of what was now the Chinati Range, and spread out in a wide apron along the north bank of the Rio Grande. From his vantage point he could see that the tendril-like fingers of molten effluvia had filled the rift valley between the Chinati and Big Bend ranges, and then cooled to form a broad coulee filled with hundreds and thousands of gullies and arroyos.

Tomás recalled being fascinated to learn (from an online-class link to a YouTube video) how flows of lava, after hardening into assortments of rolling canyons and mesas, underwent a process of erosion through a combination of wind and thousands of years of summer and autumn flash floods, which smoothed and rounded the harsher edges of the igneous rock and pulverized its top layers into the soil and dirt from which now sprouted the same scattered scrub oak, creosote bushes, and cacti that grew around Santa Teresa.

The person in line behind him was beginning to make impatient-noises, but before Tomás relinquished his lookout, he located Highway 67, the *Texas Mountain Trail,* climbing northward up the rift valley between the Chinati and Big Bend ranges. He couldn't make out the exact spot where the two ranges came together on the distant horizon, but he knew that was where the lone highway sliced through a low pass just south of Marfa, and he was more worried about traveling through that passage than about the border crossing itself. The highway there would be thick with I.N.S., Border Patrol, and Texas Highway Patrol vehicles, all stopping and searching random cars and trucks which, though they may have already made it through the crossing station in Presidio, still looked suspicious.

All six members of the immigrant band voted to cross under cover of darkness, both for concealment and so they could get as far into Texas as possible before the heat of the day came on them again. As the sun began to set, everyone took out what snacks or sandwiches they had brought with them, but, although Tomás had filled his stomach with tamales at *la feria* and had remembered to buy bottles of water for the journey, he had made the rookie mistake of forgetting extra food. Anita noticed his lack o' snack, and she smiled at him and handed him something wrapped in foil as the group of strangers sat in a tight circle eating a last meal for energy before their climb-swim-dash. As they ate, they shared their plans and dreams in hushed voices; everyone except Tomás, that is, who listened politely to the others, but kept his own, odd intrigue to himself.

Miguel was the oldest member of the clan and, having had previous crossing experience, he was appointed the clan's official flagman for the start of the footrace. After the sky was swallowed in darkness and everyone was packed up and ready to go, they all stood in line behind Miguel as he scanned the patrol road and timed the intervals between the vehicles of the Border Guard. When the time was right, he held up one hand and whispered loudly over his shoulder.

"Get Ready!"

He dropped his hand and took off around the corner at his personal top speed, and the others filed out behind him, but, when they reached open ground, the two older boys shot around Miguel and Anita, and the rest followed suit until the predicted pole positions were attained. Marcos was the first to reach the three-meter high cyclone fence, and, throwing a thick blue quilt Miguel had given him earlier over his shoulder, he scaled it in a flash and draped the blanket across its crown of barbed wire.

By the time the two older boys had hit the ground on the other side, Tomás was already swinging a leg over the top, and when Emilio was clear of the landing, he dropped the rest of the way down and chased after them across the sandy soil towards the riverbank. Holding the rucksack over his head, he ran splashing into the river and felt the cool water climbing up his overheated body as the steeply sloping river-bottom dropped away under him. His adrenaline was surging now, but, when he was up to his chin in the deepest part of the channel, the current pushed on his body much harder than he had expected, and he struggled to stay on his feet. The cash and thumb-drives were safely sealed inside a zip-lock bag and stuffed deep in his duffel, but, with his entire future dependent on the delicate little devices, Tomás didn't want to risk a full immersion. So, with one hand holding the duffel tightly on his head, he used the other to balance himself against the current, which was doing its best to un-foot him.

When the riverbed started to slope upward again, he regained some traction, so he took a look behind to see if the others had made it over the fence, and spotted Miguel pulling up the rear behind his daughter, who was just entering the river. Tomás reached the other side and climbed out of the water using the reeds and weeds to pull himself up the steep bank. As he stood on the flat top of the embankment, dripping wet from his shoulders down, the red taillights of the last patrol vehicle to pass caught his eye away to the left. But, just as the Jeep was pulling even with the distant guard-station, the bright beam of a searchlight from atop the tower suddenly hit the water, illuminating what looked like three loose backpacks drifting across the deepest part of the river.

The patrol vehicle's brake lights instantly flared to life and a billowing diffusion of red haze exploded in the Jeep's wake as it wheeled in a sharp U-turn around the base of the tower. Tomás didn't wait to see which way the Jeep was headed and took off running across the paved road as fast as his soaked clothes and water-logged Chucks would allow, making a beeline for the barb-wire cattle fence where Marcos and Emilio stood waving him on and holding as the wires apart with their boots and bare hands. When he was under the wires, he followed the boys in an all out sprint up the long, gentle slope toward the mountains, his every footfall schplotching in the dirt and the wet jeans chafing his legs. He tried his best to keep up with the other two, but they soon pulled ahead, and, though the boys had done him a solid by helping him through the fence, Emilio and Marcos never looked back again, and never saw what happened to the rest of the group as Tomás did.

At this distance, and the only light source being the headlights of the two Jeeps now in pursuit and the sweeping searchlight in the background, he could only make out silhouettes. But, just as he was about to turn and resume his flight, the searchlight halted on one of the Jeeps, which had now come to a stop and had the silhouette of Miguel pinned to its hood by the silhouette of a Border Guard Agent, who was reaching behind his back for handcuffs while holding Miguel's hands on top of his head. Tomás watched as the agent slapped on the cuffs and eased Miguel to his knees in the dirt, and it was then that he noticed the two figures in the foreground. Another Border agent was just getting through the cattle fence in pursuit of Anita, who, as far as Tomás could tell, had a fairly healthy lead on him, and he was struck by the realization that Miguel had most likely let himself be caught so that his daughter and unborn grandchild could get away. The other woman, who Tomás now realized had never given her name, was nowhere in sight.

In a few minutes, he hit a second cattle fence, climbed through it, and kept running, but, after a few hundred meters more, he felt his energy waning and stopped to catch his breath. Marcos and Emilio were now only shadowy specs amongst the scattering of large boulders farther up the dark slope and, although Tomás was out of range of the searchlight, he still felt exposed, and so started off again in search of more cover. In the duffel bag, he had brought one change of every item of clothing (except for his one pair of tennis shoes and a baseball cap), and so, when he found a rock big enough to hide behind, he stopped for a longer rest and removed his sneakers, peeled off the wet jeans & t-shirt, and wrung them out as much as he could before swapping them for their dry replacements, which he then pulled, with some difficulty, onto his still wet body.

The water bottles were now lukewarm reminders of how stupid he had been to forget extra food, and he tried to console himself with the notion that, if he was going to forget anything, at least it hadn't been the water. Without the two bottles, which now lay underneath the wet clothing in his bag, his straits would be much direr when the sun rose again. The dearth of provender was nonetheless a gaping hole in his plan, and Tomás knew he would have to find sustenance soon if he was going to make it, which meant raiding the trash barrels along the highway for scraps of food. His maps showed that there wasn't much cover of any kind along the highway corridor for many miles, however, and he didn't dare go near it until he was much further north. He decided instead to stick to his predetermined route for now, which had him traversing the eastern slopes of the Chinati Mountains as he hiked north towards the pass, far enough from the highway on his right to see it without being seen, but not close enough to the high, craggy peaks on his left for the uneven terrain to slow him down.

When he had recovered a bit, he got to his feet and shouldered his bag. Then, sucking a deep breath into his lungs, he said a prayer to St. Gabriel the Archangel, inflated his cheeks, and blew it all back out in an explosive *puff!* before stepping out from behind the boulder. A look back revealed nothing but the faint, sweeping searchlight in the distance to the south, so he continued north towards higher ground, hiking beyond the last fenced pastures and crossing a couple of dirt roads before trudging on, over or around promontories and down creek beds, hoping he was heading in the direction of the mountains. Navigating in the gullies and gulches was disorienting, and, though he had a sense that he was moving higher, he wasn't sure until the headlights on the Presidio/Marfa highway came into view on his right. But, he knew it would be harder to see the vehicles in the daylight, which meant it would be more difficult to tell when traffic thinned out enough to risk going down to scavenge.

With the moon casting its dreamy blanket of light over the hills and bluffs, Tomás' feet kept moving long after his brain had fallen asleep, his last dregs of adrenaline propelling him forward to a spot ten miles north of the Rio Grande, where he collapsed in a ditch and slept a dreamless sleep.

Chapter 22

TEXAS

By nine a.m., the Lone-Star State was already stiflingly hot. The night had been cooler, but when the sun crested the mountains of the Big Bend in the east, the temperatures increased rapidly as the border between night and day swiped westward across the arroyo-laden expanse to the place where Tomás lay in a crag on the eastern side of the Chinati Mountains. Minutes after the direct morning light hit his face, the rising heat roused him from slumber, and he fumbled for the water and drank down half a bottle before he could stop himself. He had bought the larger sized containers, but knew they wouldn't last long in this desert oven.

Tomás needed to find a creek or a pond, or even a puddle soon, so he pulled his baseball cap from the warm, damp satchel, tugged it onto his head, then consulted his maps, squinting in the glare of the sun as he looked back and forth from the glinting pages to the vista stretching out before him. If he could avoid the Border Patrol and get beyond Marfa, the risk of being caught would lessen significantly, but now, as he looked at the vast expanse in front of him, that *if* seemed a lot *IF*-ier.

He felt lucky to have made it this far thus far, but Marfa was another forty miles north of where he stood and, in the light of day, he could now see the crisscrossing dirt roads used by the Border Guard laid out across the hills and ravines between him and the highway. When he printed out the maps on the crappy printer, the machine had been low on ink and, as a result, the colors were mostly washed-out browns & beiges. The one exception was a dark, meandering line just south of where the pass cut through the low hills leading to Marfa. On his computer monitor, the twisting contours had been a deep green color that he identified as vegetation growing along the banks of *Cibolo Creek*, a seasonal stream serpentining alongside Highway 67. The creek made a wide curve around the little village of Shafter, Texas, just south of the pass, and, through the waves of heat distorting the horizon, Tomás could now see the bend of green away to the east. He picked up his pack, pulled the brim of his cap down low, and started off towards the highway, which was only three miles away as the crow flies, but covered with a latticework of dirt roads that would limit the number of viable hiding places if he heard a vehicle approaching.

Most of the scrub-oak and creosote bushes were barely large enough to conceal him, and three different times during the morning, he was forced to lay flat on the ground in random, thorny, desert vegetation, sweating it out until the Border Patrol Jeep had passed. His exposed neck and arms were already blistering in the sun and, despite his attempts to conserve water, both bottles were soon empty.

Sometime after midday, he made his way around the south side of a large bluff and stopped behind a small hill a couple of hundred meters from the highway to assess his surroundings. Just on the other side of the hill was a wide, flat, coliche-surfaced parking lot strewn with fencing materials, farming implements, and several, old, rusted-out trucks. Along the highway side of the lot opposite his hiding place sat a long, metal building, and on the lot's north end was an old, concrete structure crumbling on the edge of a natural, rock culvert. After a quick 360-degree scan, Tomás clambered over the knoll and scurried across the white coliche to the culvert, then scrambled down beside a corner of the dilapidated building into the big, irregular-shaped hole.

The big pit was three or four meters deep at its lowest part, and was the result, Tomás guessed, of a collapse in the surrounding rock shelf. He was concealed on all sides except the end opening onto the highway, so he stayed close against the rock wall as he made his way toward the gap, ready to hit the deck in a split-second, should the need arise.

Traffic was steady, but there was occasionally enough space between vehicles to allow him to get across without being spotted, if he timed it right, so he summoned whatever adrenaline had regenerated during his sleep and bolted across the distance to the road. After hopping the guardrail, he sprinted across the highway, the intense heat of the asphalt radiating up through the rubber soles of his shoes and searing his damp socks despite the fact his fast-moving feet hardly touched the surface of the road.

Once across the sizzling griddle, he scurried down an arroyo to the creek bed, but, to his profound disappointment, there was no flowing, or even standing water. The sandy soil was dry as a bone, with the exception of a couple of faint, narrow, damp stretches. In the nearly three hours it had taken him to get to this spot from his mountainside bivouac, the exertion and extreme heat had taken their toll, and he felt himself getting weaker by the minute. Panic began to creep over him as he trotted along the dry channel at the bottom of the shallow canyonette, and he imagined seeing a border patrol agent around each desperate, snaking twisting turn. But the green-leafed cottonwood trees grew in size and number the farther he went, so he stayed under their cover when possible, moving from tree to tree and following the impotent watercourse towards the little town.

Around one long, low promontory, a shallow stretch of muddy water appeared down the centerline of the creek, and Tomás made straight for it, falling to his knees in the squishy mud and using his sweat-soaked baseball cap to scoop water onto his broiling head and drink frantically, undaunted by how much silt he was swallowing. The muddy water was nowhere near cold, but after multiple dousings, his swollen, overheated brain was out of danger of being poached. He had been smart to enough to hold on to the empty bottles, and after the rehydration had cleared his thinks somewhat, he stretched the tail of his cotton t-shirt over the mouth of one bottle, then filled the other one, held both openings tightly together, and flipped the whole thing over, letting the water filter through. After repeating the trick using a different bit of shirt each time, the stagnant crick-water looked a little less lethal. Unfortunately, the method only provided one bottle of the cleanish water, but a little bit is better than nada and, as Tomás filled the other container with the muddy swill and screwed the cap back on, he was nevertheless pleased that he had thought of it.

Consulting the map and judging by the tall bluffs looming above the canyon walls ahead on his right, he determined he was only a short way from where the creek made a wide, westward bend around the village. So, he put the bottles in the duffel, shouldered up again, and continued on. Having researched Shafter, Texas on the Internet, he knew this blip on the map was considered a *GHOST TOWN* even though it boasted a current population of eleven. It had once been a mining boomtown and had accommodated as many as four thousand residents at its peak, but when Tomás peered over the steep embankment, he thought it just looked like a small version of his own village, and he mused about the *GHOST* part. A rehydrated sense of humor permitted him a chuckle at the thought.

"Eleven ghosts, maybe, heheh."

The first 'official' checkpoint on Highway 67 was in Marfa, sixty miles north of the river and the border, but Shafter was only twenty miles from the Rio Grande, and Tomás guessed it was probably a frequent stop if not an un-official headquarters for Border Patrol agents, or *Texas Highway Patrol,* and that it might even be the residence of an I.N.S. agent or two. As he walked alongside the steep western embankment, peering over the rim at the ghost town beyond, he started to see numerous, dilapidated edifices that he had failed to notice before amongst the newer houses with their shiny corrugated tin roofs. Nearly all of the colorless, weather worn structures had crumbled down to their foundations, with sections of quarried-stone walls sticking up here and there, and Tomás tried to picture how it all must have looked in the 'silver years'.

A little farther around the bend was a short row of houses and trailer homes with cars and trucks in various states of repair parked outside and, after a sweeping look around, he climbed up on the grassy bank, ran across an expanse of sandy ground, and ducked behind a metal tool shed. As he caught his breath, he peered around the corner and spied, sitting between two trailers across a dirt road from him, a wood-plank box that looked like it could be the housing of a water well. If he was right, there would probably be a faucet for a garden hose somewhere on it.

When he started off across the dirt road, however, he was distracted by beautiful Downtown Shafter as it came into view to his left. Two features in particular commanded his attention; a whitewashed church building stood just beside the highway with a tall steeple that caught the afternoon sun and reflected a bright gleam directly into his eyes, and another, even more striking spectacle much closer to where he stood tharned in the road. Beside one of the larger, metal-roofed houses, a sparkling, baby-blue swimming pool shone like a diamond in the desert, the crystal-clear water glinting on its surface in the sunlight. A wide apron of dark blue concrete surrounded the aqua of the pool and, encircling the perimeter of the entire yard was a band of perfectly manicured shrubberies.

The vision was of a fantastical oasis in the otherwise bleak landscape and, though Tomás was conscious of the danger, he was unable to stop himself and made straight for the pool for a quick, cooling dip. Slipping through a gap in the hedges, he dropped his duffel on the blue cement, and was just removing a shoe when he heard a voice from behind him.

"Hey boy!" The voice was urgent. "You need to be careful, there!"

Tomás whipped around to face the voice and squinted in the bright sunlight to fix on the source.

"Get your head down there, *mijo*," said the man in a whisper-shout. "There's two N.I.S. in church there... RIGHT THERE, son!"

Set back under the eaves of the house, in the shade of a porch, Tomás saw the silhouette of a man crouching low and motioning for him to do the same. His first instinct was to turn and run back the way he had come, but the man's warning overcame his flight response and he hit the deck, his stomach slapping on the hot, blue cement. He raised his head to see a striking, older, shirtless, Hispanic man with a mess of wild, white hair springing from his head step out into the light. Tomás guessed he was at least seventy years old, but appeared to be in better than average physical condition, and, though his hair was so colorless that it appeared to glow in the sunlight, the long, white beard that fell onto his sun-toasted chest was flecked with peppery specks. The man's only clothing was a pair of white, knee-length board shorts with wide blue stripes down the sides, and the overall affect, Tomás amused himself, was of a hybrid, Einstein/Mexican-surfer/Charleton Heston (Cómo Moses de los Diez Mandamientos!).

"Get over behind the fence!" Barked the man, pointing to the side of the house. "Through that gate there. I'll talk to you there in a minute, go-Go-**GO!**"

Tomás sprang to his feet and grabbed his satchel, then ran bent over at the waist around the end of the pool, making for the six-foot tall wooden fence beside the house. Slipping through the gate into a small grassy yard, he leaned his back against the stucco wall of the structure, panting and sweating and listening. His roasting body and sunbaked head were anticipating the cool relief of the pool, and now, even with the creek water sloshing around in his belly, the sapping heat and hunger had him dizzy.

Struggling to think clearly through the fuzzle, it suddenly dawned on him that he may have just walked into a trap. Facing him on the opposite side of the tiny paddock was a double-wide gate. What if the old man was helping the Border Patrol and he had just voluntarily entered a holding area? He could just imagine an I.N.S. paddy-wagon backing up to the loading-gate for its next haul of freshly-caught immigrants.

But he had come too far to be snared so easily. Summoning a reserve of energy, Tomás lifted his back off of the stucco wall and walked back and forth in front of the fence, jumping up and down again and again, trying to see what was happening on the other side. Suddenly, the double-gate flew open on his left and Tomás froze in mid-air as the white-haired man chuckled,

"You like a little rabbit hop-hopping up and down." He held his hands out in an unthreatening gesture. "Don't be scared, little rabbit. Heheheh. Me amo Xéro and I not gonna hurt you today, okay? It's Sunday, and it is fortunate for you that Xéro does a good thing for Jesus every Sunday. Your timing is just right. I was waiting for Church to start before I start for Marfa."

"That's the way I'm going Señor," said Tomás excitedly. "Could you..."

"Yes... yes, of course you are, mister rabbit," Xéro interrupted. "Where the hell else you gonna go from here? We ain't got much time here boy, Ssoooooo...you got the money?"

"Uh... money, Señor?" Tomás was confused and still fearing a trap.

"Your amigos said you got money, eh? Did they lie to Xéro, little bunny rabbit?"

"Pals?" Tomás asked, even more confused, until he remembered Marcos and Emilio.

"Si," said the old man. "They are already in the truck, *mijo*. They had you beat by almost three hours."

Just before the river crossing, Tomás had seen Emilio sneak a look at him when he was stuffing things in the plastic baggie, and now guessed he had seen the wad of cash.

"How much, Señor?" Asked Tomás.

"Well... usually it's five-hundred from here to Marfa but because today is the day of the Lord..." Xéro stroked his long beard as he looked off into the distant sky, "I take you for three-hundred."

"Si, Senor," said Tomás after a quick calculation. "I will pay three-hundred if you can guarantee that I will get to Marfa safely."

Xéro displayed his perfect dental work in a broad smile.

"There is no guarantee of anything in this cat-and-mouse game, mijo, but your best chance is with old Xéro." Then, with a belly laugh he added, "Hell, boy, your *only* chance is with Xéro. Do you know where you are?!"

Tomás listened as the intriguing character explained that he was on friendly terms with most of the *I.N.S.* agents who worked the line around Presidio, as well as with certain officers of the *Texas Highway Department* who patrolled up and down Highway 67 from here to Marfa. According to Xéro's brief but convincing sales-pitch, he knew their movements and habits, and Tomás got the distinct impression that he might even be in business with some of his law enforcement "friends".

Turning away from the man, Tomás dug out three, one-hundred dollar bills from his duffel. When he turned back, Xéro quickly snatched the cash from his had and, without looking at it, stuffed the money into the front pocket of his white shorts. He gave a wink and crooked a finger at Tomás, who followed him through the double-gate and around the corner to a dusty, one-car garage, wherein sat an old, faded-blue Chevrolet pickup with a dirty, banged up white camper shell on the back. As he followed behind Xéro to the tailgate, Tomás saw the two older boys who had outpaced him on the long slope smiling at him through the rear window.

"Hop in, bunny rabbit," said Xéro, as he opened the hatch.

Holding the duffel bag to his chest, Tomás climbed up and over the closed tailgate and fell into the bed of the truck as Xéro instructed the three émigrés.

"Okay boys," he said as he pulled a white undershirt on over his wild, white hair, "When I pull out of here, you three keep your heads down and don't look out the windows. Stay down flat until I open this hatch window again, comprendo?"

The boys nodded, and when Xéro shut the hatch and turned the handle to lock it, Tomás suddenly felt like a hostage in the close space. He gave Marcos and Emilio an uneasy grin and then lay down in the narrow space between the rows of burlap feed-sacks, and, just as he was settling in for the ride, the small connecting window between the truck-bed and the cab slid open, and Xéro stuck his head through.

"Okay boys," he said sternly. "I gonna drive slow, so it'll take an hour to Marfa, at least. You gotta stay laying down and covered up the whole time. No sticking your head up for nothing, si? I have a delicate relationship with these people, so don't fuck it up for me, fellas. If we get stopped, you just play dead and let me take care of it. After all, there's many a slip 'twixt the cup and the lip."

It was sweltering in the enclosed bed, but the three did as they were told and covered themselves with empty feed sacks. The vehicle's engine roared to life in the small space with a thunderous boom, making them all jump as the truck lurched forward out of the garage. With Emilio on one side of a row of sacks, and Marcos and Tomás laying head-to-head on the other, they settled in for the ride and, over the rumble of the engine and the noise of old tires on the hot highway, Marcos told him about their journey.

"We heard about him in the market," explained Marcos, "But the person who told us said that Xéro would only take two or three people at a time. So, we couldn't tell everyone."

Tomás was silent; not knowing how to respond, but grateful that he was the third.

"Besides," added Marcos, "we didn't know if we could find him, or if he even really existed."

The heat was stifling, and all three soon shed their feed-sack coverlets, but kept them close at hand in case Xéro should turn to check on them. After Marcos' admission, they all remained silent for remainder of the journey, with the exception of Xéro, whose full-throated voice rose above the noise of the road. Tomás thought his singing was pretty good, though his repertoire consisted of only one song, repeated over and over.

After an hour, the truck slowed down, made a couple of turns, and then stopped. The exiles kept silent and still, listening to the chugging motor and anticipating the sound of Xéro at the tailgate, but soon the vehicle began to roll again and, after several such stops and starts, and the sounds of increased traffic, it was clear they were making their way through the streets of Marfa. During one particularly long stop, Tomás heard a crackling voice that sounded like a low-fi, fast-food drive-thru speaker, and when the truck pulled away, it made a few more turns and came to a stop, before Xéro shut off the engine, came around to the back and opened the tailgate, which banged down loudly, and threw them each a small, brown, paper-sack, darkened with grease stains on the bottom.

Inside the sack was Tomás' very first, greasy, Texas-burger-joint hamburger and tater tots (in two, separate, greasy paper wrappers; one yellow, one white).

"You arrive in style with old Xéro!" said the man with heartfelt pride. "Not like those nasty Polleros. I got a heart. This is Xéro's Hamburger Rebate. Heheheh."

As the engaging man spoke, the boys made short work of the burgers and tots; washing them all down with, unfortunately but necessarily, the warm bottled water from their backpacks.

"You are very lucky today, gentlemen." Said Xéro. "You can get out here in Marfa or, for another two-hundred dollars, I take you on to Pecos, where I got to go pick up a load of melons for the church picnic tonight."

Tomás was reluctant to part with the extra cash, but hoped that if he could get as far as Lubbock or Amarillo, in the panhandle of Texas, he might be able to buy a bus ticket without having to show identification. With that in mind, plus the recognition that he had saved money by not dealing with the *Polleros*, he decided this was a worthwhile investment, and accepted Xéro's offer. Marcos and Emilio did not, however, and Xéro let them out in the middle of a crowded supermarket parking lot on the north side of town.

Before getting underway again, Xéro told Tomás he would have to hide in the truck-bed once again.

"These Federáles between here and Pecos... they don't know old Xéro too well, so you can't go up front with me. This drive is gonna take a coupla hours, *mijo*. You should catch a few winks, eh?"

For the first thirty minutes, Tomás stayed below window-level as instructed, but he couldn't resist seeing Texas in the daylight, and sat up. Keeping half an eye on the back of Xéro's head, he watched the Davis Mountains roll by as the pickup truck chugged its way up and over the *Wild Rose Pass*, serpentining through the rolling hills for almost an hour until the road descended to a flat plain and straightened out again. The landscape was less dramatic here, so he decided to take the man's advice and laid his head down for some much needed sleep.

—◊—

¡CRASH! the tailgate slammed open again, and he was suddenly surrounded by the voices of four young men who started unloading feed-bags from around him. None spoke directly to him, but each gave a knowing grin as the feed-bag brigade hoisted the heavy sacks onto their shoulders and walked away in a single-file towards the back of a large, cinderblock building, painted agro/industrial-green. Tomás crawled out of the airless truck-bed and was hit by a refreshing, albeit still hot breeze. He stretched his whole body so mightily that a loud grunt escaped involuntarily from his throat, but when he looked around to see if anyone had heard, they were all too busy loading and unloading to pay him any mind.

When the first group of boys began returning to the truck carrying large watermelons, Tomás set off to find Xéro. Though he had already paid the eccentric old character good money for the ride and knew that he was nothing more than an opportunistic businessman, Xéro had made the daunting task of evading the Border Patrol much easier than it might have been, and he wanted to thank him for the divinely-inspired Sunday discount, and for the bonus burger.

He found him on the backside of the building, talking to a short, stocky, mustachioed man, whose lips moved as Xéro counted out money into his palm. Not wanting to interrupt, Tomás stood waiting at a distance, but Xéro noticed him and waved him over.

"*Aquí, ven aquí!* Come meet someone, *mijo.*"

Tomás approached with a bowed head and an outstretched hand to grasp the thick, cigar-like fingers of the giant's huge, sweaty paw.

"I don't know where you are headed," said Xéro, "but I think you want to go more north, eh?"

Tomás nodded.

"Mr. Garcia drives that hay truck over there," Xéro explained as he pointed to a large flatbed truck, stacked high with bales of green, recently cut hay. "You see if you can work something out with him, okay mijo?"

"*Gracias por todos, señor,*" said Tomás.

"*Joven de buena suerte,*" replied Xéro, raising a hand in farewell as he walked away.

The truck driver was built like a fire hydrant, and he spoke to Tomás in a hoarse, whisper-voice that was gruff and humorless, but, by happy chance, he was bound for a small dairy farm near the Texas/ New Mexico state line just west of Lubbock. Using a minimum of words, the gruff man made Tomás the offer of a ride in exchange for help unloading his truckload of green, freshly-cut bales of hay when they reached their destination, and Tomás readily accepted, glad for the chance to barter with labor instead of cash. As they walked beside each other toward the truck, Tomás strained to understand the man's words through his voice, but he got the gist, which was that '*this was gonna be 'hot, sweaty work.*

He had just climbed into the passenger seat of the big cab and slammed the door behind him, when a middle-aged woman's smiling face appeared in the open window. She handed Tomás a sandwich wrapped in plastic and, as the truck pulled away, he thanked her and they both waved goodbye.

Filthy and exhausted, but reckoning that luck had been on his side so far, Tomás sat eating the delicious ham & (American) cheese sandwich and watching the miles roll by. After a while, the terrain changed from gently rolling hills with scatterings of cattle and goats, to oil fields and pastures that were tabletop-flat and nearly featureless except for the large, rolling and churning pump-jacks. The big, undulating, iron and steel machines reminded Tomás of giant grasshoppers bobbing gently up and down in the desert, and they increased in number the farther north they drove, but, as he ate, he watched the slow, steady, oscillating pumps as they sucked the oil from middle-earth, and the see-sawing motion began to make him logy. Mr. Garcia was clearly not a talker, so Tomás laid his head against the window and tried to fall asleep again, but found that it wasn't as easy this time. The knowledge that he had gotten away with something was exhilarating, but it was accompanied by the sensation that the other shoe could drop at any moment.

—⁓—

The sudden, rapid deceleration and simultaneous *fsssss* of hydraulic breaks woke Tomás with a start. He took a quick glance out of the front windshield, then shot a sideways glance at Mr. Garcia, who was looking into the driver's side mirror as he downshifted rapidly and herded the heavily laden truck onto the highway's shoulder. When Tomás put his feet on the glove-compartment door and pushed himself back in the seat to get a good angle in the mirror and saw, to his horror, the red and blue flashing lights of a Texas Highway Patrol car pulling into position directly behind them.

"What do we do, Senor?" Tomás blurted nervously. "Should I run? When you stop I will run for it across the field."

"Shut up!" Snapped the man in his hoarse whisper. "You stay put and keep your mouth shut."

Tomás felt a rush of queasiness with the sinking sensation that his crusade had literally just come to a grinding halt right along with the eighteen wheels on the gravelly shoulder. He looked anxiously at Mr. Garcia, who gave him the hand as he rolled down the window, and then rested both of his hands atop the steering wheel in a loose grip

"Just look straight ahead and don't say nothing," he whispered.

When the Texas State Trooper's hat and head drifted into view, however, Tomás couldn't help himself and hazarded a peek. The wide brim of the officer's cowboy hat cast his face in shadow and, when Tomás looked into the curved lenses of the man's mirrored sunglasses, he saw the distorted reflection of Mr. Garcia, now with a broad smile spread across his platter face.

"Good afternoon, officer," said Mr. Garcia with as little Spanish accent as possible.

The officer didn't remove the sunglasses, but his head movements indicated that he was giving the truck a thorough looking over; from the words painted on side of the door, to the inspection and vehicle registration stickers on the windshield, to the condition of the tires.

"*Bwaynose tardis*," said the Trooper in a friendly but firm Texas twang. "May I see your driver's license and proof of insurance, *por fayvor?*"

Mr. Garcia reached into his back pants pocket and pulled out an old, brown, oil-stained wallet, and grinned as he handed the cards to the Trooper.

"I didn't think I was speeding, was I officer?" Mr. Garcia hoarsely implored. "It's hard to speed with a load like this, heheh...and in this old truck."

"Who is traveling with you today, sir?" asked the Trooper, ignoring the question.

"This is my son, Tomás," answered Mr. Garcia without missing a beat. "He helps me on the weekends."

The officer's head made a barely perceptible turn toward Tomás, who grinned politely and tried not to show his nervousness as a fresh layer of sweat broke out on his face.

The officer did not return the smile, and his shielded gaze remained fixed on him for so long that Tomás thought the jig was up. His hand slipped from his thigh, and he grasped the door handle with a sweaty fist. He didn't think the officer would shoot him if he made an all-out dash through the field of ankle-high cotton on his right, but he also knew that he was fucked. One radio call and every law enforcement unit in the area would converge on him. To Texas law enforcement agencies, the call of an illegal on the run, Tomás knew, was like the starting gun of a bad, barbaric 'Running Man' movie sequel without the glamour of Maria Conchito to soften the lens. And tonight, he was the star.

"The reason I stopped you today sir," the Trooper continued, "Is because you had a couple of straps come loose up on top there, and your load looks like it could topple off on a wide turn."

The tightly-wound bodysprings of Tomás' musculoskeletal system uncoiled a millimeter, and he was just able to repress an audible sigh as Mr. Garcia opened the driver's side door, hopped out of the cab, and motioned for Tomás to do the same. While the Trooper sat in his air-conditioned cruiser under the shade of the sun visor and watched through the mirrored aviator lenses, Mr. Garcia and his 'son' climbed onto the stacked hay bales, which were indeed listing precariously to port. After five, hot, sweaty minutes, they had repaired the peccadillo, tightened the pull-straps, and were on their way once again. As the truck pulled slowly back onto the highway, Mr. Garcia gave a thank-you wave to the Trooper, then turned a summer toothed grin at Tomás, who smiled back, remembering the words of Xéro, '...there's many a slip...' Many a slip, indeed.

—◊◊◊—

It was long after sundown on Sunday night when they pulled into the entrance of the dairy farm. The only non-bovine they could find on the premises was a lone night watchman, who told them that the dairy's owner was the only person authorized to sign checks, and he wouldn't be back until six a.m. But, Mr. Garcia refused to unload the hay *"without I get a check first,"* so he and his hired-hand settled into the cab, both shifting uncomfortably throughout the night and trying to avoid touching each other as they attempted sleep.

Tomás was up first, and he climbed down out of the truck to have room to stretch himself fully awake. They were farther north now, and when he breathed the slightly less warm morning air in through his nostrils, he found that it was dryer and smelled strongly of dung. From under the seat, Mr. Garcia produced two pairs of work gloves, both of which were much too big for Tomás, and two sets of wooden-handled steel hooks for moving the heavy bales.

As the sun sparked to life atop a perfectly flat tightrope horizon, they set to work, and, as the yellow disk made its daily crawl across the sky, Tomás found it hard, sweaty work, just as the human fireplug truck driver had warned. By mid-morning, the job was done and, though his arms were wet noodles and his shoulders felt like he had given a piggyback ride to an elephant, he had worked off his debt to Mr. Garcia, who took pity on him and went out of his way to drive Tomás into the city; dropping him off in downtown Lubbock, a couple of blocks from the Greyhound bus station.

This was it, thought Tomás, waving farewell to his ad hoc boss as the empty, flatbed truck rumbled off down the brick-paved street. The only thing standing between him and the final leg of his journey was a bus ticket, so Tomás threw the strap of his duffle bag over his shoulder and started towards the depot, conscious of the many pairs of eyes that peered at him through the windshields of cars driving by on the busy, downtown street. After circling the terminal several times trying to work up the courage to approach the ticket counter inside, he chickened out and decided on plan b.

Walking past an alleyway between two tallish buildings, he spotted a couple of ragamuffins standing behind a trash dumpster who, like himself, looked like they might be transient or homeless. He approached the odd couple hesitantly but, when the woman looked up and smiled at him, Tomás smiled back and, within a minute, they had struck a deal. The waifish woman had a valid, Texas driver's license, and, with butterflies fluttering in his stomach and the promise of an additional forty dollars when and if she returned, Tomás handed her just enough cash to cover the bus ticket.

For surety, he was left waiting at the dumpster with her nonsensically-gibbering male companion, and a big, bright red, American Tourister hard-shell suitcase (with extendo-handle and wheels), which the woman had said contained all of her earthly belongings. It was meager collateral considering the amount of money he had just handed over to her, but Tomás smiled to himself at the inverted truism that 'chiggers can't be boozers'. He kept his eyes on the terminal entrance across the street waiting for her to come back out, thinking positive thoughts and trying to ignore the disheveled, dentally-challenged man and the stream of incoherent yada-yadas pouring from his muddled maw.

The minutes crept by, and when he had almost decided that the woman had fled the terminal from another exit and was already on her way to start a new life without her prized red suitcase or her babbling boyfriend, the doors flew open and she walked out, smiling and waving the ticket. Not wanting to offend the nice lady who had just helped him, Tomás grinned as he thanked her and tried not to be obvious about looking at the amount of change she placed in his palm along with the ticket and receipt. He was very aware of his dwindling resources and had judged that it was better to be safe than sorry, but, as Tomás handed the woman the promised forty dollars for her trouble, she blew his assuaging rationale all to hell with, what he considered the unnecessarily cruel disclosure that the Ticketing Agent at the counter had never asked for identification of any kind.

—⚬⚬—

The next thirty-nine hours were mind-numbingly monotonous as he sat in the rearmost seat of a packed Greyhound coach and watched the acclaimed and perpetually extolled United States of America zoom by through dark-tinted windows, his nostrils stinging from the sharp, acrid odor of industrial sanitizers and cleaning products that were, ironically, meant to disguise the smell of urine. With the tangy stench in his nose, and the deep, loud hum of the coach's diesel motor at his back, the experience would imprint itself on Tomás' brain and would, regrettably, become a permanent memory part of his first Trans-American crossing.

Chapter 23

NEW YORK CITY

O nce upon a time, when Tomás was ten years old, he and his family travelled to the sprawling metropolis of Mexico City to attend the wedding of an aunt. He recalled being surprised at how different the large city seemed from the other, big urban centers of Torreón and Durango, both of which he had been to many times before, and, as he and his family had walked through the *Zócalo*, holding hands to keep from becoming separated, all of his senses had been set alight. He was captivated by the throngs of people, and the number of cars, trucks, and buses, and his lasting impression of *Ciudad de Mexico* was of equal parts fascination and fear at the mass of humanity and at the sheer volume of traffic, which belched clouds of exhaust as the drivers honked their horns and fought for position on the roundabouts.

Now, as he stepped down from the bus on the lower level of the Midtown Manhattan Port Authority Bus Terminal, he was expecting a similar urban experience, but, after making his way from the subterranean arrival gate to the east entrance on the Main Floor, he stepped through the doors onto the sidewalk of 8th Avenue, and the kinetic rush of New York City struck Tomás smack in the faculties. Mexico City had been a buzzing hive of activity, but his first impression of Manhattan, from street level, revealed a vigorous energy that his own country's capital lacked. There was a self assured diversity here, with an added, purposeful dynamism that was instantly infectious, and he suddenly understood why New York City was frequently referred to as the capital of the world. And, it all looked and felt so familiar.

Across the street from the Bus Terminal and looming intimidatingly over the whole block, was the iconic, fifty-two story skyscraper that was the new home to the *New York Times*. If New York City was the capital of the world, then *The Times* was surely the clearinghouse for its most predominant, ascendant, and impactful news and information. As Tomás looked up at the imposing tower, cloaked in the chain-mail of its ceramic and steel exterior curtain, he envisioned it as an enormous samurai warrior; a knight errant, clad for battle and unassailable.

He was oblivious to the stream of pedestrians that zipped past or veered around him as he stood in the middle of the sidewalk and studied the building's corporate ensign, which was mounted on its facade three stories above the ground entrance; the huge letters mimicking the English Towne typeface of the publication's seminal banner. As Tomás admired the sight, an involuntary shudder rippled through him at the thought that he was standing at the hub for the acquisition, substantiation, and dispersion of the world's most important news, while, tucked into the toes of his shoes, were his fateful pair of flash drives; the contents of which certainly transcended the *National-Enquirer's* boiler-plate sensationalist fare and, he hoped, would meet the crucial criteria of *The Time's* declared "ALL THE NEWS THAT'S FIT TO PRINT".

The notion that a teenager, who had literally just stepped off the bus from a tiny village in Mexico, had the power to cause any kind of stir in the pot of world events, brought a rush of exhilaration, and Tomás felt dizzy as he looked up at the citadel with its spire stabbing into the sky. Up there, somewhere, John Maddox was sitting at his desk, unaware that his comfortable life would soon be upended, and his trespasses exposed.

Tomás stepped out of his prideful trance and walked down to the first corner, where the uniform grid of Manhattan's streets and avenues opened up and gave him a majestic view in the four cardinal directions. The urban canyons seemed to stretch on forever, and the added sounds of traffic, music, commerce, and the aroma of street-vendor's cuisine all made him feel as if he were in a movie. So many impressions of the borough had etched themselves into his imagination from books, movies, and television shows, that now, as he spun around taking it all in, the euphoric *rush* overcame him, and he had to look for a place to sit down.

Behind him was a corner drug store with a recessed entrance, and he sat down just inside, between the door and the non-stop foot traffic of the sidewalk. With legs crossed and his back to the wall, he held the satchel in his lap and braced himself for an expectedly butsis aroma as he unzipped it. During the short stops on the long bus ride, he had been able to duck into several smelly terminal restrooms along the way to rinse his river and sweat caked clothes in the tiny bathroom sinks, then wring them out and dry them using the wall-mounted, electric hand-dryers, but there had never been enough time to get the jeans completely dry, and now a strong, mildewy smell wafted into his nostrils, making him recoil involuntarily.

He heard his mother's voice telling him that he needed to look nice and smell good if he was going to meet with professional people, so he decided to locate his intended hostel first, the West Side YMCA, who he knew had laundry facilities, for a wash and freshen up before finding Brent Ames' office. By a happy coincidence, all of the people, places, and things relevant to his scheme were located within blocks of each other in Midtown West, though the Private Eye's office was a little farther south, in Tribeca. The Port Authority Bus Terminal and *The Times* building were across the street from each other at West 40th, and the YMCA was only a few blocks north of here on 63rd & Central Park West, so he zipped up the stinky satchel, tucked it under his smelly armpit, and started north on Eighth Avenue.

Crossing through Columbus Circle, he saw Cap'n Chris standing proudly atop his pedestal, surveying the prominent continent he had invaded in the name of Spain, and two blocks farther, he found the YMCA on a street corner directly across the street from Central Park. When he went inside, Tomás was discouraged to find that there would be no beds available until the day after tomorrow, so he walked to the corner newsstand and bought a copy of the *New York Times* so he could search the classified ads for other options. He stood leaning against a sign post as he read but, just as he had singled out an ad for a bunkhouse in the East Village, the newsstand man walked into his line of sight hoisting a bound bundle of magazines onto a short stack of newspapers beside the stand. The man cut the string on the bundle, and when he began setting them out on the stand, the bright, red banner of *The National Enquirer* caught Tomás' eye.

There it was, just below the headline:

HOW I CAPTURED A CHUPACABRA!!!

It was **his** story! The color photos that he had taken and developed himself were right there, printed huge on the front page! And, printed in its entirety on page two and three was his very own story! Only, the byline did not say Tomás Sanchez. The copy was credited to a *MONTEREY EL NORTE* Staff Writer.

"CHINGA TU MADRE!" He yelled out loud, but no one appeared to notice.

They had screwed him over again, but without John Maddox acting as Commander-in-thief this time. Now, *two* of his stories had been printed in an internationally distributed publication, and he had been denied the writing credit in both cases. The snub seemed absurdly ironic, especially in light of the fact that the subject of this Story of the Decade had actually come to Tomás very own window and asked him for his help.

There was no time to bellyache, however. The game was afoot and, despite his current state of personal hygiene, he had to get to the investigator's office to warn Téo. He paid for a copy of the *Enquirer,* remembering to get extra change in case he needed to make phone calls, then set off south, dodging oncoming foot traffic as he alternated between reading his own words in print and checking the corner street signs. Trying not to let panic set in, he focused on the sensation of the two thumb-drives as he walked, each wrapped in its own roll of bus-station toilet paper and stuffed deep into the toe of his shoes (one ea.). Everything would be put to right soon, he thought. He wasn't going to let *anyone* other than himself take credit for the video, which had been a singular privilege and only possible because of his close, personal relationship with the infamous creature. But, even the comfort of the knowledge of a rise above the sky above was shaken by the unnerving fact that the hugely consequential assemblage of intangible ones and zeroes was stored in virtual space on the flash-drives, and that the fragile little devices were his sole insurance policy, trump card, and lynch-pin all rolled into one (or two). At least he had been smart enough to use two drives, in the name of redundancy.

He stopped at a corner trashcan and threw away all but the *Times* classifieds and the *Enquirer,* which he folded lengthwise and stuck up under his shirt into the waistband of his jeans. Half walking, half jogging down the sidewalks of first Eighth, and then Ninth Avenues, sweat dripped down his face in the sticky, summer heat, and the wonders of Manhattan that had mesmerized him so minutes before became a secondary concern to the safety of his little brother and everyone else in Santa Teresa.

On the block where the Private Eye's office was supposed to be, Tomás saw no sign nor placard for the business, so he wiped the hand-sweat onto his jeans and reached into his pocket for the map on which he had circled the address.

468

There it was, circled in yellow highlighter on his map, and, in big, white, block-numerals on a green awning right above his head. When he walked through the door, he was hit by the strong smell of sweet curry, however, and, judging by the interior decor and the turbaned head of the man walking toward him, he guessed this was either an Indian or a Pakistani restaurant. Tomás pointed to the map he held loosely in one hand, and the man smiled and nodded, but when he asked where he could find the Investigator's office, the gentleman nodded more and smiled even bigger as he took a menu from the host station and directed Tomás to a nearby empty table. Shaking his head, Tomás stopped him and tried again, this time using the name Ames. A light bulb came on above the man's turban and the biggest smile yet spread across his olive-skinned face as he pointed to the ceiling with one hand, and to the door through which Tomás had entered with the other.

"Ames, yes yes. Third floor...floor number three!" The restaurateur rolled the 'R's heavily.

Tomás thanked the smiling curry-man and backed out of the door, noticing this time that, beside the restaurant's entrance, but under the same awning, there was an unmarked, glass door, through which he now saw a steep, narrow staircase that began just inside the door. The door was unlocked, so he climbed the claustrophobic stairwell to the third-floor and, when he turned the corner of the last flight before the landing, he heard strange, muffled sounds emanating from the far end of the hallway; music, possibly, but other-worldly and odd. He followed the sounds to the door at the end of the hall and was relieved when he saw the gold name-plate:

AMES INVESTIGATIONS

The moment his knuckles hit the door, he detected the faint smell of marijuana. There was no answer after the first, or second, or third series of knocks, but the music and the smell of *mota* told him someone must be inside. He opened the unlocked door slowly and called out,

"Hello?... Mister Ames?"

The lights were switched off, but a dozen staves of sunshine from the half-open, horizontal blinds pierced the smoky, pungent haze that hung in the air, casting stripes of light across the dark-wood paneling of the opposite wall.

"Mr. Ames?" Tomás tried again, stepping further inside.

The sounds he had heard from the hallway were louder now and they surrounded him from the shadows. He still wasn't sure if it was supposed to be music or, maybe, the soundtrack from a movie, as it had no identifiable pulse or rhythm, just faint bells and swirling synthesizers that morphed and modulated in elongated quarter-tones, creating an aural landscape which, combined with the haze and Indicaroma made Tomás feel like he had stepped into another world.

Adorning the wall, opposite the door through which he had entered, was a huge map of The Five Burroughs of New York City, push-pinned into the wood paneling at each corner and decorated all over with small, multi-colored sticky-notes. Set out a few feet from the wall map was a large, wooden desk, behind which sat a wooden swivel-chair, upholstered in studded, black pleather. On the front side of the desk was a matching, black-pleather pair of client's chairs, and when Tomás slipped between them to get a closer look, he saw that the desk's top was covered with more of the colorful sticky-notes, some of them affixed to photographs that appeared to have been taken from a distance using a telephoto lens.

He was curious to see if any of the notes or photos pertained to his own case, but, as he was scanning the desk for John Maddox's name or likeness, the music stopped suddenly, and a door in the dark wall to the right of the map opened with a click. Tomás snapped to attention and the jolt propelled him backwards as the silhouetted form spoke.

"Can I help you, kid?" The voice was heavy with New Yawwk accent.

"Yes, I'm sorry, señor, uh...sir," Tomás nervously blurted. "I... I knocked a few times...but..."

"Don' wuhrry 'bout it, kid," said the voice as the shadowy form flicked on the light switch. "I was just on my lunch break. What can I do fuh you?"

In the flittering effulgence of the fluorescent bulbs, Tomás saw a slender man who looked to be in his mid-fifties. He was a couple of inches taller than Tomás, with a salt and pepper, three-day beard sprouting from a face with a lot of character in the form of forehead wrinkles. On his feet were a pair of comfy-looking flip-flops, and, pulled down low over faded blue jeans, he wore an oversized, royal-blue New York Knicks jersey, number 33. The investigator was holding a small hand towel, which he threw over one shoulder as he leaned against the doorjamb and studied the teenager standing in his office. It gave Tomás a chance to peer into the small, sunlit room behind the man, where he saw an unmade, single bed, and heard the sound of a toilet tank refilling.

The Private Eye leaned back into the bright little room and produced a straw, porkpie hat, which he placed on top of his wet, slicked back hair.

"I am Tomás Sanchez." Tomás broke the silence.

"You're what?" Ames deadpanned.

"I'm Tomás... Sanchez...from Santa Teresa, Mexico?" He said with an inquisitive upward lilt on each word. "I hired you to..."

"Yeah yeah I know, "Ames jumped in. "I know who you aah... I mean... I... uh... You're not kidding, ahh you kid?"

Tomás shook his head no.

"Holy Shit!... *S'cuse my French*... Holy Christ!"

Having never mentioned his age in the email correspondence, Tomás knew that his youth would be a surprise, and a corner of his mouth turned up in a sly grin.

"Kid," Ames squinted at him with his head cocked. "If you're as young as you look, I'm pretty shuh that, legally, I'm not s'posed to be takin' yuh money. How old *ahh* you anyways?"

"I'm eighteen," Tomás lied.

"Rriiiight," croaked Ames sarcastically. He took a couple of steps toward Tomás, but quickly relinquished them, his nose recoiling in disgust. "*OOYAH!* No offense kid, but you look filthy and you smell like shit...*S'cuse my French*...you don't smell so good. They let you on an airplane smellin' like that?"

"I took a bus."

"Weeelll that must have been pleasant," Ames scratched at his temple with a forefinger as he thought. "Okay... well... Seein' as how I already done two weeks of work on yuh dime, let's just continue as though I didn't have any fucking..., *S'cuse my French*...like I didn't have any cockie-doodie idea how old you wuh." Then, after another beat, "How fuckin' old *AHH* you anyways, kid?"

As his eyes adjusted to the light, Tomás began to notice more details about the man, like how he walked with a slight limp, favoring his left leg, and that, when he switched on the desk lamp and started shuffling through papers and photos, Tomás saw that Ames' left forearm was curiously, considerably, more sun-tanned than his right arm.

"Okay, right," the man was officious now. "So, let me get you updated on the love triangle situation currently go..."

"Actually Señor," Tomás cut him off, "Sir...there is something I have to do first. It's urgent, but I need to use your computer, if that's okay."

"Hells Bells kid," Ames exclaimed. "Yuh payin' me full price, and that comes with one free use of my shitty compyootah." He gestured behind him to a smaller computer desk to the left of the wall map. "This thing is always bugging up on me. I gotta get a Mac."

Tomás wasn't surprised that the middle-aged man didn't use SKYPE, but it only took a few minutes to download the program and, when it was finished, he sent an email with the title line:

URGENT--TEO ONLY--URGENT

And, in the body of the email:

SKYPE-NOW

He hit SEND and took a deep breath. Now, he could only wait. The investigator had been watching from over his shoulder and was impressed by Tomás' technological adroitness.

"Wow, kid! Yuh good at this stuff, huh? Whad'jew say this program is called again?"

The Private Investigator brought his client up to speed while they waited for Téo to respond, and the amount of soap-opera worthy drama and scandal he had uncovered since their last correspondence gave Tomás some degree of vindication at having parted with such a large sum of money. This idiosyncratic character obviously knew what he was doing, and Tomás was anxious to see all the fruits of his harvest.

As he explained in the emails, Brent Ames had spoken to several co-workers and friends of Maddox, as well as former co-workers and former friends, and had even greased a few palms in exchange for whatever professional ignominy they were willing to reveal. Tomás already knew about the dry well he had hit on that front, but now the Private Dick told of the trouble he had found bubbling just under the surface of paradise in the reporter's personal life.

According to the sleuth, in the weeks leading up to her impending wedding, Victoria Magaña had been maintaining an adulterous affair with her boss at the *National Enquirer*, one Ben Rantz. The tryst was adulterous owing to the fact that Rantz was already married and Victoria was about to be as well, in theory. A couple of past associate's of Rantz, it seemed, were willing and delighted to openly talk shit about the man, and had not only given biographical and background information on him, but had delivered defamatory diatribes about Rantz as well. When the investigator told him that both the ratfinks had accepted a fifty-dollar bill for the dirt and for the promise not to mention they had spoken to him, Tomás gave another, sly grin.

Rantz was a forty-five-year-old alumnus of Cornell University, who, while climbing up the corporate ladder to attain his current position as assignment editor for the *Enquirer's* New York office, had, evidently, stepped on several heads and stabbed more than a few backs. One of those flat-headed, back-bleeders had told Ames she thought Rantz was proud of his expedient nature and viewed his own aggressiveness as competitively healthy. When she had challenged Rantz about his opportunistic leanings, he had allegedly responded, *"Hey, I just know a good thing when I see it coming."*

And, Rantz had definitely seen Victoria Magaña coming. A beautiful blonde from rural Connecticut, whose blue eyes and rosy, All-American complexion belied the fact that she was the offspring of a Mexican mother and a Columbian father. Ames had even tracked down the woman who originally introduced the ignominious couple at a mutually attended cocktail party during Victoria's senior year at New York University. The shady duo had been seen canoodling in a corner later that same night and, according to the chatty source, the editor had offered Victoria a job as his assistant that week.

Ames was standing near Tomás as he spoke, and when he could no longer bear the odor that was coming off the the teenager in waves, he motioned Tomás to one of the pair of chairs on the far side of the desk before he continued the debriefing. When Tomás expressed his amazement at how much adulterous dirt the man had been able to dig up in such a short time, the detective explained,

"Hey kid, it's my job, and I'm thorough." He tapped a finger on the desktop for emphasis. "Sometimes you gotta learn about a person's past to understand theh habits and, uhhh.... what'dya call, uhhhh... predilections. When ya do what I do for as long as I done it, you get so's you can feel when a change in somebody's routine means that theh up ta somethin' they shouldn't be."

Tomás nodded and grinned.

"I ain't quite pinned down the secrets of 'human *NAY*-chuh yet, kid," said Ames, "but human *behave*-yuh is much easier to figure out."

Ames reached into his desk drawer for a cigarette and lighter, then leaned back in his chair, lit up, and took a long draw. When he exhaled, the words billowed out with dramatic emphasis.

"Money and Sex," he said, the words billowing out with the smoke, which gave them extra emphasis.

Pointing a pistol-finger at Tomás, the Private Dick broke it down.

"It's always gonna revolve around one of those two things, kid... eventually. It really don't take much snoopin', either. People love to tell secrets on each other, especially if it's about sex or money. You just gotta find somebody that's been screwed by the person you're after in one or both of those areas, and you're off to the races. If the pump needs more priming, I introduce my confidential informant to my buddies Grant or Franklin, and then..." He flung his hands out like he was shooting craps, "...out comes the dirt."

Tomás grinned and nodded again.

"So..." the investigator gestured toward Tomás, "what'dya think, kid? Izzat kinda thing filed under human *NAY-chuh*, or human BEHAVE-yuh? Dud'n mattah anyways. Whatever ya wanna call it, it's always about..."

He pointed the finger again, and Tomás answered,

"SEX AND MONEY!?"

"You got it, kid," Ames chuckled. "Look, kid, I don't know why you wanna fuck up this...*'S'cuse my French*...why you wanna take a dump on this guy's life, and I don't need to know. Folks do things to each other for lots of reasons. Twenty-five years in this job, I've seen some crazy shit, kid...*S'cuse me*, some nutty crap...but..." he took another drag from the cigarette, "...if you don't mind me saying, it seems to me like we're doing a favor for this Maddox guy as far as this chic goes."

"It's complicated," said Tomás. "John Maddox has done much harm to some...to one close to me."

"I get it, shuh." Ames stuck out his bottom lip. "Sorry to hear that, kid. Okay then, let's get down to brass tactics. Here's what I come up with."

The investigator leaned forward in his chair, put his elbows on the desk, clasped his hands together, and steepled his forefingers.

"Awwright... In the last three weeks, the number of...hookups...between the unscrupulous pair has only increased the closer they get to her wedding day. In my experience, this kind of... *behave-yah*..." Ames raised his eyebrows and pointed the pistol again, "...is not completely uncommon. About sixty or seventy percent of the time, it's the guy doin' the deed. Sometimes it's just a case of very cold feet, or one last, quick fling before the ball and chain are welded on, but sometimes I seen it continue after the newlyweds return from theh honeymoon... don'tcha know."

The investigator picked up a short stack of photographs and dropped them in front of Tomás. The first two shots were taken with a telephoto lens and showed the two adulterers at a romantic candlelight dinner together, but, as Tomás went deeper in the shuffle, he saw much more incriminating, scandalous images and he found himself too uncomfortable to continue.

"Now..." said Ames as he took back the stack, "... this is when you gotta decide just how cruel you wanna be, kid. How far in do you wanna stick the knife?"

Tomás was confused by the more conspiratorial tone and didn't know whether the man was encouraging, or dissuading him to blow a hole in John Maddox's personal life. Ames already had the three-thousand dollars, and Tomás guessed that he had already figured out that his teenaged, Mexican client was both depleted of funds, and probably illegal to boot, but Tomás was here to do all of the damage that he could do, with every means at his disposal, and told him to proceed with a description of his ploy.

"Well, okay then," said Ames, "The way I see it, we could just send these pics to John Maddox and be done with it, or..." He leaned in, "And, this part is in two phases... see, these two fuck buddies go to the same place at the same time every day for their fuhh...S'cuse my French...for the screwing... no uthuh way ta say it, kid. Theyah like clockwork, every afternoon late. Anyways, I'm pretty sure I could arrange for Maddox to walk in on his fiancé and Rantz while theh doin' it. It's a little complicated, and it would take some expert timing, but HEY..." Ames pointed at himself with both thumbs, "I'm an expert!"

"The crueler, the better." Tomás was resolute. "What is the second part?"

Ames looked impressed and said, "Well, I got this broad, see... gorgeous little Italian firecracker...very professional... name of Samantha. She's an expert at comforting the recently jilted, if you get my drift kid. After finding his fiancé in bed wit her boss, we just drop Samantha in Maddox's path, and she does her magic.

Ames saw by the look on Tomás' face that the drift had not been fully gotten.

"See... in the right setting," Ames tried again, "...Sam is hard to say no to, if you know what I mean. She's gonna try to get Maddox to a location of our choosing, and then get him into a compromising position. And..." He clicked an 'air-camera'. "I'll be there to take photos of that scene, too."

Now Tomás look worried, and Ames thought he knew why.

"Don't worry kid, the retainer you already paid me is gonna cover Samantha's per diem, too. Considering this girl's considerable hotness, her rates are pretty reasonable, really...you'll see. Plus, which, I got a unique arrangement with this broad. I'll broker the deal and you won't have to worry about breaking any additional State, Federal or Municipal laws."

"I think I understand," said Tomás. "She is a... a prostitute, yes?"

"Well...yeah. Technically speakin'...she is a *hooah*."

"It is illegal here for a man to be with a prostitute, right?" Tomás sounded hopeful. "Is it something that he could be fired from his job for? Because, that would be great."

"Jesus, kid!" Ames was taken aback. "Uhh... no, probably not...unless he was arrested for it. But it would cause major turmoil in his life fuh shuh. And even if he should happen to forgive Victoria for schtooping Rantz, when she gets a ganduh at the photos of Maddox puttin' it to Samantha, I'm guessing that would cement their split fuh good. That's the icing on yuh cake-of-revenge, kid."

"Yes, sir," said Tomás, "that's sounds good...for a start."

"Look kid," said Ames, squinking one eye, "I know I said that you don't owe me any explanation about why you're spending all this money to get back at this guy. But...just so's I understand yuh basic beef...didn't you say in an email that Maddox had plagiarized a story you wrote?"

"Ummmm," Tomás was hesitant, "yes sir...that's right."

"Yeah well," Ames sank back in his chair, "when I poked around on the Internet, I found some articles this guy wrote for the *National Enquirer*, and..."

Tomás gulped as Ames leaned forward once again and clasped his hands together on top of the desk.

"Given the location where this one particular story took place, I figured that must mean your 'stolen' story was about this... Choopa...doo-dah...thing also, huh?"

"Chupacabra?" Tomás helped.

"Yeah, that! So, I gotta axe you straight out, kid,"

"Yes, se... ir."

"Is this some kind of elaborate prank or something? Not that it would matter, as far as I'm concerned, but I gotta say, I am intrigued by the naytchuh of this particulah caypah. For the sake and safety of my client, of course, as well as for my own protection, don't you know. But also, most cases I do are so god-awful boring and same-same, I'm glad to have something out of the ordinary for a change, at least as far as my client and his motivations are concerned."

Tomás considered lying to him, but Ames was, for all practical purposes, a paid confidant, and besides, the whole sensational enchilada was about to be served up, steaming-hot, for the whole world to chow down upon anyway. So, he decided to divulge more, if not quite all.

"Yes Señor," said Tomás. "I took some photographs of the *Chupacabra*, as you tried to call him, and they just came out in the *Enquirer* today."

He reached under his shirt and retrieved the damp, crumpled tabloid, then offered it to the investigator, whose eyebrow arched involuntarily when he laid eyes on the images.

"And..." Tomás continued, "... Once again I find, as before, that they have been thieves."

"*CHEEZUSs*, kid!" Ames interrupted; the cigarette bouncing up and down in the corner of his mouth. "You got this thing chained up here! What the hell are you up to? I knew this had to be a scam. That's a great looking costume though, real Hollywood-quality stuff."

He held the front page up towards Tomás and pointed to the photos.

"What are these, *wings?*"

"It's not a costume," Tomás was firm.

"Really? Okay, well... Photoshop or whatever." He tossed the magazine across the desk, and it landed in front of Tomás.

"The Chupacabra is real, sir," Tomás stated flatly and defensively.

Ames leaned back in his chair again and crossed his flip-flopped feet on the desk.

"Okay, now I *am* confused. Look, you don't have tah lie tah *ME*, kid... I'm on yuah team, and I'm on the clock. But I'm still not comprendo-ing yuh angle on this Chupacoopa shit. *S'cuse my French.*"

"His name is Esteban Rey Lagarto," said Tomás, becoming irritated. "And he doesn't like the word Chupacabra."

"Woah! Okay kid," Ames sat up straight and held his hands up in surrender. "Take it easy. I got too nosy... I'm sorry."

Tomás suddenly realized that, although it had felt good to tell his secret to another human being, it might have been a mistake at this stage of the game. So, he used the leverage Ames provided by backing off, to reclaim the enigmatic high ground. The reality of the situation was too absurd for anyone to accept who hadn't seen it for themselves, and he knew that, even when the video he had made was available for all the world to see, it would still be met with skepticism by many. The ace up his sleeve was down in the toe of his shoe, but he couldn't put it into play until the time was right. Ames would have to learn the whole story along with the rest of the world.

"Like you said before," said Tomás with simulated courage. "You don't have to believe my story, Señor Ames, just help me to do what I hired you for, si?"

"Huh," Ames huffed, impressed. "Wow kid! You said a mouthful theh. Yuah wise beyond yuh eahs."

Just then, the computer monitor came to life behind Ames, the flashing SKYPE icon blinking for attention.

"*Mi hermano!*" Said Tomás as he shot out of his chair. "It's my brother! Can I...?"

"Yeah, shuh, here ya go."

The detective stood and offered his swivel-chair to Tomás, who spun it around and plopped down in front of the computer. Ames perched on top of the big desk behind him, peering over his shoulder. He wasn't comfortable about the man monitoring the conversation, but with the new issue of the *Enquirer* hitting the stands today, he had to warn his brother, and mendicants can't afford to be selective.

"Hola Téo!" he said excitedly. "I made it! I'm in Manhattan in the Private Investigator's office."

The look on Téo's face showed his excitement, but when he turned his head away to call for their parents, Tomás stopped him short.

"Wait, Téo! Don't call them yet. I will talk to Mama and Papa after. First, we gotta talk about...you know who?"

Téo nodded and moved his face closer to the camera.

Ames was fascinated by the matter-of-fact way the two teenagers spoke about the strange creature to which they, evidently, had exclusive access. The Private Investigator was clearly visible on the webcam sitting behind Tomás, and so Téo spoke in code about his encounters with the thing. The younger brother confessed to being terrified that the whatever-it-was was so unsettled by Tomás' absence, confused about the timing, and unsure about what his own role was supposed to be in the *revenge* scenario Tomás had described. Téo admitted that he wished his big brother had been there for assurance and protection, and thought that the subject of their discussion had only tolerated his presence out of respect for Tomás, and out of necessity and expediency in the getting of *his* claws into the flesh of John Maddox. Téo didn't know how to gauge the thing's temperament, but knew that *it* was impatient, and was restless to reveal itself to the village people, whom, Téo was fascinated to learn, the *thing* considered *its* royal subjects. The bottom line was that the creature's fervor for revenge was reaching a critical point.

"Tell him he must wait a little longer, Téo," Tomás instructed. "Explain that I am doing what I promised I would do, but that he must... MUST wait until I return. It's too dangerous to come out without me there. What about the T.V. reporters, Téo?"

"There haven't been any television people here yet, I don't think, but your story and pictures came out in the *Monterey El Norte* yesterday, and everybody in the village is freaking out again, only worse... *todo el mundo está muy loco.* Everybody started coming to the hotel this morning asking lots of questions, but Papa and Mama don't know what to say. They both know I have gone to see... to see it... and they're not happy about that... at all. But, they promised me they wouldn't tell anyone about the cave, or about what you are doing right now. Not until you say it's okay."

The Sanchez Hotel was centrally located in Santa Teresa, and the residents of the valley already considered it a place to hear local news, if there was any to hear. Tomás had figured that when his piece came out in the *Enquirer* and the *El Norte*, the village people would descend on his family's hotel looking for fuel to stoke the engine of their gossip machine. It was just how things worked in their little burg. What he did not tell Téo was his theory that the T.V. reporters, the press, the myth-hunters and the curiosity-seekers, and even the police might not come at all. At least not yet.

Ever since Señora Delgado's photo had been published, Tomás had been regularly monitoring the Internets for any and all au courant refer-ences to Chupacabri and was worried that the brand's ascendancy could be squandered before he could play his final card. The *Enquirer* articles had started the most recent round of reported sightings and late night talk show jokes, and then the double-murder of the Delgados had kept the ball rolling for a while, but now, Tomás was concerned that the fickle fabric of American pop culture was becoming saturated by all things

Chupa, and that the most recent rotation of the Phenom was nearly played out. The added elements of Santa Teresa's remoteness and puny size made him afraid his intentionally controversial new photos might be met with only bemused dismissal, as striking as they were.

That was, until the audiovisual presentation of an unshackled, uninhibited, and unequivocal *Esteban Rey Lagarto*, the King of the Santa Teresa Valley and Last of an Ancient Breed, appeared on every major news network, moving, talking, and excoriating Maddox as he accused the reporter of genocide.

After covering the pertinent points, the brothers agreed on a time to SKYPE the next day, and then Téo called their parents in so they could see for themselves that their boy was safe. When the call ended, Tomás spun back around to see Ames glaring at him in complete, slack-jawed disbelief.

"So..." the investigator said caustically, "... you've got your little brother convinced that this...this Ray Largo is real."

"Lagarto, sir," corrected Tomás. "*Rey Lagarto.*"

"Yeah, whatEVah."

"Mister Ames, sir," Tomás cajoled "I know it's hard to believe, and I wouldn't believe it myself if he had not come to my own bedroom window but, for some reason, *Rey Lagarto* chose **me** to be his emissary. He came to me, fearing that his own life was in danger, and I vowed to help him. He had nowhere else to go."

Tomás stood up and offered the chair back to Ames, who slid into it, then leaned back and put his hands behind his head.

"Wow, okay," Ames said, processing the absurdity. "so...you kinda had me runnin' a shadow operation here, huh kid?"

"Shadow?"

"This is some crazy fuckin' shit, kid... *pah-donay mwah*...crazy fuckin' stuff. I'm used to clients seeking revenge of one kind or another. It's my bread and buttah, really, and I accomodate them. Nothin' violent or overtly felonious mind you, though I've been known to push the envelope occasionally. Most of my cases involve obtaining photos or videos that end up in divorce courts or child custody cases between couples who hate each uthuh, but this one... heheh." Ames removed his fedora and wiped his forehead with the back of a hand. "I don't know what yuh end game is here... MIS-tuh Sanchez, but I'm already in it... three-grand deep... sooo..."

"John Maddox is a bad man," said Tomás adamantly. "He has lied, deceived and stolen, and then profited from the misery of the sins he committed. This is why I have promised *Rey Lagarto* that I would do what I could to bring misfortune to the life of this *pendejo*. The vengeance I seek will belong to the King."

"Okay, well," Ames chuckled, "so much for me not knowing the full story. That sounded like it was prolly it. But... whatevah you say, kid."

Of course Tomás had left things out, but the investigator hadn't balked or refused to continue with the case, so that was a good sign. Ames actually seemed excited about the possibilities, and it gave Tomás the confidence to make his next demand/request.

"All of these things," Tomás explained, "they have to happen soon, before Maddox's wedding, which is..."

"Yeah, I got it," Ames broke in, "the wedding is next week and you wanna drop all of this on him just before it, right? That's definitely gonna suck...for him, that is."

Tomás nodded.

"But I guess that's kind of the point, huh, kid?"

"And when it happens, Señor Ames, I will be there to deliver the message that his sins have come back upon him, and that *Rey Lagarto* is having his revenge!"

"Well, okay then." Ames turned away so Tomás wouldn't see him rolling his eyes. "I got no problem with you riding along with me when this goes down, but it's gonna take me a coupla days to set the rat trap. When it's time to put out the cheese, I gotta be able to reach you fast."

He stood and pushed past Tomás to a small, black safe that sat on the carpeted floor in the corner beside the computer table. The safe's door was ajar, and when Ames squatted down and opened it all the way,

Tomás' eye was immediately drawn to the shiny silver revolver on the top shelf. But the dick didn't touch the weapon. Instead, he removed a small, black flip-phone from a lidless shoebox on the bottom shelf and, standing up with a groan, handed it to Tomás as he shut the safe door with his foot. The phone was similar to the one on which he had recorded the, soon-to-be-famous, fifty-nine-second video clip.

"Here you go, kid," said Ames. "Disposable and loaded up with pre-paid minutes. Practically un-traceable, not that that matters much in this case, but hey, you never know. Hang on to it while yuh in the city, but first... FIRST... and I mean *right now*... before you do anything elts, you gotta get cleaned up. You got a place to stay, kid?"

Tomás tried out the flip-phone with a call to the youth hostel he had found in *The Times* earlier. The nice lady who answered said she only had one bed left tonight, but would hold it for him if he could get there in thirty minutes or less. It would put him a distance away from the rest of the action, but it was cheap, and it was available. After a quick review of plans with the investigator, Ames walked him downstairs to the sidewalk, pointed out the Subway Station in the next block, and waved to Tomás as he set out again onto the muggy, city streets.

Chapter 24

The New York Subway System was fascinating to the young man from Santa Teresa, and it would have been overwhelming if Tomás hadn't studied the routes in advance. He located the hostel on the Lower East Side without difficulty and checked in at the front desk with the nice receptionist he had spoken to on the phone, who took pity on him and let him register without an I.D. after he paid in cash.

"We have a little laundry room right here in the basement," said the woman, anticipating his request with a once over and a smile. "There's usually a box of laundry soap on top of the vending machine down there, doll. But, if you can't find any, come back and let me know."

Tomás went straight to the basement with the tokens she gave him for the washing machines and, with the exception of the boxer shorts he had on, everything went into the wash, including the canvas duffel bag, and, after extracting the two thumb-drives first, his only pair of (now) filthy tennis shoes. Feeling self-conscious in just his skivvies, he hurried down the hallways with a comical gait and peeked around corners until he tracked down his bunkroom.

The room was clean and it smelled nice, but it was a tiny space for six grown men, and as he entered, he tipped his head to his bunkmates and climbed up into the only unclaimed bed, remembering the funny line his father used about a room being barely big enough to change your mind in, let alone your clothes. It wasn't how his father had said it, but thinking about home made him smile. His roomies were three French boys, all around twenty years old, and all of whom spoke passable English; one Japanese kid, who didn't speak much at all; and an older man who was grizzled around the muzzle and looked to Tomás like he might be a homeless person on furlough from the streets for the night.

Being modest, Tomás was happy to hide on the top bunk while he waited for his clothes, and he lay on his stomach, looking over the edge and listening to the conversations of his roommates as they came and went, shyly introducing himself to them if they made eye contact. He alternately chatted and napped as he waited, but his modesty didn't stop him from making several more sub rosa excursions to check on his duffel and tennis shoes, out of fear that his only possessions would be stolen. The clothes took three cycles in the old machine before they were dry, but when it was done, he packed his warm clothes into the hot duffel bag, being careful to not burn his fingers on the hot, metal zipper, then went back upstairs to the communal restroom and took his first shower since the day he had left home, scrubbing vigorously to remove all of the Funk (and half of the Wagnall's in the process).

The micro-naps, followed by the cooling shower, had him feeling rejuvenated, so Tomás decided to get a proper look at the magnificent metropolis he had come so far, and braved so many travails, to see. While he was dressing to leave, the old man was sitting up cross-legged in a lower bunk and watching him unabashedly, which made Tomás nervous, and so, after putting the little flip-phone in his front pocket, he turned away from the man to stash his wad of money.

"You watch yourself in this city, boy," the old man cautioned from behind. "Don't ever put your cash in your pockets. I usually tuck mine here, in my bikini area."

When Tomás turned back around, the old-timer was motioning to his own crotch.

—— m ——

Tomás stepped onto the sidewalk again and was re-inserted into a movie scene once more as the sights and sounds of Manhattan enveloped him in their urban tableau. After strolling through China Town and Little Italy, he then hiked north on Broadway, past Washington Square and New York University, the Empire State Building and other iconic landmarks he knew very well and was excited to see cathode-ray and pixel-free.

The late afternoon sun cast a golden glow upon the facades of the western-facing buildings and, aided by the contrasting shadows, intensified and enhanced the dramatic contours of all exposed surfaces. The effect on Tomás was an even stronger sensation that he was in a movie, or in a television show or, even better, in a great, classic novel set in this renowned "Capital of the World".

At half-past seven o'clock, he was sitting by himself on a long bench opposite the counter in a tiny pizza joint called "**JOHN's**", and, just as he had taken his first big bite of a folded-up slice, he felt the flip-phone *buzzz* in his pocket. He plopped the slice onto the flimsy paper plate on the bench beside him and, with greasy fingers, nearly dropped the phone fumbling to open it.

"Yo kid, it's time!" Ames voice was enthusiastic. "My guy at the Carlyle texted me that Victoria and Rantz just came in separately. I'm callin' Samantha right after I hang up wit you, then I'm gonna drive to the hotel. How fast can you get to my office?"

Tomás had walked so far north that he was now closer to the Carlyle Hotel than he was to Ames' office, so the Private Eye picked him up in mid-town. When he climbed into the passenger seat of the white mini-van, he saw Ames had changed into a navy blue blazer with khaki pants and a pale peach dress shirt with no tie. They greeted each other as the van peeled away from the curb, and as they sped through Central Park toward the Upper East Side, the investigator updated his client and prepared him for the night's proceedings.

"This is it, kid," Ames announced. "I started makin' calls right after you left my office, and everything just fell right into place, perfect. So we can pull this thing off tonight...like right freakin' NOW!"

He laid out the itinerary as they drove, and Tomás was once again impressed by the man's savvy thoroughness. Ames had some sort of arrangement with the owner of a hair salon across the street from the Carlyle Hotel, wherein the proprietor would surrender his parking space whenever Ames needed it for surveillance. The space was not directly adjacent to the hotel's entrance, but a few spaces down, which gave the spy a perfect view of the main doors while maintaining a degree of anonymity. It was clear to Tomás that Ames probably used this fancy hotel on at least a semi-regular basis for just this sort of operation.

With an enroute call to the salon, the Beauty Operator was already waiting in his car when they arrived, and he pulled out of the magic parking space just as they they pulled up. While Ames maneuvered into the space, Tomás leaned forward in his seat and craned his neck to get a look at the classic, thirty-five story building looming above them, the top twelve floors of which stood majestically un-opposed above the skyline of the opulent Upper East Side. The architecture reminded Tomás of the Empire State Building without its spire and antennae, and as his eyes took it all in, a sharp *RAP-RAP-RAP* on the passenger window startled him out of his trance.

His head whipped around, and he was face-to-face with the most beautiful woman he had laid eyes on in his sixteen years on planet Earth. Santa Teresa had a couple of cute, older girls, who had always intimidated Tomás into silence whenever they were around, but they didn't compare to this woman. From close range, he was overcome by the beauty of her light brown eyes and medium complexion, set off with chestnut-brown, shoulder length hair, and, completely against his will, his eyes travelled down and took a good, long look at celestial curves packed into a tight, red cocktail dress. BuhBAYum!

Tomás had seen the rail-straight, little-boy bodies of catwalk-prowling female models on the covers of high fashion journals in magazine racks in Torreón & Durango, but this woman's figure was nothing like theirs, and he was unconscious of his mouth standing agape. She held in her hand a small, shiny, gold pocketbook and, when she tapped a corner of it against the windowpane, Tomás looked up to see her glaring at him and pointing up to her face, which was pursed in a glower. Through the closed window, and above the loud blast of the van's air conditioner, he heard her say,

"Did you get a good look, kid?"

The voluptuous vision of femininity looked past Tomás with a peeved expression and raised a thumb at Ames, who popped open the automatic door locks with a CLICK. As she slid the side door open and slithered into the back seat, the investigator put a hand on Tomás' shoulder and looked at him with a pleased expression on his face.

"Kid," he said, "This... is Samantha. Sam... this is your benefactor for the evening, my client, *Tomás Sanch...*"

A sudden jerk from the head of Tomás stopped Ames in mid-word. He saw the alarm on the teen's face and, turning to the woman, he winked and said,

"It's Tomás...just *Tomás.*"

Investigator and escort had a brief, non-verbal parley that Tomás guessed was about his young age.

"Brent..." She asked, now eyeballing Tomás. "What are you getting me into here?"

"Don't worry, Sam, the kid's all right. He just wants to ride along. Right, kid? Yuh cool, ain'tcha?"

With a nod, Tomás confirmed that he was, indeed, cool, and then turned in his seat to give the stunning ball of sexiness an embarrassed smirk. As Ames laid out the plan for them both, Tomás found that he couldn't look directly in the woman's eyes, but he continued to steal glances at her other parts when he thought he could get away with it. She pretended not to notice.

"Okay, without getting too technical," Ames was all business now, "I will tell you that I sent a text to John Maddox which, on his phone, looks like it was sent by his fiancé. As far as he knows, Victoria is inviting him for one last romantic rendezvous at The Carlyle before they begin their final week as un-married people. At the end, I added:

Don't call back or text. Just come to room 1907 at 8:00 and I'll be waiting for you, wearing something special. Don't go to the front desk. Just go to the Concierge and ask for Freddie. Tell him your name is St. Tomas and he'll give you the key-card.

"I put that little joke in there for you, kid," Ames said, acknowledging the sly grin on Tomás' mug. "You see, kid, the Carlyle ain't just a hotel. They got residential suites too, and room *1907* is actually Ben Rantz's apahtment. Well, one of 'em. He keeps this one for his rendezvous with, who knows how many women. Since I started trackin' 'em, these two have been like clockwork. They do *'it'* every other weeknight at eight-o'clock and, when they finish up with the whoopee, they leave separately and go home to their 'official' partners."

"You got quite a cast of characters assembled here, Shoe," said Samantha from the back seat. "So, where do I come in?"

Tomás stared at her perfect lips as she spoke, and he could feel the blood abandoning his brain to reapportion itself elsewhere in his body.

"Well, Mon Cheri," Ames chortled, "Maddox is gonna leave this hotel in a dazed, pissed-off, confused, and vulnerable state. He'll be on foot, but we got wheels. If he doesn't seek out a bar between here and his apartment, and I'll bet dollars to donits he does, but if he don't, then we just drop you in his path and let you work yuh magic. It would be great if you could get him into our room here, Sam, but I got our regular place in Mid-town set up and ready to go also. I'll get inside the room first, whichever spot works out, and then it's up to you. You just do your stuff, and I'll get the goods."

The woman removed a compact case from her pocketbook and sat back in the car seat with her thighs together and fuck-me-pumps spread slightly apart. As she studied her flawless face in the little mirror, Tomás took the opportunity to steal a sidelong goggle at her bare knees, which were peeking out from under the hem of her tight dress.

"Well, this one's going to be interesting," said the woman. "It's got a pursue and capture deal to it, huh? Not like most of the calls I get from you, Brent.

Tomás was struck by the irony of the comment.

"By the way," Samantha added, "Amy Jo really liked you and says you should call her again soon."

Ames shot her a not-in-front-of-the-kid look, followed by an apologetic glance at Tomás.

"Did you bring the rig, Sam?" the investigator changed the subject

Samantha reached up to the shoulder strap of her dress and turned it inside out, exposing a tiny camera and microphone sewn to the fabric. Tomás saw a single wire coming out of the little device that turned south and disappeared along the inside seam of her dress.

"And the purse?" Ames asked.

Samantha opened her gold clutch to reveal a small, black box inside with a wire running to a camera mounted in one end of the pocketbook. Tomás thought it was a clever design, with the camera lens completely hidden on all but one, narrow end of the purse, where it was practically invisible inside the folds.

"As you can see," Samantha said, looking at Tomás as she closed the pocketbook, "Brent has lots of fun gadgets, and he and I use 'em a lot."

"Yeah, kid," Ames interjected, "Some of our best work has been admitted into evidence by some of the top Family-Court Judges in New York. And, this woman," he gestured to Samantha, "this woman is the best, kid. I'm tellin' ya...one of a kind, this guhl."

Not knowing how to respond to the endorsement, Tomás kept silent but nodded in hearty agreement as Samantha adjusted the strap of her dress to make sure the camera was properly positioned. Ames reached under the collar of his shirt and pulled out a wire with an earpiece at-tached, which he jammed into on ear.

"I'm glad you got here quick, Sam," said the Private Eye. "It shouldn't be much longuh. Once Maddox walks in on them, I don't foresee a pro-tracted love-fest goin' on up theh. And it's Rantz's place, so he won't be the one who comes stormin' outa these doors."

Just as the investigator said the words, a marimba ringtone sounded in his pocket, and he pulled out a smart-phone and looked at the screen.

"'BAM!!'" boomed Ames, which made Tomás jump again. "The Eagle has landed, boys and girls. This is it!"

He touched the screen with a finger, then held the phone up to his ear.

"Yeah, Mary. What's up?...okay...right.... Okay, hit me back when he's on his way down, sweet-haht."

He touched the screen again.

"At this moment," said Ames, "Maddox and Victoria are in a heated conversation at the Nineteenth floor elevatuhs. That was the housekeep-er. She's gonna tell me when he's on his way down, then we'll put in our utility player, here."

He crooked a thumb at Samantha, then began typing on the phone's screen with his thumbs.

"Now I'm telling Freddie, the Concierge, to let me know when Maddox hits the lobby."

Samantha lifted her compact case to check her face one last time, and Tomás was happy to have yet another chance to spy. The Mediterranean beauty looked in the mirror, but, finding no flaw, only smiled at her reflection and snapped the compact shut, then returned it to her shiny pocketbook.

The incongruous, under-cover-trio sat in silence and waited for Freddie's text. Although Ames had given him firm instructions to stay in the van when the action began, Tomás felt an electric, nervous thrill at being privy to the details of a clandestine operation that was about to reach its zenith, and the entire scenario brought back the familiar, yet surreal, Movie/T.V. sensation once more. Only, this time, he was part of the action... sort of.

The smart phone sounded again, but with a more urgent sounding ringtone.

"Well, well. Bemelmans it is then," said Ames, reading the text. "And, I just happen to have the bartender's cell number. Emily is a troopah. Voted Top Bartender in Manhattan two years runnin'. Also holds the unofficial 'World's Worst Lesbian' title due to her walks on the bi-side. Emily'll keep him theh till you can make yuh move, Sam."

The sub-contracted escort exited the van and hurried off across the street, adjusting her form-fitting dress as she went. As the investigator typed a text to the bartender, he explained to Tomás that Maddox had come off the elevator into the Lobby, and then gone directly into the Carlyle's vaunted watering hole, Bemelmans Bar. After sending the text, he reached back behind the driver's seat and produced a small, black bag with a long strap, which he slung over his shoulder. He turned off the engine and pocketed the keys, then looked at Tomás.

"I'm going in, kid. If Maddox starts to leave the hotel, I'll let you know with a text."

Ames leaned over Tomás, opened the glove compartment in front of him, and removed what looked like a flat-screen monitor the size and shape of a small Children's book. He touched a button and the screen lit up, and he handed the device to Tomás.

"More tools of the trade," he said with a grin.

Tomás had read about this particular new tablet on techno-blogs and was excited to be holding one in his hands. After handing Tomás a pair of ear buds, Ames gave a quick, tutorial and showed the teenager a screen from which he could switch back and forth, from Samantha's dress-cam, to the camera in her pocketbook, to the camera in Ames' own little black bag.

"When he does come out, eventually," Ames said sternly, "you gotta keep yuh head down, kid. If he sees you at this point, the whole deal might blow up on us before we have all the dirt we need. Comprendo?"

Tomás gave the thumbs-up and stuck the buds in his ears as Ames got out of the van and crossed the street. There were three camera-icons on the device's screen and, when he touched one, the icon zoomed out and filled the monitor with a live, streaming picture of Bemelmans as seen from the in-action dress-strap cam. Tomás smiled and watched the image on the screen bounce sultrily as Samantha sashayed through the bar.

The elegantly hip lounge didn't look like any bar Tomás had ever seen, but more like an expensive, ritzy restaurant with all of the patrons dressed very nicely and sitting in couples at the bar, or in foursomes at small tables, or in high-backed, upholstered seats along the wall, listening to the jazz band that he could hear paying in his earbuds. He watched as Samantha targeted Maddox at the bar and installed herself in an empty chair beside him and, for the next hour, Tomás played technical director of a Telenovela, switching back and forth from camera to camera and wiping sweat from his brow so it wouldn't drip on the screen. He was accustomed to the heat of Mexican summers but, even with the windows of the van open, the muggy, breezeless air made him wish Ames had left the engine running so he could have the air-conditioning while he waited.

With rapt attention, he watched and listened to the action inside as the call girl and the lady bartender played Maddox like a finely tuned Stradivarius. The cocktail glasses were never empty, and Samantha said just the things that Maddox, or any man who had just found his fiancé *in flagrante delicto* with another, would want to hear from an attractive, flirtatious woman.

Ames had found a seat at a nearby table with a good view of the couple and, from the investigator's bag-cam, Tomás could better read Samantha's subtle, yet unmistakable body language. The woman was quite adept in the art of seduction, and Maddox was obviously already caught in a well-designed trap, and had no inkling of the forces at play on and around him. The reporter had already been softened by the emotional blow of finding his cheating, blonde fiancé upstairs with her boss, and now this buxom brunette down at ground level had her hooks in him and was leading him down a route from which any escape was becoming less likely with every shot of whiskey and each gaze into her gorgeous eyes. Samantha was quite an actress, thought Tomás, and he quivered at the thought of what other talents she must surely possess.

Several times while watching this passion play out, Tomás heard the voice of Ames whispering to him in his ear.

"...*you gettin' this, kid? Nice one, Sam... Look at that!...Wow!...That's my girl.*"

By 11:00 p.m. the hook was set and the fish had given up any trace of resistance. When Tomás heard Samantha seductively announce that she was '...*staying upstairs tonight, if he wanted to come up for a bit*', Tomás switched over to Ames' camera, but saw only a black screen. Just then, the ear buds crackled to life.

"Okay, kid," said Ames, "I'm going up. It's radio-silence from here on. You just stay put and wait for my text. I got no idea how long it'll take but, from the look of things, I'd say not long."

Although the sun was long gone, the night was nearly as hot and every bit as humid as the day had been. Tomás was on pins and needles as the minutes dragged by, and he waited for a buzz or a beep from the cell-phone he held in his sweaty hand, and kept his grapes peeled and fixed on the hotel entrance. Now, all three cameras showed only black, but he left the tablet-device on and checked it every so often, just in case.

—⟋⟋⟍—

The radio silence gave Tomás a chance to reflect on all that had happened around him, and to him, in the last few months. From the start, he thought it outrageous and unreal that he was involved in such a bizarre anomaly, and had at times felt as if he were watching himself from outside of his body.

Beginning with the surreal encounter beside his Abuela's chicken-shack, the whole affair seemed like it should have happened to someone else and, sometimes, he wished it *had* happened to someone else; someone older or more qualified, and thus better able to deal with everything Tomás had dealt with so far. His life, post-revelation, had nevertheless been an adventure unlike anything he could have possibly imagined. To have such a relationship with a creature that he had known only as a frightening Children's Fable until he met that fable face to face, was life-altering in itself, but, because of that relationship, and the profound empathy that he had developed for the ancient race that had come to a sudden and tragic end on the hood of John Maddox's rental car, Tomás had adopted *Rey Lagarto's* crusade for revenge as his own. In his mind and heart, Tomás was now more than just an advocate for the Lizard King; the pair were partners and of one mind, possessed by a single objective.

He had only arrived in Manhattan this morning, but the operation had taken off at an accelerated pace and, as he sat sweating in the van, calculating the broiling point of the human brain and struggling to stay sharp through the haze of heat, it gradually dawned on him. If Ames were to text him now, to confirm that he had the photos and video of Maddox and Samantha in bed, then Tomás had all of the ammunition he needed to confront the reporter right here and now. He could just waltz right up to Maddox and inform the *pendejo* that he was on the shit-list of a very scary-ass Chupacabra, and that, although his slutty fiancé had helped their cause considerably, the Santa Teresa Alliance had him dead in their sights and were about to seriously eff-up his apple cart.

His adrenaline levels began to escalate as he thought about the time his father had taken him to *los Corrida de Toros* in Guadalajara, where a young Tomás had watched *los Picadores y Banderilleros* inflict many severe wounds on a brave bull, before the Matador, in the final *Faena*, delivered the *estocada* between the shoulder blades of the staggering beast. John Maddox's love life was already severely wounded and losing blood fast, and Tomás figured that, after tonight's proceedings, the wedding would surely be called off. Then, when the reporter was at his lowest and crawling on his belly, Tomás would release the video to CNN, and hopefully, coerce Maddox into returning to Santa Teresa, where *Rey Lagarto* himself could deliver the final *descabello*. Only then would the *Corrida* be truly complete, and the fatwa against Maddox fulfilled.

Tomás was hesitant to defy Ames' command to stay in the van, but when he remembered that he had paid the man three thousand dollars, making himself the substantive boss, he removed the ear buds, wrapped them around the tablet, stuck it underneath the seat, and then stepped out onto the sidewalk. After pressing the lock button, he slammed the door shut and walked around the rear of the van but, instead of paying attention to the traffic, he was rehearsing what he would say to Maddox and didn't see the the bicycle rider, who was speeding silently down the wrong side of the dark street.

The rider didn't see him either, until Tomás stepped out from behind the vehicle and, just as the bike's front wheel struck Tomás hard in the right leg, the cyclist hit his front brakes, slowing the bike but not the rider, who was launched by the forward momentum over the handlebars and into the air. As Tomás fell backwards onto the pavement with the bicycle on top of him, the dismounted rider flew overhead, spewing a stream of obscenities both before and after he the pavement.

In the immediate aftermath of the collision, the casualties' both exhaled audible groans. Tomás held his knee to his chest, rocking back and forth on the hot asphalt with his eyes clinched tight and, when the cyclist rose to his feet and began to assess his own injuries, Tomás rolled onto an elbow and moaned,

"I am sorry, sir. I wasn't looking."

The man continued to grumble obscenities as he picked up the damaged bike and limped with it to the opposite curb, pulling the bicycle out of the street, but, just when Tomás was about to attempt standing, the bicyclist stopped grumbling and shot an arm out, pointing.

"Look out, dude!" yelled the man as a Yellow Cab came barreling down on them from the east end of the street.

"Get Up! Get BACK!!"

The Taxi honked and swerved, but never actually slowed down as Tomás scrambled to safety behind the van, pulling himself up using the vehicle's bumper and rear-door handles. He looked across the street at the injured rider, who had stopped cursing, but was now giving a stern lecture on pedestrian safety and responsibility as Tomás weakly repeated his apologies and examined his own, badly injured knee, which had already soaked his torn jeans with fresh, crimson blood.

"Chinga tu...." Tomás chuffed.

What had been a trickle of adrenaline was now a gusher, and he started to regain his senses as it washed away the detritus of his trauma. Maddox's face flashed in his mind and, combined with the pain and anger of being run over, the vision helped revive the comforting malevolence he felt for the reporter. He would confront Maddox, and he would do it *now*.

His leg hurt badly, and as he started out across the street, he quickly discovered that he couldn't put his full weight on it without considerable pain. There was also the sensation of a warm, wet trickle streaming down his face from a cut on his right eyebrow and he dabbed at the bloody dribble with his fingers. By the time he reached the sidewalk in front of the hotel, the bicyclist was already back on his bike and pedaling away from the scene, still lecturing to Tomás, who checked his phone to see that, during the mêlée in the street, he had missed the crucial, two-word text. **--GOT IT!!!--**

Chapter 25

Under a canopied awning, the entrance to the Carlyle Hotel consisted of two wooden doors flanking a center, revolving, glass door. At eye-level in the upper panel of both wooden doors was a single windowpane with little curtains and, avoiding eye contact with the uniformed door-man who was standing guard at the curb, Tomás limped to the nearest window and peered through the jalousie.

His eyes were instantly drawn to the beautiful, polished marble floors and, as he was admiring them, their shiny surface reflected the upside down figure of Maddox walking across the lobby towards him. Tomás took a couple of steps back from the window and pulled himself to his full height, bracing for battle, but when the unsteady reporter reached the front, he had difficulty navigating the exit, thrice banging into the edge of the revolving door before he finally made it outside. There was a glassy, distant look in Maddox's eyes and he took no notice whatsoever as he brushed past Tomás and started down the sidewalk toward Central Park.

Falling in step alongside the man, Tomás wordlessly vied for his attention as they walked, waving his arms and trying to lean into Maddox's blurred line of vision, but it wasn't working. So, he stepped directly into Maddox's path, forcing him to stop and meet his gaze.

"John Maddox!!," he said commandingly.

"Do I know you?" Maddox asked, his swollen eyelids lifting sluggishly as it dawned on him. "Hey, yeah! Tomas. What the hell are you doing here?"

The initial smile on Maddox's lips rapidly turned to a nervous smirk as he suddenly sensed he was being ambushed. He looked around to see if the teenager was alone, and Tomás, seeing the uneasiness in the man's demeanor, felt a rush of confidence and launched into his rehearsed diatribe.

"I am here for YOU, Señor Maddox," said Tomás, pointing a finger. "You have wronged me and you have wronged my village. I have come to you as the messenger of *Rey Lagarto,* whose Queen and..."

"Whoa, Whoa!" Maddox cut him off. "Slow down a second...what are you saying to me? This is about the *Enquirer* story, right?"

Perturbed by the interruption, Tomás picked up where he had left off.

"...messenger of *Rey Lagarto,* whose Queen and only child you killed and left to die in..."

"Hold on, Tomás," the reporter stopped him again. "I don't understand what you're saying. I know you're mad about the story that I wrote, but..."

"The story that *I* wrote, *sir.*" Tomás was acerbic. "I WROTE that story. And I was stupid to let you read it. It was **my** story, Señor Juan!"

"Look, Tomás, your argument is with the *Enquirer's* legal department, not with me. They advised me to let them handle this."

"Oh, I tried that sir," Tomás spat back sarcastically. "And how far do you think I got with that? Not very far, I can tell you."

Maddox was tired, very drunk, and very recently cheated upon. His guard was down, and he was in no ways prepared for the attack as he fumbled for words, trying to collect his thoughts into a coherent defense.

"Just... wait a second," he said, squeezing his eyes tightly shut. "You were with me when I interviewed all those people. You just used my sources. Your little story was bound to be similar to mine."

The condescending comment rankled Tomás, who had already had this argument with the reporter and was ready for his bullshit justifications.

"You used several exact sentences from my 'little story', Señor Juan. Even the angle of your story was taken from what you read in mine."

Tomás stopped himself and drew a deep breath as looked up into the night sky. This was not how he had wanted the encounter to go down. They had been over this contentious point many times in the emails, and Tomás had intended to put the plagiarism accusations on the back burner for now. The timing of his master plan was critical, and he was here to first deal with the more urgent matter of *Rey Lagarto*'s missive.

"Señor Maddox" said Tomás, trying again. "I have come here on behalf of the village of Santa Teresa, and as the emissary of *Esteban Rey Lagarto*, whose Queen and unborn child you ran over with your car and left to die in the dirt of the Santa Teresa caldera."

Maddox said nothing but joggled his head back and forth in an attempt to shake out the last few martinis and make room for the new crazy shit that was now being shoveled in.

"Ohhh-Kayyy..." Croaked the teetering sot. "Is this about the talking Chupacabra? I haven't forgotten about that crap, you know. You noticed that I left that part out of my story?"

"Si," answered Tomás. "I left it out of mine also...because I was afraid. I was afraid of what would happen to me, and... to *him*. But I'm not afraid anymore, SEÑOR JUAN." He drew the reporter's name out with scalding rancor. "Soon, sir... the whole world will know that *you* have put an end to *la Raza Lagarto* and have left their Kingdom in wreck & ruin, and their King to live out his remaining life alone as the last of his kind."

"Wait," said Maddox, closing his eyes again. "I did hit something down in the crater, just before I left Santa Teresa. How did you know that?"

"Oh, I know *all* of the things, Señor. You left death behind you, and then you lied and deceived others. And now..." Tomás' voice rang with rage, "...NOW, it's time for you to PAY!!"

As he said the words, the shiny silver revolver he had seen in Brent Ames safe flashed in Tomás' head, and he imagined squeezing the big grip tightly in his hands as he pointed an accusing finger at Maddox.

"It is time for the score to be settled... *sir.*"

Maddox began to sober up from the absurdity of the teenager's words, and he tried to regain his composure, studying the face of the teenager and trying to focus on just one pair of his accuser's eyes.

"What do you mean 'the whole world will know'?" asked Maddox? "What have you done, Tomás?"

"I am sorry to hear about your fiancé, señor," said Tomás with a malicious grin. "Your girlfriend, Victoria. It is too bad for you and her, eh?"

"What the hell?" Maddox sputtered. "How do you...,"

"She turned out to be no good, sí?" Tomás twisted the knife. "Maybe there won 't be a wedding after all........ **John.**"

"HEY, what the...?" Maddox was now fully agitated. "How in the... How in the FUCK do you know anyth..."

The savage temperament of *Lagarto* suddenly possessed Tomás and he felt himself being pulled across a line that the boy from Santa Teresa would never have crossed on his own. He dug his claws in deeper.

"Yes, Señor Juan," he taunted, "I know all about Victoria and Ben Rantz. We have pictures of them in bed together. Not only that..." Tomás sank his fangs in now. "We have pictures of you and that woman in the hotel room just now."

"*WE?*" Maddox shot back. "Who the hell is *we?* What the hell is going on here? WHY ARE YOU DOING THIS?"

It was the question, stated clearly and specifically, that Tomás had been waiting to hear. He mustered as much grit and gravitas as his voice could convey, and then hit the murderer with a succinct indictment.

"John Maddox, you have destroyed an ancient and noble race by killing the Queen of, what you call, '*Chupacabra*'."

Maddox stared blankly, his mouth agape.

"She was the last *Lagarto* female," explained Tomás, "and you ran her down and left her to die with the child she carried in her belly. Then, you sped away from Santa Teresa in your smashed up car."

"Oh...my...god," muttered the befuddled reporter. "This is just...this just can NOT be HAPPENING!"

"And," Tomás added, "*Añadir al insulto,* you stole my story. A story about the very creatures you *MURDERED!*"

"Are you *CRAZY?*" Maddox asked. "You're crazy!"

"No, Señor," Tomás answered gravely. "Everything I have said is true."

Maddox's pickled brain began to grasp that, whether Tomás was mentally unstable or not, and whether or not the teenager had an angry reptilian accomplice, be it Chupacabran or otherwise---*someone* was out to get him!

It was now after midnight and the escalating kerfuffle in front the most prestigious hotel on the high-rent Upper East Side had garnered unwanted attention from hotel employees and passersby alike. As the pair of unlikely combatants yelled nonsensical accusations at each other, the small coterie of witnesses looked on, including a uniformed Carlyle Hotel security guard who had joined the doorman and was speaking into a cell phone he held to his ear.

The tipsy and exhausted reporter was reeling from the one-two punch of being cheated upon and lied to by his fiancé (again), and the realization that he had somehow been set up to discover the infidelity. Though he wasn't entirely surprised to learn of Victoria's continuing affair, he did love the girl and was deeply hurt and becoming angrier by the second. The teenager's relentless rant of '*Rey Lagarto*-THIS, and *Rey Lagarto*-THAT' rankled and annoyed Maddox's booze-addled consciousness with every repetition, and his frustration was reaching a peak when he spotted two blue-uniformed NYPD officers approaching from behind Tomás. Just as one of them reached to grab the teen accuser by the arms, Maddox slur-yelled,

"So, this is the Chupacabra doing all of this to me, huh?"

The drunken reporter pointed an index finger at Tomás and simulated firing a gun by cocking his thumb up and down.

"OKAY THEN!" spat Maddox. "I'll go BACK to your stupid fucking village and I **WILL** bust a **CAP** in this fucking **RAY** motherfucker and I'lllll finish 'em 'ALL off...furrr **GOOD!!**"

As the policemen pulled Tomás backwards by the arms, a maniacal laugh erupted from Maddox's throat that surprised even him. One of the officers spun the teenager around for a face-to-face question and answer.

"Yo, kid," said the officer. "What's going on with all the yellin', huh?"

Tomás was at eye-level with the shiny, gold name badge pinned to the chest of the tall patrolman:

B.L. SMITH

The officer put a hand up to press the button of the radio transmitter at his shoulder, and Tomás saw the colorful tattoo of a rampaging T-Rex on the back of the man's wrist.

"933--Disturbance in fronta the Cah-lyle--{crackle}--Will Advise--"

In his impetuous decision to confront Maddox here and now, Tomás hadn't considered that this might not be the best place to do it, and that it might bring the police. Now, the entire operation was in jeopardy. He felt foolish and terrified and made a quick decision to stay mum and not risk exposing his illegal-alien status by attempting an explanation. Officer Smith continued to question him, while his partner, Officer Brenon, was doing the same a few yards away with the well-dressed, but disheveled Maddox, whom everyone on the scene had just heard yelling death threats.

"What's all this about, sir?" Officer Brenon asked Maddox. "Did I hear you threaten to bust a cap in another individual just now, sir?"

With a moan and a sigh, Maddox clapped both hands to his head in exasperation, then thrust them out in front of him with the palms up in a pleading gesture.

"Okay, wait a second, Officer...wait...wait a minute. This is crazy; I barely know this kid. That other thing I said was a joke. The thing about...shooting someone? Just jokes, oss... ovfizzer."

"It didn't sound like a joke when you were shouting about harming another individual, sir."

"Yeah, well this kid has some crazy story about...ummm... well... it doesn't matter what it's about. I think he's trying to extort money from me or zumthing."

The patrolman looked over to where his partner was still questioning Tomás, then turned back to Maddox and said,

"Stay right here while I speak with the other individual over there, sir. Do not move from this spot."

As officers Brenon and Smith conferred, Brent Ames walked through the revolving door and saw what was going on. He spoke briefly to the doorman and security guard before approaching the policemen.

"Excuse me, sir," said Officer Smith, putting an arm out to stop him. "Hold it there. Do you know either of these particular individuals, sir?"

Ames held up a hand and asked for permission to reach into his jacket for his Private Investigator's license and badge. After a quick look, they handed them back.

"What is your specific involvement with these individuals, sir?" asked Officer Brenon.

Ames smiled and said "This is one of my clients, officers. And, I think this other gentleman is confused. Look at him...he can barely stand. He's obviously stone-drunk."

Both patrolmen looked over at Maddox, who was swaying on his feet slightly and mumbling to himself.

"A case of mistaken identity, most likely," said the investigator. "I think my client was just defending himself."

The gumshoe's intercession had diffused the squabble and, when the squabblers' themselves had calmed down a bit, the police made it clear that they were not in the mood for more paperwork tonight, and told both parties that if they would agree to not press charges against each other, they would all be free to leave... in opposite directions. After putting Maddox into a taxi, the police told Tomás and Ames to clear off, and investigator and client hurried down the street to the van, then pulled away from the Carlyle very slowly.

"So, I guess you did it, huh kid?"

"Yes, Mister Ames," answered Tomás, holding a wad of paper towels onto his bleeding knee. "I told him everything... well... almost everything."

"And just what *is* the 'almost' part, kid?" Ames shot a hard look at Tomás. "Forget what I said earlier about that 'Not-needing-to-know', crap. That shit is now nullified. D'ya wanna know *WHY*?"

"Yes, sir," Tomás answered meekly.

"Glad you asked! Two reasons. For one, I stuck my neck WAY out for you with those cops just now, that's why. You know, most of the stuff I'm doing for you ain't completely legal. Actually, it's not even a little bit legal, especially the cell phone hack. We're just lucky that fucker was so drunk that the cops didn't take him too seriously. *S'cuse my French.*"

"What is the other reason?" Tomás asked.

"The other reason is because this Choopadoopra crap is stahtin' to freak my shit. I mean, I'm starting to think you really believe that you've spoken with this lizard thing." He fixed a glare at Tomás and asked, "So, hows about you let me in on the rest of your little secret now, HUH??""

The man drove with his left hand, and he leaned toward Tomás, his gaze staying locked onto the teenager, who nervously tried to direct Ames' attention back to the traffic out the front windshield while he considered his response.

"Your office, Señor Ames. Let's go to your office, and I'll show you."

—m—

As Tomás opened the passenger door and stepped onto the concrete floor of the dimly lit garage on the ground level of Ames' building, he smelled the sweet, spicy aroma of curry once again, wafting through from the Pakistani restaurant on the other side of the wall. The little parking-bunker was little more-than a single-car width space nestled behind the restaurant and, apart from the large, metal, remote controlled roll-up door, there was no means of egress other than a narrow, wooden staircase that disappeared into the ceiling at the far, back corner of the garage.

Limping up the stairs behind the gimping private eye, Tomás found it curious that there was no exit on the second floor landing, which meant that the garage was only accessible from the big, rolling door and the third floor landing, where Ames' office was. His leg had stopped bleeding now, but the climb was painful, and when the close stairwell finally ended, Ames' clandestine proclivity was evident once more, as the little staircase opened not into the third floor hallway, or even inside of the office itself, but into a tiny, cedar-paneled closet behind the investigator's office. After following Ames into the closet and through the bedroom, Tomás went straight to the chair in front of the computer, removed one of his Chucks and pulled out a compressed wad of paper towels, then unwrapped it and stuck the flash drive into the USB port. While the boring little, black and white hourglass turned round and round, Ames related his own, successful photo session.

"It was great, kid," he said delightedly. "Some of my best work. Exquisite subject to work with a' course. That girl is amazing. Knows how to give me great angles."

Tomás was unable to think of a response and kept his eyes on the monitor, wishing the video would hurry and load.

"You probably missed the key-card hand-off in the lobby," Ames said boastfully. "When I knew she had him hooked, I followed 'em to the Lobby and slipped her a key card just as they were gettin' onto the eluvaytahs. Then, I hoofed it up the stairs and, while she had him pinned up against the wall down the hallway with her tongue down his throat and one leg wrapped around his, I snuck into the room and got set up in the closet. Got some great shots, kid... real Annie Leibovitz stuff. Well, more like a Triple-X version of her shit.... *S'cuse my French.*"

"Great, Mister Ames," said Tomás impassively. "That is good."

"You don't sound too excited, kid. One thing I don't understand... why'dya want me ta get the photos if you weren't gonna actually use em? You kinda blew yuh wad theh in fronta the hotel, didn't ya?"

"No, sir," said Tomás bluntly. "I will use the photos. We are not finished yet, not even close."

The monitor mercifully sprang to life and Tomás cued up the vidja. Then, he gave up the swivel chair to the private eye, so he could receive the full force of the phenomenon in which he was about to garner a role. Pulling another chair alongside, Tomás sat a few inches back so he could watch Ames' reactions without being conspicuous. The investigator would be the first person besides himself to see Rey Lagarto in action, and he didn't want to miss a millisecond of his response.

The initial seconds of the clip showed only a distorted image, but when the Lizard King finally came into focus, Ames chuckled and glanced at Tomás with a tight-lipped smile. As the fifty-nine second anomaly progressed, however, Ames' expression went from smile to confused furrow and, finally, a jaw-dropped, dumbfounded, flabbergast. When the clip was over, he didn't turn back around to face Tomás, but remained staring blankly at the monitor for several more wordless seconds before reaching out for the PLAY button.

"Yuh shitting me, right kid?" said the investigator, squinting with a more critical eye as the video began again.

"No, Mister Ames, there is no shitting. *This*... is why I have done all that I have done."

After the second viewing, Ames leaned back in his chair, put his hands flat on his face and rubbed them around. Then, as he dragged his palms slowly down his cheeks, he said,

"Well...I... dunno what to think, kid," Ames' voice was missing its usual jovial tone. "This is either a really great hoax that yuh pullin' here, or..."

"There is no hoax, Señor Ames. I took the video on my friend's cell phone, then downloaded it to my computer at home. There are no special effects. As God is my witness, señor, this is Esteban Rey Lagarto as he really is."

"Heh!" Ames chortled. "And he mentions you...by *name*. D'ya still got that phone, kid?"

"No, sir. I gave it back to Diego after I deleted the video and photos."

"So, what's the plan now?" The investigator was businesslike. "I gotta tell ya, kid, yuh retainer is pretty much used up at this point, especially aftuh Samantha's... honorarium."

"Yes sir," Tomás said abashedly. "I was going to ask about that."

"Let's not worry about it right now, kid. We'll discuss it laytuh. I figuh you got a gold mine on that thumb-drive. Is that your next move? Sell this clip to a news network?"

"Yes, sir."

The Private Eye scratched at his two-day beard and said; "Well I guess I unduhstand the hostility toward Maddox now. You're doing all of this for the, Chupa...uh...this Ray Loag-ear-toe...?"

"*Rey Lagarto*," said Tomás, peeved.

"Yeah, to be honest, I have a hard time sayin' either word."

Tomás stuffed the flash drive back in its wrapping and put it in the toe of his shoe, then began wiping the video-file from the computer's hard drive.

"Wait a second, kid," said Ames. "Let's backtrack for a second, here. What'd I miss in fronta the Cahlyle? When I walked up, I saw the face of a man whose world was crashing down around his eahs. That's what you wanted, right?"

"It's not for me that I do these things to John Maddox, Mister Ames. Even though he stole my story and put his name on it, and I would love to see him exposed for that, I didn't come all this way, or pay you all of this money just for me.

The investigator's curiosity was at full pique.

"Everything I do," Tomás insisted, "I do for Santa Teresa and for *Rey Lagarto*! This *punta* has done great harm to us *all*, and *Rey Lagarto* must be avenged! I am just the instrument... I am his weapon."

As the words left his lips, Tomás pictured the shiny silver revolver, and his eyes went to the safe in the corner of the room. The door was standing open like before, but the weapon was missing from the top shelf, and he guessed that Ames had taken it with him to the hotel. He lowered his head to sneak a sly look and saw the large bulge of a gun in the private eye's armpit, pooching out from its shoulder holster underneath the blue blazer.

"You gotta give me a second, kid," said Ames. "I gotta let all this sink in. Also, I been holdin' my fudge for hours. Be back in a coupla minutes."

Ames excused himself to the restroom, and Tomás took the time to think of his next move. He tried to think logically and dispassionately, but the words of a drunk, angry, and defensive Maddox echoed in his head.

"*I* **WILL** *GO BACK TO YOUR VILLAGE AND* **FINISH 'EM OFF** *FOR GOOD!*"

The man had threatened to **kill** *Rey Lagarto*! Tomás had heard it with his own ears, though he hadn't reckoned on such a direct, vitriolic threat from the *periodista Americano profesional.* The man responsible for the death of the Lagarto Queen and her child was now vowing to return to Santa Teresa to finish the job and make the genocide complete.

"*...FINISH 'EM OFF...***FOR GOOD!!***'

In light of this direct threat to his captain, Tomás' mission to topple Maddox's love life suddenly seemed hollow, insignificant, and misguidedly shortsighted. Beyond the desired outcome of pissing the reporter off, the *cabron* had transformed into an enraged killer, frothing and yelling and swearing his own revenge. Maddox's reaction reminded Tomás of a time as a child, when he had poked at a beehive with a stick and then paid the price with multiple stings. His father had treated the swollen, red welts on his back by applying a poultice made from a clean, white t-shirt soaked in *mescal*, and while Tomás had laid as still as possible, the cool alcohol stinging his stings with its disinfectant, he had put the lesson to memory. Now, he had poked at a hive once again, only, this time, he wasn't the only one at risk of a reprisal.

He knew what had to be done. It had been clear when he saw the reporter's raging eyes.

"BUST A CAP... FINISH HIM OFF!"

The threat had been clearly stated. And, Tomás had taken specific offense at Maddox's denunciation of Santa Teresa as a *"SHITTY LITTLE VILLAGE"*.

Would Maddox return to Mexico, Tomás wondered, and if he did, would he be able to track down *Rey Lagarto* when dozens of Military and Civil Policía had been unable to? Then, it suddenly dawned on him;

TÉO!

Maddox was a snake, and if he deduced that *la Familia de Sanchez* was involved in the cabal, he might try to force Téo to lead him to the Lagarto Palace. Tomás couldn't bare the thought of his little brother being in danger because of a beehive that he had stirred up and, if there was any chance of something bad happening to anyone he loved, or of *Rey Lagarto* being killed, Tomás would have to be their first line of defense, right here in Manhattan.

He knew that his suzerain had wanted to deliver the final, visceral retaliation on Maddox from the moment his Beloved and child were murdered, but Tomás couldn't risk the reporter getting the drop on an unprepared Lizard King. These direct threats from the man made a preemptive strike necessary and gave him all the justification he needed to deliver the retaliation here and now. But, if he was going to be the proxy, he was definitely going to need a weapon.

He heard the sound of running water through the open bedroom door, followed by the flushing of a toilet. A few seconds later, Ames reappeared in the doorway, and Tomás saw that he had removed his blazer, but still wore the leather shoulder holster, which was now empty. He liked the eccentric private dick, and a twinge of guilt twanged at his conscience at the thought of stealing *anything*, but he knew that this might be his only chance to snatch the weapon and make a run for it. This was a matter of lives and deaths, after all.

Ames reentered the office thinking out loud, half to himself and half to Tomás, and it was clear that, whether or not the investigator thought the video was a hoax, he had seen superannuated potential dollar signs while taking a piss and was now trying to insinuate himself at a deeper angle into the operation. The normally comically gruff sleuth took on a saccharine, pandering tone as he pulled his chair up close beside Tomás and made direct eye contact.

"Look, let's be honest here, kid," Ames said, "You're a smart guy, I'll give you that, but you are a kid. Yuah young, inexperienced and, I'm guessing, prolly in this country without any kind of visa. If you wanna get top dollar for this video, you need someone to represent yuh interests. You don't know the way this city works, kid, but I do. I could act as yuh agent and broker a deal for you with CNN."

Ames leaned forward and touched the toe of Tomás' tennis shoe with a fingertip, which, along with the brown-nosey buttering-up tone of his voice, made Tomás very uncomfortable.

"Your best bet for this sort of stuff," the man explained, "is prolly CNN. They kinda straddle the fence betwixt FOX News and MSNBC, politically speaking, but this ain't political. I think they'd be more likely to go for a sensationalistic piece like this, to grab ratings away from the other two, which it would do. At least at first."

Tomás kept silent. The investigator was trying to seduce him, and it gave him the creeps, but with the retainer exhausted and Maddox's personal life in shambles as planned, he didn't need Ames anymore. The investigator's efforts had been invaluable to this point, but the waters were now fully chummed. Ames smelled blood and was sidling up for a taste of the spoils, but Tomás thought he could track Maddox on his own and, while the man rattled on, he tried to figure out how he could get the gun and make a clean getaway.

"Look," Ames wheedled, "no disrespect to your convictions kid, but if this Ray Leggorto of yours does actually turn out to be a legit creature, then your video footage here..."

He tapped a finger on the shoe again, and Tomás physically recoiled.

"...This video," Ames unfurled a debauched grimace, "this could be worth a fortune...to science...and... historical shit."

Trying not to look suspicious or telegraph his intentions, Tomás excused himself to the restroom and, when he rounded the corner and stepped into the tiny water closet, he saw that his felonious task had been made easy for him... sort of.

Laid out on a hand-towel beside the sink were the disassembled and freshly washed parts of the shiny silver revolver. Next to the towel and arranged in a single row on the edge of the sink were six silver-cased bullets, standing at attention like soldiers awaiting orders. The restroom was tiny, with a shower stall, a toilet, and a sink all packed in so tight that Tomás barely had room to turn around and close the door behind him. A fresh layer of sweat broke out on his face as he fumbled with the gleaming gun parts, trying to keep his chicanery secret by not clinking metal-on-metal, and before sixty, nervous seconds had passed, he was holding what appeared to be a complete gun in his hand, with no left-over parts. He carefully slid each of the six bullets into their cylinders, then stuck the gun into the waistband of his jeans and pulled his shirt down to cover it. Opening the bathroom door as quietly as possible, he let himself out through the false back of the little bedroom closet and closed it behind him, then hobbled down the two flights of stairs into the garage, a fresh rush of adrenaline helping to ease the pain in his leg.

He squeezed past the mini-van and hit a red button on the wall beside the big door, which started the sound of an electric motor and its chain-drive pulley, and over their loud hum and squeaky squeeks, he heard the sound of Ames opening the stairwell door on the third floor.

"YO KID!" He yelled as he started down the stairs. "What the fuck ah you **dooin!?** You don't wanna do this!"

When the gap between the big, metal door and the concrete floor was wide enough, Tomás hit the deck and slid under, then rolled into a three-point stance on the sidewalk outside with his good knee underneath him. Using his hands to push himself up, he got to his feet and lurched off down the sidewalk as fast as he could, making it to the first corner before he looked back to see that Ames had yet to exit the garage. He had drawn the attention of several late-night ranglers who were just coming out of the Paki restaurant, and so changed his quick, limp-run to the less conspicuous awkward canter as he hurried off to find a subway station.

For the first time in Tomás' life, he had stolen something from someone else. But this wasn't a piece of candy or a pack of baseball cards shoplifted from the neighborhood grocery store. He knew the investigator would surely come after him. Ames knew where he was staying, so the Hostel would no longer be safe.

Chapter 26

Tomás hopped down the stairs of the subway on one leg and set out into the bowels of the city, holding on to the gun through his shirt to keep it from slipping down his pants leg. Just as he found an empty seat on an eastbound train, he felt a buzz in his pocket and realized he still had the investigator's cell phone. He pulled it out, saw that in was Ames, and guessed that, if the man had been tech-savvy enough to hack into Maddox's and his fiancé's cell phones, he would probably know how to triangulate the location of this one. Feeling like a spy from a Hollywood action movie, he popped open the compartment on the back of the phone and removed the battery.

In his haste to get away quickly, he had taken the first train going east, but it wasn't an express train. It made every station along the route and, though he tried to settle in for the ride and look cool, the doors seemed to spite him by staying open longer and longer at each stop. Tomás nervously bounced his knee up and down each time and tried to *SWHOOSH* the doors closed with his Jedi skills, but he was distracted. Even with the slow, deep breaths and relaxing thoughts he tried to force, the threats from Maddox still repeated over and over. It was kind of horrifying.

"I'll go back to your stupid fucking village, and I will bust a CAP in this RAY motherfucker. And I will FINISH 'EM ALL OFF, for GOOD!"

The slurred threats had been bellowed by a drunken man who was under attack at the time, but the conviction behind them made Tomás think the reporter's anger would survive his hangover, and, when Maddox awoke the next day, the stark reality of the damage that had been done to him would surely cause that anger and frustration to fester. Then, when Tomás dropped the video of *Rey Lagarto* into the hippodrome of public scrutiny, he hoped that the shame focused on the reporter, and the resultant carnage wrought on his life would push him over the edge. And Tomás would make sure he was there when it all went down.

When the train at last pulled in to his station, he hobbled up the stairs and started towards the hostel, planning to rescue his duffel bag from the personal-locker in the basement before Ames could find him. The man had a van, and Tomás ran as fast as he.... uh...well, he ran as fast as he *could*, in light of his injury. In light of the new developments in the plot, he wanted to contact Téo to warn him that he had ignited a spark that would soon spread to Santa Teresa and kindle a bonfire of activity and turmoil. They had planned to SKYPE again using Ames' computer, but his impulsive snatch and run had eliminated that option, so Tomás found a corner payphone, *KLUNKED* the coins into the slot, and punched the buttons for a direct International call to Mexico.

Téo himself answered on the third ring, and Tomás told him tersely to shut up and listen. After rattling off a quick debriefing, he asked Téo for a report of the goings-on at ground zero and learned that the hype generated by the cover of the new *Enquirer* had surmounted the remoteness of Santa Teresa and brought some media people, but mostly curiosity seekers from Mexico City, Torreón, and Monterey. The weirdos were finding their way to the village in increasing numbers, and the fourteen-year old added that the influx of strangers had the local citizenry all a-twitter, not knowing what, if anything, they should say or do.

When he mentioned that old Corto was becoming a minor celebrity amongst the gathered by regaling the press with his stories of encounters with the Chupacabra, Tomás had an idea.

"You must go to him," Tomás instructed. "Call him by Raphael. It's his real name. We need him on our side, Téo. The old man has spoken with *Rey Lagarto*, so Raphael will know what you are saying is true."

"What do I say to him?" Asked Téo with doubt in his voice.

"Tell him he should gather the TV news people in the square and announce that the Chupacabra will appear before them soon at *la Árbol de Homenaje*. Say that, in a couple of days from now, *Rey Lagarto* will come to prove to them that he is real, and that he will speak to them and deliver an important message."

"Why can't I tell them?" asked Téo.

"I think they will take an older man more seriously than a teenager," answered Tomás honestly."

"I guess so," Téo sounded disappointed. "When will he appear? What should I tell Corto to say?"

"I will call you one more time to let you know, but he should tell them to have their cameras and microphones ready at the tree in a couple of days from now. First though, you must go back to the cave and tell *Rey Lagarto* that the time is almost here, but that he *MUST NOT* reveal himself until I say so. When my part is finished here, I'll make the call to you and, when I do, that's when you run to him and tell him it's time for him to do what he must do."

The brothers said goodbye and Tomás limped the final two blocks to the hostel, wondering as he went if he would ever actually make it back home to see Téo and the rest of the family again. After retrieving his duffel from the hostel's coin-operated storage locker, he approached the receptionist at the front desk and tried to appear calm and casual with small talk. When he thought the woman had been sufficiently charmed, he summoned the cutest smile he could and, adding an irresistible, pleading tone to his voice, petitioned her for help.

Tomás explained that a creepy, older man had been following him, and asked her not to tell anyone that she had seen him leave. Her expression was one of mock-suspicion, but when he slipped a twenty-dollar bill across the counter toward her, she just smirked and pushed it right back.

"Thanks, sweetie," she said, "but I'll keep your secret. You keep this money. I think you might need it more than me."

Tomás grinned his crooked grin and pushed it back to her again.

"Thank you, señora, but I'm going to have good fortunes very soon... if things go well. They might now, but either way, I would feel better if you took it."

He slung the pack over his shoulder, spun around, and headed out the front doors; stopping in the recessed entrance and looking in both directions before starting down the sidewalk and disappearing into the city night.

—◊—

It was just before 2 a.m. when he set out to find another place to stay. His first idea was the West Side YMCA, but he had mentioned that place to Ames, so that was right out. There was still enough money tucked in his underwear for a hotel room, but the first five places he tried wouldn't register him without some form of identification. At hotel number six, the receptionist agreed to let him slide without an I.D. if he paid a little extra, and in cash, so he checked in under a fake name and went to find his room.

When he opened the door, he immediately saw that the room would not have passed muster with the proprietors of the Sanchez Hotel. Bordering on fleabaggery, the dump was several steps down from the hostel that he had just left, which, while not filthy like this one, had been also very meagerly amenitied. This cheap place had two attributes that would make it easier for Tomás to fulfill his mission, however. Its close proximity to both the *New York Times* building and to Maddox's apartment would make it much easier for him to stalk his prey, but, perhaps more crucially, this crappy inn provided free wi-fi access to their guests in a tiny computer room just beside the communal TV lounge in the lobby. After he delivered his video to CNN, he would need to know when it hit the airwaves, and he would need to check the Internet regularly to know exactly when his bombshell of bits & bytes was put up on the network's website.

The whirlwind of events he had been through in the last few hours, from the confrontation with Maddox at the Carlyle, to his larceny of Ames' gun, to the long walk across Manhattan on an injured leg, had all taken their toll. Tomás was frazzled, so, after a quick shower in a disgusting, pube-strewn shower stall, he climbed into the lumpy bed and crawled underneath a filthy, scratchy Army-blanket and slid between the questionably clean sheets. Exhausted though he was, however, his mind was more keyed up than ever and, after two hours of tossing and turning without sleep, he gave up, got dressed, and ventured down to the TV lounge.

Only one other person was in the dimly lit room, curled up asleep in a beige, coffee-stained club chair in the corner. The television was on with the volume down low, and Tomás tracked down the remote control, intending to change the channel to CNN, but, by the time he found the right button on the controls, the conversation between four talking-heads on the current show had grabbed his ear.

Though he was aware of the cable news network, MSNBC, he had never actually watched any of its programs, and the one currently on was called '*Morning Joe*'. It featured three men and a woman sitting around a large, oddly shaped, glass-top table discussing the very subjects Tomás had been studying in his online Political Science class. At first, the seemingly antagonistic dialogue between the show's male host and female anchor was off-putting, but it soon became obvious that there was a genuine rapport between the four people at the table and that they felt comfortable enough with each other to speak frankly, and with occasionally brutal honesty.

The set was colorful and brightly lit, with multiple cameras moving around the table, capturing the cast from different angles and creating a kinetic atmosphere that matched the passionate opinions, assessments, and theorizations of the pundits. Though the subject matter they spoke about was serious and relevant, the hosts and co-hosts kept things from becoming bogged down with a jocular playfulness that often bordered on ribaldry, and Tomás was entranced. He continued watching as a stream of guests took their turns sitting at the table and having their brains picked and/or defending their controversial positions; power brokers and world shakers whose intentions were the influencing of the interconnected worlds of politics, finance, art, and culture.

The guests and panel discussed... well...*everything*; everything that Tomás wanted to have a career writing about. Even in the midst of the current imbroglio, he still had his sights set on a vocation in journalism and, though he couldn't have foreseen the surreal series of events that had led him to this point, he fully planned to benefit from the windfall and parlay the opportunity into his dream job, somehow.

The news anchor on *Morning Joe* was particularly captivating, and as he listened to her, Tomás started to rethink his decision to take the video to CNN. The anchor controlled the pace of the show, and he was impressed at how she kept things moving along; periodically putting the kibosh on the barrage of political and pop culture references being bandied about by the panel's three, generationally-diverse males. This woman projected a more overt sheen of integrity that seemed lacking in her chortling male co-hosts and, as Tomás listened to her delivery of the top news stories, he decided that she possessed the appropriate level of gravitas needed to introduce *Rey Lagarto* to the world. She was the one.

The 'Morning Joe' crew finally signed off, and Tomás crossed the lobby to a vacant breakfast nook on the other side, where he sat alone at a small table beside the vending machines and enjoyed a Continental Breakfast comprised of Bugles and a Root Beer. Afterwards, he found the tiny computer room and sat down in its lone folding chair in front of the single, tired-looking, old DELL PC that was bolted to a small table, which was in turn bolted to the wall behind it. A red placard bolted into the wall above the computer explained in white lettering that the computer was set up to block access to pay-websites. The porn-blocker kept Tomás from being able to download SKYPE, but it would work for his purposes of monitoring the Internet.

Tomás sat down, entered his room code to get online, and looked up the address of the MSNBC broadcast center.

30 Rockefeller Center

The famous GE building; the largest concentration of broadcast television entities in New York City, if not the world, all in one mega high-rise in the heart of Manhattan. If he couldn't spark a flame of interest in a talking Chupacabra *there*, then he couldn't make it happen *anywhere*. He figured the network would have a team of 'expert analysts', who would scrutinize his video meticulously, and he smiled when he realized that it would be the ultimate test of their skills. If they rejected it as a fraud, that would mean that the 'Experts' were officially full of shit.

There was no telephone in his hotel room, and he was out of change for the payphone in the lobby. The man at the front desk had been giving him the skunk-eye all morning and, in light of the fact that Tomás was an illegal alien who had come to town fer a spell to do him some journalist-shootin', he decided not to push his luck by asking the already suspicious man to break a $100. The flip-phone was still in his duffel bag upstairs and, calculating that it would be okay to use it if he didn't stay on too long, he went back up to his room, reinserted the battery, and called the MSNBC main number.

After navigating a lengthy push-button menu, he finally reached an actual human who listened politely as Tomás rattled off an abbreviated version of his pitch. But, when he finished, the humanoid informed him that unsolicited media-property submissions could be made online and, when Tomás replied that he would rather bring what he had into their offices himself, the voice said he should call back on Monday for an appointment, and hung up with a polite but unappealable goodbye.

It seemed absurd that the scientific discovery of the decade would have to wait until Monday for an appointment but, until he could deliver the goods to MSNBC in person, he could do nothing but keep tabs on the genocidal reporter in the event that he tried to leave for Santa

Teresa before the video hit. Tomás thought it was vital that Maddox see and hear *Rey Lagarto's* excoriation and vilification for himself before Tomás delivered the final retribution.

Desperate to catch up on the slumber he had lost during his night-flight, he pulled the threadbare drapes together in an attempt to block out the daylight, then collapsed on the bed and let sleep wrap him in its comforting cocoon at last.

—⁓—

When he awoke late Saturday morning, Tomás' knee hurt much less. After enjoying a meal of two Ding-Dongs and a Mr. Pibb in the breakfast nook, he walked to Maddox's Tribeca apartment and began a surveillance that would last all weekend without once setting eyes on his wayward target. He used Sunday night to catch up on sleep once again and, when he rose early on Monday morning, he watched *Morning Joe* until eight a.m. before calling MSNBC. This time, the receptionist informed Tomás that they didn't make appointments. She said he could either submit his media material online or, if he wanted to, come in to their Website Division offices and plant himself in the waiting room until someone could see him.

Tomás had kept his nicest pair of jeans (the ones with no holes), and his best shirt clean and tucked in the bottom of his duffel for just this occasion. Now, as he got dressed, the butterflies that had been fluttering in his stomach since he reached New York got even flutterier. When he checked himself in the chipped-cornered mirror above the tiny lavatory sink, the sickening, flickering fluorescent bulb overhead added to his jitters and, after brushing his teeth and combing his hair, Tomás gave himself a last once-over, then stuffed the silver revolver deep into his pack, and set out.

In the wake of the terrorist attacks on America and New York City in particular, Tomás was sure that there would be metal detectors or some other kind of security measures in place at Rockefeller Center. When he had first arrived in town, he had seen rows and rows of personal pay-lockers at the Port Authority Bus Terminal, and so, on his was to the GE Building, he swung by the busy hub-hive and stuffed his duff, pocketed the little key with the grimy, orange grip, and headed off towards his destiny.

It took three hours, and his video was analyzed by five screeners in ascending strati of pay grades, plus a gaggle of media analysts who didn't look much older than himself but, from the first hurdle that he cleared, Tomás knew that he had them, and that they were going to make him an offer, eventually. The first network geek-sentinel had laughed when Tomás took the flash-drive from the toe of his shoe.

"Must be some pretty important stuff, huh? Heheh," the man had quipped sarcastically.

But, the snide comment only served to widen the grin on Tomás' face as he dropped the flash-drive into the d-bag's palm. With each levee he breached, he saw the same dropped-jaw reaction that Ames had upon first viewing, and by the time he was handed off to the head of the Website Division, Tomás was already enumerating his un-hatched yardbirds, confident that NBC would pull the trigger and pay him for the rights to show the video on the air.

The man at the top who made the final decision introduced himself as Bruce, and he offered what he called friendly advice to Tomás in the form of a suggestion that he seek legal counsel before signing the release. Tomás expressed his gratitude, but told Bruce that he wanted the video to appear on *Morning Joe* as soon as possible, and that he would sign the paper right now.

"Ha, that's not exactly the way it works, Mr. Sanchez," Bruce chuckled. "And, I don't think Mika would go for something like this anyway. Stories like yours...well...sort of like yours, they go up on our website first, then the news division picks and chooses as they see fit. I really have no control over what they use on the air."

It was a minor disappointment, but he knew the video would go viral once it appeared on the website, then, hopefully, the television broadcast would pick it up. When Maddox was at last outed as a liar and a murderer in the larger public eye, then, and only then, would Tomás deliver the silver-cased bullet of atonement, saving the life of *Rey Lagarto* and ending the reporter's in one, strategic shot.

He thanked Bruce, then signed one form waiving his legal counsel, and another for the licensing rights to the video before leaving the NBC offices holding a cashiers check, made out to *Tomás Sanchez*, for eight-thousand five-hundred American dollars. When he stepped onto the unoccupied elevator, he stared in wide-eyed wonderment at the valuable piece of paper in his hands. It was a tremendous amount of money for something that had fallen right into his lap, but for Tomás, the crusade for *Rey Lagarto* had ceased to be about material gain when the threats from Maddox had put him in the role of protector and defender.

There was no way he would be able to cash the check without an I.D., but he still had a little money left on him. He would worry about the check when he made it home; *if* he made it home. Having such a large sum of money at his command was exciting, but Tomás felt a sense of regret at having given up his exclusive access to the Lizard King. The bond between them was a singular gift, and he had come to think of himself as, not only as the King's ally, but the custodian of his legacy as well. Though it was *Rey Lagarto's* wish to come out of hiding and reveal himself to the world, Tomás couldn't help thinking that the bond they shared was about to be severed and lost to the world as the Chupacabra transmogrified from myth to marvel. He folded the check and stuck it carefully into his pocket.

When the lift arrived on the ground floor, he left the GE building and walked through the plaza, skirting the colorful, flower-filled concrete planter-wall that surrounded a large opening onto the subterranean level below. Tomás looked down expecting to see the iconic Rockefeller Center Ice Skating Rink that he had seen so many times on TV, but, it was summer and the rink was iceless. The gilded statue of Prometheus instead gazed down upon two dozen artisans and artists, all of them sitting or standing guard under the shade of tents or umbrellas as sweaty tourists milled about looking at the curios, paintings, and bric-a-brac displayed across folding tables.

Before he left Rockefeller Center, Tomás stopped by the Lego Store to marvel at a diorama in the large display-window in front. The scene was made entirely of *Legos* and depicted an erupting volcano with people running in all directions from the orange and red lava flows as a big, colorful dragon flew overhead. The dragon was suspended by hidden wires from above, and a motor inside it made the fearsome, firesome lizard bob up and down and flap its expansive wings. Tomás knew the scene was meant to be frightening and apocalyptic, but he found that it, curiously, somehow comforted him.

The heat was repressive and, as he started back toward the bus terminal to retrieve his satchel and gun and, he had to regularly wipe the sweat from his forehead as he walked to keep it from running into his eyes. The torpedo was in the tube now, but until the network pushed the button to fire it, his time would be spent alternately tracking Maddox and checking the Internet, so he would know exactly when the projectile hit its mark. To ensure he would have access to the hotel's computer, he had paid for three nights in advance and, when he left the Port Authority terminal, he returned to the 'Shit-hole Inn' and logged on. There was nothing yet, of course, which didn't surprise him, but he knew that this was the calm before the storm, and just checking it made him feel better.

During his stay here, Tomás had noticed that the old *Dell* was always on the last web page that he had visited. It seemed odd in light of the fact that, because the hotel was substandard, it was inexpensive, and therefore full of guests, most of whom looked youngish and foreign, like him. He had expected the little cubicle to be used more frequently, but now, as he watched the guests file through the lobby, he noticed that most of them had computer bags or cases slung over their shoulder, and it was clear that, free hotel wi-fi or not, the laptop-jockeys were seeking an Internet connection elsewhere.

He hiked to the *New York Times* building to establish a beachhead for surveillance, stopping in a deli en route for a sandwich and a pickle.

Finding the perfect vantage point directly across the street from the building's entrance, he perched on the edge of a planter-box, eating his lunch as he pictured Maddox up there...somewhere. With an effigy of the murdering *pendejo* fixed firmly in his mind, and the *Times* building looming over him like a tremendous steel giant, a rush of hot blood came to his face once again, and he felt the familiar waves of anger sweeping him up, washing away any residual apprehension he had about the task ahead. He thought better of going into the building to try and track Maddox down and, instead, after his last bite of pickle, he found a nearby payphone, dropped coins into the slot, and dialed the number for *The Times* from memory.

When the operator answered, he asked to speak to John Maddox, and was put on hold. After thirty seconds of Lady Gaga's "*PAPARAZZI*", he heard a *click*, and a voice came on the line that he instantly recognized, and Tomás quickly hung up as the reporter was identifying himself.

—⁓—

Over the next two days, he used the old call-and-hang-up ploy several more times to learn the reporter's work schedule and daily routines. When he knew approximately what hours of the day the man was likely to stay put, Tomás took those opportunities to grab a bite to eat, check the website, and use the restroom, before returning to the *Times* to pick up his tail again. He didn't know why MSNBC hadn't been put the video on their website yet, and was getting impatient. They had already paid him for it, so why weren't they showing it?

On Wednesday afternoon late, while standing sentinel at the *Times* main entrance, the gyros and spicy falafel balls, of which Tomás had enjoyed too many for lunch earlier, began to make their presence felt once again. Knowing he wouldn't be able to make it back to the hotel in time, he stopped in a corner coffee shop a block down from the *Times*.

STARBUCKS; the worldwide chain of restrooms for the homeless, and Tomás took full advantage of the facilities at this one. When he eventually came out of the lavatory, a line of twitching, convulsing customers, all of them squeezing their thighs tightly together, gave him dirty looks, and he cast his eyes floorward as he walked the gauntlet back down the hallway. Stepping into the Customer Lobby, he saw that every stool and chair in the place was occupied by the same International-student/tourist types with which his crappy hotel was thick. All were suckling at the teat of Starbuck's free wi-fi with laptops hot and humming and all manner of convoluted beverages close at hand; candy-laced, soy/chai, and bovine-secreted, *based-loosely-around-the-concept-of-coffee* drinks.

He knew he had to get back to his post before Maddox left work for the late afternoon walk to his home in Tribeca, but Tomás took a minute to wander among the tables and sneak peeks at the preoccupied patron's laptops to see what sites were being surfed. There was still no Chupacabra-meme springing up anywhere that he could see, and the continued delay gave him a sick feeling in the pit of his stomach.

Just as he started for the exit, a full-voiced blast from behind made Tomás jump. He spun around to see a shortish barista coming straight at him, arms spread wide in a magnificent display of fabulousness, and, as he approached, the singer made direct eye contact with Tomás and belted out a Broadway show-tune in a strong tenor voice:

"WHAT GOOD IS SITTING ALONE IN YOUR ROOM? COME HEAR THE MUSIC PLAY...LIFE IS A CABARET, OL' CHUM, COME TO ZE CABARET..."

Dressed in the Starbucks uniform of khaki pants and green apron over a black, collared shirt, Tomás thought he looked Hispanic and was probably a few years older than himself. The cantante's black hair was perfectly-coiffed, and he had a huge, theatrical smile on his face as his big, dramatic eyes stayed locked on the self-conscious Tomás, making him feel like he was the casting director and this guy was auditioning for the cast of *A CHORUS LINE*.

Every head in the room was now turned toward the one-man-flash-mob, and he tried to move his petrified legs in a backwards-walking retreat, but when the barista got to within a foot of Tomás, he made a snappy, military-style Leffft**FACE**, and carried his performance on through the lobby full of smiling, appreciative patrons. For more than a minute, the singer held the attention of customers and employees alike, almost all of whom seemed to enjoy the impressive performance. The exception, Tomás noticed, was one, tall, bearded, green-aproned bloke behind the bar who looked like a hipster-pirate and who, during the show and the subsequent applause, just scowled and kept on barista-ing.

With the rest of the patrons distracted, Tomás slipped out through the door and hurried off down the sidewalk, holding on to the butt of the gun through his shirt as he ran, to prevent accidental 'Plaxicocation'. He got back to his post just in time to see the reporter leave the *Times* building, and a shock went through his body when he saw that Maddox was holding the hand of...VICTORIA MAGAÑA!

He watched in dumbfounded astonishment as the couple kissed a long, passionate kiss, followed by a few short pecks, before going off down the sidewalk in opposite directions; Victoria heading north up Eighth Avenue, and Maddox crossing 40th Street going south, in the direction of the couple's shared apartment.

What did it mean? Tomás wondered. Could Maddox have forgiven his cheating fiancé so soon? That kiss did *NOT* look like a 'farewell-for-ever kiss, but more like a 'we-just-made-up' kind of kiss (in his office?). Tomás didn't want to lose the reporter, who was walking briskly away down the opposite sidewalk, so he collected his wits, darted across the busy avenue, and fell in sixty or so feet behind, being careful to keep a few pedestrians between himself and his unsuspecting prey.

Bobbing and weaving his way through the oncoming foot traffic, they passed Penn Station, hiked through Chelsea, and then turned south on Hudson Street going towards Tribeca. He struggled to match Maddox's pace as the surprisingly fleet reporter demonstrated that living in the city made one into a strong walker, and, during the course of the sweaty pursuit, the surprising new development he had just witnessed rattled around like marbles in Tomás' brainpan as he processed all of the implications and ramifications and tried to think rationally about his next move.

He had made mental notes in the past two days, while following the murderer to and from work, of places along the way that would afford him the best chance of escape should he decide to shoot Maddox in the streets. It wouldn't do to be arrested and jailed just when *Rey Lagarto* needed his help the most. But *that kiss*...did it mean that the wedding was still on?

When they reached the reporter's apartment on Franklin Street, the reporter went inside the six story building, and Tomás set about finding a nearby payphone. Maddox's building was on the northwest corner of a five-way crossroads intersection, in the middle of which sat a large traffic island that was divided into two sections. On the smaller section at the island's north end was an arched awning suspended above a subway staircase entrance and, stretching to the southern tip of the intersection was a much longer concrete cay with an inner perimeter of terra-firma, from which grew the concentration of bushes and trees Tomás had used for cover in the last few days.

Next to the subway entrance was a line of coin operated magazine racks, and at the end of the row sat one, lone payphone. Tomás jogged across the street and, with sweat drip-dripping down his face and onto his t-shirt, dug a sheet of paper out of his front pocket, unfolded it, and then dropped two quarters into the coin slot before dialing the number. While he waited for an answer, Tomás mumbled softly to himself.

"Surely this asshole won't marry that *punta bitch*."

"St. Paul the Apostle," said the genial voice of an older gentleman. "May I help you?"

"Yes, I am calling to ask about the 'Magaña-Maddox' wedding scheduled for this Saturday."

"Yes of course, young man," the priest said with an audible smile. "We have it scheduled for seven o'clock p.m."

"a-HA!!" Tomás exclaimed before he could stop himself. "Umm... thank you, sir."

He slapped one hand to his open mouth while the other hung up the phone. Looking back towards Maddox's front door, he whispered, *"So, it's back on...or...still on."*

All of a sudden, Tomás' brain blinked, and he was in a church vestibule watching the tuxedoed body of Maddox falling to the ground with a shot to the chest from the shiny silver revolver Tomás was holding in his hand. A confusion of emotions swept through his mind as he saw the bride rush to the side of her fallen groom and collapse in tears over his lifeless body, and Tomás realized that, despite his lowly opinion of Victoria Magaña, the unfaithful *punta* wasn't personally to blame for the deaths of the Lagarto Queen and the infant prince she carried in her womb. Victoria was only supposed to have been collaterally damaged at worst, but Tomás' conscience now told him that, if he were to murder her groom, and on their wedding day, no less.... *Su Corazon sería una victima.*

The taint of compassion was no good for the cold heart of a killer, and Tomás tried to stuff the unwanted emotion back down. *Maddox* was the murderer, and *Maddox* deserved the retribution from all of the destruction he had wrought, along with the consequential tears of his bride, which would fall squarely on his shoulders. These were the thoughts with which Tomás tried to embolden himself, but his empathy for a weeping bride bothered him very much and the unwelcome image would penetrate and fester.

He shook himself free of the illusion and suspended surveillance for the evening, walking back to the hotel in a glassy-eyed, mentally-fried fog as his inner demons battled it out with his better angels for control of his soul. It had been another long, tiring, sweaty day in the hot city, and his lumpy hotel bed was calling to him in a gravelly, cigarette-damaged voice, offering the few hours of rest Tomás desperately needed.

Before heading up to bed, he went to check the MSNBC website in the little computer room one last time. His eyes were weary from a day in the bright sun and bleary from all the car exhaust. He rubbed and squinted them to be sure he was seeing what he thought he was seeing on the screen.

THERE IT WAS! Not tucked into a corner of a web page, or presented as a tease with a link prompt; the *CHUPACABRA* was *the* featured story, and his video-prompt was huge at the top of the home page.

A shudder shot up his spine like the mercury in a thermometer.

Chapter 27

MORNING JOE

INT. MSNBC STUDIO; THE CAST IS HOST JOE SCARBOROUGH; ANCHOR
MIKA BRZEZINSKI; CO-HOST WILLIE GEIST; AND INTERMITTENT GUEST
CO-HOST MIKE BARNACLE

JUST BACK FROM THE TOP OF THE 3RD HOUR BREAK. SMASHING PUMPKINS
"1979" PLAYS THE CAST IN.

                    JOE
              (to audio engineer offset)
         Thank you, Kyew

Music fades out

                    MIKA
              (to producer, offset)
         Um...Chris?

                    JOE
         Oh no, Willie. Here it comes

                    MIKA
         Is this...where are you, Chris?

                    (looks around set into
                    all of the cameras until
                    she finds the red light)
         Am I going to read this, really?

                    JOE
              (in slow, pandering
              southern drawl)
         Oh come on, Mika. This is not Paris Hilton. You can
         unplug the shredder. This is the HARD NEWs BayBAAAAAY!
         Are you kidding me? An undocumented
         Chupahaha...Chupacabrahaha...coming over our borders
         to...

                    WILLIE
Yeah, I...

                    JOE
...into our country to kill the reporter who...I
mean...

              (exaggeratedly)
Jan Brewer and Rick Perry have GOT to get on the phone
with each other and...

                    BARNACLE
              (heavy Boston accent:
              Written in *International
              Phonetic Alphabet*
              w/Boston-specific
              diacritical notation)
θə Bætfoʊn, Hʰʰʰʰʰ. ɹʰznt ə Čʰupak[ɔɪ~ɔɪ]bɹa l[aɪ]k ə
bæt, s[ɒꜝ~ɒə]rt əʌ?

                    WILLIE
One more example of weak borders.

                    MIKA
You see, this is exactly what I was talking about
yesterday. This story is a JOKE! This piece literally
came from the National Enquirer, guys.

                    JOE
It's simple, really. I think Rick Perry called up
Central Casting and asked for a more interesting set-
piece to hang his Presidential run on. Rick's gonna
get the American public off of their asses and get 'em
to call their...

                    MIKA
Are you fellows really going to try and spin
this...Stupacabra poo into a serious story?

                    JOE
...to call their Representatives about border-hopping
Chupacabras taking JOBS away from our new college
graduates...

                    WILLIE
He's probably carrying, as well.

                    BARNACLE

Šua, ʤʌst kwɒl ʤl̥ä(ꜝ)]n MʌKɛin, θɹo hɪm ä boʊn fʌ
gʰadz sɛik.

                    WILLIE
Yes. McCain needs a distraction so he can forget about
Sarah...

                    MIKA
                (gesturing)
Okay, oKAY! Enjoy this one, you morons.

                (reading from
                teleprompter)

Last night, a video was posted to the MSNBC Website
that as of our air-time this morning has gone viral
with already more than a million views. The clip
features what is being called a...

                    JOE
                (feigning excitement)
Here it goes, Willie!

                    WILLIE
Wait for it...

                    MIKA
                (looking ceilingward)
A... Chupacabra...

                (looks at co-hosts with a
                disappointed scowl)
...a mythical monster that, according to Mexican and
Central American legend, feeds on the blood of
livestock animals including... GOATS; which is how the
chupacabra got its name.

                (to director, offset)
Chris, this is ridiculous.

                    JOE
GOAT SUCKER!!!

                    MIKA
Yes, Joe. The name is Spanish and translates,
literally, to 'goat sucker'.

                    JOE
                (makes double thumbs up)
Yesss. Mika, this Chupacabra is the Paris Hilton of
the, what? Let's see...

                    WILLIE
I've got this. You're not gonna believe this, but I
know this one.

                    JOE
What is it, Willie?

                    WILLIE
The Illinois and New Jersey educational systems
triumph again. The Chupacabra would be the...

                    JOE
Drum roll please, Kyew.

                    WILLIE
                (with big smile)
...he would be the Paris Hilton of the *'Capra aegagrus
hircus...suckuss'* world... I think.

                    JOE
                (laughing & holding up an
                index finger)
CorRECT, Willie! I think. Gotta give Vanderbilt some
credit, too.

                    WILLIE
Linnaeus, 1758

                    BARNACLE
I don't think Paris was sucking a goat, though. To be
fair to... the goat?

                    MIKA
                (continuing from the
                teleprompter with an even
                more annoyed look on her
                face)
The existence of the creature has until now been
discussed as either comedic fodder for the late night
talk shows, or in the stories and photos printed in
the National Enquirer.

                (looks around the table)
Yeah, comedic, guys! There you go. *C O M E D I C.*

                    WILLIE
                (with boyish smile)
Boy, those Enquirer guys were all over this thing.
First Jonathan Edwards, and now...

                    JOE
Man, those guys are good.

                    BARNACLE

d[ɔɪ~ʊɪ]n ɪ[ɒi]t

                    MIKA
                (from teleprompter)
The new video viral sensation is a full 59 seconds
long, and it shows what appears to be a reptilian
creature, standing upright and...

        (rolls eyes)
...and SPEAKING...in a garbled dialect of the
Nahu...the Nahuatl language, an antiquated dialect in
the Aztec language group, still spoken by over a
million people in Mexico today. The creature's
vocalizations are hard to understand, and NBC has
added translated subtitles for broadcast but, even
without translation, you can hear the creature
speaking the name of the reporter who filed the first
full story about the Chupacabra with the National
Enquirer in November of last year. The reporter, one
John Maddox, is currently employed as a staff writer
for the New York Times, but was working as a freelance
writer when the piece was published in the...

        (Holds her toned arms
        outstretched to her co-
        hosts, prompting...)

        JOE, WILLIE, AND BARNACLE
        (almost in unison)
The NATIONAL ENQUIRER

        BARNACLE
Scheesh!

        MIKA
        (from prompter)
In a follow-up story from the December issue of that
TABLOID, Enquirer..."Reporter"...

        (makes air-quotes)
...René Hernandez, wrote that the brutal double murder
of a woman and her son in the remote village of Santa
Teresa, Mexico, in that country's state of Durango, is
being blamed on the Chupacabra.

        JOE
I read that one on the AP wire last year.

        MIKA
Well, why don't you read the rest of this...crap.
Because I need to go throw up now.

        WILLIE
Can we watch the...?

        MIKA
Hold on, Willie.

        JOE
You're almost done, Mika. Just finish this up, then
we'll watch the clip and dissect the larger political
angle to this puppy.

                    MIKA
              (from teleprompter)
        The woman, a former Loocha...

                   WILLIE
               (helping out)
        Luchadora. Like Lucha Libré?

Mika cocks her head a squints at Willie.

                   WILLIE
        Masked wrestlers? Mexican wrestling league?

                    JOE
        Jack Black! Hilarious movie. Me and...

                    MIKA
              (ignoring the
              interruption)
        ...a former Luchadora who went by the professional
        name "La Diabolica"...

                  BARNACLE
        Kl[ɛə-æ]sɪk

                    MIKA
        ...and her adult son were eviscerated in their home in
        late November.

                    JOE
        Holy Moly.

                    MIKA
        Neighbors of the slain mother & son claim that the
        couple was killed by the Chupacabra, a heretofore
        mythical boogey-man, of sorts, thought to inhabit
        volcanic caves in a nearby caldera.

Joe wipes his forehead with the back of his hand.

                    JOE
        WHEW! I'm with Willie, let's play this clip.

                    MIKA
              (from prompter)
        According to Hernandez's article, the residents of the
        village have known of the creature's existence for
        generations, and many of them claim to have seen it
        themselves.

                    JOE
        Oh, HECK yeah. This is great

                    MIKA
              (to engineer)
        Ok, roll 'em, Tickey Moler!

Fifty-nine second video clip plays followed by a few seconds of uncomfortable silence.

                    MIKA
          I'm glad there were subtitles.

                    WILLIE
          Ahh, a boy and his Chupacabra.

                    JOE
          Named Esteban

                    WILLIE
          Yes, Esteban the Chupacabra.

                    MIKA
          Esteban, I think he said.

                    JOE
          Wasn't that an early Don Johnson vehicle? "A Boy and
          his..."

                    BARNACLE
          And what about this kid Tomás who, I assume, shot the
          video? We gotta get this kid in here.

                    JOE
          Yeah, sure. But the name Esteban, though...that's a
          very unthreatening name, really.

                    DONNY DEUTSCH
                 (from off set)
          Cross Marketing, Joe. Children's' Books; video games;
          etcetera.

                    WILLIE
          I think the Video Game Designers will put the
          threatening stuff back in, though.

                    MIKA
          Aaaaaand to wrap things up on this pile of dung...

                    JOE
          Heheheheh.

                    MIKA
                 (from teleprompter)
          Authorities from Durango and its neighboring state of
          Coahuila have made extensive sweeps of the area, as
          well as a thorough search of the caves in a nearby,
          dormant volcano, looking for the killer or killers as
          well as keeping an eye out for any animals capable of
          this kind of vicious attack. After coming up empty-
          handed on both accounts, the search was called off in
          early January, but anthropologists from Mexico City
          were subsequently brought in to examine, quote
          "Unusual Things" found in several of the caves.

                    WILLIE
Anthropologists?

                    MIKA
Hush, Willie. Almost done...ummm...

          (squints at teleprompter)
...yes, anthropologists... to study what appear to be
pictographs and stone carvings from the Aztec culture.

                    BARNACLE
Čʰupak[ɔɪ-oɪ]bɹɑ ʌɪl

                    JOE
Wow, now that's a seriously great backstory.

                    MIKA
          (from teleprompter)
Attempts to reach the *Times* reporter connected to the
story, who is to be married at a church in Manhattan
tomorrow evening, have so far been unsuccessful.

          (to co-hosts)
There.

                    JOE
Hallelujah, Mika! Ya got through it.

                    MIKA
Okay, guys? And Chris? There are literally
hundreds...thousands of things we could be covering
instead of this. This particular example of Info-
tainment, I think, is over-heavy on the latter part of
that portmanteau.

                    WILLIE
Portmanteau, NOICE! That's the word of the day. That
and Chupacabra.

                    JOE
What could you POSSIBLY be wanting to cover besides
THIS, Mika? Let's, let's, let's go back to...

                    MIKA
Well, let's see...

                    JOE
...go back to the black & white TV era. You could
resurrect Ed Morrow. Then, he could reinvigorate all
of that integrity bullsh...

                    WILLIE
Watch it.

                    JOE
Unfortunately, that boat has sailed. The micro-chip is
out of the bottle.

                    MIKA
We could be discussing education, the Keystone
Pipeline, world hunger, perhaps?

                    JOE
Alright, Mika.

                    BARNACLE
It takes a village.

                    MIKA
Moving on.

                    WILLIE
Each One Teach One.

                    MIKA
MOVING ON!!!

                    JOE
It takes a village, Mika. It takes...a...

                    WILLIE
Village.

Chapter 28

No air-conditioning penetrated the bell-tower stairwell in the big church building on 60th and Columbus, where Tomás sat cross-legged in a small storage closet halfway up the landing, holding the shiny silver revolver in his lap and sweating in the dark. Though he would be putting fresh prints on the gun soon and couldn't see the steel gleam in the dark anyway, his compulsive polishing of the weapon with the tail of his t-shirt seemed to calm his nerves a bit, and it gave him something to do with his hands until the wedding party arrived.

Everything had kicked into high gear the previous morning when the anchorperson-of-his-dreams had introduced Tomás' video on the air, and since then, he had done his best to keep eyes on his target as Maddox came and went from the Franklin Street apartment. The previous afternoon, he had even had the experience of flagging down a chase-taxi to follow a cab in which Maddox had zoomed away. Being a fan of Cop Dramas and suspenseful thriller movies, he got a special kick out of sliding into the back seat of the taxi, slamming the door behind him, and shouting,

"FOLLOW THAT CAR!"

He had stuck to Maddox like glue all day Friday as the ostensible groom met with, what Tomás assumed were, friends or relatives of the happy loving couple. Only after the Wedding Rehearsal dinner at Tavern on the Green had finished, and it was clear that the wedding party was in for the night did Tomás return to his mungy hotel room for another round of fitful sleep. When he woke this morning, he had taken a quick shower, dressed, and strapped the duffel to his back using its auxiliary shoulder straps.

After leaving the *Buttplug Hotel & Suites* for the last time, he had speed-walked south to Tribeca, all the while brooding over the fact that he was going to KILL another human being before the day was through. The less permanent option of aiming for a non-vital part of Maddox's body had crossed his mind, but a mere wound might only prevent Maddox from getting to *Rey Lagarto* temporarily. If and when the reporter recovered, Tomás' confédére would be in mortal danger once again, so he knew he had to toughen his nerve to do what had to be done. As he hiked towards Tribeca, he focused on his target and let his hatred for the *cabeza de capullo* build, so that when the moment of truth arrived, and he was pointing the gun at John Maddox, his body would obey his will, and he could actually pull the trigger. As he moved south, his resolve had grown, and by the time he had reoccupied his sniper's nest behind a bush on the traffic island, the adrenaline had really been flowing. But he hadn't been the only hunter on the stalk this morning.

Milling around on the sidewalk directly across the street from Maddox's apartment building, there had been three, sloppily-dressed, baseball-cap-wearing men with cameras hanging from straps around their necks, smoking cigarettes and shuffling their feet as they had laughed amongst themselves and waited for Maddox to come out of his front door. They had obviously been paparazzi, and Tomás had felt a rush of hot blood to his head with the euphoric realization that his scheme was working like a charm. The show had begun at last.

The teenaged, illegal, Mexican National was aware that his own name had been flung out into the world along with *Rey Lagarto's*, and he had been careful to keep his cap pulled down low and stay hidden as he peered out from under the brim and watched the goings-on a hundred feet away.

With the rising sun, the big, five-way intersection had heated up and become noisy with traffic. Just before noon, Maddox had come out to confront the scandal-pimping photo-hounds in front of his building, but the traffic noise had prevented Tomás from hearing what was said. Judging by the besieged reporter's flailing arms and red face, it had been clear that he was upset, and before Maddox turned to go back inside, he had tried to wave the shutterbugs away like an ineffectual Scarecrow shooing a murder of jaded crows. At that moment, Tomás had seen a frustrated, angry, and frightened Maddox, which was exactly how he had wanted his quarry to spend its last few hours on earth.

By mid-afternoon, the number of paparazzi had grown, but Maddox had only shown his face once more; presumably, Tomás guessed from the body language, to politely appeal to the better natures of the photogs', and ask them to leave him alone on his wedding day. The murderous, prevaricating reporter finally had a giant bull's-eye on his back, and Tomás was delighted that the man's sins and transgressions were being lime-lit, but the afternoon heat, the visceral feel of the weapon underneath his shirt, and the excitement of seeing his prey in distress, had taken his brain to a boil, and, when he had left Tribeca to get to the church before guests arrived, he was in a state.

On the final march north on Ninth Avenue, his internal rage had swept him up and expanded until it transcended his own conscious capacity and, by the time he got to St. Paul the Apostle, his enmity for Maddox was at a level he knew would be needed for him to honor his vow. Prior to entering the church building itself, he had needed another restroom break, so before the shit went down, he stopped in yet another Starbucks at the opposite end of the block from the church to do his business. By the time he had come back out, the front steps of the church were crowded with nicely dressed people from an earlier wedding just ending. The guests had cheered the Bride & Groom and pelted them with birdseed as the newlyweds ran for the open doors of a silver limousine to escape the barrage, but, when the limo zipped away, the crowd hadn't dispersed, but instead remained in a prolonged mingle on the church steps.

The paparazzi had already taken up their positions on the sidewalk directly across the street in anticipation of the Chupacabra-killer's wedding, but they had now been joined by both local, and network news teams. While technical crews pulled cable and field reporters primped for camera-readiness, Tomás had taken his chance. Pulling his cap down low, he had zipped across the street, which by then was becoming congested with slow-driving, rubbernecking drivers, and made his way around behind the cameras. He had made eye contact with no one as he circumvented the media melee and crossed the street back on the other side, then ambled nonchalantly along beside a black, wrought iron fence and down the sidewalk that separated the broad side of the church from 60th street.

Slipping through an unlocked gate in the fence, he had descended a short flight of steps into the narrow basement well, and then dropped through an open window onto the plush, wine colored carpet of a meeting room before making his way down a long hall and up the stairs to the nave. After sneaking along behind the colonnades on the perimeter of the sanctuary, he had zipped through the vestibule and up the stairs into the airless storage closet where he now sat, gently cradling the gun as he rocked back and forth with his eyes closed and channeled *Rey Lagarto* in a sort of spiritual SKYPE.

More than ever, he felt their mutual lust for vengeance merging into a unified fury and, as he listened to the voices of the Magaña/Maddox wedding guests beginning to arrive in the vestibule below, he opened his eyes in the dark and squeezed his hand tightly around the grip of the revolver, feeling the Lagarto's hot blood and fomenting savagery rise inside, guiding his thoughts and commandeering his imminent actions. The voices he heard outside were not mirthful or celebratory. There was no lighthearted laughter in these exchanges, and as people filled the vestibule, their babbling became more heated. He guessed that the scene outside the church had become even more frenetic, causing the guests consternation at having to run the gauntlet through the onslaught.

Over the grumbled murmuring, Tomás could only make out snippets of conversation, so he opened the closet door as quietly as possible and tiptoed down the stairs to the lowest landing, stopping just around the corner from the last short flight of steps leading into the vestibule. Now, he could hear every virulent, disconcerted statement and, though the words were, mostly, politely delivered, their allusions were definitely antagonistic.

In the midst of the kerfuffle, the voices of John Maddox and his fiancé began to rise over the clamor. The Bride and Groom were lobbing accusations at each other and, as the spectators turned their attentions to the quarreling pair, the collective chattering faded to a low rumble, which made the uncomfortable couple in the center ring bring their voices down in response.

"*You screwed a hooker THAT NIGHT?*" The bride whisper-shouted.

"*I had just found you and Rantz in* **BED TOGETHER, VICTORIA**!" Maddox's throat was pinched-sounding as he exhaled the words. "*Are you really gonna make this about THAT? What about the freaking* **CHUPACABRA**? *And the* **kid**, *for* **fucksake**?"

Hearing the allusion to himself made Tomás' lips peel back in a vicious sneer, and he hoisted the shiny silver revolver to his shoulder, ready to strike.

"Oh, *that* is ridiculous, John," the bride exclaimed " Just... RIDICULOUS! I wanna know what in the hell is REALLY GOING ON HERE?"

Victoria's full-voiced demand reignited the assemblage and the noise of group-bickering rose again, only louder. In the commotion, Tomás turned the corner and galloped down the stairs, skipping the last three steps and landing flat-footed on the hard, marble floor of the vestibule. He gripped the shiny revolver with both hands and held it up to his right shoulder, but... no one noticed. The guests had their backs to him, and all were fixated on the feuding couple, who had now stepped away from each other to opposite sides of the crowded space to be immediately surrounded in supportive huddles by their respective groomsmen and maids-of-honor.

When he fired the first shot into the vaulted ceiling, every head in the room snapped around in wide-eyed alert, looking like a mob of startled meerkats, and Tomás nearly laughed out loud. He lowered the gun and pointed it directly at Maddox, texting the dedication of the conscripted groomsmen, two of whom stepped in front the groom while the other three scampered for the exit.

Tomás shut one eye and kept the silver gun barrel pointed at his target while gold dust and chunks of gilded ceiling fell onto his head.

"IF YOU DON'T WANT TO SEE THIS PENDEJO DIE, THEN GET OUT.... NOW!!"

The sound of his own voice booming around the vertical vault of the vestibule surprised him, but his confident command had the desired effect. The meerkats all scrambled for the front door exit, everyone except Victoria, whose ladies in waiting were yanking her in two different directions until she pulled away from them and scuttled toward her groom as fast as her voluminous gown would allow, and Maddox, whose two, loyal groomsmen were standing in front of their protectee with chests puffed out in false grit.

"Get out of here, Victoria!" John yelled resolutely. "I am NOT kidding...GO!"

The banished bride wanted to defy the command, but then she took a closer look into the targeting-eye of the rage-filled teenager and decided that she would, indeed, make her escape, following her maids out the door, which clicked shut behind her.

Tomás took a step toward the three remaining men, which caused the groomsmen to close ranks even tighter, but John pushed the guards apart and stepped out in front, tapping his head with one finger and pointing a stiff finger at the assassin with the other as he said.

"You really *ARE* crazy, aren't you Tomás? You did all of this to me, didn't you? What the hell, you little bastard? Are you taking orders from this Chupacabra thing? Is *that* what I'm supposed to believe?"

Tomás locked his arms out straight and steadied his aim, squeezing his hand tighter around the grip harder and curling his finger around the sweet-spot of the trigger.

"His name..." Tomás hissed through clenched teeth, "...Is **Esteban Rey Lagarto**...and **THISs**...is from *HIM*!"

He had a clear shot at Maddox from the bowtie up, but both attendants saw the teenager's body stiffen a split second before he pulled the trigger, and the darker haired one leapt in front of the bullet just as the **BOOM** boomed around the room.

"TAYLOR!" Shouted Maddox, falling to his knees over the body of his friend.

Tomás didn't hesitate, but followed his target as it dropped, and fired again.

¡BOOM!

He knew the bullet had hit its mark because he saw Maddox fall backwards, but Tomás didn't stick around to see his victims bleed. The taller, bearded groomsman came at him with arms spread wide and fingers splayed like the claws of a charging grizzly bear, but Tomás sprang backwards to evade the attack, and then dashed through the sanctuary doors and into the nave.

Bolting down the center aisle, the weight of the swinging weapon in his right hand threw him off-balance and thwarted an all-out sprint. When he reached the altar steps, he made a hard right and paused in front of the first row of pews, but saw that the grizzly bear had not followed him in. The frantic groomsman was instead bouncing around on the threshold between sanctuary and vestibule, pointing wildly in Tomás' direction to alert two early-arriving NYC cops to his escape route. So Tomás turned and dashed through the open doorway beside the vestry at the front corner of the chapel and shagged it down the stairs and back into the basement.

Without looking back, he sprinted to the end of the corridor and ducked into the meeting room he had entered through earlier. After circumnavigating the chairs of a long conference table, he shot across the room's thick, wine-colored carpet and attempted a triple-jump at the open portal, but he was hampered by the bulky weapon in his hand, and his body slammed helplessly into the wall underneath the window. His heart was racing as he grabbed a chair and shoved it under the window, then, stepping up onto it, he set the silver revolver on the sill, placed his palms on the ledge, and was ready to hop up into a sitting position when he heard a voice behind him that he recognized instantly.

"I believe you got something that belongs to me, kid."

—⁓—

In his office at the headquarters of the *National Enquirer* at the southern end of the island, Ben Rantz was working late. He had been slaving over a hot computer for hours, but couldn't seem to get any work done.

Weeks earlier, he had received an invitation to the wedding of the woman with whom he had been philandering intermittently for the past year and a half, but, in spite of the official notice for the impending nuptials, his tryst with Victoria Magaña had continued until eight days before the wedding. For Rantz, the intervening week had passed in melancholy, but now, a whirlwind had whipped up, and he would have a front row seat for the reaping. He had resigned himself to the end of the affair, but didn't have the luxury of ignoring the wedding itself, which was supposed to be happening at this very moment a few miles away. The disturbance in and around St. Paul's church made the Magaña/Maddox wedding integral to his job at the tabloid and, as the action in midtown ramped up, he sat at his desk and switched back and forth from desktop to laptop; one eye on real-time updates from Internet sources, and the other on a raw, live feed from CNN, who had arrived on the scene even before the guests had arrived.

The network newshounds had been reporting for the past ten minutes that the groom and one of his groomsmen had been shot by Tomás Sanchez, and that the teenaged assassin was believed to be still hiding in the basement of the church. Now, Rantz glared at the computer screens as a phalanx of police officers filed through the front doors, followed by two different, four-person teams of EMT's to treat the casualties. When the church doors burst open a minute later, he saw that one of the teams was carrying an occupied stretcher, which they proceeded to schlepp down the steps and shove into a waiting ambulance. Two of the Paramedics hopped in behind it, slammed the doors, and, with lights and sirens on full blast, the emergency vehicle maneuvered impatiently through the throng of bystanders before zooming off down Columbus Avenue.

The editor watched breathlessly as two EMT's hurried back up the steps to the church door, only to be met by the other Paramedic team, who had left their stretcher inside the vestibule and were shrugging and pointing confusedly this way and that. When Rantz refreshed the web page on his laptop, he quickly found out why.

Several independent Internet sources were now reporting that one of the victims, *New York Times* reporter John Maddox, had suddenly vanished. The police were keeping the media at a distance, so there weren't any shots of the actual crime scene, but the CNN website said that Maddox had indeed been shot, but that, during the ensuing confusion of people running in and out of the church, the injured man had somehow disappeared. Now the police were not only dealing with the shooter in the basement, they were simultaneously occupied with a search for his wayward and wounded victim.

When the church doors opened again, a queue of bridesmaids wearing bright, fuchsia dresses filed out, followed by two EMT's who were standing on either side of a distraught Victoria and gently holding her by the elbows as they helped her down the steps. On his big, desktop computer monitor, Rantz had three separate windows open, each with its own live feed from one of the three top cable news networks, and he watched as all three cameras converged on the bride in a near-simultaneous zoom shot. While she wiped tears from her eyes with the back of one hand, the other was holding a black tuxedo jacket, which was wet with invisible blood that had besmirched her dazzling white dress with smudges of crimson. Rantz knew instinctively that this was the footage that would be looped, and then run ad infinitum on every twenty-four-hour news network in America.

The spectacle was red meat for the media-crocodiles, and the editor knew it would surely be the defining image of the bizarre, and still very fluid story. Despite his cynical nature, Rantz cared for Victoria, and part of his heart and a portion of his penis wanted to rush uptown to her side, but he knew a great story when he saw one, and knew that he couldn't risk missing the bigger story, whatever his personal feelings.

He hit the refresh button once more and was watching the spinning rainbow beach ball of death go round and round, when movement in the cubefarm outside his office door caught his eye. Through the maze of chest-high cubicles, someone was coming toward him quickly, and, when he finally recognized the face, Rantz stood up from his desk and steeled himself for a confrontation.

John Maddox was black and white and red all over as he rounded the last cubicle and walked with long, unsteady strides towards the office door. Rantz noticed that the disheveled man's tuxedo jacket was missing and that he was holding a blood-soaked rag to the side of his head, trying to stem the flow that had turned the right half of his white shirt scarlet. As the bloodstained casualty stepped into his office, Rantz saw that the man's face was also bright red, but not from the wound. The editor was speechless, but the enraged groom was not and, as he lowered the blood soaked rag to reveal that the top of his right ear was gone, Maddox thundered,

"That God-dammed thing tried to have me killed!!!"

PART V

Chapter 29

*This is CANDACE TREVIÑO reporting from SANTA TERESA, MEXICO,
the remote village believed to be the home of a teenager accused of shooting two
NEW YORK TIMES employees during a wedding in Manhattan this past
Saturday.*

*The teenager, one TOMÁS SANCHEZ, is thought to have entered the
United States illegally sometime last week, and then travelled to Manhattan
with the intention of settling a vendetta with the intended groom, NEW
YORK TIMES staff writer, JOHN MADDOX.*

*In a bizarre twist, several wedding guests claim they heard the
shooter say that he was sent to assassinate MADDOX on the orders of a
CHUPACABRA; a mythological creature thought by some to inhabit parts
of Mexico and Texas. Until recently, debates about the existence of the
CHUPACABRA have been mostly tongue-in-cheek, but the residents in
SANTA TERESA blame the creature for a brutal, double-murder that occurred here in November of last year.*

*Prior to the killings, the NATIONAL ENQUIRER printed a story about
the CHUPACABRA in question, written by the groom, who was at that
time a freelance reporter. The piece featured interviews with residents of the
SANTA TERESA VALLEY who, according to Maddox, not only believe in*

the CHUPACABRA's existence, but claim the creature actually has the ability to speak a human language; an obscure dialect of the Aztec NAHUATL language still spoken in parts of Central Mexico today.

[camera shot widens]

At this moment, I am standing in the SANTA TERESA village square, where locals have been known to leave live sacrifices to the CHUPACABRA in the form of livestock animals tied to this old tree stump. Next to me right now, I have a local man known simply as 'CORTO', who acts as a WATCHMAN over the tree and claims to have interacted with the CHUPACABRA on several occasions.

"It's actually Raphael."

"Mr. CORTO, how do you respond to critics who would claim that this is all an elaborate hoax?"

"What creetics, meess? Are you the creetic? You are asking me this? Well señorita, you steeck around for a while. You will find out soon enough. Then you won't be creeti*SIZE*ing old Raphael no more."

"Can you tell me about this symbol carved into the tree, CORTO? What does it mean?"

"Me amo RAPHAEL. Well... It is the Chupacabra, sí?"

"The police have searched caves in the surrounding area and have not been able to find the creature. Do YOU know where the CHUPACABRA is hiding, CORTO?"

"Eets **RAPHAEL!** And no....I do not."

"What, if anything, CAN you tell us regarding rumors that the CHUPACABRA will come to this tree and allow itself to be photographed and filmed?"

"Sí, I can tell you about that, okay. Esta tarde, this afternoon, todos nosotros pobladores... ummm...all of us Santa Teresans...we will gather at the tree. Then at seex o'clock, HE will come."

"How do you know that the CHUPACABRA will come to this location this evening?"

"Yooouu don't worry so much about that, señorita. You just have you cameras ready, sí?"

"Is it true that you have communicated with the creature on several occasions, and, do you plan to speak to it...or...HIM, tonight?"

"Oh yes, I have talked to heem, yes...okay? And I gonna talk to heem some more today. Okay, I got to go now. These other camera peoples want to talk to me."

"Alright, thank you for speaking to us, CORTO."

"RAPHAEL!!" [Shouting as he walks away]

"As you can see, behind me are more than a dozen television and news crews from both Mexico and the U.S., along with over two-hundred Curiosity Seekers; Conspiracy Theorists; Crypto-zoologists; and Scientists from Universities around the world. And, tonight, they will all find out if they have once again been duped by clever pranksters, or if a zoological anomaly has indeed been discovered in this sleepy little village.

We will bring you more from the scene as this strange story develops.

Reporting from Central Mexico, this is CANDACE TREVIÑO for CNN."

—ɯ—

The Sanchez Hotel was packed with guests, and Tomás' parents had to press extended family members into service in order to accommodate the overflow. In addition to dealing with hotel patrons, the proprietors were besieged by the media, as well as varying degrees of weirdos, all wanting to know where their son was, and asking a hundred other questions to which they had no answers.

In a way, it was a blessing that the distraught Sanchez's were kept so busy because, by now, they were very aware of what Tomás had being accused of doing in America. They were beside themselves fretting over his whereabouts and safety, but the activity in and around the hotel had kept the full weight of their worry at bay for the time being. They were bracing themselves for an even worse final outcome, however, and compounding their concern about Tomás was the fact that Téo had now gone missing as well.

The sudden, overwhelming influx of people to the little village had the natives in a tizzy and, in the middle of the melee, Corto was holding court as a de facto master of ceremonies. His colorful personality and droll comments provided an obvious focal point for the news cameras and, as Corto seemed to be the only one in the village who claimed to know anything about when the real star of the show would show, all eyes watched him for cues.

When John Maddox pulled off the Torreón highway and drove down the dirt streets of Santa Teresa in his rental car, he saw long lines of vehicles on both sides of the road and ended up parking almost a mile away from the town square. Climbing out into the oppressive, late afternoon heat, he and his associate/interpreter René Hernandez threw their backpacks over their shoulders and started walking.

In the wake of the debacle at the wedding, the paparazzi and news media had set up camp in front of John's New York apartment. Some of them had followed him to LaGuardia Airport early this morning, but he had avoided commenting on the status of his situation, and, when René had approached him at the gate just before the flight, the two reporters had struck a deal. Because John was inextricably linked to the narrative of the phenomenal saga, and René intended to capture the follow-up Piece de Resistance for the *Enquirer,* they had agreed to a symbiotic arrangement wherein René would stick close by him and translate as the story's finale played out.

When the pair reached the village square, they saw a throng of gawkers gathered in a wide semi-circle around *los Árbol de Homenaje.* The crowd was at least ten deep all the way around, and, as John and René pushed and shoved their way through the crowd, they were cursed and grumbled at in several different languages. They got as close to the big stump as the horde would let them and saw that all eyes were watching a small, brown calf who stood alone on the sparse patch of grass with one end of a rope looped loosely around its neck, and the other end wrapped around the thick, whitewashed stump. The spectacle of oblation was at the hub of attentions, with news cameras occupying strategic spots closest to the stump at both ends of the semi-circle, and a cadre of *Policía* in between, hoping to prevent the mob from advancing further.

Since John's face had been shown ad nauseum on television and across the Interwebs for the past two days, he tried to avoid eye contact with anyone, but the Americans had blown their cover by bulldozing their way to the front, and he was now aware of heads turning and eyes glaring at him. The news cameras hadn't picked up on it yet and were still focused on the calf and the stump, but the fanatics and aficionados who stood all around John and René had clearly marked him as the reporter who was the archenemy and victim of both the Chupacabra and his teenaged sidekick, Tomás Sanchez. René stood close and translated the whispered comments from people nearby.

"They're all saying that you've come back to kill the thing. Everyone seems to think you have a gun." After a beat, René leaned away and looked sideways at his colleague with the afterthought, "You don't have a gun on you... do you?"

John didn't answer. He had spotted Corto standing in the shade under the awning of the bakery, surrounded by camera crews and waving his arms in exaggerated flourishes to entertain the TV viewers at home with his impressions of the Chupacabra.

In the hot, afternoon sun, the assemblage grew more and more restless and, when six o'clock came and went with no sign of the headline act, a dissatisfied and displeased rumble began to ripple through the crowd. Soon, shouts of laughter and mock anger began to be directed at Corto, who took on a pleading tone as he implored the doubters and dissenters to be patient, but by seven-thirty, it was clear that many in the group believed they'd been conned, and some started to amble off toward their cars.

The news cameras remained pointed at the white stump and at the hapless calf, who seemed curious but unconcerned as it chewed its cud and returned the stares of a thousand eyes. But John noticed that even the camera crews were starting to pack up their equipment; smoking cigarettes and snickering amongst themselves as they lazily wound cords and occasionally checked their shot-alignment and focus. Even with the encircling crowd eyeballing him regularly, John had managed to avoid being spotted by the media, but when he unintentionally made eye contact with an attractive female CNN correspondent in the bullpen, she made *him*.

The woman immediately set the video hounds on him, and John and René had to backtrack through the restless, shifting horde to avoid being collared; serpentining this way and that as they moved towards the back of the crowd again. They had almost made it to the open concourse when a collective gasp erupted from the crowd like a burst of steam, and every head in the plaza turned to face them.

John and René froze in place before the sea of wide-eyed, gawping faces, but, with the exception of a few eyes still on him, every face was tilted up and looking over their heads at the roof behind them. Before he had the sense to turn, René grabbed his arm and spun him around just in time for John to see the Chupacabra fold its bat-like wings and drop into a three-point-stance onto the roof of the hardware store behind them. The Lizard King stood to his full height and, stepping to the roof's edge and hooking his hind talons over the lip, he thrust out his chest and flexed his shoulder blades, making his wings rise slightly off of his back in a half-opened position.

For the past fifteen minutes, Esteban had observed the throng of Workers with a predator's eyes from the safe distance of several thousand meters up, and when he noticed people starting to leave the square, and then saw Téo standing behind the hardware store, waving his arms wildly in their prearranged signal, he had descended quickly to the flat rooftop. Just as he touched down on the soft, hot, black tar, he spotted John Maddox directly below him at the near edge of the crowd. But, hundreds of eyes were fixed on him, and *Rey Lagarto* was torn between addressing his gathered subjects and diving straight at the murderer.

This was the moment Esteban had visualized in a thousand savage fantasies ever since his Beloved and child had been violently ripped away from him, and he wasn't going to let the moment slip away. He gripped the ledge with three clawed extremities, and then leaned out over the roof's edge and pointed a long, clawed finger directly at Maddox. Then, taking a deep breath, he summoned his most commanding *Hissss,* and, when the *Nahuatl* tongue effervesced from his fanged mouth with a shrill, gurgling, raspy shriek, the people standing around John and René parted like the Red Sea.

The two journalists were left standing alone in the bull's-eye as the Workers vacated in all directions, many skedaddling for the porches, where they crammed together under the eaves, freaked-out-scared, but not wanting to miss any of the action.

René felt conspicuous and conflicted. He had wanted to part with the rest of the sea, but felt obligated to stay with his targeted colleague, and so, he stood as behind John as possible and spoke into his ear.

"He's talking that Aztec shit," said René, frustrated. "I can't translate this stuff, but I know he's pissed off."

"Thanks for that." John's ventriloquist-style response was sarcastic. "Hang on, I've gotta get this."

In one motion, he lowered his left shoulder and reached his right hand into the unzipped opening of his backpack. Esteban saw the move and leaned out over the lip of the building even farther, the stucco ledge crumbling away under his talons as he spewed his vengeful diatribe at John, the words of which were unintelligible to all but a few of the spectators. His wings were arched over his back in a ready posture and, when he saw John pulling something out of the bag, he crouched to spring, but, in the penultimate moment, a gunshot exploded with a terrific...

"¡BOOM!"

The noise triggered a collection of terrified yelps and screams in the plaza that rent the air with a cacophony almost as loud as the shot itself. Esteban pushed off from the roof with his powerful thighs and launched himself into the air, but he didn't spring at Maddox. Instead, he leapt straight up, opened his wings with a WHOOSH, and flapped them frantically; cupping drafts of hot air with rapid, pulsing contractions that pushed his body skyward.

Just as John was spinning towards the source of the blast, he caught a last, peripheral glimpse of the winged lizard as Esteban banked in a hard left turn to evade a possible second shot. John and René turned to see Tomás standing just ten meters away on the flat top of the big, white stump, his elbow bent close to his body to support the weight of the shiny silver revolver he held to his shoulder with its still smoking barrel pointing straight up into the air. Tomás glared at John from across the breach, and when he saw that the reporter had only pulled a small video camera from his backpack, he started to lower the gun. But, as his trembling hand was coming down, he was grabbed from behind and pulled backwards by both arms, causing him to lose his grip on the heavy weapon.

The gun fell from Tomás' hand, hitting the hard ground with a second, explosive ¡**BOOM!** and discharging a wild bullet that pierced the belly of the calf a few yards away and knocked the animal to the ground. In the ensuing pandemonium, people ran in all directions, yelling and screaming as the calf lay writhing in the dust, bleeding and bleating in convulsing paroxysms. René had hit the deck and was laying flat on the ground beside his associate, yanking at his pants leg trying to pull him down, but John had turned back around and was standing immobile, frozen in shock, watching the Chupacabra wing its way into the distant sky.

René fumbled for the cell phone in his pocket as he scrambled to his feet again. Jabbing a finger at the screen, he speed-dialed the *Enquirer,* then held the phone to his ear. As he waited for Ben Rantz to answer, he surveyed the chaos all around and saw Tomás being held face down in the dirt by police officers as, in the sky beyond the hardware store, the Chupacabra was now only a dot on the horizon, shrinking away smaller and smaller in the screens and monitors of dozens of cameras and smart phones.

"¡LAS CUEVAS, LA CALDERA!"

The cries were scattered at first, but they spread rapidly around the square, and the horde started to break up into smaller groups and disperse in every direction. The plaza emptied quickly as dozens of excited spectators streamed around both sides of the hardware store for a better view of Esteban flapping his way toward the caldera, but most of the congregation ran this way and that in an all out race for their cars.

After *la Policía* had handcuffed Tomás, they pulled him up off the ground and quick-marched him to a waiting squad car parked on the plaza's edge, then shoved him into the back seat and slammed the door behind him. As the cruiser sped off towards the caldera, its spinning tires threw clouds of dust at the news crews and their field reporters, who were all sprinting for their respective News Vans.

In their rush, most of the cameramen had grabbed their portable cameras, but abandoned the bulk of their equipment in place in the village square. One crew, however, had inadvertently deserted their talking head as well. The CNN field reporter who had spotted John in the crowd before was standing near the calf when it was shot and, after the police had the gunman pinned to the ground, eliminating him as a threat, she had tried to comfort the wounded animal. When it was clear that the poor beast was in its death throes, she left the calf's side to look for her crew, but they were nowhere in sight. In fact, there was no one left in the plaza but herself and the old man, Corto, who was standing beside the white stump a few feet away, looking at her with a twinkle in his eye and a sly grin on his face that said *'I told you so'*. The reporter looked at him with a shrug and flashed a sincere smile of acquiescence, then tipped her make-believe hat to him before turning back towards the bakery. Taking a seat on the worn planks at the edge of the wooden porch, she pulled out her cell phone and reached out to her AWOL crew.

—∿—

Rey Lagarto's coming out party hadn't gone the way he envisioned it and, once again, he could place the blame squarely on the shoulders of John Maddox. Though he hadn't stuck around to see if the bullet that Tomás fired had killed Maddox, Esteban knew that any chance of a reunion between *Lagarto* and *Worker* had, at that moment, gone up in gun-powdery smoke. When he saw the murderer pull something from his bag, and then heard the loud bang of the gunshot, he had leapt from the rooftop and flown for safety as fast as he could flap, but now, as the maelstrom in the square shrank behind him, he remembered that he had absolutely nowhere to go.

For days, *Rey Lagarto* had been a refugee from his home, returning to the Palace only thrice to verify that his front door was still congested with Workers. He had complied with the game plan Tomás had devised, but when the time came to reap the rewards, it had all gone terribly wrong, and now he was without any kind of refuge. If the cluster of Workers at his front door had been impenetrable before, he knew that it would soon be forced inward when the stampede coming from the village arrived at the *Palace* entrance and flooded the cubbies, dens, sleeping chambers, and *Throne Room* of his ancestral home.

With so many folk in and around the village square, the tree-hole had been inaccessible for days as well, but on the previous three nights, Esteban had waited for darkness to fall, and then slipped into the back part of the Palace through the smallest vent; creeping like a thief in the night into his *OWN HOME*. The entrance to the narrow passage was in an overgrown field on the northeast edge of the village that Workers rarely visited these days and the opening itself, which was barely wide enough for him to squeeze into, was hidden between two big hunks of rusted metal that once were cars. On each occasion, Esteban had stolen into the Palace and crept close enough to his front door get a look at the interesting assortment of Workers who were blocking it, careful to stay out of the range of flashlight beams. He had observed, gathered just outside of the cave opening, inquisitive Workers with cameras; uniformed Workers with badges and guns; and other, scruffier-looking and strong-smelling Workers, who remained separate from the others and yelled out requests for an audience with *Rey Lagarto,* in his native tongue, no less.

When he made his aerial escape from the roof in the square, he had flown in the direction of the caldera out of panic and habit, but now his only thought was to circle back and slip into his ancestral home through the back door one last time. As far as he knew, the Workers had never discovered the opening of the tiny vent, so he figured he could hide in the back end of the Palace for as long as possible, and when the swarm swept through the front door and into the throne room, he would scramble back up the escape hatch, pop out in the auto-graveyard, and then... just... *fly*.

Tomás had once described for him a magical device that many Workers possessed, which allowed them to see long distances in the daylight, and Esteban guessed that he was surely being watched now as he flew. So, as he approached the dormant volcano, he made a conspicuous descent towards the crater, hoping to confound his pursuers with the conceit that he was winging his way back to his front door. Flying low, he skimmed the tops of the trees that grew up the side of the sloping cone, and when he reached the crater's edge, he plunged down into the caldera, then hooked a quick, sharp left-hand curve just above the thicket and coasted beside the cliff face for several hundred meters. With a few forceful flaps to increase his air speed, he veered out away from the rock face, banked hard to the left once more, then flared up over the rim of the crater and sailed low over the desert flora, making a wide circle away from the dust clouds being kicked up by the convoy of vehicles racing down the road to the caldera.

When he reached the junkyard, he spotted his landing-pad below and dropped onto the rusty hood of a formerly blue 1971 Plymouth Satellite, then hopped to the ground on all fours and scrambled down into the vent-hole headfirst. Quickly slithering his way to the bottom, he dropped onto the pumice floor of the corridor and stood dead still, listening for the voices and trying to determine if the mob had begun their inevitable, maniacal invasion of his residence.

Though the mutterings were louder and more animated than they had been on his previous incursions, it didn't sound like the caravan from the village had hit the door yet, so the King crept forward for a final look at his Royal Palace, knowing he might not see any of it ever again. Despair washed over him as he scanned the Throne Room one last time, taking in every pillar, every pool, every pedestal, and every *stalag*, be they *mite* or *tite*.

Too soon, the muttering voices rose to a choleric clamor, and he knew the crazed throng of Workers had breached the entrance and spilled into the front hallway. Pulling a big breath of the cool, damp air deep into his lungs, he turned to leave, but, he didn't hurry as he should have. Crushing despair weighed on him as he marched despondently towards the escape-vent, passing the dens, sleeping chambers, and niches that had been cleaved, carved out, and sculpted by the claws of his ancestors, millennial moons ago. When he reached the vent opening, he stood underneath it and glanced back through swollen eyes once more. Then, *Rey Lagarto*, the last King in an ancient, sustained lineage, reached through his dysphoria and summoned the spiritual will and the physical strength to save himself.

He bent his knees in a crouch and was ready to spring up into the vent, when he heard a sudden, close sound, soft, yet piercing the darkness like a sunbolt and resonating over the clatter of the fast approaching horde. Then, a sweet, strangely familiar voice spoke his name.

"Xipilli"

—⚇—

The marooned CNN reporter sat gingerly on the splintery wooden porch-slats of the Panadería, staring at the screen of her iPhone and trying to reach her producer and camera crew. When the Chupacabra had beat its airborne retreat from the rooftop, the ensuing exodus was expeditious and complete, leaving only herself and the old man behind in the deserted plaza. She was not at all happy about being left behind, but at least her camera crew's gopher/gapher had thought to text her and let her know when they reached the cavern entrance.

As she sat there, missing the story of the decade and waiting for another update, she was forced to listen to the jabberings of her loquacious porch-mate as he repeatedly muttered a mix of English, Spanish, and *Nahuatl* to her, indirectly.

"They'll be back," was the only phrase she could understand. "They'll all be back."

When she could stand it no longer, the reporter decided to ask Corto to keep his blabbering to himself, but when she turned around, the old man had fallen silent and was standing up, drop-jawed, and pointing into the distance. Following his line of sight to the ribbon of deep orange that now separated the earth from the sky, the reporter saw two shapes winging their way towards the western horizon. She had been staring at the screen of her phone for the last seven minutes and her vision was blurred, so she squinched her eyes tightly and blinked hard a few times to reset her eyesight. But the nictitation didn't get rid of her double vision, and she still saw two Chupacabras, flying one above the other.

Corto suddenly regained his voice and shouted excitedly,

"Dos! Dos!!" Hay dos de ellos. ¿Puedes verlas, señora? DOS, hay DOS!!"

Her brain suddenly slipping into gear, the reporter jumped up and ran to the far end of the porch, where her crew had left behind one large camera sitting atop a tripod, still aimed at the roof above the hardware store. She searched frantically for the ON switch as she spun the camera around to point at the new target, wishing she had paid more attention to the crash course in basic camera operation her cameraman had offered her. With no time to waste, she gave up in frustration and scrambled for her cell phone, swiping again and again at the stubborn unlock-slider, which always seemed to freeze up when you needed the phone in a hurry.

In the few seconds it took to access the phone, her mind flashed to the infamous, washed-out celluloid footage from the 1970's that she had seen on the YouTubes of a blurry, furry 'Bigfoot' lumbering through a sepia-hued forest, and when her camera app opened at last, she held the phone up with both hands and pointed the lens at the flying shapes.

As the image came into focus, she saw, against the deep red backdrop of the sky, the distinct silhouettes of two *Chupacabri,* the movement of their wings synchronized in an elegant, aerial ballet as the figures grew steadily smaller, and finally vanished into the darkening void of night.

EPILOGUE

INT. MSNBC STUDIO. MORNING JOE REGULAR CAST IS SEATED AROUND THE
TABLE.

First segment: 6:00 a.m. Eastern Daylight Savings time. After
the titles package, the Doors "Not to Touch the Earth" plays
loudly over the video of the Chupacabra standing on a roof and
threatening John Maddox in the Nahuatl language.

Music fades out as the aerial camera shot descends to the table
of co-hosts.

                    JOE SCARBOROUGH
                  (Boldly)
          I am the Lizard King...I can do anything!

                    MIKA BRZEZINSKI
          Welcome to Morning Joe. It is July Twenty-first, and
          with me on set are...

                    JOE
                  (Excitedly)
          There's no time for that, Mika.

                    WILLIE GEIST
          No time for pleasantries or punctiliousness.

                    JOE
          This is Big, BIG news, Mika. How can you do the
          introductions so coolly after seeing THAT!?

                    MIKA
          Well... I still don't want to believe this is real. I
          guess I'm still processing it.

          JOE
            (To everyone)
Well ladies and gents, it's hard to deny it at this
point. There are camera shots of this thing from every
angle and with expensive, professional microphones
pointed at it and picking up its...

          WILLIE
            (helping)
Speech?

          JOE
...the speech.

          MIKE BARNACLE
All over the Internet now.

          MIKA
To me it sounds not so much a speech as a direct
threat toward this Times reporter. You can see it
right there in the captioning.

          WILLIE
Yeah, this thing was ready to pounce before that...

          JOE
            (interrupting)
YES! The gun goes off, and it's the KID!!

          BARNACLE
This kid is determined.

          WILLIE
Crossing the border twice?

          JOE
I wonder which was easier, coming or...

          WILLIE
            (laughing)
Coming or going, heheheh.

          BARNACLE
What I wanna know is, do all the Networks have an
Aztec translator on the payroll, or have they sourced
it out.

          JOE
Who knows? This Chupacabra... I hope he's not trying
to interfere with our political system here. How many
of these things are out there?

          WILLIE
Well, we saw the two...

                    JOE
                (to director)
        Yeah. Hey Chris, could we see that other...

                    MIKA
        The nice sunset shot, please Chris.

The shaky, camera-phone video footage plays showing two
Chupacabras in flight, barely visible against a nearly dark sky.

                    WILLIE
        Now that's just romantic.

                    BARNACLE
        It is sweet. Looks like a mating pair to me.

                    MIKA
        Here's what gets me, guys. Just like the Jonathan
        Edwards piece, the National Enquirer started this
        whole thing.

                    JOE
                (Sarcastically)
        That's just good investigative journalism, Mika. We
        haven't heard the last of this story, though. I can
        tell you.

                    WILLIE
        I hope this Rey...

                    MIKA
                (Squinting at the
                teleprompter)
        Ummm, letsssss sseeee...Rey Lagarto.

                    JOE
                (pumping his fist)
        YES! The Lizard King... King Lizard! That was the
        music tie-in, right, Kyew? That was perfect.

                    MIKA
        Soooo, like I was trying to say. We went from this
        Enquirer cover in October of last year...

Mika holds up the magazine for the camera.

        ... To this...

                    JOE
                (Like an excited child)
        Oh, boy. Here we go!

                    WILLIE
        Yesssss!

> MIKA
> ... to the front page...

> JOE
> (to Barnacle)
> FRONT page!

> WILLIE
> Above the fold.

> MIKA
> (Irked & vexed)
> The front page of the Gray Lady herself.

Mika holds up the New York times for the cameras.

"CHUPACABRA HIRES MEXICAN HITMAN TO RUB OUT TIMES REPORTER"

ABOUT THE AUTHOR

It is very awkward to write about Kyle Abernathie in the third person, so I won't. After thirty years as a songwriter and working musician on the road with bands and as a solo performer in my home town of Lubbock, Texas (birth, and resting place of Charles Hardin "Buddy" Holley), I was in desperate need of a new creative outlet.

Revenge of the Chupacabra is my first effort as a writer, but I hope I have found a new vocation. Much of that depends on you, the reader of this awesome story, so please don't let me down. Share it with others and send them links to my website (kyleabernathie.com) so they can experience the misadventures of Esteban Rey Lagarto as you have, and I can then afford new typewriting ribbon for my macbookair. Kyle Abernathie thanks you for giving this opus a whirl. Good day sir, madam, or other.

CPSIA information can be obtained
at www.ICGtesting.com
Printed in the USA
LVOW13s1736270317
528626LV00011B/1269/P